The Dungeon House

Books by Martin Edwards

Lake District Mysteries
The Coffin Trail
The Cipher Garden
The Arsenic Labyrinth
The Serpent Pool
The Hanging Wood
The Frozen Shroud
The Dungeon House

Harry Devlin Novels
All the Lonely People
Suspicious Minds
I Remember You
Yesterday's Papers
Eve of Destruction
The Devil in Disguise
First Cut Is the Deepest
Waterloo Sunset

Suspense
Take My Breath Away

With Bill Knox
The Lazarus Widow

Collected Short Stories
Where Do You Find Your Ideas? and other stories

Historical
Dancing for the Hangman

The Dungeon House

A Lake District Mystery

Martin Edwards

Poisoned Pen Press

First Edition 2015

10 9 8 7 6 5 4 3 2 1

Library of Congress Catalog Card Number: 2014951275

ISBN: 9781464203183   Hardcover
      9781464203206   Trade Paperback

Poisoned Pen Press
6962 E. First Ave., Ste. 103
Scottsdale, AZ 85251
www.poisonedpenpress.com
info@poisonedpenpress.com

Printed in the United States of America

To Helena

Twenty Years Ago

Chapter One

"Tell me his name."

"Whose name?"

"I'm not stupid, Lysette."

Malcolm Whiteley rested a hand on an armchair to steady himself. His chest felt tight, as if steel arms were crushing him in a murderous embrace. Was this how heart attacks began? He'd know who to blame if he finished up in intensive care. Was that what she wanted, to clear him out of the way, leaving her free to screw around, and spend all his money on her fancy man?

"I never said you were stupid. What's got into you, Malcolm?" The voice of reason, soft and refined. "Look, you're sweating. Remember what the doctor said about your blood pressure. You paid a small fortune to join that gym in Ulverston, and how many times did you go there—once, twice?"

"There's nothing the matter with me."

Lysette's frown said: *You couldn't be more wrong.* Her eyes flicked to the bottle of Chivas Regal on the sideboard, and the empty tumbler. Yes, he felt light-headed, but no way was he drunk. He'd only swallowed a mouthful to calm himself down after arriving back home. Not knowing where she was, or who she was with, or what she was doing.

"Take it easy, sit yourself down."

Actually, he wanted to grab her by the shoulders and shake some sense into her. Yet her green-eyed gaze hypnotized him, and he found himself stepping back, and lowering his bulky frame on to the sofa.

"That's more like it."

She parked herself next to him, keeping between them a couple of inches of hand-crafted Italian leather, the best money could buy. Her perfume had cost a packet too, even in the duty-free on their way back from Aruba. Leaning toward her, he breathed in, but all he could smell was the citrus tang. Not the faintest whiff of booze or sex. He felt like the detective in her favourite TV crime show. Canny and grizzled, determined to drag out the truth, however long it took. What was his catch-phrase? *"There's been a murder."* Well, not yet there hadn't, but if she took him for a fool, she was making the biggest mistake of her life.

She sighed. "What's up, more hassle about the business?"

"This isn't about the business."

"What, then?"

Brow furrowed, lips slightly parted. A picture of innocence, butter wouldn't melt. You couldn't deceive Malcolm Whiteley that easily.

"Where have you been all evening?"

"I told you before you rang Gray. Don't say you weren't lis-tening?" Over the years, she'd perfected the art of putting him in the wrong. "I went over to Cheryl's, to make sure she was clear about the arrangements for tomorrow. I love her to bits, but she can be dizzy."

A faint smile, but she was watching him like—yes, like a suspect under caution. Easy to spot her game—buying time while she tried to deduce how much he'd found out, how much was guesswork. It was so unlike him to confront her, he'd assumed surprise was the only weapon he needed to make her blurt out the truth.

Lying came easily to her. Funny, he'd never realised until today. In business, you expected people to lie, that's how the world works. Slutty women out for a good time lied constantly; it was in their DNA. Lysette was different. She exuded class. He'd chased her since she was sixteen, and even when she fled to

Leeds after leaving school, and took a job in a bar, not for one moment did it cross his mind to wave the white flag. She'd said she needed space, and all that women's magazine crap, but he'd pursued her, and in the end she came back home, to Cumbria and an engagement ring. He'd always trusted her. Discovering she kept dark secrets hurt him more than he could bear.

"It's half ten," she said. "Is Amber still out?"

No way would he let her distract him. "Amber is fine."

"I don't like it, she's only sixteen."

"Joanna gave her a lift, and if anyone is going to drive carefully, it's Joanna. Anyway, Amber knows better than to do anything stupid." The words *not like some* hung unspoken in the air.

Lysette shrugged. "So what have you been up to, Malcolm?"

"You didn't answer my question."

He closed his fingers around her wrist, feeling bone beneath the sheer silk. So tiny, Lysette, pretty as a doll and just as fragile. He could have made her shriek with pain if he'd wanted, but she didn't bat an eyelid. It wasn't courage, simply confidence. She was so sure she was untouchable.

"Because I've no idea what you're talking about."

"Bollocks."

She wrinkled her nose, to show she could smell the whisky on his breath. "We have a big day ahead of us, don't forget. So much to do. At least Cheryl is sorted."

"You weren't with Cheryl."

She pulled free of his grip, and pointed to the telephone. It squatted on an occasional table they'd picked up at an antiques fair in Keswick. Victorian rosewood with marquetry inlay. Absolute bargain, she reckoned, and she was the expert; she never missed an episode of *Antiques Roadshow*. He just wrote the cheques.

"Ring her up and ask her yourself."

He remembered the fat, sweaty dealer ogling Lysette as she haggled over the table's worth. That smelly old slob, what a loser. By the time she was done with him, the bloke was ready to give her the table as a present. Considering how little they paid, he might as well have.

"No point." This sounded like an admission of defeat, so he made up for it by raising his voice "Is there?"

"I've no idea what you're shouting about."

"Cheryl's your mate, isn't she? You'll have primed her."

"All right." Her eyes narrowed, but he hadn't provoked her into losing her cool. "I'll ring her myself."

She bustled over to the telephone, fizzing with energy, an actress giving the performance of her life. What man with red blood in his veins wouldn't give his right arm to be with her for one night, just one night? The envious glances cast his way gave him more of a buzz than the thrill of someone spotting his Tiffany gold watch, or swerving for safety as his Jaguar XJ flew past. One rule was set in stone. Other men could look, but never touch.

"Don't waste your time," he said, as she picked up the receiver.

"Who's wasting time? You want to check on me, hear what I've been up to, who I've been with. Cheryl can give you chapter and verse."

"Put it down."

She started to dial. "No, we need to sort this out, once and for all."

He snatched the receiver from her hand. "Forget it."

"For God's sake, Malcolm."

She put her hands on her hips. The plain white shirt and brand new Gucci jeans suited her, but she'd look smart in a bin bag. Even when she was in a bad mood, she looked fantastic. Eye shadow purple, cheeks tinged with pink, lips a shocking shade of red. She never walked out of the door without putting her face on, not even to see her old school friend, so the make-up wasn't proof that she'd been with a lover, but he didn't have a shred of doubt. Never mind evidence, never mind clues. Any decent detective would say, it's all about gut instinct.

"All I want is to know his name." He banged the receiver down on the cradle.

Not true, of course. He also wanted to lock his hands around the other man's neck. To watch the bastard's eyes bulge, and hear him gurgle in terror once he understood what would happen next.

"You're having a rough ride," she said "All this trouble over the business would be bad enough, even if Ted wasn't dying."

Through the full-length glass doors, you could see the garden lights changing colour. Red, green, yellow, blue, then back to red. Vivid splashes illuminating potted plants on the patio, and the bushes and the new summer-house beyond. Tomorrow the grounds of the Dungeon House would teem with people, brimming with envy and admiration. He needed to straighten things out with Lysette before the first guest arrived.

"The business isn't a problem. Gray reckons the new board is just playing a game. As for Ted, he's a waste of space. I won't shed any tears when he's six feet under."

She put her hand to her mouth. "You don't mean that. He is your brother, after all."

"Stop changing the subject."

He found her expression impossible to decode. Not so long ago, she'd adored him. It wasn't too late for them, even now. Once she rid herself of the boyfriend, they could start again and make everything right. He believed that was all that stopped him from losing the plot, good and proper.

"What's got into you, Malcolm?"

He snorted with laughter. "Question is, who have you let get into *you?*"

She didn't blush with shame, just pursed her lips, and took a step toward the door. "If you're going to hurl filthy insinuations, I'm off to bed. You'd best do the same. Tomorrow's going to be a long day. You need to sober up, and start thinking straight."

"It's not Ted, is it?" He was itching to wipe the disdain off her face. "For God's sake, you've not…"

"Enough!" Still no embarrassment, only anger. "Listen to me, Malcolm. I can understand why you're sorry for yourself because you sold the company and now the buyers want to rat on the deal. I can understand you drowning your sorrows while I'm out seeing Cheryl. But I can't understand these needlessly offensive remarks. Not only about me, but your own brother. A sick man! You ought to be ashamed of yourself. Tomorrow morning, I hope you will be."

That was it. She'd crossed a line. Scrambling to his feet, he snatched hold of her arm. She tried to pull away, but he was too strong.

"All right. Not Ted, then. Tell me it's not Robbie?"

"Let go! You're hurting me!"

And he'd hurt her some more if she kept pissing him about. Yes, he could put up with a good deal, but every man had his limits.

"Robbie Dean?" He tightened his grip. "Years younger than poor old Ted. Is it Deano you're screwing?"

She lifted her free hand, as if to slap him, but he seized it before she could land a blow. As she wriggled in his grasp, he pushed her back against the wall. There was nothing she could do. He stood right in front of her. She was breathing hard. It was weird, he'd not felt this excited in a long time.

"You're making a terrible mistake."

"Not me, Lysette. After you left this evening, I waited five minutes, then set off for Gosforth myself." He couldn't resist a smile of triumph. She was still panting. Was she turned on too? Women were strange, you never could tell. "Left the Jag in the lane a hundred yards away from Cheryl's cottage, and had a good look round. The lights were on, her Mini was in the drive. Not a trace of your Alfa. One thing about a car painted canary yellow, there's no missing it."

"You *followed* me?"

"Yeah, lately I've been worried about you."

"About *me?*"

Her eyes almost popped out of her head. Anyone would think he did have his hands round her throat. He relaxed his hold. Maybe now she'd see reason. Pity she'd made it such hard work.

"You've not been the same lately. Pushing me away, I couldn't make head or tail of it. And you've been going out more at night. I know Cheryl's your mate, and you're glad she's come back home again, but even so. Come on now, answer the question. Robbie Dean?"

A strange glint came into her eyes. "I think you're going mad."

"I'm the sanest man you'll find for miles around, and that's a promise. Okay, say it isn't Deano. Who, then? Please don't say Gray Elstone. Please, I'm begging you. I wouldn't know whether to laugh or cry."

"Not Gray," she whispered. "Not Robbie, either."

"Tell me who."

She sucked in air. "Ben came back home early today. He'd been up all night investigating a robbery, and just wanted to chill in front of the telly. He'd taped a documentary from the week-end, so Cheryl and I went out together, and left him to it. One of her tyres has a puncture, so she borrowed his car. We went to a quiet pub in Seascale, and talked about tomorrow. I wanted to make it go well for you. I wish I'd never bothered." She glared at him. "Satisfied?"

Oh yes, she loved climbing on to that moral high ground as much as other folk enjoyed scrambling up Helvellyn. He wasn't in the mood for her condescension.

"It's Scott Durham, isn't it?"

She blinked, said nothing.

Gotcha!

"Be honest with me, Lysette."

She put her hands up, and for an instant it looked like a gesture of surrender. Then she shoved him away from her.

"Go to bed, Malcolm. Before we say anything else that we regret in the morning."

"It is Scott, isn't it?"

Deep down, he'd always been sure. He just didn't want to believe it.

She opened her mouth, but no sound came. Outside, the front door slammed. Amber was home.

"I'm back!" she bellowed."Night, night."

He heard his daughter's feet, running up the open treads of the wooden staircase. Lysette frowned, like a bookie calculating odds.

"I'm going up as well."

"Not before you admit it."

"Malcolm! You're obsessed." Amber's arrival had given her time to dream up a counter-attack. "Seriously, love, you've got a problem. Yes, you've had a tough year, but that's no excuse for this paranoia. There's this doctor in Ulverston, he's a member of Scott's art group, I'm sure if I asked, he'd be willing to have a chat with you."

"Don't tell me he's shagging you, as well as Scott."

She slapped his face before he could move a muscle to defend himself. His cheek stung. How did she get up the nerve, after what she'd done to him?

"I'll be in the spare room, and I'm locking the door. Don't even think about disturbing me. Tomorrow's a big day, and you haven't got long to sober up. When it's over, we'll thrash this out, once and for all."

She flounced out of the living room, banging the door behind her. He'd never known what *flounce* meant until now. All at once he felt a hundred years old. His knees were aching, the unreliable bastards. He hobbled over to the sofa and put his head in his hands.

Sweat soaked his shirt, and the pinching waistband of his trousers reminded him of his abandoned diet. How long had his gut hung over his belt, when had his hair started thinning, and his eyesight begun to lose its sharpness? Time was passing, his life was careering in the wrong direction, like a lorry out of control.

Cheek smarting, head throbbing, he heaved himself to his feet, and poured whisky into the tumbler. He downed it in one, and trudged across the hall to the study. His lair, his private kingdom, a sanctuary looking out toward the Irish Sea. A computer sat on a desk, and a small bookcase stood beside the radiator. He yanked a key from his pocket, and unlocked a cupboard facing the window.

Inside lay the Winchester, polished and smooth. He took it out, and started stroking the barrel. Strange, the comfort given by the caress of a weapon. A mysterious impulse prompted him to raise the barrel to his lips, and he tasted the kiss of cold, hard steel.

Chapter Two

Joanna Footit squinted through her bedroom curtains. Seven forty-five, and already sunlight streaked the painted stonework of Ulverston. Perfect weather for this afternoon's barbecue at the Dungeon House. Across the road from her flat, scarlet begonias blazed in hanging baskets, and bunting fluttered above cars humming through the labyrinth of streets.

Two burly traders were manhandling crates in the direction of the market hall, and she dodged out of their line of vision. She looked so dreadful before she got herself ready. As for the see-through nightie, she meant it for Nigel Whiteley's eyes only. She'd definitely not given up hope of getting back together with him. Far from it. Her parents were on holiday in Filey, and she was staying overnight at their cottage in Holmrook. You simply never knew what might happen.

Nigel was bound to fancy the pants off Amber, who wouldn't? But whatever Amber thought, Nigel wasn't interested in a serious relationship with a kid her age, even if Amber was sixteen going on twenty-six. Amber was Nigel's cousin, and besides, Joanna was sure he preferred more mature women. Last week-end, she'd bumped into him in Ravenglass, and he'd greeted her warmly, with a kiss on each cheek. He'd even asked if she was going to the barbecue at the Dungeon House. When she said yes, she was helping out, he'd grinned and said he'd better volunteer too.

On the grapevine, she'd heard that he'd gone out with two or three other girls, but nothing serious, nothing that lasted. Give her another chance, and he wouldn't regret it. The prospect of seeing him again made her knees weak. What happened at the barbecue today might change her life forever.

Her flat was carved out of a converted loft space in the town centre. There was a sweet shop at street level, and a watch repairer's on the first floor. The landlord, a local businessman, was one of Gray Elstone's clients. When she'd complained about being fed up at home, Gray said the chap owed him a favour, and offered to have a word. The flat was tiny, with barely enough room for her clothes, let alone all her books, but the rent was next to nothing. She was saving a fortune on petrol, now that she no longer had to commute back and forth from Holmrook.

Did Gray's kindness have an ulterior motive? Soaping herself in the shower, she imagined her boss lurking outside, summoning up the nerve to part the plastic curtain and get an eyeful. He was thirty-eight, and had never married. If he'd had a girlfriend, nobody knew about it. People pulled his leg, calling him a Gray bachelor, and worse. Yet he was interested in women, not men, she was sure of it. More than once in the office, she'd caught him sneaking a glance at her when he thought she was preoccupied with her work. Three times in the past month, he'd invited her for a quick drink after work. Different pub each time, as if he didn't want to be seen to be making a habit of it. But he'd kept his hands to himself, and hadn't so much as brushed against her "unintentionally", far less ventured a peck on the cheek when she said she really must be going. Perhaps he simply wanted to be friendly.

Amber said he was a dirty old man, but that was Amber for you. Gray was impossibly ancient as far as she was concerned. They'd talked about him last night, after their trip to the Film Club at the Roxy. A Danish movie, all sub-titles and full-frontal nudity. Amber lied about her age to get in, but it wasn't worth the effort. After five minutes Amber started yawning and saying she preferred the real thing. Half an hour in, Joanna surrendered to the inevitable, and followed her friend to the pub round the corner. Amber told the leering barman she was nineteen, and he was happy to take the size of her boobs as corroboration. "Of course your creepy old boss wants to get inside your knickers," Amber had said. "Who wouldn't?"

That was one of the things Joanna liked about Amber. It was impossible not to feel like an ugly sister, squashed next to her on the plush banquette. Quite apart from their very different looks, they hadn't much in common. Amber wasn't interested in history or reading, and turned up her neat little nose when Joanna extolled the virtues of *Pride and Prejudice*. But Amber was fun to be with, and generous with her compliments. She never missed an opportunity to boost Joanna's ego. Might her kindness have an ulterior motive, did she reckon that sticking close to Joanna somehow brought her closer to Nigel? Each time the thought slipped into Joanna's mind, she swatted it away, as if fending off a wasp about to sting.

"Gray is a respectable professional man. He's a chartered accountant, for goodness sake."

"Honestly, Jo, you have no idea what men are like."

Amber had slept with three boys, and had shared the gory details with Joanna. She certainly wasn't backward in coming forward, but she was too young for Nigel. He was a real man.

"Gray is kind. Look at how he sorted out my flat. How many bosses would do that for a member of staff?"

"Wants you at his beck and call," Amber diagnosed, taking a slurp of shandy. "No chance of throwing a sickie and taking the day off to soak up the sun when the office is so close the head honcho can pop in at lunchtime for a so-called welfare visit. Trust me, Jo, it's your body he's after."

Joanna giggled. "I don't think so."

Would it be so terrible if Amber were right? Suppose things didn't work out with Nigel; suppose he wasn't willing to try again? Her mother's mantra was that a girl couldn't hang around forever. Gray Elstone was no Pierce Brosnan, but looks weren't everything. He had good manners, and a nice house, with the mortgage paid off.

"Mum reckons he's pervy."

"She didn't say so!" Joanna was startled. Mrs Whiteley seemed too polite to talk like that.

"Not in so many words. But the way his tongue hangs out when he's watching her and thinks no-one's looking, well…all I'm saying is, if he touches you or anything, you don't have to stand for it. Take him to an industrial tribunal. He'd cough up thousands to keep his name out of the papers."

"He's not like that. Really."

"Oh well, don't say I didn't tip you off. All set for tomorrow, then?" Amber had allocated enough time to trashing Gray, and was ready to return to her favourite topic. "You're sure Nigel will be there?"

Joanna didn't want to mention the conversation she'd had with him. Best keep her cards close to her chest. "According to Dad, he will."

A disingenuous answer, but plausible. Nigel's father and Joanna's were old mates. They'd played in the same football team for years, and after age took its toll and they were no longer able to run or tackle, they'd stood in the cold and rain, cheering Nigel on. The Whiteleys lived five minutes away from the Footits, and the two families were always in and out of each other's houses. After Linda Whiteley lost her long battle with breast cancer, Mum took pity on Ted and his boy, and they often came round for meals or a trip to the chippie. Both Joanna and Nigel were only children, and for years she'd acted like his older sister, though barely twelve months separated them. When he didn't make the grade as a footballer, and was forced to take a job in Malcolm Whiteley's company, it hit him hard. Working for his uncle, he'd said in a rare moment of self-revelation, felt like a punishment for failure. She'd become a shoulder to cry on. And eventually, something more.

Amber fiddled with a beer mat. "I was afraid my dad wouldn't let Nigel come."

"Why? It's Nigel's dad he fell out with, not Nigel."

"He's a pig-headed old bugger. I keep saying he ought to let bygones be bygones and make it up with Uncle Ted before it's too late. But he's not going to blink, those were his very words. I said it's not about blinking, it's about common humanity, but he simply won't listen."

"You never told me what Ted did to make him so angry."

Amber gave her a meaningful look. "It's all to do with Mum."

"You don't mean he and she…?" Joanna was agog with shock and excitement.

"Sorry to disappoint you." Amber's teeth flashed. "There was nothing in it. Far as I know, anyway. Uncle Ted was just flirting, and she probably gave him too much encouragement. Dad went apeshit. He can't bear anyone so much as giving her a second glance."

"Must be hard for your mum. It's not her fault she's so lovely."

Joanna wondered what it felt like, to look so good that you drove a rich man wild with jealousy. Lysette Whiteley was the most gorgeous older woman she knew. Not that she knew her very well, but whenever their paths crossed, she seemed pleasant and kind, never more so than after the accident. Every time they met, she asked how Joanna was getting on, and sympathised about how awful the car crash must have been. Very ladylike, Amber's mum, no airs and graces. Yet to hear Amber after they'd had a row, you'd think her mother was a cross between Margaret Thatcher and the bunny-boiler in *Fatal Attraction*.

Anyway, the barbecue was guaranteed to be fantastic. Amber's mum and dad would be on their best behaviour, and so would Gray. She knew from the invoices that Malcolm Whiteley was Elstone and Company's most valuable client, and she didn't mind Gray offering the services of his secretary (correction, PA—he'd written the new job title into her contract after her last pay rise) as an extra pair of hands. Robbie Dean would be there too, unfortunately, but she'd put behind her the way he'd behaved at Seascale that night. All she cared about was spending the afternoon with Nigel.

〉〉〉

"You two had a row?" Amber demanded as she tipped her breakfast things into the dishwasher. "I mean, you've not spoken a word to each other all morning."

"All morning?" Her father strove for jollity, but the shadows under his eyes told a different story. Despite the time he'd spent in the sun this summer, his skin looked sallow. No wonder his doctor was worried. She hoped he wasn't going to have a coronary or something, and leave her on her own with Lysette. "Give us a chance, it's barely nine o'clock."

"I'm the lawyer, better leave the quibbles to me." She wasn't a lawyer, of course, but the plan was for her to study law at York or Leeds. This was her father's idea; he liked to say he'd never known a solicitor to starve. Mum's idea of humour was to trot out the line that Amber was ideally suited to becoming a lawyer, given how much she loved an argument.

"Nothing to fret about." Malcolm patted her head, as if she were still nine years old. Anyone else, and she'd have smacked his face. "We're suffering a bout of pre-barbecue stress, that's all. Big day for us, princess. Lots of important guests, we need to make sure they all have a great time."

He'd coated himself with after shave, but up close, the stench of last night's booze was unmistakable. Lately, he'd been drinking too much, and on his own too.

"Even those scumbags who bought your company?"

"Even them. Don't forget, they paid through the nose for the privilege."

The breakfast kitchen stretched from the front of the house to the back. French windows gave on to a paved area, and the pink, cream, and yellow blooms of the rose garden. A large, fiercely trimmed lawn sloped down toward the summer house, and a low hedge surrounding the lily pond. Robbie Dean stood on the grass, putting up a green canvas gazebo.

Deano was stripped to waist, muscles rippling. He spotted her, and raised a hand. Was that a smirk on his face? Yes, she was still in her pyjamas. Deano fancied her, she felt sure, but he wasn't her type. She turned away to face her father.

"Weren't they threatening to take you to cleaners?"

Her father bit into the last piece of toast. "No fear. Gray is on top of the situation. Worst case scenario, we botched the small print of the deal. A breach of the warranties and indemnities, just a technicality. Nothing to lose sleep over."

Amber didn't have a clue what warranties and indemnities were, but she was certain he was fibbing. She'd persuaded Joanna to indulge in some industrial espionage, borrowing a key without Gray's permission, and sneaking the confidential takeover file out of a locked filing cabinet. Jo reported that Gray had consulted some pricey barrister in London whose advice was stuffed with dire warnings about fraud and tax penalties. Whatever this meant, now wasn't the moment to make an issue of it. If the new company chairman, that slimy greaseball Morkel, so much as touched her arm, she'd scream the place down, and insist on her father calling the police. Serve the scumbag right. In her mind, she pictured Nigel rushing to comfort her.

"What are you wearing this afternoon?" her mother asked.

"In this weather?" A sweet smile. "I thought the crop top and those shorts I bought in Aruba."

Her mother winced, but kept her mouth shut. Amber had made a bet with herself that she would be spared the *stop-dressing-like-a-hooker* lecture. Neither of her parents could afford to waste energy on an argument, with so much still to do. Specially when they were so keen, so pathetically keen, to pretend they were the perfect family.

How come no-one saw through the bullshit? For no-one did, not even Jo. Since selling the business, Dad had reinvented himself as a member of the idle rich, spoilt for choice between playing golf and quaffing champagne, with the lovely Lysette as his adoring soul-mate, a devoted wife and doting mother. Depressing to think people were so gullible. Everyone except her. And Nigel, of course.

"You're looking very...um...summery this morning, Joanna."

Gray Elstone held open the door of his Honda Legend with an old-fashioned courtesy Joanna rather liked. His compliment was awkward, but so was Gray. Six feet three, hopelessly uncoor-dinated and possessing an Adam's apple with a mind of its own.

His clumsiness and shambling gait matched his ham-fisted way with words. A numbers man, he found comfort in balance sheets and profit and loss accounts. Whenever conversation veered toward stuff that normal people talked about, like pop music and fashion, he became twitchy and inept, and started chewing his mangled fingernails. Joanna arranged herself carefully on the passenger seat, making sure she wasn't showing too much leg. Gray needed to keep his eye on the road. To be involved in another accident would be too much for her to bear.

"Thanks, Mr Elstone. Lovely morning for it."

"Gray, please." He wagged his finger playfully, to the bemusement of a woman crossing the road in front of them. "Now, now, what have I told you?"

"Sorry, Gray." She bestowed a brilliant smile on him, and tightened the seat belt. "So we're heading for the cash and carry first?"

"That's right." They moved out into the line of traffic waiting for the lights to change. "Save our host and hostess a job, eh?"

Malcolm Whiteley had delegated the food shopping to them. Amber found it hilarious that Gray tolerated acting as his client's dogsbody. Anybody else would be embarrassed, she said, especially when her Dad was semi-retired, and Gray worked at full pelt. Joanna didn't see it the same way. Malcolm's fees had paid for this big brute of a car, and for a chunk of Gray's new detached house. When your key client asked you to jump, the only question you asked was, "How high?"

Although the takeover was done and dusted, Malcolm remained a key client. He still rang up every five minutes. The potential litigation with the new owners of the company was causing both men a lot of grief. The difference was, Gray charged handsomely for the time he spent dealing with it. Things weren't as one-sided as Amber imagined. Malcolm had made Gray rich. In return for financial security, bending the knee to the guy who held the purse strings was a small price to pay.

◇◇◇

"Deano looks as though he's working up a thirst. I'd better ask him if he wants a coffee. Or something."

Lysette had moved to the window, her gaze lingering on Robbie Dean's bare chest. An act of deliberate provocation, Malcolm thought. He couldn't detect any clue that she was in the mood to kiss and make up. Had she spent the night working out how to hit back at him, and opted for a campaign of taunts and humiliation?

Fists clenched behind his back, he said, "Yeah, go ahead."

Surely Deano would never make a move on Lysette? Since the death of that girl he'd been seeing, he didn't seem to have anyone special, but Lysette was way out of his league. Lately, she'd pretended to take an interest in him, but this was a blind, Malcolm would stake his life on it. The more he mulled things over, the more certain he was that Lysette was diverting attention away from the man she was really screwing. Scott Durham, it had to be. She liked to think of herself as artistic. Creative, a free spirit. Load of bollocks.

Malcolm marvelled at his own self-control. He could feel— actually *feel*, without so much as looking in a mirror—a vein throbbing at the side of his head. In the face of endless provocation, it was a miracle he kept so calm. How many other men had to cope with this amount of shit?

Lysette had spent the night in the spare room, and he'd collapsed on to the bed before he had time to undress. Lysette would have called it a drunken stupor. She could be bitchy when she was in a bad mood.

Amber padded upstairs to put some clothes on. About time too, though she didn't intend to wear that many clothes by the sound of it. Lysette kept shooting herself in the foot, making a fuss about Amber's tarty dress sense. Kids liked to shock their parents, and Amber was addicted to making them squirm. Hence the piercings on nose and lip. What had happened to the little girl who used to sit on his knee, and tell him how much she loved him?

Where had it all gone wrong? All those years spent slogging his guts out, working round the clock, building his firm to secure their future. It wasn't easy money, hiring out skips. After expanding into waste management, he'd taken plenty of short cuts to make sure work kept coming through the door. Kill or be killed, that was the choice when you worked in waste.

Lysette poured coffee into a decorated gardener's mug, adding heaped spoonfuls of sugar. Neither of them uttered a word. She opened the glazed door and strode out on to the patio.

"Here, get this inside you!" She held aloft a mug emblazoned with the legend *Raindrops Keep Fallin' on My Shed*.

Sweetness and light. If only people knew. Shit, was that a tremor in his hands? Not the effects of the booze, he was certain, just one more symptom of the stress he was battling. Better steady his nerves. A quick swig of whisky was all he needed, while his wife—his *wife!*—was outside, flirting with Deano. A bloke with a young woman's death on his conscience, for God's sake.

> > >

The loaded trolley had a mind of its own. As Gray Elstone wheeled his shopping outside, he almost collided with two people coming in to the cash and carry, a man and a young boy who skipped out of his way at the last moment, nimble as dancers.

"Sorry, sorry!" Gray gasped. "Oh, it's you, Scott."

Of course. Joanna recognised the man now. A client of Gray's with no idea about finance, one of those hapless sole traders who dumped a barrow-load of receipts and scribbled apologies for records at the office a week before the deadline for filing his tax return, and expected his accountant to wave a magic wand, and turn the mess into something coherent and credible that wouldn't tempt the Revenue into launching an investigation. Unlike the second hand car dealers and window cleaners Gray acted for, at least Scott Durham could plead artistic temperament as an excuse. He made a living flogging watercolours, tourist fodder with innumerable different perspectives on Wastwater and Windermere.

"Hello, Gray." Scott spotted her, skulking behind her boss. "Hi there. Joanna, isn't it?"

God, he'd remembered her! They'd met several times, but had only exchanged brief pleasantries. She'd never dreamed she'd made any impression on him. Scott was only a year or two younger than Gray, and couldn't have been more different. Fair-haired, boyish, with piercing blue eyes. He was wearing a white tee shirt, and black jeans that showcased his bum. Amber reckoned Mrs Whiteley had a secret crush on him. He supplemented his income by teaching art, and Lysette was a member of a group he led. This spring, she'd enrolled for some one-to-one tuition. According to Amber, her dad was livid.

"Hi." She felt as shy as a schoolgirl. Handsome older men like Scott Durham had that effect on her.

He surveyed the overflowing trolley. "Stocking up for the barbie, Gray? Don't tell me Malcolm wants to deduct the cost of his sausages and burgers as a business expense?"

Gray could be relied on not to rise to the bait. Sure enough, he turned his attention to the artist's companion. The boy was about thirteen, slightly built, and wearing a Liverpool football shirt. Pretty kid, with a bird's nest of curly blond hair. No mistaking the resemblance to Scott in those small, neat features.

"So who's this?" Gray asked with forced jollity. "Not your famous son, by any chance?"

The boy shook his mass of curls. "I'm not famous."

"Gray likes to have his little joke, Josh," Scott explained. "He means, I've been telling everyone you're gonna be a star. The next Bon Jovi."

The boy rolled his eyes. "I'm not that good."

"Think positive!"

Gray beamed down on the lad. "I hear you're entertaining us with the guitar this afternoon."

"Singing one or two of his favourites," Scott nodded. "Trust me. He'll wow the crowd."

"I'm sure he will. Anyhow, we'd better get moving. Plenty to do before the festivities begin."

"Yeah, I've come to pick up a bottle of Bolly for Lysette and Malcolm."

"Splendid. Just as long as you don't try to claim the bubbly against tax!" Gray's geniality was heavy-handed, but at least he made an effort. "Shall we make tracks, Joanna?"

Scott treated her to a dazzling smile. "Lovely to see you."

She cleared her throat. "I'll see you later."

"I'll look forward to it."

She trotted after Gray into the car park, spine tingling. No wonder Amber said her mum liked Scott. He was a charmer. But Lysette was married, and too old for him anyway. She'd celebrated her fortieth birthday a few months ago. Spending a fortune on cosmetics papered over the cracks, but nobody could stop the ticking clock. Oh well, she ought to think positive herself. Suppose Nigel wasn't interested in getting back together again? Scott Durham might not be so far out of reach after all.

The whisky had done Malcolm a power of good. Simply a matter of gathering strength for the afternoon. The Whiteleys' barbecues were legendary, but he felt like a man preparing to face a public ordeal. Just as well he still had his self-control.

He'd locked the door of his study. You couldn't be too careful. If Lysette saw the Winchester, she'd go bananas. She didn't have the faintest idea of its existence. The rifle was an heirloom. His father enjoyed shooting, and had encouraged his sons to pursue the same hobby. Ted soon lost interest, but Malcolm was keen until he fell for Lysette and started spending every spare moment chasing her. The old man had made him a gift of the rifle, and three boxes of Eley Club ammunition, not long before a stroke claimed him. "Don't tell that wife of yours", he'd whispered.

No, Malcolm hadn't uttered a word. Lysette loved antiques, but she had a thing about guns, and had a sentimental distaste for the idea of shooting living creatures. He caressed the rifle, casting his mind back to his teens, hearing his father's gruff instructions on how to cock it, ready for firing. It was a .22 single shot target rifle, full size with a long barrel and fairly rudimentary sights. Light as a feather, and the recoil pad made it comfortable to hold. He'd not fired it for years, but he'd maintained it in good condition, and the ammo was long-lasting.

A few nights ago, he'd woken up from a crazy dream in which he'd acted as a one-man firing squad in some godforsaken Latin American country, gunning down blindfolded bandits, one after another. That same day, he'd taken the rifle out in his car to the lonely dunes at Drigg, just to make sure it still worked. The shots didn't make much noise at all, he'd disturbed nothing more than a flock of gulls.

He couldn't explain, even to himself, what had prompted him. Anyway, he found it oddly reassuring to know the rifle fired as well as ever. People let you down, but you could always rely on the Winchester.

Chapter Three

"The Dungeon House?" Ben Kind said to his host. "A sinister name for somewhere so idyllic."

His airy wave took in the lily pond and lavender bed, the winding beck and the distant sea, shimmering in a haze of heat. The view beyond the grounds of the house had scarcely changed since Roman legions marched down from the fort at Hardknott to their garrison on the coast. You could tune out the hum of conversation, and even Amber's favourite rock bands screeching from the temporary loudspeakers.

A sudden peal of laughter from Amber's friends knotted Malcolm's stomach. They were mocking the way he'd stumbled over his words in welcoming everyone to the annual Dungeon House barbecue. He'd kept his speech brief, on Lysette's strict instructions, and despite having drunk more booze than he'd intended, he thought he'd got away with it. But Cheryl struggled to keep her face straight, and the ghost of a smile flickered even on her boyfriend's poker face.

Ben Kind unnerved him. It wasn't simply that the man was a police officer. This wasn't some local PC Plod, but a flinty Mancunian who'd cut his teeth detecting serious crime in the city before meeting Cheryl, and leaving his missus and kids to be with her. According to Lysette, the wife had begged Ben to come back, but Ben Kind was determined to make a new life for himself in the Lakes. A stubborn man, judging by the set of his jaw, someone who stuck to his guns. Those dark eyes seemed to read your thoughts, and his cynical jokes implied that anyone living in a big house must have paid for it with ill-gotten gains. Malcolm wouldn't want to be on the other side of an interrogation conducted by Ben Kind.

"This name, Dungeon, goes back centuries." He chewed his steak. Red meat, there was nothing tastier, and fried onions complemented it to perfection. "Not that we have our own underground prison cell, if you're in search of an overflow for Millom Jail."

"You've got mustard all over your chin," Lysette said. "Here, use this."

Snatching the paper napkin without a word, he wiped the yellow smear away. Lysette had hung her daubs inside the summer house. She reckoned her painting had come on leaps and bounds since she'd started taking lessons from Scott Durham. What else was the bastard teaching her? His nephew Nigel and his accountant, Gray Elstone, were cooking in the gazebo, while Amber and Joanna served from trestle tables covered in gingham cloth. Deano and two lads who helped him in the garden were in charge of the booze, giving host and hostess a chance to mingle.

Not that Malcolm was in the mood for social chit-chat, least of all with a detective inspector. It wasn't as if he could quiz Ben Kind about the alibi Cheryl had supplied for Lysette's tryst with her secret lover. The policeman's abandonment of marriage for someone pretty, vivacious, and unworthy had set a disturbing precedent of betrayal.

Ben downed a mouthful of lager. His self-assurance made Malcolm's flesh creep. What had Cheryl been saying, were she and Ben poking fun at him behind his back? Adultery meant nothing to this pair. Ben's divorce was nowhere near finalised. Lysette said the wife was fighting tooth and nail, but she'd never win.

"You saw the deep split in the rocks beyond the stretch of grass where everyone is parked?" Malcolm demanded. "*Dungeon* means fissure."

"As in Dungeon Ghyll?" Cheryl gave Ben a lover's smile. "That's a marvellous spot, in Great Langdale. We must go walking there, one of these days."

Lysette nodded. "Dungeon Ghyll is fantastic, but we have our very own tiny sandstone quarry, the other side of those trees. Robbie Dean is turning it into a garden."

"Wonderful," Cheryl said. "Hey, why don't we check on progress?"

"I'll lead the way." Lysette adjusted her Ray-bans. "We don't want any accidents. Robbie hasn't put railings around the top path yet, and there's a twenty-five foot drop. Are you coming, Malcolm?"

He shook his head. In the quarry garden, she'd be out of harm's way. He needed to keep a close eye on Scott Durham, and make sure he didn't sneak off somewhere to be alone with her. Lysette had volunteered Durham to look after the music this afternoon, and Malcolm hadn't come up with a good excuse to wield a veto. "Supersonic" had given way to Whitney Houston, wailing "I Will Always Love You." Shit, was he sending Lysette a romantic message, coded in his choice of music? Malcolm wouldn't put anything past the man. Right now, Durham was chatting to his son, the curly-haired wannabe pop star. The kid had performed a handful of songs like "Blaze of Glory," prompting the guests to clap like mad, even though you could see better on television talent shows any day of the week.

"Gray says Morkel wants a word," he said. "I'd better speak to them."

"Business!" Lysette yawned. "Okay, we'll leave you to it."

Making his way down the slope, Malcolm felt a burning sensation behind his breastbone. Heartburn, or simply indigestion? He'd probably over-indulged in the steak and kebabs. Comfort eating, yes, but who could blame him?

Might Ben Kind, not Scott Durham, be the man Lysette was seeing? What if Ben had taken Lysette to some hotel last night? The way he'd dumped his wife and family revealed a ruthless streak. Perhaps continued close exposure to Cheryl had made him realise she was a pain, and he'd taken a fancy to his lover's best friend. Would Lysette have dared to ask Cheryl for an alibi if she was sleeping with her best friend's lover? Or was it a daring bluff, had she never bothered with an alibi because she was banking on her husband's reluctance to humiliate himself by checking with Cheryl?

No, no, it had to be Scott Durham. Back when Lysette was sweet sixteen, a weedy, four-eyed loner in her class had written a fawning poem about her, and she was so flattered, Malcolm had to deal with him. The poet was a cry-baby, and next time Lysette spotted him in the street, he scuttled off in the opposite direction. But Scott Durham wasn't as soft as he looked, even though people pitied him because he'd lost his wife, and admired his tireless fund-raising for the hospice where she'd died. He was a keen fell-racer, and kept himself in shape. It would take more than a knee in the groin to scare off Scott Durham.

"Malcolm, how the devil are you? Thought I should come over, matter of courtesy."

A hand the size of a shovel thumped him on the back as he heard the South African voice in his ear, consonants spat out like bullets from an Uzi. Hansie Morkel was about the least courteous person you could wish to meet.

"You talked with Gray?"

Morkel mopped his brow with a red handkerchief. The heat was unrelenting, and he was overweight and out of condition, the legacy of too many expense account dinners. Corpulence was all that he and Malcolm had in common.

"I asked a few questions, he had no answers. Not much of a dialogue, to be candid with you. Malcolm, the board will consider a resolution of no confidence in you at its next meeting. Meantime, consider yourself suspended from duty with immediate effect. The lawyers asked me to give you this."

He thrust an envelope into Malcolm's hand. "Give my best to that lovely wife of yours. And thanks for the invite. Impressive place you have here. Take my advice, and enjoy it while you can."

Malcolm's head was swimming. He stuffed the envelope into his pocket unopened. "Don't...don't under-estimate me, Hansie."

A grin cracked Morkel's face. It was like watching a rock split in two. "Truth to tell, Malcolm, my mistake was over-estimating you. As well as the value of your shitty little company. Ah well, we live and learn, eh?"

With a derisive laugh, he strolled away in the direction of the makeshift car park at the back of the house. Malcolm's chest felt on fire. What had possessed him to jump into bed with those South African thugs? It was like selling your soul to the Mafia. No way would he surrender, even if they set out to bankrupt him. The Durham kid's song said it all. If he did go down, he'd make sure he went in a "Blaze of Glory."

"All right, Malcolm?" Robbie Dean asked.

"I've had better days." No point in bullshitting Deano. "Fancy a pint?"

"Sure."

Deano's expression never gave much away. He wasn't the sort to offer well-meant advice to go easy on the booze. His indifference to others was a strength. Malcolm's problem was that he cared too much. Most of all about Lysette.

"The lawn is bone dry," Malcolm said as they reached at the bar. "Two pints, Dave, thanks. Remember when it pissed down last August, and finished up like a mud bath? See those bare patches."

"I'll put the sprinklers on full blast tomorrow."

Malcolm lifted the plastic tankard. "Cheers."

Deano wasn't the most skilled plantsman in the world, but he didn't mind putting in a shift, and how many homeowners had a one-time football star on the payroll? He was a far better player than Ted's son, Nigel, and after he was picked for England schoolboys, some good judges had predicted he'd go all the way. Preston North End signed him on, and only a bad tackle that tore his cruciate ligaments had kept him out of the first team. While trying to regain his fitness, he went out clubbing one night with Nigel and two girls. One of them was Gray's PA, the girl who was potty about Nigel. Robbie took a bend too fast, showing off to the pretty blonde in the front passenger seat, and veered off the road and into a tree. Neither he nor the blonde girl was wearing a seatbelt. She went through the windscreen, and was dead on arrival at A & E.

Thinking aloud, he said, "Life's a bugger."

Robbie Dean's moody face stared over the rim of his glass. "You never said a truer word."

People were drifting away, and an elderly couple Malcolm hardly knew came up to say cheerio. He mumbled pleasantries, keeping one eye on Scott Durham, but the bloke was on his best behaviour. He and Lysette must have made a pact: do nothing to stoke up suspicion. Cooking had finished for the afternoon, and Gray Elstone, angular frame draped untidily over the iron-work bench outside the rose garden, signalled to him. Gray had forgotten to take off his ketchup-stained apron, making him look like a butcher taking a break from bloodthirsty work. His grimace was usually reserved for funerals and bad news from the Revenue.

"You spoke to Morkel?"

"Uh-huh." Malcolm took another swig. "He gave me this envelope. Inside are my marching orders. I nearly shoved them up his arse."

Gray winced. "Morkel hinted he'd drop all claims if you walk away from the business and repay sixty per cent of the purchase price. A clean break."

Malcolm almost choked on a mouthful of ale. "I'll break his fucking neck first. Chuck away everything, in return for a measly forty per cent? He must think he's fucking well tipping a servant back in Joburg. It's a joke."

"Don't fly off the handle." Gray nibbled his thumbnail. "Bad for your blood pressure. Honestly, you need to think about his offer. It's an opening shot, my guess is that he'll settle for fifty-fifty. We might even squeeze out better terms in return for a quick deal. At least he's prepared to compromise. The alternative…"

"The alternative is to see him in court." He laughed, more raucously than he'd intended, and some folk nearby, including Scott Durham and his kid, looked round to see what he found so funny. "Dead easy."

"You can't win, Malcolm. The consortium's pockets are deeper than Wastwater." Gray's Adam's apple bobbed unhappily. "The man's talking about bringing in the Fraud Squad, never mind pursuing a civil claim."

"Relax, it isn't gonna happen." Malcolm made a lordly, sweeping gesture with his hand. "Trust me."

"Of course I trust you, Malcolm." A nervy lick of the lips. "The problem is, that makes me part of an endangered species."

Malcolm slapped him on the back. "You worry too much. Leave everything to me. I know what I'm doing."

"Your very words when I suggested you look at that offer from the American venture capitalists. Instead, you bit Morkel's hand off."

To be rebuked by Gray Elstone was like being mugged by a boy scout. Malcolm was so startled, he didn't even lose his rag.

"Past history."

"Sorry." Gray's voice was barely a whisper. "It's just such a disastrous situation that we are…"

His hands were shaking. It wasn't the drink, the man was terrified. Malcolm hadn't sussed that until now. Crazy to be talking doom and disaster out here in the sunshine in the loveliest place on God's earth, but if he sank, Gray would sink with him. They'd finish up sewing mailbags together. Even if somehow Gray wriggled off the hook, what did the future hold for a dodgy accountant who was as ugly as sin?

"Don't worry. I've got a plan."

Gray's crumpled expression registered a vote of no confidence in his client's forward thinking. No point in wasting any more time trying to inject some backbone. With a dismissive grunt, Malcolm abandoned him to his misery, and stumbled up the slope to the gazebo, where Nigel and the girls were clearing the trestle tables. At the sight of him, Amber made a face.

"Dad, you're staggering."

"I've not recovered from having my eardrums shattered by that rock rubbish of yours. Oasis, you call them? Desert would be nearer the mark. Not a patch on the Beatles."

"They're fantastic, actually. And you're pissed."

"I'm fine. Mind your language, princess."

"Why are you slurring your words, then? When it comes to bad language, you're a million times worse than me."

"I only wanted," he said with careful dignity, "to see how you kids were coping. And to thank you for all your help, of course."

"No problem." Nigel was keen to act the peace-maker. "We've had fun, haven't we?"

Malcolm had never been close to his brother, even before the recent bust-up over Lysette, yet he had a soft spot for Ted's lad. Tall, broad-shouldered, with a devil-may-care glint in his eye, Nigel reminded him of his younger self. He understood business, and was ready to do whatever it took to succeed. After Morkel's takeover, Nigel had moved on, and set up a claims management company, hustling for compensation on behalf of people injured in accidents. Ambulance chasing was a dirty job, yes, but someone had to do it. Nigel would go far. Ted lacked his son's drive, that was why he lived in a crummy terraced house, and couldn't afford 24/7 personal care to see his illness through to the end.

In sentimental moments, Malcolm saw Nigel as the son he and Lysette would never have. She'd suffered a series of miscarriages, and both her final pregnancy and Amber's birth were a nightmare. At one time it was touch and go whether mother and child would survive. The medics were brilliant, and everything worked out fine, but Lysette made up her mind that one near-death experience was enough. She'd insisted on Malcolm undergoing a vasectomy. He'd hated the thought of it—who wouldn't?—but eventually surrendered to the inevitable. Nothing illustrated more clearly the depth of his devotion. And how had she repaid him?

"Thank Christ that's over for another year."

Amber's tone was sulky, her pretty mouth contorted into a pout. Her slender, tanned body looked stunning in that skimpy crop top and bikini pants, whatever her mother said, but Nigel hadn't made enough of a fuss of her. Sensible lad, he was way too old for her. Malcolm wasn't ready for Amber to have a serious boyfriend. Plenty of time for that, she was still only a kid, even if her curves said otherwise. It had been very different with him and Lysette. They were made for each other.

Joanna Footit said, "Oh, it's been a lovely day, Mr Whiteley. Thanks so much for inviting me."

Her pale cheeks glowed, her voice cracked with excitement. Joanna and Nigel had been canoodling in the back of Robbie Dean's car the night he drove it into a tree. Although both of them walked away without a scratch, the horror of the crash had left Joanna an emotional wreck. Only Nigel escaped with no scars of any kind. Born survivor, that lad, cool as you like. At long last Joanna seemed to be sorting herself out, and that strapless dress made the most of her slender figure, even though she was the ultimate titless wonder. At least she had long, long legs. Nigel's hand had sneaked on to her bum, but he could surely do a lot better than Jo Footit. Never mind, if she distracted him from Amber, good luck to her.

"He only wanted another lackey," Amber grumbled. "Isn't that right, Dad?"

"We couldn't have managed without Joanna," Nigel said.

The compliment made the older girl simper. Only the other day, Lysette had predicted that Joanna and Nigel would get back together. Lysette had become a sort of surrogate mum to Nigel, and Malcolm often wondered if she used him as an excuse to see more of Ted. Truth was, he'd fretted about her interest in other men for as long as he could remember. As the mocking refrain of a boy band version of "Love is All Around" thudded in his ears, he told himself that the difference now was that he was *sure*.

"Hi, guys!" Cheryl shouted. "Any of that Bolly left?"

She and Lysette emerged from the rose garden, both jigging along to the music. Malcolm had never liked that bloody song; now he detested it. Ben Kind strolled behind the women, keeping an eye on everyone, Malcolm glanced over his shoulder, and noticed Scott Durham, taking care to look out to sea. Unlike Cheryl, Lysette wasn't showing much flesh. She had a thing about skin cancer, and liked to cover up whenever the sun shone. Malcolm didn't mind. Her body was meant for him alone.

Amber brightened at Cheryl's approach. One of her long-running gripes was that Cheryl was much nicer to her than Lysette, which always provoked her mother into saying that was because Cheryl didn't know her well enough. Once, the girl had even asked Malcolm why he hadn't married Cheryl instead. There'd been no question of that. Cheryl was sexy and constantly pestered by boys, but Lysette was quieter, cleverer, more sophisticated. Malcolm only ever had eyes for her.

"It's boiling," Amber complained. "Look at me, I'm sweating cobs."

"I prescribe a glass of Bolly, darling," Cheryl said. "Now your guests are melting away, forget the buck's fizz. Your Dad's cellar has two whole racks full to bursting with vintage champagne."

"So you do have a dungeon in your house?" Ben Kind said. "Even if it only accommodates alcohol?"

"I'd love to be incarcerated down there," Cheryl announced. "You can lock me up and throw away the key. Just me and the booze."

Amber sniggered. "I bet Ben has an even better idea. Every policeman owns a pair of handcuffs, doesn't he?"

"Do you know our helpers, Ben?" Lysette asked quickly. "This is Joanna, who works for Malcolm's accountant. Her parents live down the road."

"Not in a mansion anything like this," Joanna said quickly.

"We'd have invited them if they weren't living the high life on holiday."

"In Tenby." Joanna blushed. "Not exactly Tenerife, is it? They rent a cottage every summer. I…I'll probably stay in their house tonight, keep an eye on the place. Keep it safe from intruders."

She gave Nigel a shy smile. Amber stretched in a slow-motion yawn, watching him from the corner of her eye as he withdrew his hand from its resting place on Joanna's backside.

"What wild, exciting lives some people lead," Amber murmured.

"And this is Nigel," Lysette said. "Malcolm's nephew."

"You're a detective?" Nigel was intrigued. "Not on duty, though?"

Ben weighed up the young man as they shook hands. "Cheryl says I'm never off duty."

"Ever met a psychopath?"

"A few." A lazy grin. "Mostly they were members of the legal profession."

"Nigel, sweetie," Cheryl said hastily, "what's the latest about your dad?"

Nigel frowned. "Not so good. The doctors say he's got six months. Give or take."

"Oh, sweetie, how awful! Give him my love, will you?"

"Sure." Nigel bowed his head.

"Tell him I really will pop in and see him this next week."

"I'm sure he'll be glad to see you."

The silence was filled by Celine Dion. "The Power of Love." Malcolm cleared his throat noisily. "I'm going inside."

The tittle-tattle was doing his head in. Instead of shedding crocodile tears for that useless brother of his, why didn't anyone care about how he felt? If he stayed outside, soon Scott Durham would give in to temptation and join them. No way could Malcolm bear Lysette promising to visit Ted—even though he had sent him to Coventry—and exchanging jokey small talk with the man she was shagging.

Enough was enough. Soon they'd see he wasn't powerless, and understand he was still the master of his fate. You didn't mess with Malcolm Whiteley.

Chapter Four

"Malcolm! Are you awake?"

He forced open gritty eyes. Lysette stood in the doorway of the study, hands planted on her hips. She'd changed into a slinky green dress, dangerously high heels compensating for her lack of inches. He'd crashed out in the armchair, sprawling awkwardly, one hand squashed under his head. His fingers felt numb, and a cramp in his legs made him wince as he tried to shift position.

"What…what is it?"

"We're all going down to Ravenglass for a meal. Obviously, you don't want to come."

What if he insisted on joining them? Her disdain made it clear that was the last thing she wanted.

"I…I'm not…"

"No. Stay here, and sleep it off." Her features were taut with strain. "Can't say when we'll be back."

Daylight was fading. Must have been out for longer than he'd imagined. Fighting the grogginess, he managed to string two sentences together.

"I was dog tired. I needed to rest my eyes."

"Recover from your drunken stupor, you mean." She sniffed. "You stink like a brewery, Malcolm. Open the window, can't you? You're a complete and utter shambles. As for welcoming our guests—you made a spectacle of yourself. I felt like throwing up, I was so embarrassed."

Never had she spoken to him with such contempt. Choking with rage, he tried to haul himself on to his feet, but before he could straighten himself, she'd marched out into the hall, heels clattering on the new wooden floor like tracer bullets. He heard her yell at Amber to jump in the car. The front door slammed, and the Alfa's engine roared into life.

He'd fallen asleep with his mouth open, and his throat felt scratchy. Hobbling to the kitchen, he filled a glass from the tap. An old man's face glared back from a gold sunburst mirror on the wall. Bloodshot eyes, sunken cheeks. Shit, he looked like a down-and-out in designer summer wear. He moved gingerly, testing tender muscles and creaking joints. Another reminder of the passing years. Back in the day, he could go on a bender, and then spring out of bed at the crack of dawn, fresh as a daisy and ready to take on the world.

He splashed cold water on his face. What was Lysette playing at? At least with Amber around, she wouldn't dare to get cosy with Scott Durham. Presumably Cheryl and Ben Kind were tagging along for the meal. Had she asked Durham to join them? Surely she wasn't that stupid. Or was she tiring of the affair? Secrecy and lies, exciting at first, became squalid once laid bare. If Durham had asked her to move in with him, that would mean taking on the son, the wannabe Bon Jovi. She wasn't the maternal type, her constant squabbles with Amber proved that. What if the boot was on the other foot, and she'd started getting too intense? Durham might easily have second thoughts. Lysette was high-maintenance, and commitment never came cheap. Plenty more fish in the sea, especially for a baby-faced artist with a winning smile, and a sob story about his wife's losing battle with cancer

Stretching his arms, and sucking in air, Malcolm gave the face in the mirror a mocking grin. Not quite dead yet, eh? Like the song in that film. "Always look on the bright side of life." Even when you're being crucified.

Outside, the sky was streaked with orange and red. A shepherd's delight sunset, the sort Durham drooled over. How much money did his paintings rake in? His cottage was no bigger than a phone box, he drove a rusty old Ford, his jerseys were holed by moths. Quite a come-down for Lysette. Would she really fancy slogging through the divorce courts, knowing he'd fight her every inch of the way?

He lay down on the living room sofa, and stared through the window with heavy-lidded eyes. The garden was empty. You'd never guess that a few hours earlier, these grounds had thronged with people and life. Robbie and his crew had dismantled the gazebo, and shifted the trestle tables, while Durham had taken away his sodding loudspeakers. The spreading oaks cast shadows, the summer house was in darkness. The Dungeon House estate was still as a graveyard.

>>>

When he woke again, he was starving, but his head hurt, and he had a sickly feeling in his stomach, so he made do with a round of unbuttered bread. He'd been kidding himself with that brief flash of optimism. How likely was it that Lysette had dumped Durham? Her fretfulness was provoked by a husband who couldn't stay sober, not even when hosting a party for the neighbourhood. What if she came home this evening, and locked him out of her room again?

No! He banged his hand down on the table so hard that for a moment, he thought he'd cracked a bone. Lysette wasn't going to pull that trick again. He simply wouldn't allow it.

He blundered back to his study, taking the Chivas Regal and a tumbler for company. Pouring himself a generous measure, he spilled most of it on the Axminster. No problem, plenty more where that came from. He prided himself on keeping his cellars well-stocked. For as long as he could remember, he'd dreamed of becoming a sort of lord of the manor. When business was booming, once or twice he'd indulged a flight of fancy by lodging a bid for country houses at auction sales, but something always held him back. Nothing captured his imagination until his first viewing of the Dungeon House. Talk about love at first sight. The house stood on a wooded knoll between Holmrook and Ravenglass, and had once been a hive of industry, buzzing with men and machinery. Sandstone quarried here built cottages in Ravenglass, and other villages dotted around the Western Lakes. The Dungeon House was more than a home; it was a slice of history.

Selling up was unthinkable. An Englishman's home was his castle. But castles required a vast amount of upkeep, and he'd spent eye-watering sums on redecoration, roof repairs, and new central heating. To pay back sixty per cent of what he'd made from selling his company would cripple him. Fifty per cent? Same difference.

A sharp pain stabbed him in the guts. Early warning of a stomach ulcer? Stress did that to people, it was a well-known fact. Not so long ago, he'd been as fit as a flea, now he was odds-on for an early grave. When was the last time he'd managed a full twenty-four hours without a drop of the hard stuff? He needed booze the way a one-legged man needs a stick to lean on.

Selling the company was the turning point. Each year, waste management became more cut-throat, and creative accounting could only take you so far. The offer from Morkel's consortium was timed to perfection. Too good to be true? Well, yeah, so it had proved.

Once the celebratory Caribbean holiday was over, things started going awry. He'd assumed Lysette would jump at the chance to spend more time with him, but she kept heading to places like Buttermere and Ennerdale Water, to sketch or paint. Or so she said.

He savoured the whisky's tang. No better medicine. For months he'd been sleeping badly; his GP prescribed Temazepam, but after he began to suspect Lysette of an affair, he started having nightmares for the first time in his life. Once in a dream, he'd discovered his wife naked in bed, legs wrapped around a smooth-skinned man wearing nothing but a goat's mask. Malcolm had seized hold of the goat's horns, determined to tear off his enemy's disguise. Instead, his own fingers were ripped away, leaving his hand a bloody stump. He woke in a cold sweat, to find his wife sleeping peacefully beside him.

When she'd lost interest in sex, his suspicions crystallised. At first, he gave her the benefit of the doubt, knowing her appetite was almost as healthy as his. Once or twice he'd drunk so much that he was incapable of performing anyway, but lately she kept whining that she had a headache or wasn't in the mood. And that wasn't all. Several times, she'd hurriedly silenced her chirruping phone for no obvious reason, making excuses that wouldn't convince a child. One afternoon when she was out sketching, he rifled through her things until he found a folder of credit card statements. None of her purchases looked dodgy, though he cringed at the sums she frittered away on clothes. At least he'd put his mind at rest—until Robbie Dean had set him wondering again.

"Saw your missus in Seascale yesterday, while I was filling up the van."

"You did?" She'd told him she'd spent the afternoon at Wasdale Head, had rhapsodised about the light playing on the surface of the lake.

"Yeah, gave her a wave, but she didn't wave back."

"Too busy enjoying the sea breeze, I suppose?"

Robbie shook his head. "Dunno. When I glanced round again, she'd dipped out of sight."

That evening, he'd told Lysette that Robbie had seen her. She brushed it off, pointing out that he'd admired the watercolour of clouds scudding over the peaks of Great Gable and the Scafells, her afternoon's work. It sounded convincing, but panic flickered in her eyes before she recovered her nerve. You could paint clouds and mountains any time. Had she stockpiled watercolours, to corroborate her alibis? Next chance he had, he resumed his search of her personal belongings. Her bank statements proved more mysterious than the credit card transactions. She'd made a series of sizeable cash withdrawals. Unusual for someone who never liked to carry much money in her purse. What was she spending the money on? Gifts for her lover surely couldn't account for all of it. Hotel rooms for their assignations surely explained the rest. Seascale boasted several hotels and guest houses, and if she wasn't making use of them, why else would she be there? In a small town she disliked, nestling under the brooding bulk of the nuclear power station at Sellafield?

The only puzzle left to solve was the identity of the boyfriend. Scott Durham had his cottage, and Gray Elstone lived on his own. Robbie did too, for that matter, in the cottage where his grandfather had brought him up after his parents died. Why bother with a hotel, unless the sheer danger of it all was part of the appeal? He thought the culprit must be someone else, someone he'd never even met, until it occurred to him that her hotel visits might coincide with times when Josh Durham was at home from school.

The sound of the Alfa pulling up outside jerked him back to consciousness. Hearing someone fling open the front door, he called out, "Amber, is that you?"

His daughter looked into the study. She was wearing a party dress that showed far too much flesh. Her hair was tangled and her cheeks were stained with tears.

"You're pissed. The stench in here is disgusting."

"What's up? Who made you cry?"

"What do you care? I hate you. And I hate Mum."

She turned away, and ran up the stairs. He heard the click-clack of Lysette's heels as she came inside, and struggled to his feet. Okay, it was now or never. His life was falling apart. Time to start putting it back together again.

"Lysette!"

She appeared in the doorway. Her face looked stretched, her expression unnatural, like a woman who'd undergone too much cosmetic surgery. "What do you want?"

Anyone would think he was the one at fault. "Who upset Amber?"

"She's fallen out with Nigel, that's all. She finally woke up to the fact that he's more interested in Joanna. We were in the restaurant at the Eskdale Arms, but she was an embarrassment.

In the end, Nigel went off with Joanna, and Amber's wailed all the way home."

"Who else was there?"

"Gray, and Ben Kind, and Cheryl, why do you ask? Robbie was drinking in the bar, and playing darts. Oh, and Scott Durham turned up later on, after he'd taken Josh back to the cottage." Her green eyes were cold. "Happy?"

"It's you I want to be happy, Lysette."

"That's not true, is it?" Her voice trembled with anger. "What you want is for Malcolm Whiteley to be happy. The man with the big house and big dick. Successful in business, and brilliant in bed. Adored by his family, and…"

"Lysette!" He put up his hand. She was needling him into doing something he'd regret. "We need to talk."

It was a good line, the sort of shit peddled by those women's magazines she lapped up in the hairdresser's, but she shook her head. "You'd never listen to me."

"I'm all ears."

She breathed in, as if summoning up her courage. "Okay, Malcolm, you asked for it. Tomorrow, I'm leaving. My solicitors will be in touch. I want a divorce."

He swallowed. "I don't think I'm hearing you right."

"I said you wouldn't listen."

"You haven't even got any fucking solicitors!"

"As a matter of fact, I have. It's one of many things you don't know about me."

He grabbed her by the shoulder. "What else don't I know? Tell me that. I know you're shagging Scott Durham, you little whore."

"Let go of me." She struggled, but his grip was too strong for her to escape.

"You seriously think I'd surrender you to that pathetic toe-rag?"

"Surrender me? You talk like I'm something you bought in a raffle."

He was breathing hard. "Lysette, you're not leaving me."

The instant he relaxed his hold on her, she wriggled free. She was panting, and her cheeks were crimson.

"You're so wrong. Tomorrow, I'm off, and I'm never coming back. We're finished, Malcolm, and if you don't sort yourself out, you'll be finished too. Look at you. Your life's a mess. Everybody thinks you're a swollen-headed oaf. They only tolerated you because you had money, and now that's dribbling away, you'll soon find out who your friends are. The real question is whether you'll find any at all."

She ran out into the hall, and up the staircase. He hesitated before following. She'd reached the half-landing and was staring back at him. Taking care not to fall, she took off first one of the high-heeled shoes, then the other. He took a stride forward, and she threw one of the shoes at him. It struck him on the forearm, a glancing blow that didn't hurt but took him by surprise. As he hesitated, she spun round and raced off barefoot, up to the third bedroom. Not moving a muscle, he listened to her fiddling with the key in the lock.

"Bitch," he mumbled.

That was it, then. He'd tried everything, now he'd run out of options. Nobody could blame him for what happened next.

⟩⟩⟩

For a long time, Malcolm sat in the armchair in his study, endlessly polishing the barrel of the Winchester. His mood was almost serene, thanks to the Chivas Regal. The long struggle was over, the uncertainty at an end. Once hope died, it was easy to move forward, and do what had to be done.

He heard a noise. Lysette, unlocking the bedroom door? She'd thought better of her defiance, perhaps, and wanted to talk. Too late, too fucking late. He sat very still, straining his ears. The soft sounds could only be Lysette's footsteps, as she inched down the staircase, desperate not to disturb him. So she'd decided not to wait until tomorrow after all. She'd probably been listening out, waiting to see if he went up to bed, and leave the coast clear. Hoping that drink or pills or exhaustion had knocked him out.

Quiet as a ghost, he picked up the rifle. Energy surged through him. He was about to seize control of his life again.

The study door was ajar. Nudging it open with the butt of the Winchester, he waited for Lysette to appear into his line of vision.

Yes, here she came, in tee shirt and jeans, a zipped and bulging airline bag in her hand. All ready for a quick getaway.

But if he couldn't have her, no-one else would.

As he lifted the rifle, something caught his eye through the window, from the darkness of the garden. A gleam of light, coming from the summer house. Another malfunction in that extortionately pricey lighting system? No, the summer house wasn't connected up yet. Was someone out there? No, it was impossible.

He heard Lysette gasp, and realised she'd seen him. And she'd seen the Winchester. Now he'd reached the point of no return, he felt drained of energy. All he wanted was for it to be over.

"Malcolm, no!"

He took a pace forward. Another stride would take her within arm's reach. Not that she needed to be so close. The Winchester would do colossal damage at this range. Upstairs a door opened. Was that Amber? He couldn't allow himself to be distracted.

His eyes met Lysette's. He saw no sign of contempt or hatred now. Only terror.

"Put that thing down!"

Her voice was a cracked whisper. Probably she was calculating whether she dared make a dash for the door.

But it was too late.

Now

Chapter Five

"Heard the news?"

Les Bryant didn't wait for an invitation to sit down at the table where Hannah Scarlett was chatting to DC Maggie Eyre. One beefy hand held a mug of strong coffee, the other a half-eaten Cumberland sausage in a bap, dripping brown sauce onto the tiled floor of the cafeteria. He curled his lip at the sight of Hannah's lentil soup and Maggie's tuna rice salad.

"Don't tell me, let me guess," Hannah said. "New research has revealed that meat eaters' life expectancy is longer than previously thought. They are now expected to survive until their sixtieth birthday."

"You're a cruel and heartless woman, DCI Scarlett." Les was just three weeks away from his sixtieth. "Don't worry about me. I'm a born survivor."

True enough, Hannah supposed. It wasn't merely that, years after retiring from West Yorkshire Police, and despite occasional health scares, Les still worked as hard as detectives half his age. He was on contract as a consultant to Cumbria's Cold Case Review Team, and somehow his post had survived the scything-down of jobs conducted by the grim reapers of Finance and HR. To everyone's surprise, he hadn't even committed career suicide by saying something utterly inappropriate when Hannah and her team were summoned to a photo-opportunity with the Police and Crime Commissioner.

"You'd be amazed how much fitter I feel since I went on the veggie detox." Her aim was to show solidarity with her friend and colleague Fern Larter, after Fern was placed on a strict diet following a diagnosis of hypertension. The sight of a juicy steak still provoked feelings of lust, but she had no intention of confessing to Les. "Seriously, you ought to try it."

"I'd sooner stick pins in my eyes. To be fair, you're not looking terrible on it." Les gave her slim figure the sort of appraising gaze nobody else would dare. "Take it from me, the feelgood factor is nothing to do with the crap you're eating. It's Daniel Kind who's put a smile on your face. How is he, these days?"

Hannah glared, while Maggie tried to suppress a grin. "Fine, thanks. Now, what about this breaking news? I'm all ears."

Typically, Les strung out the tension, gnawing at his bap, and wondering out loud why no slick marketing man had rebranded long sausages rolled into circular coils. Why not call them Cumbria sausages? The historic county of Cumberland had vanished forty years back, when all was said and done.

"The name's a reminder of the good old Cumberland pig." Maggie's family had farmed for generations. "The boars died out in the Fifties. My granddad owned one of the last in the county. So sad the breed disappeared."

"Tragic." Les finished his hot dog, and burped shamelessly. "All right, then. Another teenage girl has gone missing. She set off from her home, just outside Ravenglass, on Saturday morning, and nobody's seen her since. Name of Shona Whiteley."

Maggie leaned forward. "You're not suggesting there's a link with the Lily Elstone case?"

"Who knows?" Les sucked in his cheeks. "Admitted, the circumstances aren't one hundred per cent identical. Young Lily was knocked off her bike, wasn't she? Shona said she was catching the bus on Saturday morning, forty-eight hours ago. She was supposed to be spending the night at a sleepover with a friend in Eskdale Green, and the alarm wasn't raised until yesterday evening when she was due back. But the girls are much the same age. Lily was fourteen, Shona's fifteen, and the places they were last seen are only a few miles apart in west Cumbria."

"Is that all?" Maggie had never mastered the art of hiding disappointment. She was desperate to come up with something fresh, but it was hardly unknown for teenagers to go missing. Even in the Western Lakes, it had happened several times since Lily vanished without trace. Each time the kid had turned up safe and sound. Usually the explanation was a row with the parents.

"He's just ratcheting up the suspense," Hannah told her. "Our Mr Bryant is more of an old ham than any of your grandad's Cumberland pigs. Come on, Les, spit it out. And I don't mean that bloody sausage. Did the two girls come from the same village, or attend the same school?"

"Not as far as I know. But there is a link between their fathers."

Maggie's eyes widened. "You're talking about the accountant, Gray Elstone?"

"And Shona's dad, yes. Name of Nigel Whiteley. Ring a bell, Hannah?"

"Uh-huh." He peered at her across the little table, smug as a quizmaster when an answer teases the tip of a contestant's tongue. "Whiteley, Whiteley…"

"You'll kick yourself when I tell you."

"Was he…?"

"The Dungeon House killer?" Les' bleak smile resembled a "before" picture in a commercial for cosmetic dentistry. "You're getting warm."

"But his name wasn't…"

"Nigel? No, you're right. The man responsible for the murders at the Dungeon House was Malcolm Whiteley. He was the uncle of this Nigel Whiteley."

"Ah." Hannah pondered. "Gray Elstone was a friend of Malcolm Whiteley, wasn't he? His financial adviser?"

He applauded lavishly. "Go to the top of the class. Not sure he was such a great adviser. Whiteley's finances were in meltdown at the time of the shootings."

"Small world, eh?" Maggie said. "Though I don't see what this has to do…"

"The world's even smaller than you think." Les sat back, ready to play his ace. "You'll never guess where Shona Whiteley was last seen."

"Try me," Hannah said.

"At her father's home, before she set off to catch a bus."

"So?"

"These days, it's called Ravenglass Knoll. Twenty years ago it was known as the Dungeon House."

〉〉〉

Joanna Footit wasn't even watching the television when Nigel Whiteley's face appeared on the screen. She liked to keep her set on in the background, even in the morning, when there was nothing on worth watching. It was company, especially when Darcy was at his most aloof; it was true what they said, dogs have owners, but cats have staff. The regional news was on, and Joanna was hoovering the living room carpet in her pyjamas, looking even more of a sight than usual. She was waiting for the local weather forecast, although if anyone had asked, she'd have struggled to explain why she followed the weather news with almost religious devotion. It wasn't as if she spent a lot of time out of doors.

"All we want is to have Shona back, as soon as we can."

That voice, oh God! The timbre was imprinted in her brain. She'd misheard Nigel's name when the reporter mentioned it, but she'd never mistake the sound of him. Fumbling with the switch of the vacuum cleaner, she tripped over the lead in her haste to catch sight of him on the screen.

Yes, there he was, tall and square-jawed. He'd aged well. His hair was short and flecked with grey, but it made him look distinguished. He wore a sombre suit, and an expression to match, but he was still the Nigel Whiteley she'd once adored.

The news item was brief, but she played it back half a dozen times until she had the story off by heart. The gist was that Nigel's daughter had vanished into thin air. A photograph showed Shona at a party, giving a thumbs-up to the camera. An attractive girl, with shoulder-length dark hair, and a brace on her teeth. Good cheekbones, inherited from her dad.

"Shona has never done anything like this before." Nigel said. "I'm desperately worried."

Shona had told him she'd arranged to stay the night with another girl, and it wasn't clear to Joanna whether the friend was actually expecting her. You never got the full story on television. Sometimes, Joanna knew, this was due to "legal reasons", a phrase which covered a multitude of sins. The police liked keeping their cards close to their chest.

Pausing the television, Joanna made herself a cup of Nescafe. Perched on her favourite chair, she sipped slowly, and asked herself what could have happened to Nigel's daughter. The obvious assumption was that she'd run off with some lad, but if the police took the same view, would the story make the TV news? Then again, Nigel was a wealthy man these days, and the rich were different. They had influence with the media.

Nigel's name cropped up in the papers now and then. He was sometimes described as one of the North West's leading entrepreneurs. His company, Accident Payback, was highly successful, but courted controversy. She'd read news items accusing them of encouraging people to make false claims, and putting up the insurance premiums of innocent motorists. For Nigel, it was water off a duck's back; he insisted he was performing a public service. Joanna supposed he was right, and found it impossible not to dwell on what-might-have-been. This wasn't foolish fantasizing about a celebrity who was hopelessly out of reach. Her spine tingled at the memory of him running his hands along her body.

If only Robbie Dean hadn't crashed his car, things would have been so different. The accident might not have harmed her physically, but it had destroyed her nerves. They had a name for it now, post-traumatic stress disorder, but back then, everyone thought she should just be thankful she'd survived in one piece. She and Nigel were the lucky ones, but Joanna didn't see it that way, not for a long time.

She pressed the TV remote. Nigel spoke directly to the camera. "Shona, love, please. All I want is to hear that you're safe and well."

Heartbreaking to see him in such distress. Joanna knew what heartbreak felt like. She'd been so happy that final night, that terrible night of The Last Supper. They'd kissed and made up on the foreshore at Ravenglass. She had a good job, a little nest egg in the bank, and the man of her dreams. It felt like Heaven

Except that, in the space of a few hours, came the blood-soaked Hell at the quarry garden.

The Dungeon House nightmare had destroyed her fragile recovery from the horror of the fatal car crash. She'd lost the ability to think straight. Malcolm Whiteley had so much to answer for. It wasn't just that he was a murderer. He'd ruined her life, and, yes, Nigel's too. Money didn't count for everything, and Nigel looked so pale and drawn. Twelve months ago, when she'd read about the death of his wife from pancreatic cancer, she'd almost got up the nerve to drop him a line and offer her sympathy, but at that stage Eoin was still around, and the moment had passed.

"You're not in any kind of trouble. Just get in touch, and let me know you're okay, yeah?"

Nigel was distraught, naturally, but Joanna's instinct told her the girl would turn up safe and sound. Teenagers often did ridiculous things. The authorities would pull out all the stops to find her, but would the joy and relief of reunion with Shona be enough to answer all Nigel's prayers? Joanna suspected he was suffering from a deeper unhappiness. Pain was visible in his dark eyes. While everyone hunted for the girl, who was taking care of him?

>>>

"If we're raking over the past," Hannah said, "let's do it in my office, and let someone else grab this table."

"You've not finished your soup," Les said. "What's wrong, too many lentils?"

"It got cold while I waited for you to tell us about this Whiteley girl."

He bared his teeth again. "No loss. Why not forget the veggie experiment, and grab yourself a pork pie, build yourself up? With you in a minute. Just let me collect my bits and pieces."

Hannah watched his retreating back. "He's getting worse."

Maggie laughed. "You did tell me to watch him and learn."

Not long ago, Maggie had split up with her fiancé, and further dismayed her parents by deciding to prioritise the job, rather than marriage and raising a family. She was aiming for promotion, though with salary budgets under tight control and competition fierce, the odds were against her. Hannah was giving her more responsibility, with Les acting as her mentor. In the last forty-eight hours, Maggie had fronted a press conference about the case, under the watchful eye of a woman from PR, and made a fleeting appearance on local TV. She'd done well, and resisted the journos' invitations to promise a swift and miraculous solution.

Lily's bike had been found in a ditch next to the lane she cycled along to reach home, but no trace of her had ever been found. It looked as though she'd been knocked off the bike and abducted, but without a body—assuming she was dead, of course—there was little to go on. But you never knew what diligent re-examination of witness testimony might turn up. In her heart of hearts, Someone knew the truth about what had happened to the kid, and the best way to find that someone was through patience and determination. Qualities that Maggie possessed in abundance.

"Selectively, was what I had in mind. Come on."

"I've heard of the Dungeon House," Maggie said, as they walked down the corridor. "Some nutter gunned down his family? And now his nephew's daughter is missing."

"I'm hazy about the details. Believe it or not, I was barely into my teens when the murders took place. But a colleague told me about the case, years ago."

"Is that right?"

Hannah coughed. Why on earth did she still feel a pinch of embarrassment about mentioning his name? "Yes, my old boss, Ben Kind."

Maggie nodded. Ben had retired not long before his premature death, and she'd never worked with him. But she was familiar with his name, and the fact that Hannah was seeing his son, Daniel. A small world, yes, that was the Lake District. So often around here, one person was connected to another. One of the lessons Les drummed into any colleague willing to listen was that a good detective needed to understand the significance of the connections. Especially those that people didn't want you to discover.

"Dare we risk a coffee?" Maggie asked.

Even the quality of the hot drinks had fallen victim to austerity measures, but Hannah said, "Yeah, I need a caffeine boost. Let's risk it."

They stopped at the machine, and carried three alleged cappuccinos into Hannah's room. At one point, her office had been due to be sacrificed on the altar of cost efficiency, but in the end she'd shifted to a smaller room, commanding a view of the car park. Beggars couldn't be choosers and she was glad to keep her own space. Open plan working was supposed to help communication, and undoubtedly saved money, but she often yearned to shut the door on the hubbub outside, and work out in her head what to do next. Blue sky thinking, this was called, when practised by divisional commanders. For a humble DCI, it looked dangerously like self-indulgence, but Ben had taught her that it was easy for police inspectors to feel the need to run around like headless chickens, and plenty did just that. She dared not think what he'd have made of the cult of budgets and bureaucracy, with its sacred rituals of process, form-filling, and spreadsheets, where worshippers prospered, and heretics who queried the crime statistics were cast into the outer darkness. Slavish devotion to protocols, systems, and key performance indicators were as comforting as blind faith, but proper detective work demanded the courage to use your initiative, and a little imagination.

A small circular table and three chairs were squashed into the space, but she'd done little to personalise the room. Her only concession to interior decor was to line the window sill with potted plants that she kept forgetting to water. She'd chosen them for their supposedly indestructible qualities, but even the spiky green and white leaves of the sanseveira seemed to be praying for a transfer to the typing pool. Throughout her career, she'd striven to keep her work and her private life in separate compartments, though she hadn't always succeeded. So, not a single photograph, not even of Daniel Kind. Their relationship was still in its early days, and Hannah was undecided about its future. In theory, only a handful of people had a clue that she and Daniel were a couple, but the office grapevine ensured almost everyone in the building was up to speed. If only police intelligence were equally efficient. No crime in the county would go unsolved.

She tasted the coffee. "You were about to give me a heads-up on progress with Lily Elstone."

"We've had a number of responses to the appeal, which Linz and I are following up, but nothing jumps out as a likely breakthrough. I'm disappointed."

"Les is right. Looking for leads in a cold case is like looking for love. Got to kiss a lot of frogs before you find a prince. Hey, speak of the…"

Les bustled in, arms full of papers and lever-arch files. He plonked himself down on the vacant chair, and spread everything out over the table. To watch him at work, you'd think the technological revolution had never happened. Probably he thought a tablet was what you swallowed to cure a hangover, and an Android was a creature out of a sci-fi movie.

Turning to Hannah, he said, "How much did Ben tell you about the Dungeon House?"

He took it for granted that they'd discussed the case. Les knew Ben had taken a shine to Hannah, and he'd heard the gossip that their relationship went beyond the strictly professional. Rumours of an affair were exaggerated, but her involvement with his son meant Hannah still tended to turn pink and defensive whenever Ben's name cropped up.

"Years back. I forget the details."

"All right, I'll begin at the beginning. Are you sitting comfortably?"

He grinned at the two women, and Hannah realised he enjoyed being centre stage again. A reminder of the old days, when he was the SIO mapping out how his team should conduct an inquiry.

"Once upon a time there was a big bad businessman whose name was Malcolm Whiteley. He made his money in waste management, which I thought was just a posh term for running a scrap yard. In fact, play your cards right, and it's a licence to print money. There's a lot of waste that needs managing, apparently. Whiteley built up his operation over the years, and bought out rival concerns. Along the way, he earned a reputation for operating on the windy side of the law."

"Worked a treat, didn't it?" Hannah pointed to a yellowing photograph of an Arts and Crafts house among the papers Les had laid out on the table. "He bought a mansion on the proceeds."

"Yes, he developed a taste for the high life. Conspicuous consumption, don't they call it? The Dungeon House stood on a rise, looking out toward Ravenglass. In the grounds were the remains of an old sandstone quarry. The building was in a rotten state of repair when Whiteley moved in, and he spent money hand over fist, creating his dream home. He was one of those work-hard-play-hard types, and toward the end he was drinking like there was no tomorrow. Usually, that sort goes in for chasing expensive women, but there's no evidence that Whiteley had eyes for anyone but his wife. Things might have turned out better if he had. He'd married his childhood sweetheart, a girl called Lysette, and everyone agreed she was a stunner. Tiny woman, below five foot, but stylish and charming. Whiteley idolised her. They'd been together since their school days. Their only child, Amber, was sixteen at the time of the killings."

"Was the marriage happy?"

Hannah winked at Les. Maggie had taken to heart the advice which Hannah, in her turn, had once been given by Ben Kind. Finding out about the people in the story helps you to find out who committed the crime.

"To outward appearances, yes."

"But?"

"The story goes that Lysette was playing away from home." Les took a mouthful of coffee, and looked as though he wanted to spit it out. "Call this cappuccino? Breach of the Trade Descriptions Act. I bet the Whiteleys owned a decent coffee maker. They were the couple who had everything. Only snag was the usual one. Everything wasn't enough."

Snippets of the story were coming back to Hannah. "Didn't Whiteley run into financial trouble?"

"Yes, he sold his company and made a packet, but the buyers started stamping their feet. Questions arose about the accounts, and there was a strong suspicion Whiteley had taken too many short-cuts to save time and money. Breaches of hazardous substances regulations and what-not. They put him under pressure to refund a large chunk of the money he'd been paid. His problem was that he'd blown most of it."

"So he couldn't afford to repay?" Maggie asked.

Les turned to her. "Gray Elstone—the money man, Lily's dad—was very close to Whiteley. You could say that Elstone knew where the bodies were buried, if that wasn't tasteless, in view of what happened. Elstone insisted there was no risk that Whiteley would be bankrupted, even if he was forced to cough up some money to settle litigation."

"He would say that, wouldn't he?"

"Correct. Elstone was in it up to his neck, and it suited him to play down any suggestion that the people who purchased the business were misled. But he admitted Whiteley had frittered away a small fortune. He'd have needed to draw in his horns."

Hannah nodded. "According to Ben, Whiteley's self-image depended on being seen as a man with a Midas touch. Grand house, gorgeous wife, glamorous teenage daughter."

"On the day of the killings, he hosted a barbecue in the grounds of the Dungeon House. An annual event, loads of people invited. He was losing the plot big style, and had a skinful before anyone arrived. He insisted on making a speech of welcome, but only succeeded in coming across as a drunken loser. Some guests were amused, most of them cringed. Nobody imagined he was about to go on a killing spree."

"Did anyone have any idea he owned a rifle?" Hannah asked.

"Ted Whiteley, his brother, knew. The rifle was a Winchester that belonged to their father, and he taught his lads how to use it. Ted wasn't fussed about guns, but Malcolm enjoyed shooting. When the father died, he left the Winchester to Malcolm. The brothers didn't get on, and there was a big row some time before the killings. After that, Malcolm never spoke to Ted again, even when Ted was diagnosed with terminal cancer. He'd given Ted's son, Nigel, a job in his business, but after the takeover, Nigel left, and became an ambulance chaser. He and his uncle remained on speaking terms, and he helped man the bar at the barbecue. Ted, the dying brother, wasn't invited."

"What an utter shit," Maggie said.

"Of course, after the killings, people said they'd always thought there was something seriously wrong with Malcolm Whiteley. Not sure if it was really true. After a crime as horrendous as that, everyone jumps on the bandwagon."

"Understandable," Maggie said. "Hard to have sympathy for a family annihilator."

"Family annihilator, eh?" Les plucked at a hair growing in his nostril. "American term, is it? Something you picked up off the telly?"

"It's a well-established phenomenon," Maggie retorted. "A man—well, usually it's a man—murders his wife and one or more of his children, and then kills himself. It's becoming more common, nobody knows why."

"You're assuming," Hannah said, "that Malcolm Whiteley did kill Lysette and Amber before he shot himself."

Maggie glanced at the newspapers on the table. "Has anyone suggested that he didn't?"

"Yes, as it happens," Hannah said. "Ben Kind believed the whole truth about the Dungeon House murders never came out."

Chapter Six

Joanna switched off the television. She was feeling peckish, and didn't have much in the fridge. Better nip out to the convenience store. She could treat herself to a cheese and mushroom toastie at that new coffee shop in the centre of Lytham. These pangs in her stomach were unfamiliar. Since finishing at work, she'd lost her appetite. Was she feeling hungry because she'd seen Nigel's face up close again, out of the blue?

"Told you what a good-looking chap he was," she murmured to Darcy.

Darcy, a glossy Siamese, curled up in his basket, feigning supreme indifference. His jealousy amused Joanna. Fresh competition for her affection wouldn't go amiss.

Seeing Nigel again reminded her of the afternoon they'd taken the ferry across Windermere, before walking through the woods near Hawkshead. Not long ago, she'd dreamed about that day, reliving every magic moment. Heartbreaking to wake up, and find herself no longer a young woman with high hopes for the future. Doctor Chanderpaul was right, she'd got herself into a downward spiral. Yet it was all very well for outsiders to harp on about thinking positive. First, you needed something to think positive about.

Infused with an energy she hadn't felt for ages, she showered and dressed. Almost noon, naughty, naughty, but she'd fallen into bad habits. Sometimes she spent the whole day in her pyjamas. With time on your hands, things preyed on your mind.

The deli and the shops were more than a mile from her bungalow. This would be further than she'd walked for weeks. She usually caught a bus to the doctors' surgery, but she needed the exercise. Doctor Chanderpaul had warned against getting old before her time. The skies were cloudy, and she took an umbrella, to be on the safe side. No sense in getting completely carried away.

She locked the front door behind her, still cheered by the unexpected sighting of Nigel. At least she had happy memories, souvenirs that money couldn't buy. One thing she'd never envied Nigel was his wealth. She guessed it had brought little happiness, just like it never brought happiness to that hateful uncle of his. Nigel had spoken so movingly about his missing daughter. If only she could offer him comfort at a difficult time.

"Nice to see you out and about, Joanna." Edna Butler, who lived three doors away, paused in the act of wheeling a bulging shopping trolley through her front gate. "You're on the mend, I hope?"

"Tons better, thanks."

"Grand news, though you do look a bit pale, if you don't mind me saying so. And thin as a rake. Good to get a blow of air, bring some colour to those cheeks."

Joanna's tight smile was more like a grimace. She'd always hated people going on about her appearance.

"You must pop round for a cup of tea. I'll bake a Madeira cake in your honour, how about that? Are you doing anything tomorrow afternoon?"

Edna, a widow in her late sixties, talked incessantly, mostly about relatives Joanna had never met, and hoped never to meet. The price of a cup of tea at Dunromin was two hours of genteel boredom. Three or four hours, if you were really unlucky, and she insisted on your staying for an early supper and a game of Scrabble.

"Thanks, I'd love to." Joanna hesitated. Lies didn't spring readily to her lips; it was the price of being well brought up. "Unfortunately, I won't be here."

"What a pity. Not to worry, shall we say Wednesday, instead?"
A tinkly laugh. "Or Thursday, come to that? My social calendar
isn't exactly chock-a-block. It would be lovely to have a natter.
You did say you've taken early retirement, didn't you?"

Yes, she'd agreed to the phrase with the insurance brokers
who employed her. It sounded better than *sacked* or *redundant*,
yet it carried a whiff of premature old age and mothballs. Joanna
had been signed off work with stress, and her manager, wanting
to reduce staff levels, but fearing a claim of unfair dismissal or
disability discrimination, had offered a generous exit package
if she volunteered to go quietly. Joanna didn't really need the
money, but it was an easy way out, and her habit in life was to
take the easy way out.

"I…I'm not…"

"Say yes! It will be a tonic for you." Edna's beam out-dazzled
the yellow tulips lining the path to her front door. "We can have
a right old chinwag, just the two of us. You might like to come
along to the W.I.'s next meeting. We have a guest speaker talking
about the history of cockle fishing in Lytham."

"As a matter of fact," Joanna said, "I'm going away. Get some
sea breezes in my lungs."

"How lovely. Whereabouts are you going? Not Morecambe,
by any chance? My cousin's youngest lives there."

"Back to the Lakes," Joanna said quickly. "We used to live
in Cumbria, on the edge of Holmrook. I called the bungalow
after the village."

"Ah, the Lake District! Walter and I used to love Bowness."
Edna had evidently never ventured as far west as Holmrook.
"Where are you staying?"

"Ravenglass." Joanna spoke without thinking, but of course
it was the perfect destination. Ravenglass, where she'd last been
happy with Nigel. "On the coast."

"I'm sure it's marvellous," Edna said. "When will you be back?"

"Not sure, to be honest." Joanna gave her neighbour a brilliant smile. "I'm hoping to catch up with an old friend of mine.

By the by, Edna, could you do me an enormous favour? Would you mind taking care of Darcy while I'm away?"

⟨⟩⟨⟩⟨⟩

Maggie stared at Hannah. "Surely there's no doubt what happened?"

Les gestured toward the headlines screaming from old newspaper cuttings. *Three Dead after Rifleman Rampage. Suicide Husband Killed Wife and Daughter.* "Not if you believe what you read in the Press."

"Which we never do," Hannah said.

He gave her a sly grin. "Over to you. Tell us about Ben's take on the case."

"He and his girlfriend—Cheryl, his future wife—knew the Whiteleys."

"So I discovered when I looked up the files. They even had dinner with Lysette and Amber Whiteley and some others a few hours before the killings. They were interviewed, but nothing in their statements suggests Ben had a particular theory. He didn't take part in the investigation, because of the personal link."

"Cheryl was Lysette Whiteley's oldest friend. It's coming back to me now." Hannah closed her eyes. In her mind, she heard Ben's husky voice, telling the story. "As I recall, they'd known each other since primary school. Two pretty girls, popular with the boys. Cheryl played the field, but Lysette never got the chance. She and Malcolm started going out together, and that was that. Fate sealed."

Maggie winced. Hannah could read her mind. The young DC's journey through life had seemed pre-destined, but she'd had the courage to strike out on her own.

"You can always escape, if you want to enough."

"I'm not saying Lysette was a coward. Whiteley was hardworking and faithful, and crazy about her. Millions of women settle for much less. He made money hand over fist, and bought a palace where they could live happily ever after. The fly in the ointment was Lysette's boredom. Her interests were very different from his, and the cracks showed as their daughter grew up. Malcolm thought the sun shone out of Amber's backside, but

Lysette thought he spoiled her rotten. When Amber misbehaved, they quarrelled over how to discipline her. The marriage was in trouble, long before Malcolm realised it."

Les was curious. "Cheryl told you all this?"

"No. this came second hand, from Ben. Cheryl and I were never…close."

"Uh-huh."

Hannah felt herself colouring. "Cheryl introduced him to Malcolm and Lysette Whiteley after they moved to the Lakes. When he transferred to the Cumbria Constabulary, they came up to her old stamping ground, near Gosforth, and were invited to the Dungeon House more than once."

"What did Ben make of Whiteley?" Maggie asked.

"They were chalk and cheese. He said Whiteley was matey enough, or at least thought it didn't hurt to be on good terms with a cop. Lysette he liked. She was fun to be with, and didn't spend her life talking about herself, or showing off how much money they had."

"Did he realise the marriage was on the rocks?"

"Yes, Cheryl hinted that Lysette was seeing someone else."

"Who was the other man?"

"Ben didn't know for sure. Cheryl wasn't in on the secret. Lysette was very discreet, but the smart money was on a local artist. Lysette enjoyed painting, and he gave her one-to-one tuition. Cheryl suspected that wasn't all he was giving her. Though Ben also wondered about the man who raised the alarm after the shootings. The head gardener."

Les whistled. "Doing a Lady Chatterley?"

"It crossed Ben's mind. But he admitted it was very unlikely."

"What exactly happened?" Maggie never liked discussion about a case to be sidetracked. "When did the gardener find the bodies?"

"Sunday, the day after the barbecue. He turned up to finish tidying the grounds after the barbecue. There was no sign of life in the house, but he had a key to the outbuildings where the gardening equipment was stored, so he didn't give the Whiteleys a second thought—or so he said."

"Working on a Sunday?" Maggie's suspicions were aroused. "That's devotion to duty for you."

"It's no different from your dad's farm," Les pronounced. "The job's never done, with a garden. Why do you think I started work again after I retired? I was fed up with breaking my back, digging and hoeing, that's why. Came back for a rest."

"Tucked away in the grounds were the remnants of an old quarry," Hannah said. "Whiteley was transforming it into a landscaped garden. At some point, the gardener's work took him there, and he found two bodies lying on rocky ground at the bottom of the quarry. Malcolm Whiteley, with his face blown off, and his rifle by his side. His daughter Amber, sprawled next to a boulder with her head bashed in."

Maggie winced. "Not the sort of thing you ever forget."

"He ran back to the house, but nobody answered the door. It wasn't locked, and when he pushed it open, he saw Lysette. She was lying in the hall in a pool of blood. Like the others, she'd obviously been dead for hours. He dialled 999, and waited for the emergency services to arrive. From the start, it looked like a classic case of murder followed by suicide."

"What did they think was the sequence of events?"

Hannah cast her mind back. "Malcolm shot Lysette first, and this was either witnessed or discovered by Amber. She ran for her life, and her father followed her out of the house. A path ran around the top of the quarry. There were no railings, and the drop was sheer. He pushed her, or possibly she fell. The forensic evidence showed she hadn't been shot, but died from the impact of hitting the ground. It looked as though Malcolm Whiteley checked she was dead, then shoved his rifle in his mouth, and fired."

"Good riddance," Maggie said.

"I gather everyone agreed about that."

"So what niggled Ben Kind?"

"The precise timeline was never clear. By the time police and ambulances turned up, more than half a day had passed since the shootings. The assumption was that Malcolm and his wife had a row, and he killed her. A bag was found at the Dungeon House, filled with Lysette's things. Presumably she'd broken the news that she was walking out on him for good, and he snapped. What happened to Amber was the unanswered question. It seemed likely she'd run out of the house, and her father followed her. Perhaps he meant to calm her down, who knows? An unfenced path, as I say, skirted the top of the quarry, and one way or another, she went over the edge. The drop was enough to kill her, even if she hadn't hit her head on a rock."

"Sounds plausible."

"Ben didn't deny it. But he felt the SIO settled too quickly for easy answers."

"Who was the SIO?"

"Desmond Loney."

"Oh." Maggie'e eyebrows shot up. "Say no more."

Desmond Loney had risen to giddy heights in the force, largely on the strength of an undeniable capacity for putting in the hours, coupled with an imperturbable demeanour suggestive of wisdom and sound judgment born of long experience. A classic case of appearances deceiving. His career, Hannah reflected, was one long story of investigative incompetence. Some of his mistakes hadn't surfaced for years, and others no doubt remained undiscovered, ticking away quietly in the filing cabinets like unexploded bombs. When his luck finally ran out, he'd snatched at the chance of spending more time with his family, his holiday home, and his pension pot, enjoying a premature but well-upholstered retirement while his former colleagues laboured long and hard to clear up the mess he'd left behind. Hannah's team had been called upon more than once to re-examine cases where his habitual blind optimism and instinctive faith in his least reliable officers had led to clues being missed, and crimes remaining unsolved. Maggie's own career had not quite overlapped with his, but she belonged to a new generation of detectives for whom Desmond's reputation amounted not only to a legend, but also a dreadful warning.

"Ben had no time for Desmond, but to be fair, the man was under intense pressure, and public scrutiny. The Dungeon House shootings were one of the bloodiest crimes that Cumbria had seen in years. It was brutal and shocking, and people were very frightened. The national media descended, the force was in the spotlight. The temptation to draw a line under the whole horrible business was almost irresistible, and Desmond wasn't the man to resist it. He made it very clear that the police weren't looking for anyone else in connection with the incident, and exuded confidence and calm at every press conference."

"Can you blame him?" Les asked.

"Ben did."

"But why?" Maggie asked.

"He couldn't believe—and Cheryl couldn't believe—that Whiteley would have killed his own daughter. Whatever the man's faults, everyone agreed that he adored her."

"It's a classic pattern with family annihilators," Maggie said. "A man decides to end his own life, and can't contemplate his children living without him. So the bastard murders them. It's a vicious, perverted kind of love. Most of all, these people love themselves."

"True. And we have gained more experience of these cases, unfortunately, since the deaths at the Dungeon House. But Ben had other reservations. He wasn't sure the forensic work in the quarry was as thorough as it should have been. There hadn't been any rain, so it seemed unlikely that the girl had slipped over the edge of the quarry. The path wasn't fenced, but it was quite wide. Would Malcolm really have pushed her to her death, rather than shooting her? Why the change of M.O.? Killers don't usually switch methods like that."

"Paper thin," Les murmured. "Was that it?"

"No, there was something else. A witness claimed to have seen someone fleeing the scene that night."

"Any I.D.?" Maggie asked.

"This chap was driving along the lane that passes by Dungeon House. He was taking it slowly, because he'd been out on the ale, and was probably well over the limit. He came forward a few days after the murders, and said he'd nearly hit someone who ran out into the road in front of him. He swerved, and managed to avoid a collision, at the price of hitting a dry stone wall. This person seemed to come out of nowhere, and had vanished by the time the man got out of the car. The car was damaged, but he managed to drive home in one piece. When he sobered up and went back over the incident in his mind, he reckoned it occurred right outside the gates to the Dungeon House. The gates were never locked, and he thought the person he saw had run out from the grounds."

Les made a sceptical noise. "Don't suppose he came up with anything as useful as a clear description?"

"No such luck. But he claimed that he'd seen a man, dressed in a woman's clothes."

Joanna's expedition proved a triumphant success, and she arrived home exhausted yet elated. Her spur-of-the-moment decision to decamp to Ravenglass meant there was no need to stock up with food, but she'd enjoyed her toastie, and treated herself to a carrot cake. Just as tasty as Edna's, she decided over a blissfully solitary cup of camomile tea, even if shop-bought. For good measure, she'd bought herself three new outfits. Quite a spending spree, but she could afford it. She'd hardly opened her purse for months, except for bare essentials. Her illness might prove a blessing in disguise. The sales girl had boosted her morale by admiring her trim waist, and in the changing room mirror, Joanna had persuaded herself that she really was capable of looking svelte. So often lately, she'd felt closer to sixty-plus than forty-plus, but her legs were as slender as ever, and at least her breasts weren't big enough to sag. On her way home, she felt young again. She'd rediscovered the spring in her step, and the only reason she'd caught the bus back was that she was weighed down by her parcels. All this thanks to that glimpse of Nigel on the telly. The next step must be to see him in the flesh. What would he make of her?

"What do you think, Darcy?" she giggled "A flame-haired temptress?"

Ravenglass was an inspired choice as somewhere to stay. She was right to trust her instinct. Such a pretty spot, where the National Park met the sea. Full of historic significance, an old railway line and Roman remains. Seascale didn't compare, and as for Millom and the Furness Islands, forget it. Ravenglass was perfect.

Joanna had never booked accommodation online. In fact, she'd not had a proper holiday for the past three years. Since those nightmarish months with that conman Eoin, she'd withdrawn into herself, relying on Darcy and the television for company. No wonder her health had suffered, along with her work, but it wasn't too late to make a fresh start. She picked up the phone, and started making enquiries.

Within twenty minutes, she'd secured a room in a guest house for a fortnight. The place sounded snug, and the proprietor eager to please. You couldn't ask for a more beautiful location, over-looking the estuary, and the price per week was very reasonable, all things considered. Joanna's luck was turning at long last. She hugged herself with delight.

"I'll see you when I see you," she told Darcy. "This will be quite an adventure."

〉〉〉

"I'm guessing the mystery transvestite never came forward?" Maggie said.

"And was never traced." Hannah took a final taste of the cappuccino before giving up on it. "Desmond decided early on that the witness was pissed, or a time-waster, or both. To be fair, everyone in the team agreed. We all know that any major incident attracts sensation-seekers."

Les grunted. "Like pigs in muck."

"The Dungeon House killings provoked a flurry of unlikely stories from losers gagging for a share of the limelight. A Masonic conspiracy led by the people who bought Malcolm's company was behind the killings. The Whiteleys hosted regular swing-ers' parties, and Malcolm became jealous when Lysette started enjoying them too much. You name it. There wasn't a shred of evidence to back up the wildest theories. The inquest decided that Lysette was murdered, and Malcolm committed suicide. As for Amber, they recorded an open verdict. Logically, you couldn't argue."

"But?"

"Ben knew the witness. This was a bloke who liked a drink, and wasn't chasing fifteen minutes of fame. He never uttered a word about what he thought he'd seen to anyone outside the police, so the Press never got wind of it. Ben felt Desmond should have taken his story more seriously."

"Any men in the Whiteleys' circle known to have a taste for dressing up as women?" Les asked wryly.

"None. Ben had a quiet word with the witness, and tried to persuade Desmond to take him more seriously, but Ben was a newcomer, and his views didn't count. We all know it takes time to gain respect when you join a new force. People hate loose threads, they prefer narratives with a beginning, a middle, and an end. Nobody was sure whether the girl fell or was pushed, but Malcolm Whiteley was obviously the villain of the piece. Desmond's team wasn't looking for anyone else, and once the inquest was over, they had every incentive to wind down the investigation."

Maggie was growing restive. "I can't see any connection between those three deaths, and Lily Elstone's disappearance. Even allowing for her father being Malcolm Whiteley's financial guru."

"I'm not saying there is one," Hannah replied. "The burning question is whether there's a link between what happened to Lily, and the disappearance of Malcolm's niece. Who's in charge of the search for Shona Whiteley?"

"Ryan Borthwick," Les said. "Billie Frederick is on his team, and the FLO is Grizzly. I've already had a word with her."

Griselda Hosein, he meant. Plump and maternal, she made a very sympathetic Family Liaison Officer. In that job, you needed to be a good listener, and Grizzly was skilled at picking up clues to family secrets.

"What does she have to say?"

"Nigel's charming, she says, but a loner. He was married to a much older woman, who died a year back, but he doesn't want mothering. Already he's made it clear that there's no need for Grizzly to hang around. She can report when there's some progress, but that's all he wants from her."

"Any suggestion he might have harmed his own daughter? Killed her in a rage, and hidden the body?"

"Absolutely none, in Grizzly's opinion. She's convinced he adored Shona. As for concealing the remains, he does own a large garden. The house doesn't actually have a dungeon, but there is a wine cellar, and Grizzly persuaded him to show her round, just in case he'd buried her there. Nothing to report, except that it's full of rare vintages worth a fortune. He doesn't drink them, they are strictly an investment."

"Shocking waste," Hannah said. "How the other half live, eh?"

Maggie stood up. "Chances are, Lily's case and Shona's are entirely separate."

"True, but we can't take it for granted," Hannah said. "The same goes for the Dungeon House killings. Three teenage girls connected to the Whiteleys and, over the space of twenty years, bad things have happened to all of them."

Les levered himself to his feet, and waved at the papers covering the table. "I'll leave you in peace to digest the stuff I've dug up. For starters, there's one particular question I'd like answering,"

"I can guess," Hannah said. "Nigel Whiteley is made of money, or so it seems. Rich enough to pick and choose where he lived. So with its horrible history, why of all places did he set up home in the Dungeon House?"

Chapter Seven

Each time Hannah returned to Brackdale, she found something else to love about the narrow, wooded valley, criss-crossed by streams, and surrounded by steep slopes. In the depths of winter, when the fields were silent, and the fells shrouded in snow, you felt you were in a world of your own. Especially at Tarn Cottage, with its mysterious garden snaking below the shadowy bulk of the Sacrifice Stone. Daniel's home stood close to the coffin trail, where centuries ago the dead were carried over the tops on pack-horses for Christian burial in consecrated ground. Not another house was in sight, and when darkness came, Tarn Fold seemed to Hannah as remote and mysterious as anywhere in England.

Spring-time was different. Light flashed through the trees, and danced on the clear water and uneven rocks, making the ancient landscape seem fresh and young. She parked at the end of the rutted track, and walked toward the cottage, breathing in the lemon scent of the magnolia blooms, and spotting two white butterflies with orange-tipped wings flutter around the camellias beneath the shade of a rowan tree. Daniel appeared from around the side of the house, barefoot, and wearing dark glasses and shorts. At the sight of his lightly tanned skin, she felt desire stirring. He clutched a fat airport thriller in one hand, and waved with the other.

"Thought I heard the car. I was out by the pond. Good day?"

"Fine." She kissed him, and pointed to the paperback. "Flogging yourself to death, I see."

"Coming to live here taught me to seize the moment. Or at least the sunshine. Tomorrow it may bucket down. I need it to, so I won't be distracted from finishing my talk for the local publicity tour. I've been shaking off the remnants of jet-lag out in the garden."

"Are you really going to find inspiration in a Scandinavian serial killer novel?"

"You'll hate me for saying this, but I'm tempted to write another book about murder. My agent says the American publishers won't commit until they see sales figures for *The Hell Within*. They're nervous about my becoming typecast as a murder maven. I see their point, but I'm not in the mood for yet another orthodox social history. Murder intrigues me, I can't help it. You're a bad influence."

He'd arrived back in England thirty-six hours ago, after a fortnight spent on the road in the States, promoting the American hardback of his newly published history of homicide. Five hundred pages sparked by a fascination with the work of a long ago denizen of the Lake District, Thomas De Quincey.

Hannah had never come to terms with the concept of considering murder as a fine art. She'd seen too much of the misery it caused. Yet she shared Daniel's fascination with the motives that led to murder. So had Ben Kind, despite his frequent reminders that the CPS were only interested in proof, not psychology. For Hannah, as for Ben, solving the puzzle of why one human being might wish to end the life of another was the ultimate challenge for any detective.

She ran upstairs for a quick shower, and changed into a halter top and jeans. After she and her ex, Marc Amos, had sold their house in Ambleside, Daniel had invited her to stay at Tarn Cottage while she hunted for a flat. They'd never spoken about living together long-term. Thank God he was perceptive enough to realise it wasn't what she wanted. Too soon, too risky. She needed somewhere of her own. So she'd gone ahead, and exchanged contracts on a flat in Kendal. It was handy for Divisional HQ, and work was her anchor. Completion wasn't far away, and the prospect of moving in excited her. It reminded her of being eighteen, eagerly anticipating the liberation of student life.

"I'll leave some clothes and a toothbrush here, if that's okay," she'd said. "After that, let's see how things go."

He'd nodded, and said fine, and they'd left it at that.

Finishing with Marc had bruised her. They'd been together for a long time, and she'd always have a soft spot for the guy, but he'd had his chance, and now she meant to look ahead. So—what did her crystal ball reveal? She and Daniel had become lovers not long after the death of an old friend. Coupled with the break-up with Marc, the death had left her numb with loss. Daniel had also suffered bereavement; his fiancée's suicide had been a catalyst for his move from Oxford to the Lakes. Her inner pessimist warned it was too good to last. Secretly, she expected they'd finish up as they'd begun, as friends, not lovers. Their lives were so very different. He was a well-known historian, a minor celebrity, and one of these days, the lure of the life he'd abandoned would surely prove too strong.

A lager and lime awaited her outside. That crazy cipher garden, with its eccentric planting and paths leading nowhere, seemed to symbolise her unlikely relationship with the son of the man whose patience and encouragement had made her a half-decent detective. This morning, Daniel had proposed cooking dinner, which probably meant raiding the freezer and shoving whatever he found in the oven. He really wasn't perfect. Then again, neither was she.

"Your dad's name cropped up today."

He lifted his dark glasses. "Really?"

"If you've caught the news bulletins, you'll know a teenage girl has gone missing."

"I saw something at lunch-time, though I didn't pay attention until I heard Ravenglass mentioned. That's where I'm giving the first of these talks." Now he was back in Britain, his next task was to promote *The Hell Within* locally, talking to audiences in venues around Cumbria over the next fortnight. "When you hear something like this, you always hope she's simply run off with a boyfriend. Whatever the truth, it must be agony for the parents, not knowing where she is."

In idle moments, Hannah had wondered what sort of a father Daniel might make. They'd never talked about having a child together. It was almost a taboo, as it would involve a commitment that neither was ready to make. The closest they'd come to discussing it had been when Daniel once said his parents had married too young. Ben's desertion had hit his kids like a hammer blow, and Daniel was determined not to make the same mistakes. Ben only realised how much he'd missed, how badly he'd messed up, when it was too late to make amends.

"Nigel Whiteley is a single parent. His wife died a year ago. Your father knew him. Nigel's aunt was Cheryl's best friend."

"Is that right?" The sunglasses masked his eyes, but his tone was as cool as a November breeze. He'd never had much time for the woman he blamed for breaking up their family. Though Hannah had to admit, it took two to tango. Ben had been a fool.

"The aunt was shot by her husband twenty years ago. His teenage daughter also died, and Malcolm Whiteley shot himself."

Daniel swore. "Dad knew these people?"

"Whiteley held a barbecue at his home on the day of the shootings. A big event, he fancied himself as a country squire. Ben and Cheryl were both invited."

"This wasn't the Dungeon House case?"

"You remember it?"

"Very well. Not that Dad and I ever discussed it, of course. I read it up in the papers. After he moved to Cumbria, I devoured anything I could find that concerned crime in the county. I was desperate to know what he was up to. He was a big hero of mine, even after he left home. The crime-buster, the great detective. I kept reminding myself of that when Mum and Louise complained about him being a lousy husband and father. The killings were a big story, and I remember my disappointment when Dad's name wasn't mentioned. At that tender age, I wanted him to come up with the vital clue, the one piece of evidence that everyone else overlooked....hey, what's amusing you?"

Hannah couldn't help laughing. "You know, it's funny. There's just a chance—an outside, outside chance—that he might have done precisely that."

❯❯❯

Joanna decided on an early night. She'd done so little for so long, she must take care not to over-do things. Tomorrow was bound to be taxing. As soon as she came back from the manicurist, she'd set off for Cumbria. Not by train, the journey was dreadful—two or three changes, depending on when you travelled, and sometimes it took more than four hours. Utterly ridiculous, given that Ravenglass was no more than one hundred miles away. She'd resolved to drive, even though she was out of practice, and would need to take extra care on the busy roads. Her confidence had collapsed after she'd scraped a bollard in a car park while trying to reverse into a tight space, and other than a few sorties to the nearest parade of shops during a bus strike, she hadn't sat behind the wheel since her last day at work. During her illness, she'd made up her mind to sell her Polo and rely on public transport. Thank goodness she'd lacked the energy to carry out her plan. In the Western Lakes, you didn't want to be at the mercy of the buses.

Before having her tea, she closed the curtains, and stripped to her underwear. Two Christmases ago, someone had given her a DVD of yoga exercises, but a new year's resolution to give them a go had lasted less than a week. She tried a few gentle stretches, nothing too ambitious, and found she enjoyed it. Amazing how a sense of purpose changed your mood. For the past year, she'd felt like a punch bag, battered into submission at home and in the office. Deceived and eventually deserted by a boyfriend she'd adored. Detested by the new Head of Claims, a slip of a girl who had slept her way to the top, and loved to find fault with loyal, long-serving workers. She'd lost Eoin and she'd lost her job, no wonder she'd lost confidence all over again.

People said you should never go back, that it was a mistake to try to recapture the happiness of youth, but Joanna thought they were wrong. If the present was bloody awful, why not chance it? What was the worst that could happen?

The Lake District was where she belonged. Her mother came from St Bees, and her father from Barrow, and they'd settled down half way between, on the edge of Holmrook. They'd died within a year of each other, and her inheritance had paid off her mortgage. With hindsight, she understood that her bank account had appealed to Eoin more than she did. Thousands of pounds she'd loaned him, and she'd never see a penny back. Thank goodness she'd caught him out in a string of careless lies about what he was spending the money on before he bled her dry. No wonder she'd succumbed to depression.

Before getting ready for bed, she watched the national news, in the hope of an update about Nigel's daughter. Nothing doing, but the regional bulletin covered the story. To Joanna's disappointment, the snippet merely recapped the item she'd seen in the morning. At least it gave her one more opportunity to admire Nigel as he addressed the camera.

He was being interviewed outside his front door. How well she remembered the Dungeon House, and how shocked she'd been, when she learned he'd made it his home. You'd think that after what had happened…well, nobody could say it was a lucky house. Still, Nigel and his daughter seemed to have been happy enough there, despite the death of that woman he'd married. Happy, at least, until Shona had disappeared.

What must it feel like, to lose a child? Or to give birth to one, come to that? Joanna had never been the maternal type. If ever anyone hinted she must be disappointed not to have had kids, she insisted in all honesty that a family had never been high on her agenda. If the right man had come along, things might have been very different, but the men she'd slept with over the past twenty years had proved unreliable lovers, and would have made hopelessly unreliable fathers. Poor Nigel had been the best of them, by far. If only…

Who was that? Heart pumping, she froze the picture, and rewound for half a minute. Yes, she wasn't mistaken. There he was, walking away in the corner of the picture, a brawny man in a black sweatshirt and denim jeans, opening the door of a van, and oblivious to the fact that he was in the shot as the camera panned along the imposing facade of the Dungeon House. The van bore his name, but in any case, that walk of his, a sort of limp with a swagger, was unmistakable.

A ghost from the past.

Robbie Dean, oh my God.

Nigel's oldest friend. The man who had killed Carrie North, and nearly all four of them. The man who had once put his bare hands around her throat when she'd discovered his shameful secret.

"I need to talk to Cheryl," Hannah said.

"Good luck with that." Daniel eased his hand under her top.

"Hey, shouldn't you be getting on with writing up your talk?" They were on the sofa in the living room, with Ellie Goulding crooning in the background.

"A job for tomorrow," he said, as his fingers began to explore. "Let's take it easy this evening. If my brief encounters with Cheryl are anything to go by, you'll find tomorrow hard work."

"You're not kidding. She never liked me."

"Did she see you as a threat?"

"Because I liked your dad?" she asked lazily. A delicate subject, this. Until now, they'd only ever skirted around it. "She had nothing to worry about. We were never more than friends. I didn't believe in mixing business with pleasure, and neither did he."

"He did meet Cheryl through work."

"Even so." She smiled as his hand slid up to her breast. "He certainly never did what you're doing now. Cheryl struck me as insecure. Not her fault, necessarily. Before she met your dad, she had bad luck with men. She was terrified of losing him, and he felt sorry for her. She'd lost her parents young, and later she lost her best friend, in horrific circumstances."

Daniel withdrew his hand. "Your best friend died too."

"Uh-huh. I suppose it gives me a better insight into Cheryl's experience. Losing your parents is desperately hard to cope with, but it's part of the expected order of things. When someone you've grown up with dies suddenly, it's a reversal of nature. It shouldn't happen. You've lost someone close to you, and received a sharp reminder of your own mortality, at one and the same time." She took a breath. "I'd never really thought about dying until…"

"Yeah, I know." He wrapped his arm around her. "Do you really need to talk to Cheryl?"

"It's not my idea of a fun day out, but she can tell me more about the Whiteleys, Gray Elstone, and their circle. It's appalling, how much they've suffered. The killings at the Dungeon House, the Elstone girl vanishing, now Shona Whiteley."

"You don't seriously believe the cases are connected?"

"Not directly, no. Malcolm Whiteley killed himself and Lysette, and presumably was responsible for Amber's death. But we can't rule out a link between what happened to Lily, and Shona's disappearance. Cheryl knew Gray Elstone, and Malcolm Whiteley, and whatever her faults, she's sharp. Ben said Cheryl was a good sounding board, especially in their early years together, before they got on each other's nerves. They must have discussed his suspicion that the whole truth never came out about Amber's death."

"This mysterious missing witness Dad told you about?"

"His greatest strength as a detective was his instinct. If he thought there was more to that drunken driver's story than met the eye, I'd back his judgement over Desmond Loney's, any day."

"And you want to talk to Cheryl rather than send Maggie?"

"If Maggie talks to Cheryl, she'll get the brush off."

"Cheryl won't be overjoyed to see you."

"Trust me, the feeling will be mutual, but the two of us go back a long way, and I've the best chance of finding out anything worth knowing." She sighed. "I'll wear my body armour."

He laughed, and his hand resumed its journey underneath her shirt. "Okay, but you're not putting it on just yet."

〉〉〉

Joanna found sleep elusive. Tired as she was, her mind wouldn't stop buzzing. It wasn't merely excitement about tomorrow's trip to Ravenglass that kept her awake, there was also the shock of seeing Robbie Dean again. She'd scarcely thought about him for years, and it had certainly never occurred to her that he'd be working for Nigel. The legend on the van said *Deano Garden Services*. He and Nigel had been friends since they were kids playing football together. Robbie never said much, and Joanna had always felt rather afraid of him, but Nigel admired and envied his sporting prowess. Everyone predicted stardom for Robbie. Nigel never made it as a footballer, but neither did Robbie, in the end. The injuries he'd sustained in the crash that killed poor Carrie saw to that. His pelvis was fractured, and one knee cap broken, leaving him with a permanent limp, and his dreams of football fame shattered. Nigel had talked his uncle into giving Robbie a job as a handyman and gardener at the Dungeon House. Quite a comedown for a boy who'd once had the world at his feet. Twenty years on, he was still working at the same place.

She hauled herself out of bed, and told Darcy about what had happened all those years ago, while she made herself a mug of Ovaltine. The cat purred contentedly, and settled himself back in his basket as she carried the mug to her bedside table, and snuggled under the blankets, waiting for her drink to cool.

What would she do, if and when she returned to the Dungeon House, or whatever Nigel called it nowadays, and once again her path crossed with Robbie's? It was a question for another day. No point in letting it spoil everything. Yet as she took a sip of Ovaltine, she reflected on life's ironies. Everyone remembered Malcolm Whiteley for a shocking crime, but in his own strange way, Robbie Dean was just as frightening.

Chapter Eight

Ravenglass again, after how many years? Fifteen, Joanna calculated, as she drove down Muncaster Fell toward the sea. She'd last come to the village with her parents, during a visit home, when they went for a trip on La'al Ratty. They'd parked at the terminus for the narrow gauge railway, and never ventured as far as the waterfront. She'd not set eyes on Main Street since the night of The Last Supper. After leaving the Lakes, she'd concentrated on making a new life for herself, and even when she returned to Holmrook to see Mum and Dad, she steered clear of Ravenglass. Too many memories. Remembering was just one more form of self-harm. But time healed even the deepest wounds. She'd loved this village once, and now she felt ready to fall in love all over again.

As she passed under a bridge carrying the railway north to Whitehaven, the sunlit estuary lay out in front of her. On impulse, she pulled up next to the Green. After the long, circuitous drive, her calves and thighs twitched with cramp as she levered herself out of the elderly Polo and into an invigorating breeze. Motorway driving forced you to take your life in your hands, and even on the quieter roads, the traffic was terrifying if you were out of practice. Thank goodness she'd made it, and now she was all goose bumps. She'd not felt so alive since her first date with Eoin. This was an adventure, and not having a clue what might happen next was part of the fun.

Taking a seat on one of the bright blue benches, she looked out across the dunes. A raised embankment of grass protected the low-lying cottages from floods as well as providing a green open space overlooking a foreshore of shingle, sand, and mud. Three rivers met here, making a natural harbour. No wonder the Romans had chosen this as their port. To think this view was once admired by soldiers of the Twentieth Legion! Roman ships carried goods from this northernmost edge of their territory to the rest of the Empire, but after the legionnaires marched away, Ravenglass did not die. Saxons and Vikings came and went, King John granted merchants a Charter to hold a weekly market and annual fair, and fishermen plied their trade along the coast. When the estuary silted up, ships could no longer dock at the end of Main Street, but trains brought iron ore down from Boot to the station, so it could be transported on the coastal line. Although the mines had closed down, the railway was preserved, and the Ratty became a tourists' delight. Yes, Joanna had something in common with this place. She was a survivor, and so was Ravenglass.

The sunshine was deceptive, and the late afternoon chill persuaded her not to linger. Hurrying back to the Polo, she threaded through the vehicles parked on either side of Main Street. The village had once been a stopping point on an old road that crept along the coast by way of shallow fords and ramshackle bridges, but these days the street narrowed into a dead end, bounded by huge flood-gates.

The Eskdale Arms stood on its own on the estuary side of the road, and the Saltcoats View guest house was separated from it by a tiny car park. She'd wondered if seeing the pub again would revive such dreadful images of the night of The Last Supper that she'd change her mind, and scurry back home. To her surprise, she felt no more than a pang of melancholy. This new Joanna lived for the moment.

She carried her suitcase to the front of the Saltcoats View. Inhaling the fragrance of grape hyacinths crammed into hanging baskets on either side of the door, she rang the bell, and a loud voice invited her to walk right in. A middle-aged man with thinning, sandy hair and the worst comb-over she'd seen in years sat with a steaming mug of tea in his hand, and a copy of *The Cumberland News* spread over the counter in front of him. Nigel Whiteley stared grimly from the front page, beneath the headline: *My Agony: Missing Teenager's Father.*

"My name is Joanna Footit. I booked yesterday for a fortnight."

He bestowed a cheesy grin, and extended his hand. "Ah, yes, Ms Footit. Or may I call you Joanna? My name's Quiggin, pleased to meet you. Alvaro Quiggin, would you believe? My mother came from Almeria, and that was her dad's name. She married a Manxman, and when I was born they named me in grandad's honour. Never mind, it's quite a mouthful, and as the song goes, you can call me Al."

Joanna hadn't the faintest what song he was talking about, but shook his hand anyway. As she filled in the registration form, and went through the usual palaver with her credit card, she was aware of his sidelong appraisal of her figure. Her illness had left her painfully thin. In her schooldays, nasty boys had nick-named her Stick-Insect, but words no longer hurt her. At her age, better to be a Stick-Insect than a Heffalump. Her new skirt was short enough to display her legs to full advantage, and for the first time since she'd sent Eoin packing, she felt attractive. Desirable.

You-Can-Call-Me-Al hauled her suitcases upstairs to a small but thankfully *en suite* room with chintzy decor and watercolours of Lakeland beauty spots on the wall. "Nice and comfy, eh? Watch yourself under the shower, the nozzle can be temperamental. In that cupboard, you'll find a kettle and a basket with sachets of tea and coffee. There's a map as well as a guide book in the top drawer of the dressing table, if you're planning excursions or need any information about the area."

She smiled. "Thanks, but I won't need a map."

"Oh really? Regular visitor, are you?"

"I grew up nearby and my parents lived at Holmrook until they died."

"So what brings you back here?"

Obviously she didn't intend to utter a word about Nigel. Certainly not until she'd decided how best to approach him. The merit of her cover story was that every word was true. "I've recently recovered from a long illness, and Ravenglass seemed the perfect spot to complete my recuperation. Healthy sea breezes…"

"Oh aye, we've no shortage of sea breezes! Won't take a jiffy for you to get the colour back in your cheeks. If you come from these parts, you'll easily find your way around. Ravenglass never alters much. Revisiting old haunts, eh?"

"And looking up old friends." Her eye caught the flamboyant signature on a landscape of Wasdale hanging next to the wardrobe. "Gosh, is that by Scott Durham? Is he still around?"

"The artist? You know him?"

"I did—very slightly. Twenty years ago."

"Well, well." You-Can-Call-Me-Al beamed. "You've come to the right place. The Eskdale Arms next door offers our residents a ten per cent discount on evening meals. Scott lives in Seagull Cottage. He's a regular in the saloon bar, and never misses a quiz night. Pop in for a bite to eat, and you'll probably bump into him. Likes his pint, does Scott."

The conversation with Cheryl was never going to be easy. Hannah hadn't seen or spoken to her since Ben's funeral, a dismal occasion on a winter's day when the rain never let up. The two of them had exchanged brief and civilised pleasantries at the door of the church, but Hannah's mood matched the weather, and she kept her distance from the grieving widow. Cheryl had looked good, she'd had to admit, as they stood under umbrellas around the open grave. Black suited her. So did the pallor of mourning, and the opportunity to be the centre of attention, bereaved and brave and rather beautiful.

Her call took Cheryl aback, but surprise soon gave way to suspicion. "Malcolm Whiteley? Of course I knew him. Lysette was very dear to me. Why on earth do you want to rake over the ashes twenty years on?"

"As I said, I run the Cold Case Review…"

"Yes, yes, I read about in the papers. I was taken aback, to be honest."

"You were?" A mistake, this, affording Cheryl a chance to twist the knife.

"Absolutely, I thought you preferred investigating crimes in the here and now. You seemed very ambitious when you were young."

Hannah glared at the sansevieria. Wasn't its alternative name mother-in-law's tongue? It wasn't as sharp as Cheryl's scorn. "I suppose none of us are getting any younger."

"Time is precious, yes. Which makes me wonder, frankly, why it's worth wasting time over an old story."

"Easier to explain when we are face-to-face."

A pause, followed by a long-suffering sigh. "You always were very persistent, Hannah. Wouldn't take no for an answer."

Was that another dig? Did Cheryl believe she'd spent her formative years in the police pestering an unwilling Ben Kind for sex? Hannah ground her nails into her palm. Cheryl hadn't lost that knack of winding her up.

"Are you free tomorrow morning? How about eleven o'clock? I'm happy to visit you in Grange. Don't worry if it's not convenient. You tell me when and where."

An ungracious sniff. "No, that will do. Might as well get it over with."

"Thanks very much, Cheryl." Hannah wasn't a naturally untruthful woman, so she preferred to think of her parting words not as a lie, but as satire. "It will be lovely to see you again."

>>>

Maggie bustled in half an hour later. "I've fixed up a meeting with Lily Elstone's mum tomorrow. Les said he'd come along. I'll do the talking, but he reckons I could do with a minder."

"Not a bad idea."

Anya Jovetic was notoriously volatile. Once, she'd scratched the face of a journalist whose questioning upset her. A mother whose teenage daughter vanished never to return could be forgiven the occasional outburst of anger and desperation, but there was always a risk that Anya Jovetic would take out her misery on the wrong person. She should be pleased about the case being reviewed, but she'd never be satisfied until Gray Elstone was under lock and key.

According to Anya, he was a sexual deviant who couldn't handle a mature woman. She claimed that he'd molested Lily, and that when the girl had resisted, he'd killed her to keep her quiet. Three years ago, a vast amount of time and resource had been devoted to investigating her allegations, but there wasn't a shred of evidence to support them. Lily hadn't confided in anyone about the supposed abuse, and school friends insisted that she was closer to her father than her mother. Even Anya had to admit that she'd never suspected Gray of misbehaving with Lily until the girl's disappearance.

It also turned out that Anya carried a truck-load of baggage. Enquiries in Split, her hometown, established that her own father had been sent to prison for indecently assaulting young girls, and she'd accused a former lover of something similar, although nothing had ever been proved. Some officers on the original team of investigators had a theory that it was her temper that had driven Lily away.

"Would you mind talking to the father?" Maggie asked. "He might open up more to you than to me."

"Because he knew Ben, and so did I?"

"That's part of it. When I told him that we were reviewing the case, he said all the right things, but seemed wary, perhaps because Anya has accused him of all sorts. And now this business about Nigel Whiteley's daughter complicates the picture."

"Okay, I'll give him a ring."

One more task for the to-do list. The mantra in the public sector nowadays was *Do more for less*, and Hannah had lost a sergeant and some admin back-up. She was overworked, and it made sense to delegate whenever she could. The snag was that she was a detective who had been sucked into management. What she loved about the job was detection, not filling in spreadsheets and attending endless meetings. Anyway, there was just an outside chance that Maggie was right, and she'd be able to tease some new information from Elstone to cast fresh light on the three-year-old mystery of his daughter's disappearance.

Once You-Can-Call-Me-Al left her in peace, Joanna unpacked before taking off her shoes, and lying down fully clothed on the bed. Eyes closed, mind spinning. She'd never dreamed she'd ever set foot inside the Eskdale Arms again. That meal after the Dungeon House barbecue represented a watershed, not only in her life but in so many others. No wonder she thought of it as The Last Supper.

For twenty years, Joanna had banished that night from her mind. The horror of it all had driven her from the Lakes. Later, fresh entanglements gave her more than enough to fret about, without allowing old ghosts to roam. Now she'd returned to Ravenglass, must she face up to the past? Or was it best for her to don her rose-tinted spectacles, and forget everything other than how much she cared about Nigel?

She dozed for half an hour, but once she'd got up and washed her face, she decided to fit in a walk before something to eat. As she wriggled into her jacket, she considered Scott Durham's take on Wastwater. Yellow sunlight played on snow-covered fells and lit the surface of the grey-blue lake. A pretty picture, subtle hues harmonising with the room's pale pastels. He was a talented artist, nobody could deny it. Yet was something lacking? She detected no hint of the secretive nature of those inky depths, or of the claustrophobia that the dark scree slopes always induced in her. Scott had turned a blind eye to Wastwater's sinister side.

Perhaps he too liked to pretend that the horror of the Dungeon House had never happened.

On her way out, she passed You-Can-Call-Me-Al, who was still perusing the story about Shona Whiteley. The photograph of the girl differed from the one shown on television. No sexy party dress this time, but a rather severe school uniform, navy blue, striped with magenta. Her braces were even more prominent in this picture.

"Off for a constitutional, Joanna?"

"I fancy a breath of air. The driver has left me with a stiff back."

"Yes, it's quite a journey, getting here from pretty much anywhere." He sneaked another glance at her figure. "You'll know that well enough, being a local lass yourself. No short-cuts to Ravenglass, eh?"

She hurried outside. His interest was flattering, but faintly creepy. Perhaps he saw it as part of his job to befriend residents. If he was lonely, she sympathised. It had been so long since a man had taken an interest in her that she was out of practice. Even Eoin—hindsight left her sadder but wiser—had regarded her more as a meal ticket than a lover. Anyway, she didn't fancy You-Can-Call-Me-Al. Her mind was filled with a single question. How would Nigel respond to the brave new Joanna?

Striding along the sea cobbles of Main Street reminded her of old times. Gulls wheeled and swooped overhead, and a burly fisherman loaded up his van. As a kid, she'd thought Ravenglass was like an island, and she still did. The tiny promontory might be part of mainland England, but it felt remote from the everyday world, surrounded by lakes and mountains and sea, miles from anywhere except a nuclear power station.

A cottage painted canary yellow caught her eye. Wisteria clambered around the canopied front door, bluebells covered every inch of the postage-stamp garden, and pansies and pinks spilled from a window box and two hanging baskets. This selfsame cottage appeared on one of the watercolours hanging in her room, and Joanna guessed it was Scott Durham's home even before she saw the carved log house sign. Seagull Cottage was picture postcard pretty, though anyone who stared at it for long enough might suffer a sugar crash.

A man of middle height opened the front door, and locked it behind him. He had an envelope in his hand. At first glance, the famously handsome Scott Durham hadn't worn too badly, even if the tweed jacket complete with elbow patches, corduroy trousers, and scuffed Hush Puppies suggested a middle-aged schoolmaster rather than an artistic free spirit. His fair hair was greying, but as thick and untamed as ever. On closer inspection, however, he'd developed a paunch, and he looked in need of a shave.

As he closed the front gate and turned into Main Street, they came face-to-face. He did a double-take that was almost comical.

"It's…it's not Joanna?"

Forty-eight hours ago, she'd have found this encounter impossible to imagine, but now she felt confident, ready for anything. When he moved closer, to make sure he wasn't hallucinating, she noticed his cheeks were threaded with veins. The brilliance of those blue eyes had faded, and she caught the smell of alcohol on his breath.

"How nice to see you, Scott. It's been a long time."

"Yes." He rubbed a stubbly jaw. "What…what brings you here?"

"Oh, revisiting old haunts, you know. I came on impulse, to be honest. I've booked into the Saltcoats View."

"You're staying here?"

"Yes, yes, for a fortnight." She hesitated. "At least."

"Holiday?" he grunted.

"I'm a lady of leisure these days, I come and go as I please." She smiled. "I live in Lytham, and I worked in St Annes for years, but I was poorly, and my boss suggested a severance package. An offer I couldn't refuse, you might say. It left me footloose and fancy free, so I said to myself—why not go back to Ravenglass?"

He swallowed. "Like you say, it's been a long time."

She pointed to the cottage. "Such a lovely place. And your paintings are on the wall of my room."

"Yes, Al Quiggin's a good customer, even if he does haggle me down on price."

"Hefty discount for bulk purchases?" She laughed. "I'm so glad to see you're still painting. And drawing inspiration from Ravenglass!"

He indicated the cottage. "There's a rickety old conservatory at the back, looking out over the estuary. I use it as my studio."

"Marvellous! Have you lived here long?"

"Since Josh left college."

"Josh, yes, I remember him well." The boy was a blur to be honest, she could just about picture him strumming his guitar at the fateful barbecue. The curly fair hair was all she remembered. "What is he up to now?"

"Why do you ask?"

His abruptness took her aback. "No reason, Scott, just curious. Such a nice-looking lad, is he married?"

Overhead, a gull wailed. Scott glanced up to the sky, as if he suspected the bird of mockery.

"He went into teaching."

"Oh lovely!" Something made Joanna persist. "Teaching music, I expect? Passing on his enthusiasm to the young folk?"

"Yes," Scott said through gritted teeth. "He teaches music."

"Here in Ravenbank?"

"No, no. At a private school. Now, if you'll excuse me." He waved the letter. "Things to do. You know how it is."

She was on the verge of pointing out that he'd missed the post anyway, but something in his demeanour stopped her. "Hopefully we'll bump into each other again. I gather the Eskdale Arms is your local?"

He made a non-committal noise. "Got to be on my way. Bye, Joanna. Take care."

He strode off in toward the village, leaving her to reflect that he hadn't asked a single question about how she was, or what she'd been up to over the past twenty years. Typical man. Not an ounce of curiosity.

How strange to walk back into the Eskdale Arms after twenty years. At first glance, the only change was the arrival of a huge television screen in the saloon bar, where once a dartboard was the centre of activity. Even the aroma of beer and steak and onions seemed reassuringly familiar. A group of men were watching some football match, and she mistook their loud collective groan for an unkind comment on the arrival of an unaccompanied woman. In fact, one of the players had just missed an open goal.

A colourful poster pinned on the wall caught her eye. There was a photograph of a chap she'd seen once or twice on television a few years ago, a historian called Daniel Kind. He was coming here in a couple of days' time to talk about his new book. The subject was the history of murder. Even in the warmth of the pub, she found herself shivering. Would he talk about the deaths at the Dungeon House?

The large oak table where they'd eaten The Last Supper still occupied the same nook. That night, she'd sat in the corner, with Nigel at her side, their legs touching under the table. Chatty and charming, he had paid close attention to everything she had to say, ignoring Amber's self-absorbed prattle. When the younger girl's increasingly clumsy attempts to chat him up failed, she lapsed into monosyllabic surliness. Joanna recalled her twinge of sadness at the thought their friendship was unlikely to survive.

She could picture the faces around the table as if it were yesterday. Scott Durham had turned up late, after giving Josh a meal at home, and Joanna remembered wondering why he'd bothered to come. Did he really carry a torch for Lysette? The pair barely exchanged a word all evening.

Cheryl had changed into a low-cut top and tiny skirt, and was giggly after an afternoon's drinking. Her partner Ben watched and listened, and made sure she didn't make a fool of herself. His taciturnity made Joanna wonder if policemen could never be completely off duty.

Malcolm Whiteley was conspicuous by his absence, and by common consent, the barbecue wasn't discussed, nor was his excruciating drunken speech of welcome. Lysette seemed tense, and more than once she bit Amber's head off. Joanna shivered. To think that, a few hours later, both mother and daughter were dead.

In this day and age, pubs couldn't survive simply by selling beer and traditional chicken in the basket. The dining area had been extended, taking in most of the old beer garden, so that outside there was just a tiny paved area, and steps leading down to the sand. She claimed the last vacant table before ordering a vegetable balti with garlic and coriander naan bread, plus a small glass of house white to wash it down.

Her thoughts turned to Nigel. She'd need to pick her moment in contacting him. Poor soul, he was bound to be preoccupied while his daughter remained missing. She'd be happy to help take his mind off things, but obviously, tact was required. Scott Durham might be in touch with him. If Scott came into the pub, she'd wheedle out any information he had about Nigel.

The food arrived, but Scott Durham was a no-show. Surely he wasn't avoiding her? Never mind, perhaps she'd track down Gray Elstone. He'd lost a daughter, just like Nigel. Surely there was no connection? Because of her medication, she had to be careful how much she drank, but a couple of units wouldn't do any harm. Dr Chanderpaul's pills were doing the trick. The doctor had sympathised about the set-backs she'd experienced, but urged her not to waste time feeling sorry for herself, and the advice was spot on.

A roar of pleasure erupted from the football spectators in the bar as someone scored. Joanna was in an equally good humour. This little adventure was like a shot in the arm. No longer did she feel like one of life's victims. She was infused with energy and a sense of purpose. She was making things happen.

Chapter Nine

Joanna polished off a croissant and orange juice in the pub the next morning before setting out down Main Street. No more lazing around in bed for the new Joanna. The sun was shining, and the vagaries of the climate here meant she'd better take advantage of it while she had the chance. She was familiar enough with the laid-back ways of Lakeland folk not to be startled by the sight of a middle-aged woman in a fleecy white dressing gown standing at the end of the street, throwing sticks for a spaniel to fetch.

The curtains at Seagull Cottage were open. Was this a good time to speak to Scott Durham about Nigel? On impulse, she rang the doorbell. No answer. She peered through the window into an untidy front room. Watercolours and ink drawings covered every inch of the walls, and half a dozen of this morning's newspapers were scattered over the dining table and armchairs. There was no sign of Scott. Presumably he'd seized the moment, and headed off to paint or sketch while the spring weather stayed fine.

The beach lay beyond the flood-gates. The land facing her on the other side of the water was owned by the Ministry of Defence, and the Eskmeals firing range. A sinister notice warned that it was "dangerous to touch any shell, bomb, missile or strange object found on the sands or beach." *Strange object?* The mind boggled. As if the possibility of being shot wasn't enough. Just thinking about the guns of Eskmeals reminded Joanna of Malcolm Whiteley's horrific crimes, and she turned away with a shudder.

Walking round the point, she followed the shoreline behind the houses, back in the direction of the Eskdale Arms. The urge to climb over the rocks, something she'd last done in her teens, was impossible to resist. A rusting anchor was stuck in the mud, and you could see the willow sticks from the old salmon traps. Traces of the old coast road still remained, and someone had even parked an ancient Ford Anglia on the shore. Here she'd once collected fragments of Georgian pottery and coloured glass from in between the stones, though she'd never fulfilled her ambition of picking up a long lost Roman coin.

The Esk, the Mite, and the Irt joined together here, but although a footbridge ran alongside the railway viaduct, toward Saltcoats and the caravan park, she intended to go round in a circle, and return to the guest house. No point in hanging around Ravenglass in the hope of a word with Scott Durham.

Half a dozen houses backing on to the shore boasted conservatories, and Joanna identified the most dilapidated as Scott's studio. Set into the concrete sea wall below was a back door—locked, she couldn't resist trying the handle—giving access to the foreshore. Steep steps ran up to the house, with an iron spiral staircase leading up to the studio from the tiny garden. She imagined Scott sitting up there on the other side of the floor-to-ceiling glass walls, drinking in the view. Why had he been so grumpy yesterday? Seeing her must have opened old wounds. If Lysette was the love of his life, perhaps her death left scars that never healed.

The rocks were slippery, and the gusts of wind gaining strength, but somehow she kept her footing. The cold morning air had cleared her mind, and a fresh thought struck her as she scrambled down. Those newspapers in Scott's cottage—why had he bought so many? He hadn't collected a pile of yellowing copies of *The Whitehaven News* or something, but rather a mix of nationals as well as the latest locals. She'd spotted the *Telegraph*, *Guardian*, and *Mail* amongst others. Why would an artist take such an interest in what was going on in the outside world? He was checking out a particular story, Joanna thought.

At once she realised what it must be. Scott was researching the disappearance of Shona Whiteley.

>>>

"That girl is still missing."

Daniel was in the kitchen of Tarn Cottage, listening to the news on Radio Cumbria, as Hannah looked in to say goodbye. Spread out in front of him on the kitchen table was a sheaf of notes, background material for the talk he was preparing. "Heard the latest on Shona Whiteley?" She frowned. "Not looking good."

"No, she was last seen on Saturday morning, and today's Wednesday. A long time for a sixteen-year-old to be away from home."

"The more time passes, the more likely it is that she's been taken against her will. Her father must be frantic. It's only a year since he lost his wife. I'll see if I can get an update at HQ before I set off for Grange."

"Good luck with Cheryl."

"Thanks, I'll need it." She kissed his cheek. "Maybe I will get myself kitted out with body armour. Just in case, eh?"

>>>

"An accountant called Gray Elstone?" You-Can-Call-Me-Al was standing in the doorway that led to his private office. "I certainly do know the name, Joanna. He does my books."

"I used to work for him, a long time ago," she said. "I thought I'd look him up."

He gave a thoughtful nod. Her skin prickled, and she wondered if he was mentally undressing her. He reminded her of one of Gray Elstone's clients, a corpulent middle-aged businessman who thought his audit fees entitled him to fondle her backside whenever she made the mistake of getting within range. She was glad the reception counter separated the pair of them.

"Old flames of yours, Scott and Gray?"

She flushed. "Not at all. They were both quite a lot older than me."

"Of course, of course, I didn't mean to…." He coughed, to signal a hasty retreat into platitudes. "Nice chap, Gray, salt of the earth, I'm sure he'll be over the moon to see you. His office is in Seascale, but you probably knew that?"

"No, we lost touch a very long time ago. In those days, he was based in Ulverston, and lived nearby. But I seem to remember he came from Seascale originally."

"Yes, and he has a big house on the cliffs, two minutes from the office. There's nothing like getting back to your roots, is there? Not that I plan to get back to mine in a hurry. Then again, I was born in a two-up, two-down in Benwell, so can you blame me?"

He gave a throaty laugh, but Joanna didn't join in. Once again, he'd baffled her. She had no idea where Benwell was, but she suspected Benwell was doing just fine without him.

"DI Borthwick still thinks Shona left home voluntarily."

Billie Frederick conveyed her disagreement with a shake of her tight black curls. She was one of Cumbria Constabulary's few detectives with West Indian heritage. Her family had come over from Jamaica when she was a child, and although her father and brothers were medics, she'd joined the police after leaving school. A no-nonsense character, always blunt and often bolshie, Billie was a small woman with a loud voice. Her inexhaustible supply of scathing one-liners made her the life and soul of any party as well as a scarily effective negotiator on behalf of the Police Federation. Management had learned from bruising experience that you didn't mess with DC Wilhelmina Frederick, and so had plenty of criminals.

"Why's that?" Hannah asked. "Was she unhappy at home?"

"Not according to Daddy. Question is, how much does Daddy really know about his little darling? Grizzly reckons he's a smart guy, but how many men are that smart when it comes to their teenage daughters?"

"There were no clues on her laptop or her phone, were there? Not on her Facebook page, or anywhere else. Nothing to suggest she was planning to do a bunk."

"One theory is that she left her phone at home on purpose, because she had another phone, ready for use."

"Any evidence to support that?"

"We found a girl from her class who reckoned she saw Shona fiddling with a brand new iPhone on the last day of term before the Easter break."

"The day before she disappeared."

"Right. When she asked Shona if it was a present from her dad, she was told it belonged to a friend, and Shona had just borrowed it out of curiosity. According to the classmate, she seemed evasive, as if she'd been caught out. We've not been able to track down whoever supposedly lent the phone."

"Was the classmate a close friend?"

"Shona doesn't have many friends. Let alone people she confides in. That's one of the things complicating the inquiry."

"And there's no trace of the girl she was supposed to be seeing over the week-end?"

"Nothing. The story she told her father was untrue. Unless she didn't tell him that story after all." Billie leaned forward. "There is another possibility. Want to hear it?"

Hannah grinned."I'd be heartbroken if you didn't tell me. Gobsmacked, too, to be honest."

"Ouch." Billie rocked with laughter. "What if darling Daddy did something to Shona, and made up the story to cover his tracks?"

"Grizzly reckons he's devoted to her, doesn't he? And hasn't the house been searched?"

"Grizzly's too nice. And yeah, we've had a look round, but I doubt the kid's buried under the floorboards. The grounds are extensive."

"You really think Nigel Whiteley is a murderer?"

"Hey, nobody around here knows better than me about the dangers of stereotyping. But we've got to face facts." Billie grimaced. "This man's uncle was a killer, and one of his victims was a teenage girl. I'm not talking sexual abuse here, not necessarily. Just about a violent temper snapping. Let's face it. It's in the blood."

〉〉〉

Seascale was a few miles up the coast, on the far side of the sand dunes at Drigg, but to reach it by road from Ravenglass, you had to drive inland and zig-zag out of the National Park. As Joanna drove along the front, above the cliffs, she thought the resort hadn't changed much in the past twenty years. She parked next to the rebuilt battlements of an old stone fortress. Below a reinstated cannon, a plaque commemorated the people killed a few years back by a demented gunman called Derrick Bird. Although Bird's madness was very different from Malcolm Whiteley's, he'd destroyed even more innocent lives.

The narrow wooden jetty had been rebuilt, and three anglers were trying their luck. The smell of fish and salt took her back to seaside trips of her childhood. The waves were choppy, the breeze bracing, and she strolled to the end of the jetty before looking back at the buildings perched on the low cliff. With the coming of the Furness Railway, Victorian speculators planned to transform the village into "the Eastbourne of the North", but the money ran out, and the grand hotel-lined promenade never got past the drawing board. Seascale remained tiny, peaceful, and half-forgotten until the government built a munitions factory, and then replaced it with a nuclear processing plant. In the Fifties, so many atom scientists lived in Seascale that it claimed to be the brainiest village in Britain. Most of the boffins moved on, but Sellafield remained, a vast sprawling blot on the landscape. During her childhood, Joanna had recurrent nightmares about being burnt to a cinder in an atomic explosion, or turned into some sort of radioactive zombie. But time acclimatised you to almost anything, and the night of The Last Supper had taught her that the worst dangers were those you never dreamed of.

She walked back toward the old water tower, with its red stonework and conical roof. Thank goodness nobody had bull-dozed it in the name of progress. In no time, she found Elstone and Company's offices, which occupied the floor above a tea shop rejoicing in the name of The Odd Women. Her pleasure at tracking down Gray soon gave way to uncertainty about what to do next, and she dithered on the pavement until the decision was snatched from her hands. The door marked with the name of Gray's firm swung open, and the man himself strode out. Ungainly as ever, he cannoned into her.

"Hello, Gray."

He gave a little gasp. "Joanna?"

She smiled. "Glad you still recognise me."

"Good Lord, of course." He'd lost an inch or two of height, thanks to a slight stoop, and he still bit his fingernails, but he'd had his teeth whitened, and his shirt and tie looked expensive. He peered through rimless spectacles. "Your…um…hair, I mean… it's still very…um…eye-catching."

"Thanks." She took it as a compliment. The numbing misery of her younger days returned only when someone like Eoin was unkind about her appearance, and made her think her appeal lay in her bank balance, not in her womanliness. "It's lovely to see you again."

"Yes…um, and you, of course." He drew breath. "What on earth are you doing here, of all places?"

"I'm staying in Ravenglass. Decided it was time to get back to my roots. The man who runs the guest house told me he's a client of yours. Is his name really Alvaro Quiggin, or is he pulling my leg?"

"Alvaro? Goodness, yes, nothing less than the truth. Um…nice chap. Well…" Gray seemed unsure where the conversation was going. So was Joanna. It was one thing to map out an encounter in your mind, quite another to conduct it according to plan when the moment arrived. "Can you spare the time for a cuppa?"

"How kind. I'd love that." Nothing ventured, nothing gained. "I'm sure you're rushed off your feet without wasting your time chewing the fat with an old secretary from twenty years ago."

Gray hesitated, and she feared she'd played her cards badly, giving him a chance to escape. "No, no. I was only popping out to the florist's. I don't have any more client meetings till this afternoon."

"Well, in that case…" Joanna waited to see if he was going to explain the trip to the florist's, but he simply smiled, and said that The Odd Women did a very good Darjeeling.

Walking into the tea shop, they were greeted by home cooking smells, and the fragrance of herbs. Gray whispered, "In case you're wondering about the name of this place, the owners are two…um…lesbians. Nice women, Molly and Pat. Jolly good fun. They're clients of mine, and they're making a go of the business, though it's never easy out of season."

"I suppose it helps that they have a sense of humour."

Gray allowed himself a smile as they took a table in the window. "They are also a very cultured couple. As you can see."

He pointed to a framed print showing a Victorian novel, lavishly bound. The author was George Gissing, the title *The Odd Women*. A small buxom woman in her fifties came to take their order, and greeted Gray like an old friend.

"Molly, this is Joanna. She used to work for me, more years ago than either of us cares to remember. Another keen student of literature and history, if I remember correctly. You were a fan of Jane Austen rather than Gissing, isn't that right?"

"Still am, actually." How wonderful that he remembered.

"Pleased to meet you." Molly's handshake was firm. "Gray's told you about Gissing, then?"

"Never read him, I'm afraid."

"Unlucky bloke, George, but he could write. As a boy, he came here on holiday. Even in those days, Seascale wasn't exactly Blackpool, but he fell in love with the place. When he came to write an important feminist novel, where did he set a crucial chapter of *The Odd Women*? In Seascale, where else? So that's a pot of Darjeeling for two, and a plate of scones?"

As she bustled off, Gray gave a nervous laugh. "You live and learn, eh?"

"I suppose we've both done a lot of that in the last twenty years."

"Very true." He sighed. "So what have you been up to, all this time?"

Joanna had planned what to say about her life during the last twenty years. She needed to rehearse for her meeting with Nigel. Not that she meant to lie, naturally. She was simply aware that many people would think she'd had a miserable time, and she didn't want to come across as sad or desperate.

"Oh, this and that. When I left home, I didn't have a clear idea about what to do. I only knew I needed to get away from Cumbria, after so many awful things had happened to me here. You'd been very kind, it was nothing personal. I moved to Manchester, but city life didn't suit. I met a boyfriend who was a dyed-in-the-wool Mancunian, so I stuck it out for as long as I could, but in the end I left him, and finished up in a flat in Lytham. After Mum and Dad died, I spent my inheritance on a bungalow, and worked in an insurance broker's."

He glanced at her hand, searching for a ring. "You never married?"

"No, no." It was her turn to give a nervous laugh. "Came close a couple of times, but never made it to the altar. My last boyfriend treated me unkindly, and I was ill for a while."

"Sorry to hear it. You do look pale, but not to worry, the Ravenglass air will do you a power of good."

"Absolutely. My firm wanted to cut back on the secretarial side, and they gave me a package. Now I'm feeling more like my old self, and I'm ready for a fresh start."

He looked startled. "You're not thinking of coming back here permanently?"

She smiled. "Don't worry, Gray, I'm not here to beg for my old job back."

"Sorry, I didn't mean...actually, I might well have a vacancy before long, as it happens. But I rather thought...when you left, you were in quite a state. So it's a shock to see you here...a nice surprise, of course, I don't..."

She held up her hand. "Please don't apologise, Gray. You're right, it's a bolt from the blue, seeing me again after so long. But my story isn't very exciting and doesn't take long to tell. How about you? I was so sorry to read about..."

"About Lily?" The Adam's apple bobbed. "Yes, it was dreadful. Still is. I mean, you keep hoping, but…"

He'd never been good at finishing difficult sentences, and nowadays his voice trailed away more often than ever. Molly brought the tea, and Joanna took charge of pouring. She reached across the table, and brushed his hand. His flesh was cold to touch.

"From what I gather, she vanished out of a clear blue sky."

"That's right, the day the police knocked on my door and broke the news, it was the worst of my life. To make matters worse, my ex-wife blames me for Lily's disappearance."

Joanna's voice rose in outrage. "You were her father! To have your daughter go missing on her way to school, and never see her again, it doesn't bear thinking about. How could anyone imagine that was your fault?"

He made a wry face. "You'd have to know Anya. In her opinion, everything was my fault, from the English weather to the immigration laws."

Joanna buttered a scone. Much as she wanted to turn the conversation to Nigel, she couldn't help being curious. "Do you want to talk about it?"

"Not in any detail, if you'll forgive me. It's still very raw—the not knowing, I can't imagine anything worse." His head dipped, and for a moment, she thought he was about to cry, but he sniffed loudly and kept his voice steady. "Obviously, my life's been turned upside down more than once. First, the Dungeon House shootings. Terrible for Lysette and poor Amber, of course, but not very good for me."

She nodded. Rumours had spread though the Lake District that Malcolm Whiteley was a crook, and that Gray was mixed up in the funny business. She'd heard that Morkel's gang had threatened to sue Gray, and that the Fraud Squad was taking a close interest in his books.

"You sold your practice, didn't you?"

"It was the best solution in the circumstances. I had a rocky couple of years, but the worst didn't happen. Morkel was scared off by the publicity over the shootings, and although I had to jump through countless hoops to satisfy the police, and the professional regulators, in the end they found other people to persecute. But I was sick of private practice, and I tried my hand as a freelance for a while. Then I went on holiday to Florence, and met Anya outside the Duomo."

"How romantic!"

He blushed. "She'd fled from Croatia because of the fighting, and was working as a tour guide. To cut a long story short, I fell head over heels, and she came over as soon as we could make the necessary arrangements."

He nibbled at his scone. "When I married her, it was the happiest day of my life, at least until Lily was born. Such a beautiful child. The image of her mother, not me, thank goodness. When I was offered a partnership by an elderly accountant from Seascale, who wanted someone to buy him out in due course, I thought I'd mended my broken life, so you couldn't see the join."

"Marvellous. It's not true what they say. You can go back."

"Mmmmm, well. Unfortunately, Anya didn't really want me as a husband. Just as a meal ticket."

"Sound like Eoin and me."

He gave her a rueful smile. "You and I have something in common, don't we? I did my best to keep the marriage afloat, but my best wasn't good enough. She found another fool with a fat wallet, and walked out on me. Eventually I surrendered to the inevitable, and agreed to a divorce. Lily was nine by that time, and Anya was very difficult about allowing me access, but I hired the sharpest family lawyer in the county, and he negotiated terms I could live with. Anya made things as hard as possible, but Lily was spending a week with me when she went missing. Normally, Lily only stayed with me at week-ends, but Anya had found yet another boyfriend by then, and he'd booked a romantic trip to the Maldives. So reluctantly, Anya let her stay with me."

"And you never had any idea what happened to Lily?"

"There were a thousand false leads, a thousand false hopes, but no real clue. Nothing. To this day, I can't believe what happened. But there is one thing I do believe."

She looked him in the eye. "What's that, Gray?"

"I believe," he said, voice faltering, "I believe that Lily is still alive. And regardless of whether I see her again, I'll believe that until the day I die. And you know what hurts me most of all, Joanna? Apart from losing my daughter, that is?"

She shook her head, and he bent toward her.

"It's that Anya suspects me of murdering Lily."

"No!"

"She's persuaded the police to re-open their investigation. They're treating it as a cold case, and the senior officer has rung me to fix an appointment. Naturally, I'm pleased about any development that gives us a chance of finding out the truth. And whatever poison Anya has dripped into the detective's ear, she's crazy if she still thinks I killed Lily rather than lose her."

Joanna gaped at him. Gray would never hurt a fly, she was sure of it.

"But—why?"

"Because," he said bitterly, "Anya was talking about leaving Britain for good to live in France with her fancy man, and she meant to take Lily with her. She believes I'm as bad as Malcolm."

"Nonsense!"

He smiled wanly. "I'm glad you're on my side, at any rate."

"Of course!"

As she poured more tea, Joanna wondered if it was tactless to introduce Nigel into the conversation. Fortunately, Gray solved the dilemma for her, clearing his throat noisily as a prelude to changing the subject.

"I suppose you've read the news about Nigel Whiteley's daughter?"

"Yes, yes, it's dreadful."

"The police have been in touch. Not heard from them for ages, and now they're talking to me every five minutes. They want to pinpoint any connections between the two girls. Teenagers do leave home, of course, but two unexplained cases in the same neck of the woods is unusual, even if they are three years apart. The fact that Nigel and I are acquainted interests them. Understandably, I suppose."

"Were Lily and Shona friends?"

"They'd never even met. Lily was slightly older, and they went to different schools."

"But…things like Facebook…." It was her turn to leave a sentence unfinished. The world of teenage girls and social media was alien to her. All she knew of it was gleaned from television and the *Daily Express*.

"Who knows? When Lily disappeared, her computer was carted away, but the IT people never found anything to explain where she'd gone. I'm sure they will check Shona's laptop, and phone records and such-like, so if there was a link between them, it'll show up. It seems far-fetched to me."

Joanna drained her cup. "I feel so sorry for you…and Nigel."

"This morning, the detective in charge of the cold case unit rang to fix an appointment. Not that I'm likely to be much help. I can count on the fingers of one hand the number of times I've seen Nigel since the Dungeon House…."

"You don't act for him, then?" Joanna felt a stab of dismay.

"Good heavens, no. I doubt he'd touch me with a bargepole, given the fuss over Malcolm's company sale. Thankfully, not everyone holds that against me. It's taken years, but I've rebuilt my client list. Enough to afford a lovely home here, and pay Anya more than she deserves in alimony. Nigel's made his own way."

"I gather he made a huge success of his business?"

"Yes, he made a lot of money from paying people peanuts to hand him the right to sue for compensation for accident injuries. Real or imagined. Like Malcolm, he has an eye for the main chance."

Joanna bridled. "Nigel is nothing like Malcolm."

"No, no, I've put it badly. They both had an opportunistic streak, but Nigel's much smarter."

This seemed like damning him with faint praise. "He's a very different *person*."

"Oh, certainly. He was never a boozer, not like Malcolm. And thank goodness, he doesn't own a gun. As far as I know."

Joanna shivered. "I wish there's something I could do. He and I were such good friends. I did wonder if…."

Gray took the hint. "I'm sure he'd be glad to hear from you."

"You really think so? I feel…well, a bit awkward."

"No need for that, Joanna. You were good friends. Come back to the office with me for a moment, and I'll give you his details. I sent him an email expressing my sympathy when I heard the news about Shona."

"Did he reply?"

"No, actually. Of course, he has a lot on his plate at present."

Molly arrived to clear the table. "Was that all right?"

"Lovely, thanks," Gray said.

"You made me curious about this man Gissing," Joanna said. "You said he was unlucky?"

"Too right," Molly said. "His first wife was a prostitute who drank herself to death. The second went bonkers, and died in an asylum. He was sent to prison for theft, and died young, some say of syphilis. Pat reckons he was ruined by drink and money and sex. Then again, who isn't?"

Chapter Ten

Cheryl—Cheryl Johnson, as she now was—lived in a smart bungalow a couple of lengths away from the old Art Deco Lido. A fortnight after taking her degree, Hannah had come to Grange one Saturday with a boyfriend, and swum in the saltwater baths after they'd walked up Hampsfell, and had a picnic by the little stone tower known as the Hospice. A couple of months later, the boy moved to a new job in London, and that was the end of that, but she retained happy memories of the Lido. For the past ten years, it had rotted away while a new indoor baths was built at eye-watering expense. The new pool won an award for architectural merit amid much fanfare, before closing down due to "structural problems". Hannah supposed this said it all about experts on architectural merit. One day, she hoped, the authorities would come to their senses, and restore the Lido to its former glory instead of frittering money away on vanity projects that turned into white elephants. But she wouldn't bet on it.

The bungalow was set back from the road in a large corner plot dominated by a magnolia tree in full bloom. It wouldn't have come cheap in this Mecca for affluent retirees. Cheryl had a knack of landing on her feet, and Hannah gathered that Mr Johnson wasn't short of a few bob. The curtains at the bay window fluttered, and as Hannah walked up the path, Cheryl opened the front door. Her unsmiling expression made it clear that she was eager to get the interview over and done with.

The new husband had suffered a coronary last autumn, hence this move to a one-level home close to the promenade and shops. His recovery was going well, Cheryl said, and he was out on the golf course this morning. Hannah presumed this meeting was timed to coincide with his absence. Perhaps Cheryl expected Hannah to compare Johnson unfavourably with Ben.

Cheryl fiddled with an elaborate Italian coffee-maker, while Hannah made admiring noises about the kitchen and its array of shiny gadgets. They took their drinks into a large front room tastefully decorated, spotlessly clean, and as full of character as an airport lounge. Cheryl was, Hannah thought, fighting a losing battle with the passage of time. Her wrinkles ran deep, and she'd gone overboard with the make-up to compensate. The trouser suit, elegant and expensive, didn't quite disguise the fact that she'd put on half a stone. Nor did she move with the briskness Hannah remembered. Was life with the rich husband taking its toll? As she perched on the edge of her armchair, her eyes were narrow with suspicion.

"Right, then." Cheryl's arms were folded, her body language defensive. "I suppose we have to remember this isn't a social call. You're here in your capacity as chief of the cold case unit. This job of yours is newsworthy, isn't it? Though presumably very different from working at the cutting edge."

Hannah's coffee tasted bitter. "Yes, I do find the work fascinating, specially when the past connects up with the present. Not that it's always easy to join the dots."

Cheryl snorted. "Can't be any dots to join between what Malcolm Whiteley did, the fact his accountant's daughter vanished, and the disappearance of his nephew's girl. The cases are years apart. Totally different, anyone can see that."

Hannah was determined to exude calm. "Some of the same individuals are involved, so it makes sense for us to eliminate the possibility of a connection. As I said on the phone, my team is reviewing Lily Elstone's disappearance. And I wanted to ask you about Gray Elstone."

"Not clapped eyes on him for twenty years. Gray was up to his neck in Malcolm's dodgy business affairs, and after the shootings, he ran for cover. I didn't even know he'd married, let alone had a daughter. Pretty kid, going by the photos in the papers. Obviously she must take after her mother. Gray wasn't in the front row when good looks were handed out."

"What did you make of him?"

Cheryl shrugged. "I only knew him through Lysette. Malcolm was hand in glove with Gray. There was talk afterwards that Gray had fiddled the company books, and that Malcolm lost the plot when his fraud was discovered. Not sure about that, but Gray would never have had the guts to stand up to Malcolm."

"Did he strike you as dishonest?"

"No, he was simply a weakling." Cheryl wrinkled her nose. "Not the sort of chap who would harm a fly."

Hannah had met a number of chaps who wouldn't harm a fly, but had done terrible damage to fellow human beings. "Would you say the same about Nigel Whiteley?"

"Again, you're asking about someone I knew briefly, a long time ago. Nigel was a young man with an eye for the main chance. Confident and determined. Malcolm fell out with his father, because he had this ridiculous idea Ted was pursuing Lysette."

"Was it such a ridiculous idea?"

"Yes, Ted was just an ordinary bloke. A football crazy widower. The big disappointment of his life was when Nigel failed to make the grade as a soccer player. Lysette liked Ted, but I can't believe it went any further than that. She wanted to be a peacemaker, she hated the thought of the brothers not speaking to each other, especially when Ted was diagnosed as terminally ill. But Malcolm was jealous, and bore grudges. Hence his rampage with the rifle. At least Nigel wasn't crazy." Cheryl smiled to herself. "He was good-looking, and popular with the girls. Even on that last night, the night of the shootings, they were all over him."

"Which girls?"

"Poor Amber fancied him rotten, and so did her friend. Joanna. Odd-looking girl who worked for Gray Elstone. Gray obviously fancied her, but she only had eyes for Nigel. Anyway, she was a good deal younger than Gray."

Hannah put down her cup. "Gray was interested in young girls?"

Cheryl's eyes widened. "Don't get me wrong. If he'd been after Amber, Lysette would have hit the roof. Joanna was in her early twenties. She'd suffered health problems, stress-related. Anorexia, alopecia, you name it. She'd grown up with Nigel, and they dated for a while. It was painfully obvious that she was desperate for them to get together again. He was sweet to her that last evening, when we all went for a meal in the Eskdale Arms. All of us except Malcolm, that is. Nigel and Joanna were the first to leave. They went off together, holding hands. Though if you ask me, Nigel was simply being kind because he felt sorry for her."

Joanna followed Gray up the steps to his office. The clatter of heels on the narrow staircase brought back memories of the climb up to that poky flat in Ulverston. Gray led her through a door at the top into a small reception area. A watercolour of a Lake District beauty spot, in Scott Durham's familiar style, adorned each of the four walls. Presumably Gray still acted for Scott. A young Asian woman with crimson lipstick and matching fingernails was on the phone, trying to understand what the caller was saying.

"Sorry, sir, please can you speak more slowly? You say the Revenue…?"

The caller rang off, evidently tired of trying to make himself understood, and the woman greeted Gray with a shrug of frustration. She had long, jet black hair, and her slickly tailored business suit looked like the work of some expensive designer. Not easily paid for on a receptionist's wages.

"He talked so quickly, I couldn't…"

"Not to worry. Another time, put him through to Olive, and she will take a message. Have you had time to look at that spreadsheet?"

The woman scowled at her computer screen, and shook her head. "No, it has been busy since you left."

"Never mind. Yindee, this is Joanna Footit. Many years ago, Joanna used to work for me."

"Ah." Yindee raised elegant eyebrows. "You will have to tell me all Gray's secrets."

Joanna giggled. "My lips are sealed."

A door opened, and a grey-haired woman emerged. As she handed a buff folder of papers to Yindee, Gray performed further introductions. This was Olive, his PA. Her face resembled a hatchet, the younger woman's was shaped like a heart. An unspoken tension told Joanna that Olive and Yindee were not bosom pals.

"We'll only be five minutes," Gray said, ushering Joanna through a door marked with his name. Olive gave him a crisp nod, Yindee the helpless smile that seemed to be her default expression.

As she sat down, Joanna thought that business computers might be smaller and many times more powerful than they were twenty years ago, but not much else had changed. Gray was a tidy man, and neatly labelled lever arch files filled his shelves. There was a filing cabinet, a laser printer, and a paper shredder. He'd bought his first shredder shortly before she stopped working for him. They were unfamiliar machines in those days, but she guessed he'd had the shredder working overtime as soon as he heard what Malcolm Whiteley had done.

He closed the door, and gave his nervous cough. "Perhaps I should mention that Yindee and I are...um..."

Light dawned. She'd been slow on the uptake, especially given that she'd noticed Yindee's diamond ring. Now Gray's whitened teeth and smart clothes made more sense. No wonder Olive looked as though her nose had been put out of joint, and Yindee could get away with an air of disgruntled incompetence.

"You and she are engaged?"

"Well, yes, I'm glad to say she's done me the honour...um... her birthday's coming up. Hence my trip to the florist's."

"Congratulations! How long have you known each other?"

"We met in Bangkok when I was on holiday last year, and it was…gosh, love at first sight." He ventured an apologetic smile. "Arranging a visa was complicated, and it helped for her to have a job ready and waiting. Between ourselves, it's not working out terribly well, but I only ever saw reception work as a temporary expedient. Yindee's English is improving all the time, but her real love is modelling with clay. A client of mine is helping her start a little business, selling at craft fairs and so on. As you can see, she has real talent."

He gestured to a small clay bust of a man's head and shoulders occupying a corner of his desk. The spectacles were undoubtedly Gray's, the rest a flattering image. Much younger, and borderline handsome.

"How marvelous!" Craning her neck as she looked around the room, she saw the screensaver on Gray's computer. A soft focus head-and-shoulders studio portrait of a young woman was the only other personal touch in the room. Fair hair, bare shoulders. Her appearance triggered an unexpected memory. "That isn't…?"

"Lily, yes." He bowed his head. "The last photograph taken of her, only a month before she disappeared. I paid for her to have a session with a professional photographer in Carlisle. Anya was furious, said I was trying to buy her affection, letting a young girl pose like a tart. Nonsense, the shots were all in perfectly good taste. Thanks to Anya, the photographer was put through the third degree by the police, just in case he'd taken a fancy to her. Ridiculous."

"It's just that…." She didn't know how to put it.

"The pictures printed in the press were different, you're right. That was Anya's doing. I told her that it made sense to publicise the very latest photographs, just in case anyone recognised her. Anya would have none of it, even though the older snaps showed Lily with short, mousy hair, looking younger than her age."

"She doesn't look her age there."

"No." There was an unmistakable pride in his voice. "Quite the glamorous young lady, isn't she? Anyway, let's not…"

"No, no, sorry." She paused. "You don't think Nigel will mind if I get in touch, do you?"

"I'm sure he'll be glad to…catch up." He fiddled on his keyboard, and glanced at the screen. "Here we are. Shall I print off his details?"

"Thank you." The printer's whirr masked the tremble in her voice as she asked the sixty-four-thousand-dollar question "Am I right in thinking Nigel isn't…with anyone at the moment?"

Gray chewed at a hangnail. "I really have no idea. When I saw him on television, his comments seemed to imply that he's single."

She said eagerly, "Yes, I saw that. It makes it so much more difficult to bear, being on your own, when something like this happens."

"Yes," Gray said. "That's what I found. Since Anya left me, there's been nobody else—until I met Yindee."

"And Nigel? His wife died twelve months ago, didn't she?"

"Yes, a brain tumour. She was a good deal older than Nigel, in her late fifties, but even so, it's no age. Very sad."

Joanna lowered her eyes, but she found it impossible not to feel a tremor of excitement. Surely Nigel would be glad to see a friendly and familiar face, as he waited for his daughter to come home? On the subject of familiar faces…. "Speaking of that television report, I noticed Robbie Dean outside Dungeon House."

"It's called Ravenglass Knoll these days," Gray said. "Nigel changed the name of the house as soon as he moved in. As a matter of fact, I do Robbie's books. Nigel gave him a long-term contract years ago, and there's more than enough work at Ravenglass Knoll to keep him going. He has a couple of chaps working for him on a self-employed basis. I'm the first to admit Robbie isn't my cup of tea. Surly fellow, always has been. But an accountant doesn't need to like his clients. He simply has to make sure they pay the right amount of tax."

"So Robbie works for Nigel?"

"He and the Whiteleys go back a long way, don't they?" He frowned. "He was drinking in the Eskdale Arms that night, wasn't he? The night of the shootings."

〉〉〉

"Tell me about that day," Hannah said. "The barbecue, and the meal you had together."

Cheryl glared. "This morning, in the newsagents, I saw the tabloids are using Shona Whiteley's disappearance as an excuse to crawl over what happened at the Dungeon House. Prurient, if you want my opinion. Anyway, didn't Ben tell you all about it? The pair of you spent a lot of time…talking to each other."

Hannah let that one whistle past her. "He did speak about the case, but it was years ago, and he was an outsider. You came from that part of the world, you were close to some of the people."

"I was only close to Lysette," Cheryl retorted. "She and Amber have been buried a long time. We all know what Malcolm did. Let his poor wife and daughter rest in peace, that's what I say."

"I want to make sure we cover all the angles."

"I suppose you learned that from the trial you messed up." Cheryl gave a tight, humourless smile. "Someone called Rao, wasn't it? I read about that in the papers, too."

Hannah took a breath. She'd anticipated a frosty conversation, but the hostility in the woman's voice verged on hatred. For a wild instant, she imagined Cheryl stalking her at a distance, scouring reports in the Press and on television, hoping to read about her not-so-brilliant career veering off the rails. But no way would she let Cheryl have the satisfaction of rattling her.

"Yes, we all make mistakes, don't we? I try to learn from mine." A frosty pause. "You and Lysette Whiteley knew each other from way back, didn't you?"

Cheryl held her gaze for a moment, then looked out through the window. "We were best friends. She was lovely, caring, funny, and she deserved better luck. Both her parents died before she was ten, and she was brought up by a miserable old maiden aunt. She didn't have any other family, I was closer to her than anyone. She could have had her pick of men, but once Malcolm got his hooks into her, he never let go."

"You disliked him?"

A sigh. "No, actually, not till the end. He was smart, driven, you could see he'd make something of himself. But Lysette was artistic, and there wasn't a cultural bone in Malcolm's body. Attraction of opposites, you might say. Obviously she was flattered to be wanted so much."

She stared blindly through the bay window, and Hannah guessed Cheryl was recalling her early days with Ben. She'd bewitched a savvy, seen-it-all cop into leaving his job, his wife, his children. Who wouldn't be exhilarated, to wield such power?

"They only had the one child."

"Amber's birth was horrendously difficult. Lysette was an only child herself, and she'd never been that maternal. So she decided enough was enough, and told Malcolm he had to get his bits snipped."

Why hadn't Cheryl and Ben had kids together? It wasn't a question Hannah had dared to ask him, and she could scarcely quiz Cheryl out of sheer curiosity.

"So she became a stay-at-home mum, while Malcolm worked round the clock, building up his business?"

"That's right."

"What was Amber like?"

"I didn't see a lot of her as she grew up. I'd moved to Manchester with a boyfriend. Malcolm spoiled Amber rotten, I'm afraid, and it turned her into a teenage diva. When Lysette tried to rein her in, she was rude and rebellious. I told her it was a phase, and the silly girl would grow out of it. The tragedy is that nobody will ever know, thanks to bloody Malcolm. It's incredible. He idolised that girl. When I heard he'd run amok and killed her, I couldn't believe it."

"Yes, it is hard for you and me to credit." Hannah tried again to establish common ground. "But there are people who think the world revolves around them, and can't believe their children will want to live without them."

"It's only men who behave so selfishly," Cheryl snapped. "What woman in her right mind would murder her own child?

Malcolm was insanely jealous. Lysette couldn't so much as smile at another fellow without him flying into a temper."

"Did she give him much to be jealous about?"

Cheryl hesitated. "Lysette had a great deal to put up with, but she was a loyal wife."

"There were rumours about affairs. How much did she tell you?"

"Nothing." A pause. "Well, toward the end, yes, there was someone. When Malcolm had pushed her too far. After he sold the company, his behaviour became intolerable. No wonder she wanted…some comfort."

"Where did she find it?"

"She took up painting. There was a professional artist, a man called Durham, who gave her lessons. He was a good-looking, sympathetic, widower…I suppose she succumbed to temptation."

"She told you about the affair?"

"Certainly not, she was obsessively discreet. Malcolm had a violent streak, and years earlier, he beat up a boy from school who took a shine to her. She was frightened he'd do the same, or worse. When I came back to the area, I had Ben in tow, and she'd never have wanted to get Malcolm into any trouble with the law. So she kept her mouth shut."

"Then how did you know she was involved with someone?"

"The night before Malcolm went berserk, she asked me for a favour. She wanted to catch up with a friend, but she didn't want Malcolm to find out. If he asked me, she wanted me to say we'd spent the evening together. To cover her tracks, she came to our house, but only stopped for a couple of minutes. Ben knew nothing about it. It was just between me and Lysette. Our little secret."

"Didn't you ask about this friend?"

"I trusted her to tell me when she was ready. I didn't know how far things had progressed, and I had no intention of subjecting her to the third degree. She deserved a breather. Life with Malcolm was suffocating her."

"You're sure this friend was a man?"

"I knew Lysette better than anyone," Cheryl said. "Trust me, it was a man. Blokes swarmed around her like bees with honey. Not that she encouraged them. All I wanted was for her to find happiness. And Scott Durham was definitely an improvement on Malcolm."

"Did this man Durham ever admit that he was seeing Lysette?"

"Denied it till he was blue in the face." Cheryl swallowed some coffee. "I don't blame him. Who in their right mind wants to be mixed up in something so terrible? To be seen as the person who caused such a tragedy?"

"So it might have been someone else? Not Gray Elstone, presumably?"

"You must be joking."

"And not Malcolm's brother?"

"Ted? No way. That really would have driven Malcolm to... no, it's unthinkable. It must have been Scott. Though at one time I did wonder..."

"Yes?"

"There was Robbie Dean, though he was much younger than Lysette. He'd grown up with Nigel, and they were both mad keen on football. Robbie was a good player, but a bad influence. He'd take Nigel drinking, and the two of them used to watch porn together, so Malcolm said. He seemed to think it was a huge joke. Robbie was involved in a car crash which wrecked his career, and he finished up working for Malcolm as a sort of handyman and gardener. He was certainly fit, but Lysette wasn't the sort to go in for a bit of rough."

"And he was rough?"

"I never cared for him. He was moody to the point of rudeness. Lysette used to joke that he was the strong, silent type. He'd stand and stare at you, as if he was picturing you in his mind, without your clothes on. To be honest, he was at it again, that very last night."

"Really?"

"Yes, he was in the bar, throwing darts. Stupid game. At one point, he came over to talk to Nigel, but he wasn't part of our group. That was just Lysette and Amber, Gray and Joanna, and Nigel. Plus Ben and me, of course. Scott turned up later on. His teenage son had played guitar and sung a few songs at the barbecue, and he'd organised a meal for the boy before joining us. The idea was to have a nice, relaxing evening after the barbecue."

"And was it relaxing?"

"Anything but. Amber was vying for Nigel's attention, but after the main course, Nigel asked Joanna if she fancied a walk along the foreshore, and Amber wasn't invited. They wandered off together, hand in hand, all very romantic. He and Joanna had cycled down to the pub, and I remember her dropping a heavy hint that her parents were away from home, so they'd have the place to themselves."

"How did Amber react?"

"She was in a foul mood all through the desserts. The rest of us lingered over coffee, winding down after a lovely day in the sun. Ben did his best to lighten the atmosphere, and told some funny stories about stupid criminals he'd known, and even more stupid chief constables. But Amber spoiled the evening, sniping at Lysette at every opportunity. Such a pity that's my last memory of her."

Cheryl pulled a tissue from her bag, and blew her nose noisily.

"I'm sorry to put you through this, Cheryl."

"No, you're not!" Her cheeks were pink with indignation. "This is what the police do, isn't it? Making life worse for people when you should be helping put things right."

"My best friend was murdered," Hannah said softly. "I think about her every day. I hope you're going to tell me that the pain lessens."

"No," Cheryl sniffed. "When you lose someone to murder, the pain never goes."

Time to draw breath. "Can I get you something? A glass of water?"

"All I want is for you to go away."

"I will get out of your hair in a minute, promise. First, I just need to ask a couple more questions. Did anything happen between Lysette and Scott to make you suspect they were… involved together?"

"Not at all. They were very discreet. I think Scott was terrified Amber would say something to her dad, just to spite Lysette."

"Would she have done that?"

"It's perfectly possible. In the end, she announced she had a headache, and wanted to go home, so we all went our separate ways. Never dreaming, of course, that by the time we woke up the next morning…"

She dabbed her nose with another tissue.

"Ben told me about a witness who supposedly saw someone outside the Dungeon House that night. Did he talk to you about that?"

"I remember." Cheryl made a face. "The witness was someone Ben knew from the cricket club. The chap was an alcoholic, and everyone in the team seemed to drink like there was no tomorrow. It wasn't sensible for a detective inspector to keep company like that, and cricket's a boring game, anyway. The shootings were big news, and a lot of rubbish was talked. Conspiracy theories, you name it. I said to Ben, the man was probably hallucinating when he'd had a skinful."

"Ben didn't agree?"

"No, he insisted the chap wasn't a fantasist. He could be very obstinate, could Ben. You only saw one side of him. I never believed for one second that anyone else was involved. Malcolm went mad, simple as that."

Ignoring the sideswipe, Hannah said, "Ben wasn't satisfied."

"It wasn't his case. That prat Des Loney was in charge. Ben was miffed because Loney wasn't interested in making a simple case any more complicated. To be fair, this was one time when Loney was right."

"Ben's instinct never let him down."

Cheryl gave her a long, lingering look. "Oh, I'm not sure that's right at all. Sometimes he got things very, very wrong."

Hannah couldn't restrain herself any longer. Through gritted teeth, she said, "Look, Cheryl. Whatever you may think, I never slept with Ben."

"Oh, I know that." A false laugh, more like the squeal of a wounded animal. "I could read him like a book. But secretly, he wished you had."

Chapter Eleven

Nostalgia lured Joanna back to the dunes at Drigg that afternoon. As she steered the Polo into the almost deserted car park, she told herself that people who said you should never go back were wrong. Seeing Scott and Gray again had boosted her confidence. Surely Nigel would be glad to see her after so many years? His daughter's disappearance had turned his world upside down, and even a strong man needed someone to lean on.

A tiny grey-haired woman in a quilted bodywarmer was returning to her Toyota, accompanied by a bouncy Labrador. "Bit of a nip in the air!" she called.

Joanna waved back with a smile. Drigg's long, sandy beach was perfect for folk walking their dogs, but nobody else was around. And yes, it was as blustery as ever. Tiny grains of sand blew into her eyes and hair. The terrain along this stretch of coast was gentle, yet Drigg never lost its mood of lonely wildness.

On the way here, she'd wondered whether the old look-out post had been pulled down—or fallen down—but she spotted it at once, a small brick building perched on a low rise above the beach. Skylarks sang as she ploughed through the mud and the grey-green marram grass, and it only took a couple of minutes to reach her destination. The look-out had lacked a door for donkey's years, and she walked straight in. Once upon a time, this was an observation post for a gunnery range, and a few rusty metal fixings for a long vanished telescope still survived.

Hard to imagine shots being fired in such a peaceful place, but then again, she'd have thought the same about the Dungeon House. Her own memories of the look-out were very different, very personal. She stood still, staring out toward the polished blue water.

In this confined space, she'd lost her virginity to Nigel Whiteley. One summer evening, he'd brought her for a walk along the beach and the dunes, and they'd finished up in the look-out. She'd known all day that she was going to surrender to him, but she made him wait until the sun was setting before letting him take her by the hand to the little brick building, and take off her clothes. For all his eagerness, he'd behaved tenderly, realising she was scared of being hurt, and shy about allowing him to see her in the nude, after so many years when they'd been more like brother and sister. She'd wondered if part of her appeal for him was the fact that she wasn't an easy conquest. Finally, his determination not to take no for an answer had earned its reward.

As they rested afterwards, she caught sight of an adder slithering in to join them. With a scream of terror, she ran out of the look-out post, stark naked. Thank goodness so few people frequented Drigg dunes. Nigel pulled on his pants and padded after her, laughing until the tears ran down his face.

"Would you believe it?" he'd said. "A serpent in Eden."

"It's not funny. Adders are poisonous."

"It didn't bite you."

She looked at the red mark on her tiny left breast. "Not like you."

"Badge of honour. It'll make a nice bruise, sort of a souvenir. Come on, let's have a skinny dip."

So vivid was that scene in her mind, it might have been yesterday. No adders were sliding around today, at least none she could see. She strolled out on to the sand, watching the black-headed gulls swoop over the dunes. Thank goodness her first time had been somewhere special. There was history here—settlers had come thousands of years before the Romans—as well as romance. When people spoke about Drigg, they often grimaced, although it was home to a nature reserve and a site of special scientific interest, but in her mind it *was* romantic, with the waves lapping against the sand, and the sun peeping through the clouds. Never mind the snakes, and the high wire fence that separated the lonely shore road from the low level nuclear waste repository. That evening at Drigg, she'd experienced an intensity of happiness unlike anything she'd known before. Or since.

〉〉〉

"What do you make of Anya Jovetic?"

Hannah and Maggie Eyre were having a catch-up in the briefing room. The younger woman grimaced. "A glamorous gold-digger with a vindictive streak and a deep distrust of the British police."

"You two really bonded, then?"

"She demanded to know why we still haven't arrested her ex-husband. I tried to explain that it was difficult without any evidence that he'd done harm to their daughter, but she wasn't impressed. The satisfaction she showed when we agreed to review the case has vanished. Just like Lily."

"Nothing to implicate Elstone?"

"Nothing. She's just cutting up rough because of their financial arrangements post-divorce. Reckons he used his accountancy wiles to hide lots of assets. Not sure why she feels so hard done by, with her designer clothes, and an open-top sports car parked outside her detached house. She's a busty blonde who looks like she's stepped out of a centerfold. Her boob job and hair extensions probably cost more than I earn in six months. She gives Elstone no credit for bringing her over here in the first place, and I'd say the closest she came to true love was when he showed her his credit cards. She's annoyed because he's found another young woman. A Thai girl, this time. Looks like his M.O. He lacks confidence with women, so he scuttles overseas in search of attractive foreigners who want some bloke to carry them off to England."

"Why would Elstone hurt his own daughter?"

"She can't come up with a plausible reason. Apparently, he's no great shakes in bed, but not even our Anya can point to any girl he's ever mistreated. He doesn't seem to have a temper. She says he was hell to live with, but that's par for the course with most men, isn't it?"

Hannah laughed. "They aren't all hopeless."

"Les wasn't best pleased when I said the same to him." Maggie reached into her bag. "Lily had a makeover shortly before she went missing. Her dad arranged for her to have a professional photo shoot, it was something she'd mithered about for ages. She fancied herself as a model, but Anya was dead against it. If you ask me, she didn't want the competition. She looks quite different in these photos, much more mature than in the pictures that were widely issued at the time of her disappearance."

She tossed a couple of prints onto the table, and Hannah said, "I see what you mean."

"I thought we could publicise these shots, see if they jog any memories."

"Good idea." Hannah considered the young woman posing for the camera with a provocative half-smile. "Attractive girl."

"Doesn't look her age, does she?"

"No," Hannah said, "she certainly doesn't."

What impelled Joanna to take a detour to Lower Drigg? Curiosity, she supposed. She felt an inexplicable urge to see where Robbie Dean lived. Lower Drigg barely qualified as a hamlet, comprising just a couple of small farms and a solitary cottage scattered along a long, winding lane that eventually looped away from the dunes, and met the shore road again near the railway station. Half way down the lane, she spotted a van outside the only cottage in sight. She slowed down to a crawl, and saw it was Robbie Dean's.

The old Joanna would have reversed the Polo, and driven away at top speed, but returning to Ravenglass had emboldened her. You couldn't remain scared forever. Life was a lottery, you could never be sure what Fate had up her sleeve. You never knew. Robbie might even have spent years regretting his unkindness toward her. A flight of fancy, perhaps, but today Joanna felt lucky.

She pulled up on the verge, leaving just enough room for other vehicles to pass. Not that traffic ever built up in Lower Drigg. Tourists didn't flock to see nuclear waste dumps, and anyone who strayed out here might be surprised that the landscape lacked a menacing blue hue. Only the high security fence and warning signs supplied clues to what was stored in those sealed vaults far below ground.

No sign of life behind the grubby net curtains. The cottage was built of grey stone, and had none of the charm of Scott Durham's home. A couple of squat outbuildings were visible beyond the garage, and the grounds were separated from the dunes by a barbed-wire fence. They were laid mostly to lawn, while rhododendrons had colonised the border. Unless something special was hidden round the back, Robbie had made no effort to advertise his talents as a gardener. Perhaps only the hardiest plants flourished so close to subterranean stores of radioactive sludge.

"Hello!" she called. "Anybody at home?"

She heard a noise. Someone was moving behind the garage. It must be Robbie, but he wasn't answering.

Perversely, this strengthened her resolve. She'd done nothing wrong, and he really ought to treat her with the respect she deserved. When he'd crashed his car, he might have killed her as well as Carrie.

"Robbie? Robbie Dean?" Still nothing. Even as a young man, he'd been anti-social. Leopards didn't change their spots, but she decided to give it one more try. "You remember me, don't you?"

Suddenly he came into her line of vision, moving with that swaggering limp she remembered so well. The long-handled shears held in his fist shone in the light. The blades were pointing at Joanna's heart.

>>>

Desmond Loney's reluctance to meet for a chat about the Dungeon House case equalled Cheryl's, but Hannah had long suspected that the old goat fancied her, and in the face of a tongue-in-cheek charm offensive, his resistance crumbled.

"Police work isn't what it was," he complained. "The job's all about form-filling and diversity awareness nowadays. Load of codswallop, in my humble opinion."

There wasn't much that was truly humble about Desmond. He was quietly spoken, but buoyed by an invincible self-esteem.

"The bureaucracy can be a nightmare," Hannah agreed. "Like you used to say, you can't beat…"

"Good old-fashioned bobbying? Spot on, Hannah, I always knew you'd go far. Seen you on the telly a time or two. When we've been in England, that is. Pammy and I spend half the year in our holiday home in Paphos."

Les Bryant put his head round the door. Hannah mouthed, *Good old fashioned bobbying,* and he whispered, "Desmond Loney?" *How did you guess?* she nodded.

"I'm lucky to catch you, obviously. Is tomorrow convenient, before you jet back to the sun, you lucky fellow? It will be good to catch up on your news, maybe pick your brains."

"I wouldn't do it for anyone, young lady," Desmond Loney said with complacent magnanimity. "But you could always twist me around your little finger."

The moment she put down the phone, it rang again: Billie Frederick, with an update on the Shona Whiteley investigation.

"Good news. At last, we have a credible lead. A motorist has come forward to say she was driving down the lane that runs past the Whiteleys' house, and she caught a glimpse of a girl answering Shona's description. She was getting into a car which was tucked away on the grass verge, under some trees."

"Make and description?"

"Ever the optimist, Hannah." Billie sighed. "The witness was taking her family off on a short holiday, which is why she's only just got in touch. Unfortunately, at the time, she wasn't paying attention. Her mother was nattering away, and she was trying to hush her kids, who were bickering on the backseat. All she can tell us is that it was a small car. Possibly black, but she can't be certain."

"Does the time of the sighting fit?"

"Perfectly. According to Shona's dad, she'd left the house ten minutes earlier. If this was Shona, it sounds like a pre-arranged meeting, rather than a casual pick-up."

"So she may have run off with a lad."

"Let's hope so. If this is some romantic escapade, there's a chance she's safe and well."

"But no information about a possible boyfriend?"

"Nothing." Billie sighed. "It's not like a teenage girl to be so discreet. We can only pray she hasn't got herself mixed up with whoever abducted Lily Elstone."

>>>

In the sky above Lower Drigg, gulls were squawking. On the ground, the hands holding those wicked shears, were shaking. Robbie Dean was angry, not nervous. Joanna's body was rigid with tension, but somehow she kept her voice calm.

"Hello, Robbie. Is this how you greet an old friend?"

His forehead was lined, and his hair was thinning, but he remained stocky and muscular, and quite unmistakable. He was staring as if unable to believe the evidence of her eyes.

"Joanna?"

"How are you?" From somewhere she found the guts to switch on a smile, and hold out her hand. It was as if she'd become another person, fearless and in command.

"What the fuck are you doing here?"

"Charming!" She gave a little laugh, to show she wasn't mortally offended. "I'm staying in Ravenglass. I arrived yesterday."

"For fuck's sake. What for?"

"A holiday, what else?" Something prompted her to add, "It's been utterly wonderful, revisiting old haunts. This morning I had a look around Seascale, and just now I went for a wander on the dunes."

He seemed lost for words, so she kept talking, not for one moment taking her eyes off the cruel blades. "I saw poor Nigel on television, and your van was outside the house. So I realised you must work for him, just like...."

She'd meant to say, *just like you worked for Malcolm*. But it sounded too much like an accusation, as if bad luck followed him around. Staring at her in disbelief, he still kept a grip on the shears.

"Won't you put them down? For a moment, I almost thought you were going to stab me."

She tittered, to show how absurd was the very notion. He glared, but took a step back. Opening the back of his van, he put the shears inside.

"Can't be too careful," he muttered.

Joanna wanted to yell with delight. She'd faced him down! But it still wasn't wise to annoy him. She waved at the CCTV camera fixed under the roof of the house. "So I see."

"I keep my England schoolboy cap and the other souvenirs under lock and key. There's a trade in football memorabilia, my stuff is worth a packet."

"Better than a pension," she said, forcing a giggle.

"I'll never part with them."

Robbie Dean the sentimentalist; who would have thought it? She looked around at the empty, windswept landscape. "I suppose you're not used to visitors?"

"You can say that again."

"See a lot of Nigel?"

A dismissive shrug. "I was helping the lads to cut ivy back at the house this morning."

"How is he?"

"His daughter's missing. How do you think he is?"

"I'm sorry, I didn't mean…."

His brow furrowed. She could almost hear cogs turning in his brain as he tried to make sense of her unexpected reappearance. An unpleasant smile sneaked across his face.

"The look-out post is still there, y'know."

"So I see." She gave an embarrassed laugh.

How did he know about the look-out post, and what it meant to her? Instantly, she answered her own question. Nigel must have told him. Oh God, had he boasted to his friend about getting inside her knickers? She could picture the two young men laughing at her expense as they watched a blue movie together. Back in the day, she'd have been mortified. Men were so childish about sex.

They stood in silence, staring at each other. Did Robbie see in her the girl he'd known twenty years ago? She'd blocked him out of her thoughts, just as she'd blocked out so many things. In her mind, catastrophe and Robbie Dean went hand in hand.

"You still haven't told me why you came here. This place isn't on the way back to Ravenglass. It's a detour."

"Yes, but…it's good to catch up, isn't it? Gray told me that he acts for you."

"Gray?" He seemed appalled. "You went to see Gray fucking Elstone?"

"I bumped into him in Seascale."

"Hell of a coincidence." He sounded like a hard-nosed cop in mid-interrogation, scornful about her so-called explanation for her movements.

"Not really." She felt provoked into justifying herself. "How many people live around here? A couple of hundred in Ravenglass, the same in Drigg? Seascale is scarcely Brighton. It's not surprising that I should come across a few people I used to know. I've met Scott Durham, too."

He shook his head. "Unbelievable."

"Not really. A trip down memory lane, let's call it. Long overdue, to be honest. You may have heard, my parents died, and…."

He wasn't the sort to offer condolences about her bereavement. "You haven't seen Nige?"

"No, but…I'd like to."

"Why?" He almost spat out the question.

"Why not? He was a good friend, and I'm desperately sorry about what's happened to his daughter."

He peered at her, as if trying to detect some ulterior motive. "Is that why you're here? To have a snoop around, and then try and find out from me about Nige?"

"Hey, Robbie, no need for nastiness. We were…friends, remember?"

"Friends?"

His bafflement seemed genuine. And it was true, she would never have described him as a friend. He might once have been a football star, but he never made her go weak at the knees the way Nigel did. Not before the crash, and not after it. And certainly not that night at Seascale.

"We stuck by you after the crash."

"You had a fucking breakdown," he snapped. "You weren't in any fit state to stick by anyone."

"You know what I mean." It was like being slapped on the cheek, but at least she knew what to expect from him. *Sticks and stones may break my bones, but words will never hurt me.* "I didn't blame you for what happened, even though the car crash nearly killed me, as well as Carrie."

"Don't talk about Carrie," he muttered.

She took no notice. "When we smashed into that tree, I was sure I was going to die. It was terrifying, can you wonder I was upset? But I never let you down. When the police asked me, I said everything you and Nigel wanted me to say. I'm sorry about what happened, but it wasn't my fault."

He took a breath. "Yeah. I suppose so. Yeah. Sorry."

An apology from Robbie Dean! That had to be a collector's item. Inwardly, she exulted. Her new-found confidence was giving her the courage to say and do things she'd never have dreamed of.

"That's all right. It must be a shock, seeing me here without any warning."

"Yeah, just a bit."

He shifted from foot to foot, his hesitancy strangely reminiscent of Gray Elstone's. Was he going to invite her in? She very much doubted it. It wasn't Robbie's style to chat over a brew. But she sensed a subtle alteration in his manner. The naked aggression had vanished, thank goodness, and he seemed unsure of himself. Had he ever truly been attracted to her? She doubted it, though with men, you could never quite be sure. Most likely, her sudden reappearance in his life had brought embarrassing memories flooding back, and he was desperate to be rid of her, but she was determined to exact a price. Given that he worked for Nigel, he could help her to make contact with the man who *had* loved her.

"You asked why I want to see Nigel. I hate to think of him upset, not knowing what has happened to his girl. And his wife died. It must be so hard to cope on your own."

"And you...think you can help him to cope?" He spoke slowly, as if working out the answer to a riddle.

"I'd like to do what I can. A trouble shared, and all that. It would be lovely to see him again. It might even take his mind off Shona for a while."

He shook his head. "Spoiled rotten, that kid. Proper little madam, if you ask me."

"Even so, she's missing. Perhaps someone's taken..."

"Nobody's holding her captive," he interrupted.

She stared at him curiously. "You think she's run away from Nigel?"

"What else?"

"Like I say, the police obviously haven't ruled out kidnapping."

"No ransom demand," he said. "She's off with some man, you can bet on it."

"A boy? Someone from school?"

"A man," he repeated. "She's trouble, that one."

She stared at him. "Do you know where she's gone?"

"No!"

She'd struck a nerve—he was almost shouting. The only other time she'd seen him this rattled was on the night of the car crash, when they were together in the ambulance. He'd recovered consciousness, only to be told that Carrie was dead, and she'd watched tears trickle down his cheeks.

"Okay, calm down. I only..." A thought occurred to her. "Shona didn't ever...flirt with you, did she?"

"No way!" He was breathing heavily, fighting for calm. "You shouldn't poke your nose in, Joanna. It won't do any good."

"I'd love to see Nigel again." She paused. "Are you going back to the Dungeon House this afternoon?"

"Ravenglass Knoll," he said. "It's not been the Dungeon House for twenty years. Nige is seeing the police this afternoon. They are due to give him an update."

"Don't worry," she said recklessly. "I wasn't hoping for a lift. I haven't forgotten what happened last time I was your passenger."

He took a step forward, and for a second she thought he was going to start strangling her again. "And you think I have forgotten?" he demanded through gritted teeth.

"No, no, of course not. Sorry, Robbie, that was uncalled for. It's just that…"

"What are you after?"

"Would you let Nigel know I've come back to Ravenglass? Please?"

"Is that it?"

She dug her bag out of the Polo, scribbled her mobile number on a scrap of paper, and handed it to him. "If you could ask him to ring me? Or I can give him a call, if it's easier. Will you do that, Robbie?"

"All right. Now, I have things to do. You'd better go."

She felt like dancing, she was so exhilarated. Her skin tingled, her heart beat faster. Soon she'd see Nigel again, she was sure of it. As for Robbie Dean, for as long as she could remember, he'd scared her. His mood swings were so intimidating. Yet she'd faced him down. And although she wasn't quite sure how, she'd managed to turn the tables. Today, he almost seemed more scared of her than she was of him.

"How was Cruella?" Daniel asked as Hannah walked through the door.

She kissed his cheek. "May I be bitchy?"

"Please, be my guest."

"Getting old. Grumpy. It won't be long before we can describe her as *raddled* without risking an action for slander. Tell you what, though, her tongue's still as sharp as a Stanley knife."

"The interview wasn't a total success, I take it?"

"Oh, I got what I wanted, her first-hand impressions of the Whiteleys' circle at the time of the shootings. In a nutshell, the sun shone out of Lysette's cute little bum, and Malcolm was the devil incarnate. All of which may not be far from the truth, to be fair. As far as she's concerned, the case was solved, and I shouldn't waste taxpayers' money asking questions about it."

Daniel slipped his hand inside her shirt. "And the Mysterious Missing Witness?"

"She was distinctly unimpressed. As far as she was concerned, your dad revelled in making life complicated."

"Given the mess he made of our family life," Daniel said, "I suppose I can't argue."

〉〈〉

"Are you staying for the quiz?" the waitress asked, as she cleared Joanna's table in the Eskdale Arms.

"Oh, I don't…" As Joanna reached for her bag, she heard a familiar voice. Scott Durham, responding to a greeting at the other end of the bar. "On second thoughts, yes, why not?"

"Another drink, then?"

"A Sauvignon Blanc, yes, please." Although there had to be a limit to hedonism. "Just a small glass this time."

"I'll get you an answer sheet. Unless you're joining a team?"

Joanna giggled. "I'm not sure anyone will have me."

"Don't be so modest, love." A large man in a Fair Isle pullover leaned over from the next table. "Join up with us, if you're not fussy about winning. We're short of two of our regulars tonight."

As she opened her mouth to answer, Scott ambled in, and the Fair Isle man greeted him like an old friend. "Hey up, mate. Thought you weren't coming. We're already a man down. Bob Evans' wife has been taken poorly. But I've just recruited another member, this young lady here."

Scott hesitated before giving her a thin smile. "Hello again, Joanna."

"What? You're already acquainted? Blimey, I always knew you were a fast worker, mate. Aren't you going to introduce us, then?"

"My name's Joanna," she said. "I used to live in Holmrook, a long time ago. I've booked in next door, and lo and behold, I ran into Scott last night."

The only empty seat left at the table was next to her. Scott wavered before realising there was no escape, and made the introductions. The Fair Isle man and Walter, a small, taciturn chap with a hearing aid who made up the rest of the team, both lived in Waberthwaite. They all chatted amiably through the first three rounds of questions, in which Joanna performed creditably on history and literature, whilst revealing a profound ignorance of pop music and politics. When the Fair Isle man, whose name was Kelvin, headed for the bar to order a fresh round of drinks—Joanna played safe with orange juice this time—Scott asked if she'd had a good day.

"Lovely, thanks. Went for a walk on the shore this morning. Your studio has a marvellous position."

"Thanks, it's not bad." She wondered if he'd invite her to take a look round, but no joy. He seemed more distracted than ever, and she asked if he was okay.

"Yes, fine. Sorry, I'm just a bit preoccupied. Usually, I'd have been the first to figure out those anagrams."

"The painting's going all right, I hope?"

"Yes, yes." He took a surreptitious peek at his mobile, for perhaps the fifteenth time that evening. Whatever text he was hoping to receive showed no sign of turning up.

"I do hope things sort themselves out. Whatever they are."

"Thanks." He was offering no clues. "So you've been exploring Ravenglass? Did you go for a trip on the La'al Ratty?"

"No, no, the train is a treat for another day." She wanted to draw him out. "I've been meeting one or two other old friends, as it happens. Gray Elstone, for instance. Were your ears burning? We had a cuppa together in Seascale, and he told me he still acts for you."

"You met Gray?" His eyes almost popped out of their sockets. Anyone would think she'd confessed to an assignation with Daniel Craig. "What on earth for?"

"I used to work for him, remember?"

Kelvin returned with the drinks, and Scott gulped down a large mouthful of beer. "Yes, yes, of course you did. Sorry, I was just….I forgot, that's all."

"He told me his ex-wife was horrid to him. She even accused him of being responsible for his daughter's disappearance."

"Unthinkable," Scott said. "You know Gray. He was a good father."

"You think that Lily is dead?"

He looked bewildered. "There's always hope, I suppose, in the absence of definite news. But really—three years is a long time."

"What do you think happened?"

"How would I know? It's a mystery."

"What if the same thing happens with Shona Whiteley, and she never shows up? Do you think one person could be responsible for taking both girls?"

"No!"

His vehemence took her aback, and out of the corner of her eye, she saw Kelvin exchange a look with Walter. She suspected the older men shared a tacit disapproval of any outpouring of artistic temperament on a quiz night. Before she could say anything else, the quizmaster was asking them to name the highest mountain in Oceania.

Ten minutes later, when the sketchiness of her geographical knowledge had been brutally exposed, she murmured in Scott's ear, "Robbie Dean told me that Shona is rather spoiled. I suppose it's not surprising. Nigel's probably making up for the fact that she lost her mother. Can't have been easy for either of them."

"You've talked to Dean?" Plainly, he had no wish to discuss Nigel and Shona.

"Yes, he lives out near the dunes."

"You were in his car that night he crashed, and his girlfriend was killed, weren't you?"

So Scott remembered. "Yes. It was a long time ago. Bygones should be bygones, don't you think?"

The quizmaster bellowed into his microphone that the time had come for teams to exchange their sheets and mark each other's answers. This was evidently Scott's job. She watched him jotting down the ticks and crosses in his neat hand, concentrating on the task, oblivious to the groans that echoed around the pub whenever a mistake was exposed.

"Hello, there." You-Can-Call-Me-Al loomed over her, a foaming pint clutched in his hand. "Got your feet under the table already, Joanna! A key member of a red-hot quiz team, no less!"

"Actually, we've finished in fourth place."

"Not to worry. It's not a matter of life and death."

"Nope," Kelvin said. "It's more serious than that."

"Can I get you lads a drink? Joanna, can I tempt you?"

Scott scrambled to his feet. "I need to be off, thanks all the same. Goodnight, all."

Before Joanna could say anything, he was gone. She mumbled an excuse about wanting to be up early in the morning, and ignoring You-Can-Cal-Me-Al's protestations, headed for the door. By the time she got outside into Main Street, there was no sign of Scott. He must have made it to Seagull Cottage in record time.

Never mind. Tomorrow she'd call Nigel, and see if he was willing to meet up. It had been a productive day. And now she even knew about Puncak Jaya's claim to fame.

Chapter Twelve

"How lovely to hear you again, Nigel."

"It's…been a long time."

That gorgeous husky voice in her ear again. He sounded uncertain, but who could blame him? She squeezed the mobile into her palm.

"Twenty years."

"Robbie rang and told me you'd be calling. He says you look the same as ever."

"Goodness, he's the last person I'd expect to indulge in flattery."

Except that perhaps he hadn't meant to flatter her. She told herself not to be so negative. You led a happier life if you thought positive.

"So…" Nigel paused, as if steeling himself. No need, he had nothing to fear from her. Absolutely nothing, she only wanted to help. "What you have been doing with yourself these past twenty years?"

"Nothing too exciting, if truth be told." She gave a modest laugh. It was spitting with rain, and she felt awkward conducting this conversation on the pavement outside the Eskdale Arms, but she'd needed to escape from You-Can-Call-Me-Al. He seemed keen to get to know her better, and she wouldn't put it past him to eavesdrop. His latest gambit had been to invite her to share bacon and eggs in his private kitchen at the back of the guest house. She'd excused herself by saying her GP had put her on statins, and she needed to keep her cholesterol count down.

"Not like *you*," she said, when it became apparent that Nigel wasn't about to respond. "Mind, I wasn't in the least surprised you became so successful. I always knew you'd make it one day."

"What's brought you back here?"

That question again. "Oh, I don't know. I fancied a change of scene, and wanted to look up some old friends."

"You've heard about Shona?"

He made it sound like an accusation. "Yes, yes. I'm so sorry that you've had such a worry to contend with."

"A worry," the quiet voice repeated. "Rather an under-statement."

Her cheeks burned. Thank goodness he wasn't there to witness her embarrassment. All she could do was grovel, and hope he would forgive.

"I'm sorry, Nigel, truly. Rotten choice of words. It must be appalling for you. You lost your wife not long ago, didn't you? And now this."

She paused, but when he remained silent, she asked, "What's the latest news?"

"There is no news." His voice was unsteady. "The police don't seem to have a clue. They say…but anyway, you don't want to hear me go on."

"Of course I do. Why do you think I told Robbie I was keen to get in touch? If there's any way I can help, just say the word. I thought you might be glad to chat with an old friend. After all…we went through a lot together in the old days. You could talk to me about Shona. I'd love to meet her." She hesitated. "I'm sure you will be reunited soon."

He didn't reply. Wondering how to give her the brush-off without seeming to be rude? She held her breath.

"I'm lousy company at present."

"Doesn't matter," she insisted. "It would be wonderful to see you. Talk over old times."

"Almost being killed in a car crash? About the night we spent in a pub with my aunt and my cousin, hours before they were murdered by a maniac?" She'd forgotten the sarcastic bite of his humour. "They aren't the best memories. We were jinxed."

"There were plenty of happy times," she retorted. "Yesterday afternoon, I went on a pilgrimage to Drigg. Went into the old look-out post, remember?"

A pause. "I haven't forgotten that, Joanna."

"Me neither," she murmured.

He coughed, as if buying time while he racked his brains for a response. "I remember the adder frightening you."

Pleased, she laughed. The touch of mockery didn't bother her. All that mattered was to win his confidence. He was in a fragile state, with his daughter missing, it was understandable.

"Funny, I thought about the adder yesterday." She paused. "I'll never forget that day, Nigel."

She heard an intake of breath. "Cherish your memories. You'd be disappointed in me if we met."

"Nonsense. I'd love to see you. No hidden agenda, I promise."

"You always were very persistent, Joanna."

He spoke as though persistence was a vice, but she didn't care. His resistance was weakening, must be. "Go on. You've nothing to be afraid of. I don't bite!"

A heavy sigh. "All right, I'm sorry, I don't mean to be brusque, it's just that…would you like to come over here sometime?"

"To the…house?"

"Ravenglass Knoll, yes." He emphasised the name.

"I'd love to, Nigel. Thank you so much."

Once the Dungeon House had boasted two lichen-encrusted stone gateposts, with nothing in between. Anyone could walk up the drive. Now an iron electric gate barred the entrance, an eight-foot tall fence ran along the boundaries of the property, and signs warned that the premises were protected by camera surveillance 24/7. Above the intercom box, the house's new name was carved defiantly into a chunk of green slate. Joanna couldn't blame Nigel for trying, but Ravenglass Knoll would always be the Dungeon House. When he'd given her the security code, he'd said that over the years, a good many sensation seekers had noseyed around the place, drawn by its association with bloody murder. *Dark tourism* was the fashionable term. He thought it was sick, and Joanna agreed.

Joanna leaned out of her window, and keyed in the code. The gates opened soundlessly. How much did all this security cost? Nigel had always wanted money, now he had it to burn. Did Shona feel like a princess trapped in a gilded cage? The gates closed behind her as she drove up the slope toward a large circle of gravel close to the garage block, where he'd told her to park.

The trees were clouds of cherry blossoms, purple and pink, and she could smell newly mown grass. Robbie and his men had made the grounds look even lovelier than she remembered. Her heart thudded as she caught sight of the four familiar half-timbered gables. She'd always adored the mellow architecture of the house. A disciple of William Morris had designed it for a wealthy Victorian merchant, the sort responsible for so many large houses dotted around the Lakes. Many were now upmarket hotels, but she felt glad this one had remained in private hands, even if she couldn't understand why Nigel would want to live at the Dungeon House.

Sorry, would she never get it right? Ravenglass Knoll.

He must have been watching out for her, since the door opened seconds after she pressed the bell. In navy blue sweatshirt, jeans, and trainers, he looked slim and fit. She wondered whether he would greet her with a kiss on the cheek, but it didn't happen. His handshake was quite gentle, not the aggressive grip that some men used to assert their masculinity.

"Come in, Joanna. I've made us some coffee, and we can take it out on to the terrace, if you don't mind the breeze."

"That's kind, thank you," she said, following him into a kitchen that deserved to feature in an ideal home magazine.

"You're looking well," he said. "I bet you're not an ounce heavier than when I last saw you."

"At least I've never needed to diet. Like I said on the phone, I was poorly for a while. The pounds dropped off me."

He organised two mugs of coffee, and put a small box of chocolates on a tray. "Belgian, your favourites, right? I'm assuming you still like them?"

"You have a fantastic memory." This was unbelievably touching. Her knees felt weak.

"For some things. Others, I prefer to forget."

"Believe me, I know the feeling."

"You're recovering from your illness?"

"Absolutely. I finished with my partner, and signed an exit deal with my firm, and now I'm feeling a hundred per cent better. Unshackled from my bonds."

At the press of a button, the glass doors giving on to the sitting area slid back, and he led her out through a pergola festooned with voluptuous clematis blooms, mauve and cream, and a fragrant wisteria. The low yew hedges were much as she remembered, but the summer house that had been Malcolm Whiteley's pride and joy was no more. In its place stood a spherical lounger, four yards in diameter, with bronze-tinted windows and timber supports. Nigel pressed a tiny remote control in his hand, and a door slid open, to reveal cushioned seating which ran all the way round. In the middle of the pod, a television screen hung above a mini bar. She followed him inside, exclaiming at the comfort and the views.

"Very futuristic!"

She caught a flicker of the old familiar zest as he said, "You should see it lit up at night."

"I'd love to!" She coughed. "Never mind me, you're looking very fit."

His face darkened. "I've lost weight half a stone since Shona disappeared. Losing your only child has a more drastic effect than any diet. These biscuits are for you, by the way. I'm hardly managing to keep anything down."

"I'm so sorry." Instinctively, she rested her hand on his. For a moment, she feared he would flinch, or pull away, but he didn't react. It was almost as if he didn't notice. "Is there any news about Shona?"

"Nothing credible," he said bitterly. "I speak to the police constantly, and they still seem to think that she may have run off with someone she knew. I don't believe it for a moment. She wouldn't have been able to hide it from me. I'm not blaming them, they are doing their best. What terrifies me is the thought that Shona has been abducted by a pervert. For all anyone can tell, it's the same person who took Gray Elstone's daughter."

"You haven't thought about talking with Gray?"

"What good would it do? Two grown men, crying on each other's shoulders? Not for me, thanks. " He stared out toward the horizon. "To tell you the truth, I feel bad because I didn't contact him when his girl went missing. Never crossed my mind that one day I'd be in the same boat. The worst is that, from that day to this, nobody's heard anything of her. Who knows what the man who took her did? Buried her in woods, threw her body down a ravine, rowed across a lake, and dropped it into the deepest part?"

She shivered. "There's always hope, Nigel."

He turned to face her. "You think so?"

"Look at me," she said, and was rewarded by the intensity of the way his dark eyes scrutinised her. "Not so long ago, my life scarcely seemed worth living. No partner, no job, no reason to get out of bed in the morning. My health was rotten, and my doctor was really worried. And now I'm back on my feet, as you can see."

"I can see," he said slowly. "How did you manage it?"

"I'm on medication," she admitted. "But there's more to it than that. Doctor Chanderpaul said I needed to start liking myself again. To be honest with you, the turning point came when I saw you on television."

His eyebrows lifted. Did it excite him, that he still exerted such power over her? She hoped so. Nigel was someone who needed to be in control. How he must loathe his present helplessness, relying on the police for news of Shona, and unable to do anything to save her.

"You're kidding."

"No, honestly. I remembered the life we all had together up here." She hesitated. "They were good times, weren't they?"

"You had rough days along the way."

"Like when Robbie crashed the car? At least you and I weren't hurt."

"No, but you were…upset for a long time."

Even now, the memory of the shattering impact as the car hit the tree filled her with horror. It had taken her years to get over it. Nigel was made of sterner stuff. He'd dusted himself down, and got on with his life.

"They have a name for it nowadays, don't they? Survivors' guilt."

"You had nothing to be guilty about."

"I lived, and that poor girl died. And the crash wrecked Robbie's life." She looked straight at Nigel. He really was a handsome man. The years had treated him kindly. She supposed having all that money helped. "You stuck by him, though. Then—and now. You pay him to take care of your garden."

"It's not an act of charity. He's not expensive, and he doesn't do a bad job." Nigel gestured through the windows of the lounger. "As you can see."

"The garden is gorgeous." She hesitated. "Though I must say I never understood why you and he were such good friends."

"He was a wonderful footballer. With a ball at his feet, he was a magician. I felt proud that he was my mate." He gave a bark of laughter. "Perhaps I'm fascinated by unusual people, Joanna. Like you, I suppose."

"Oh, there's nothing fascinating about me."

A crooked grin. "I don't agree."

She gulped some coffee, trying to hide her delight. "To be honest, I've not felt remotely interesting for a long, long time."

"You treat life seriously," he said. "It's a mistake to take everything to heart. Best live for the moment."

"I suppose so."

"I assumed you'd have married, and brought up kids."

"I rather expected things would turn out that way myself," she admitted. "That's what I wanted, I suppose. Life as a wife and mother."

"You can't have wanted it enough. Otherwise, you'd have made it happen."

This was the Nigel she remembered. Life was simple. Make up your mind what you want, and go for it. No dithering. He'd set himself the goal of seducing her, but once he succeeded—she saw it with hindsight—his interest began to fade. Even before the car crash sent her into a tailspin of misery and despair, she was losing him. Afterwards, she'd felt inadequate, a freak. It came as such a thrill on the day of the barbecue to discover he still cared for her. And then Malcolm Whiteley went berserk with his rifle, and destroyed everything.

"After I left Cumbria, I floundered, didn't know what to do with myself. And I'm the first to admit, I'm a hopeless judge when it comes to men. My last partner was a businessman, or so I thought, but he spent the money I lent him for a new venture on another woman he'd met through the Internet. If I hadn't stumbled across the truth by having a peek at his phone messages, he'd have bled me dry."

"Not an easy ride, then," he said quietly.

"You can say that again." For a dreadful moment, she thought she was about to cry, but somehow she managed to hold back the tears.

He gave her hand a quick squeeze. "Care to take a walk round the grounds?"

"Thanks." Her heart was doing somersaults. "I'd love to."

"There's one thing I wanted to ask you," Joanna said. "I hope you don't mind."

She was following Nigel along a curving path of stepping-stones cut into the lawn, past a border blazing with crimson camellias, and toward a rock garden bounded by a low stone wall with aubretia spilling over it. He halted, but didn't turn round.

Was he afraid she was about to say something lovey-dovey and embarrassing?

"What is it?"

"It's about this house. I mean, it's fabulous, of course, but I couldn't help wondering…"

The stepping stone path led to an oak tree with a wooden bench running around it. Bright yellow celandines shone from the grass beneath the branches. He sat down, and gestured for her to join him. His face was stripped of any expression.

"How I could bear to live here, after everything that happened?"

What a relief that he'd read her mind. Putting the question into words herself would have sounded judgmental, as if she were accusing him of not caring enough about Lysette and Amber, and their dreadful fate.

"I don't want to be nosey…"

"You were always nosey, Joanna, but don't lose too much sleep over it." His thin smile didn't quite rob his words of their sting. "Okay, I'll satisfy your curiosity. If you must know the truth, I'm here because of a promise I made to my dad before he died."

"Your dad?"

Ted Whiteley had succumbed to his cancer a few months after the shootings. She'd heard the news from her parents. Ted had died in the same hospice as Scott Durham's wife. No flowers, by request, but Joanna scribbled a note of condolence to Nigel, and sent a donation to hospice funds. He hadn't acknowledged either. Secretly, she'd been dismayed. He was grieving, of course, but she'd still hoped he would drop a line, or even, seeing that she'd put her phone number in the note, give her a ring. But… not a word.

"Yes," he said. "Before he died, he made me promise not to sell up."

Light dawned. "Of course," she said. "After the shootings, your dad was Malcolm's next of kin. I suppose Lysette had no close family?"

"It came as a total shock," Nigel said. "The lawyers told Dad that the house was in Malcolm's sole name. He was a real male chauvinist, you know. With Lysette and Amber dead, the property passed to Dad. The final tragedy was that, after years of struggling to make ends meet, he became rich overnight, when he was too sick to enjoy the money."

"How ghastly."

"You said it," he muttered. "The last thing I wanted was to come and live here, in the house where my uncle had killed his wife and my cousin."

"I can imagine." She hesitated. "Poor Amber, she was so young."

"Yeah, she wasn't such a bad kid. Vain as hell, mind."

"I liked her very much."

"Her dad spoiled her. No wonder she became such a diva." He looked her in the eye. "I suppose people say I made the same mistake with Shona. At least I have the excuse that her mother battled a brain tumour for a long time. I felt I had to make up to Shona for having her childhood torn apart."

"I'm sure you are a wonderful father."

"Not really." He finished his coffee. "You always see the best in people, Joanna. It's a rare quality."

Her cheeks were burning. Did he share her regret that things had not worked out between them? She was daring to hope.

"I don't know," he began tentatively, "whether you want to see the quarry garden?"

"Oh. Well…"

"Perhaps it's not a good idea." He was studying her face with genuine concern. "After what happened there."

"I suppose…we all have to learn to confront our demons."

"I guess that's right," he said quietly. "Is that why you've come back here?"

"That's part of it, I suppose." She hesitated. "I'd seen Scott Durham and Gray Elstone already before I called on Robbie."

His eyes widened. "You have been busy."

"Are you still in touch with Scott?"

He frowned. "We've bumped into each other once or twice over the years. Good old Lake District, eh? You can never escape from the past."

"Perhaps we shouldn't try to escape from it," she said. "I ran away because I couldn't deal with what happened, but it didn't make me happy."

He was watching her closely. "You'd had a rough time. I should have been kinder."

"You were young. To have such a flaky girlfriend must have been a pain." Her throat felt dry. "I didn't blame you for getting bored with me. Though I wish you hadn't told Robbie about… the look-out on Drigg beach."

Nigel flinched. "Tease you about it, did he? I'm sorry, Jo. It was just…lads talking. I suppose I boasted about my conquests. Not that there were many of them."

"Robbie is…" She didn't know how to describe him.

"He fancied you, you know."

"No, he only had eyes for Carrie. Nobody could replace her, certainly not me." She paused. "He didn't confide in you, did he?"

"How do you mean?"

"I know he's your friend, and you've always been so loyal to him. But there's plenty you don't know. Did he tell you about Seascale, for instance?"

He looked baffled. "What about Seascale?"

"Six weeks before the barbecue, he and I bumped into each other one evening at Seascale. He bought me a few drinks in a seedy pub, and as it grew dark, he took me down to the beach. He'd always intimidated me, I could scarcely believe it."

"Like I said, he fancied you."

"Not enough," Joanna said. "He took me to a quiet spot below the cliffs, and pulled my knickers down. I was tipsy and in the mood. I'm not making excuses, it was just one of those things. But he couldn't manage to…"

He stared at her. "Seriously?"

"Yes." This was the first time she'd ever told anyone what happened that night, and at once the words came out in a rush. "It was incredible. Embarrassing. Robbie Dean, the glamorous football star, was impotent."

For a few moments, they sat together in silence. "There," she said, "I've shocked you, haven't I? The respectable Joanna."

He gave her a wary grin. "You were never quite as respectable as you liked to crack on. But…how did he react?"

"As you might expect," she said "Badly. He said some very cruel things to cover his blushes. Blamed the way I looked, said I didn't turn him on. It wasn't even as if I laughed at him, or tried to make him feel inadequate. And then he put his hands around my throat. I was terrified he was going to strangle me."

"Steady on." Nigel swallowed. "Robbie's not the easiest, but I've never known him attack anyone. Never."

"Looking back on it, I suppose it was just on the spur of the moment. He did hurt my neck, but I wriggled free, and when I ran off along the beach, he didn't follow."

"Uh-huh." He took a breath, as if making a decision. "Still want to see what he's done to the quarry garden?"

Chapter Thirteen

Linz Waller, a DC in Hannah's team, had dug out the paper-work for the deaths at the Dungeon House. The witness who claimed to have seen a man dressed as a woman near the scene of the crime was called Anton Friend. Hardly a common name. Hannah asked her to see if Friend could be traced. If he hadn't been inconsiderate enough to die in the meantime, she wanted to have a word. Would he stick to his story after all these years? And, if he did, would she find it as persuasive as Ben had done, or conclude that he was simply an alcoholic time-waster?

Desmond Loney had celebrated his retirement by moving from Carlisle to the coastal haven of St Bees. Hannah had arranged to see him before driving south for a meeting with Gray Elstone in Seascale. St Bees lay a few miles outside the National Park, but was the starting point for the coast to coast walk, and she cherished a vague fantasy of trekking across England along with Daniel. If they stayed together long enough, if he didn't get bored with her.

The clouds of early morning cleared during her journey, and by the time she arrived in the village, the red sandstone of the old and unexpectedly impressive priory church was resplendent in the sun. St Bees Man was buried here, she remembered, the perfectly preserved remains of a medieval knight, which had been discovered wrapped in a shroud. He'd died a violent death, according to the experts, but that was one cold case she'd never be asked to investigate.

The Loneys' retirement bungalow was called The Cop Out. Desmond wasn't devoid of a sense of humour, but most of his colleagues would say that his career had been one long cop out. Switching off the ignition, she spotted Desmond by the side of the bungalow, planting a wicker hanging basket with herbs. Tall, stoop-shouldered, and vaguely raffish in a panama hat, he'd put on weight since she'd last seen him. When he turned at the sound of her car, she could almost hear his body groaning with the effort. He beckoned with his trowel, and kissed both her cheeks by way of greeting. She caught a whiff of damp earth and stale beer. He'd always liked a drink, had Desmond, and his unsteadiness on his feet wasn't accounted for solely by arthritis.

"We save a fortune growing our own," he boasted, as he led her round the back to a tidy patio equipped with a table-cum-firepit, and four aluminium chairs. "See over there, behind the hydrangeas? Strawberries, potatoes, cucumbers, you name it."

"Retirement's suiting you," Hannah said, as Pamela Loney served soft drinks and milk chocolate digestives.

"I need to lick the garden into shape in time for summer." Desmond gave his orange juice a resentful glare, and Hannah guessed he wouldn't need much of an excuse to bring out the booze.

"How lovely," she said dutifully, although she much preferred the eerie wildness of Daniel's cipher garden to these neatly striped lawns, and the regimented tulips in the weed-free borders.

"I keep that busy, I've no idea how I ever found the time to go to work," he chortled. "Mind, I can't do exactly as I please. Pammy insists on keeping me in order, don't you, love?"

Pammy, a muscular ex-midwife with features as bleak as Scafell Pike, pursed icy lips before making herself scarce with the practised discretion of a career policeman's wife. Hannah allowed Desmond five minutes to update her on the state of his diabetes, interrogate her about his least favourite former colleagues, and tut reproachfully at news of a couple of undeserved promotions, before turning to the deaths at the Dungeon House.

"It was a long time ago. These other cases you mentioned, the two girls who have gone missing. You're surely not telling me they are connected to what Malcolm Whiteley did?"

"Gray Elstone was Malcolm's accountant. Nigel is his nephew. What happened at the Dungeon House must have affected their lives. I'm looking to get a full picture."

Desmond snorted. "You can have too much information. Clouds the issue more often than not, mark my words. When I hear all this bollocks on the telly about intelligence-led policing, I want to puke. You can't beat an experienced copper's gut."

He patted his substantial stomach for emphasis.

"I'm interested in your view of how events unfolded that night."

Lifting the panama, he scratched his shiny bald head. "It wasn't much of a mystery to me. Whiteley was in financial trouble, and jealous over his missus. While she went out carousing after the barbecue, he drank himself into a rage. When Lysette and the girl arrived back from the pub, the kid went up to bed, and he confronted his wife about her affair. One thing led to another, and he shot her. Young Amber heard the commotion, came downstairs, and saw what her dad had done. My bet is, he threatened her with the rifle. She panicked, and made a dash for it. Poor kid was in her night-clothes, not wearing any shoes. She never had much of a chance. He followed her out to the quarry path, and pushed her over the edge."

"Why not shoot her, same as he did his wife?"

"Perhaps he didn't want to make such a mess of her," Desmond said. "Trust me, Lysette's face wasn't a pretty sight. I'm not even saying he meant to kill the girl. Possibly all he wanted was to shut her up. On the other hand, he may have decided all of them would die. That's the pattern in this kind of case. These blighters think their family can't live without them. Absolutely bonkers, of course, but there it is."

"There was no proof that Malcolm laid a finger on Amber," Hannah said.

"What do you want, CCTV evidence?" He shook his head, and took another mouthful of coffee. "His body was found in the quarry, close to hers. Once she was dead—because he pushed her, or she slipped, or jumped to get away from him—he'd nothing left to live for. So he blew his own head off. Good riddance, in my book."

"Cheryl didn't care for Malcolm, but even she struggled to believe he'd murder his own daughter."

Desmond's frown conveyed his opinion of Cheryl. "One way or another, he was responsible for the kid's death."

"What about the man who saw someone running away from the Dungeon House that night?"

"The drunk driver?" Desmond rolled his eyes. "Ben Kind harped on about that. What about him?"

"Perhaps someone else was there at the scene."

"Doing what, exactly?"

Inspiration struck her. "Suppose Lysette's lover showed up, to check she was okay. Malcolm had behaved badly at the barbecue that afternoon. The boyfriend might have worried about her, or even guessed what would happen. Or perhaps they had a late night assignation."

"So he turned up in disguise as a woman?" Desmond was incredulous. "Pull the other leg, it's got bells on."

Hannah winced. On second thoughts, perhaps it wasn't such an inspired piece of guesswork. "Did Scott Durham admit to being Lysette's lover?"

"Denied it vehemently. So what? He would, wouldn't he? Nobody wants to be blamed for three deaths."

Desmond was a past master at dodging blame, so he was probably right.

"You weren't convinced?"

"Nah. He claimed they were just good friends. Admitted to exchanging the occasional hug, but said it never went any further. They were just two tactile people, according to Durham. He must have thought I was born yesterday, but it wasn't my job to put him in the dock. He'd not committed any crime."

"And the drunk driver's evidence?" Hannah chewed on a biscuit. "Why would he lie?"

"The clue's in the word drunk. He was way off beam, trust me. I could feel it in my gut." Desmond belched with smug sell-confidence. "The world's full of attention-seekers. Perhaps he was mistaken. Or dreamed it. The story didn't make sense. A bald man dressed as a woman? Who would that be? And why lurk around the Dungeon House at midnight?"

Put like that, who could argue? Yet something Cheryl had said surfaced in Hannah's memory. A fresh idea formed in her mind, almost making her choke on the biscuit crumbs, but Desmond was too busy mounting an old hobby horse to notice.

"Look," he said in the amiably patronising tone that reminded her why she'd always yearned to kick him. "Ben wasn't a bad detective, but he had too much imagination for his own good, and when he got a bee in his bonnet, he could be a right pain in the arse. You were young when you worked with him. Impressionable. He wasn't bloody Sherlock Holmes, I'll tell you that. Anyone else would have spotted early on that Cheryl was bad news. But what did he do? She wasn't bad looking, you could understand him fancying a bit of rumpy-pumpy on the side. But ditching his wife and kids, to waste the rest of his life on her? Way over the top, if you ask me."

Hannah bit back her anger. Desmond knew she'd been close to Ben; had he been jealous? He'd had a reputation in the force for fancying a bit on the side himself. Her visit had given him the chance to take a shot at his dead colleague, and he didn't intend to miss an open goal. What really hurt was that, for once in his life, his aim was true.

Giving her a crafty smirk, he said, "Good thing Ben Kind wasn't on my team. Or maybe it's a crying shame. I could have taught him a thing or two, young Hannah, I'm telling you straight."

Hannah had planned to ask more questions about the investigation, and the people in the Whiteleys' circle, but she couldn't take any more of Desmond Loney. He wasn't stupid, and he wasn't a bad man, just an indifferent detective with an inflated view of his own abilities and a fatal fondness for the easy way out. Her own failing, like Ben's, was that she seldom even noticed easy ways out, far less took them.

Getting to her feet, she said, "Thanks for your time."

"Going already? Thought you might like a spot of lunch. Pammy does a decent salad." He contemplated his stomach with a rueful grin. "The doc has told me I need to lose a bit of weight. Says I enjoy the good life too much. Bloody spoilsport. Anyway, we can wash down the green stuff with a lager and lime or a spot of vino. What do you say, Hannah, love?"

"No, I'd better be off. Work to do. Grateful for your time." She considered his fleshy, well-fed jowls. If he didn't watch out, Desmond would soon become as pickled as the original St Bees Man. "I'll let you get back to the good life."

>>>

The quarry garden had metamorphosed into a lush green paradise, tucked between the sheer rock sides of a steep ravine, in which majestic ferns flourished, and a graceful palm tree grew. Purple-chequered snakes' head frittilaries nodded on either side of a stepping-stone path that led to a dark pool covered with lilies. As Joanna followed Nigel through the yews and limes she remembered so well, and down to the path that ran around the top of the quarry, she had her first glimpse of the garden spread out thirty feet below. Her flesh crept. Despite all the effort that Robbie Dean had put into making the quarry garden a work of art, for Joanna, it would always remain a crime scene. A man had died here, together with his daughter, her friend.

"Are you all right?" Nigel asked.

"Mmmmm."

"Your teeth are chattering." He hesitated, then slipped off his linen jacket, and put it around her shoulders. "Better?"

"Thanks." She was so afraid she might drop down in a dead faint, or burst into tears, or find some other way of making a fool of herself. And then Nigel would want nothing more to do with her.

"Looks as though nothing's changed here for a thousand years, don't you agree?" He spoke in a loud, bright voice, smothering her anxieties with a blanket of bonhomie. "Yet if you cast your mind back, this was a wilderness. Overgrown with brambles, and strewn with boulders. You really had to watch your step, it…"

He let the words trail away, and his face creased with dismay. Joanna gritted her teeth. The fracturing of his self-assurance gave her fresh heart. Nigel needed her as much as she needed him. There was no hiding from the truth. Those violent deaths had ripped her away from Nigel, from that day until this.

Now they were back together again, and she simply refused to let what happened wreck her happiness all over again. This time nothing and nobody would stand in her way.

"It's going to be all right," she said. "I promise, Nigel."

Hannah drove to the beach car park to catch up on her emails and phone messages before setting off for Seascale. A triumphant Linz Waller announced that it had taken her next to no time to track down Anton Friend. He was alive and well, and still living in the same property at Santon Bridge. Six or seven miles from Gray Elstone's office, in other words. Perfect. Some days nothing went right, but today was shaping up nicely. Hannah decided to try and see Friend before her meeting with Lily's father, but first she had another call to make.

"Cheryl, this is Hannah. Sorry to disturb you again, but I just wanted to check something about that pub meal on the night of the Dungeon House shootings. You mentioned the girl with alopecia, the PA to Gray Elstone."

"Joanna Footit, you mean? What about her?"

"I don't know much about alopecia, but doesn't it sometimes cause you to lose all your hair?"

"That's right, it happened to Joanna. After she was involved in a fatal car crash, apparently she had a sort of meltdown. Stress, depression, whatever you want to call it."

"So Joanna was…bald?"

"Yes, poor thing. She was rather odd-looking to start with, tall and skinny with boobs the size of thimbles, but of course the hair loss made it a thousand times worse. Her embarrassment was excruciating, by all accounts."

"You didn't know Joanna well?"

"No, we only ever met in passing. Lysette told me her hair had been red and thick and rather luscious before it all fell out after the car crash. She was a bright girl, but she mucked up her A Levels, and didn't go to uni. For ages, she refused to wear a wig, and became a virtual recluse. Eventually her mum and dad persuaded her to see sense."

"So she wore a wig?"

"Yes. It never looked quite right, if you ask me, but it still made a huge difference. Little by little, she regained her confidence."

"And she was wearing the wig at the barbecue?"

"Correct."

"I don't suppose you can remember what she was wearing that night, when you had the meal in the pub?"

"It's not an evening I'll ever forget, every little detail is engraved on my memory. The last time I saw my oldest friend." Her voice trembled, and Hannah waited. "Joanna had on a lacy top and a very short red skirt. Her legs were very long, they were far and away her best feature, and she made the most of them that night."

"Your memory's brilliant. Thanks very much, Cheryl. I suppose you don't know where Joanna lives nowadays?"

"No idea. After she left the Lakes, I never heard any more about her. Her parents lived at Holmrook, you could try them, if they're still alive." A sigh. "I spent long enough living with Ben to know I'd be wasting my time asking you what this is all about?"

"Probably nothing. But I'm grateful for your help."

"Just don't get it into your head that Joanna was mixed up in anything dodgy. She was one of life's victims, that girl, you only had to look at her to see that for yourself."

Hannah ended the call, and made for the tearoom, where she succumbed to the temptation of Hartley's ice cream. A treat she deserved, she assured herself, after Desmond Loney's sniping at Ben, and her brainwave about Joanna Footit. But a fresh question nagged at her. If Joanna was the person Anton Friend had seen outside the Dungeon House on the night of the shootings, what on earth was she doing there?

As she drove past the menacing bulk of Sellafield, a possible answer struck her. Joanna and Amber Whiteley were friends. When Malcolm Whiteley went berserk, the girl might have rung Joanna for help. Her friend came from Holmrook, which was close by. Dialling 999 would have been a more sensible plan, but nobody from the Dungeon House had contacted the emergency services that night. Had Joanna stumbled on the bloodshed, and fled in panic? If so, why hadn't she told anyone? Was it because she'd had a second nervous breakdown?

Santon Bridge straddled the River Irt, and its main claim to fame was that, each November, the local inn hosted the World's Biggest Liar competition, in honour of a former landlord renowned for tall tales. Politicians were presumably barred from entering because they'd have an unfair advantage. Anton Friend's cottage was across the road from yet another Lakeland tearoom, and luckily he was at home, mowing his postage stamp lawn. An affable, burly man with a plump, grey-haired wife who insisted on supplying tea and scones, he told Joanna that he'd been in a sorry state at the time of the Dungeon House killings. His first wife had recently left him for an Australian, and taken their three young children with her to the other side of the world. Having been made redundant from his job in the labs at Sellafield, he'd spent a large chunk of his pay-off drowning his sorrows in the pubs of Wasdale.

"In a funny kind of way, you could say that Whiteley's rampage saved my life," he said. "What he did was so shocking that somehow it brought me to my senses. You don't expect crimes like that in such a lovely part of the world. It seems…wrong. A chap I knew at the cricket club persuaded me to get some help, and I've not drunk a drop of booze from that day to this. I found myself a job in Whitehaven, where I met Moira, and I've never looked back."

So it was true, Hannah thought grimly. Every cloud really did have a silver lining. Yet there was something quietly impressive about this man in his early sixties who had managed to turn his life around as a result of a brief encounter with a human tragedy.

"That chap wasn't Ben Kind, by any chance?"

"That's the fellow! Decent bloke, and not a bad cricketer. Bowled a mean off-cutter, did Ben. I was sorry we lost touch after he and his girlfriend moved from Gosforth. She didn't fancy being a cricket widow, so that was that. He was a policeman, probably retired by now. Name of Kind. Did you know him?"

"I'm afraid he died a few years ago." Hannah cut short his expressions of regret. This wasn't the moment to be sidetracked by sentiment. "Can you tell me again about the person you saw that night?"

"It's a very long time ago, obviously. But I can still picture him. As I drove past the entrance to the Dungeon House, he came racing out from the drive. Panic-stricken, I'd say. I had the shock of my life. You don't get many transvestites in this neck of the woods. I had to swerve to avoid hitting him as he ran into the lane. Thank Heavens I missed him, there were only inches in it."

"Can you describe the person you saw?"

"Tall and skinny, and as bald as a billiard ball."

"You said in your statement that he was wearing a jacket, but it wasn't buttoned up, and you could see he was wearing a skirt underneath."

"Yes, it was bizarre. It was a short skirt, and his legs were bare. I think he had some kind of sandals on his feet."

"Can you recall the colour of the skirt? It doesn't seem to be mentioned in your statement."

"It was red."

"Are you sure? There were no streetlights, and it must have been pitch dark."

"But my headlights were on, of course," he said with a touch of impatience. "I admit that I only glimpsed the fellow for a split second, but it's not the sort of thing you forget in a hurry."

"And it was a short skirt, you say?"

"Very. He had long skinny legs. I'm pretty sure they were bare."

"Did you catch sight of what else he had on under the jacket? A shirt, perhaps?"

He frowned. "I think it was a woman's top, rather skimpy. Not a man's shirt."

"Colour?"

"I don't know. It looked like something thin and diaphanous. Not very warm for that time of night, even after such a sunny day. Lacy, perhaps, but I couldn't swear to it. Sorry."

"No need to apologise, Mr Friend, you've been really helpful." Hannah had to fight back the urge to fling her arms around him. Her wild guess was spot on, and Ben had been right to take Friend's statement seriously. So much for Desmond Loney's fat, useless gut.

"Ben Kind was the only one who didn't regard me as a nutter. I'm sorry to hear he's passed away. He'd left his wife and kids for this new girlfriend, but he used to beat himself up about it, after he'd had a few drinks. Thought he'd done the wrong thing. I often wondered if he'd go back to his family in the end."

"He never got round to it," Hannah said. "Now, please think carefully about my next question. Is it possible the person you saw was a woman?"

Anton Friend gaped at her. "But he was bald."

"Even so." He deserved a clue. "Women can suffer hair loss as a result of illness."

"I suppose so." He considered. "If it was a woman, I'd be very surprised. She was unusually tall. Over six feet. Not to mention flat-chested."

"So might the person you saw have been a tall, flat-chested woman who had lost her hair?"

Anton Friend leaned back in his armchair, wrinkling his forehead as he wrestled with the conundrum. "Well, yes, I suppose it's possible. But who in the wide world would fit that description?"

Chapter Fourteen

Five minutes into her meeting with Gray Elstone, Hannah found herself feeling sorry for him. It wasn't her habit to sympathise with accountants or lawyers, and it wasn't very professional of her, but she could never quite forget that the people she interviewed were not merely suspects, victims or villains, but also human beings.

If Anya Jovetic was right, and Elstone had killed Lily, then lied through his teeth and covered up the crime for the past three years, he was a monster. Hannah struggled to believe it. He might not convince as a Don Juan, but that didn't make him a paedophile or a child killer. Instinct told her he was as devastated about Lily's disappearance as he claimed. But a still, small voice of caution in her head muttered a reminder that he might simply be devastated that he'd lost control, and done something terrible that he now bitterly regretted.

They sat in his office, sipping rather unpleasant tea brewed by Yindee. Another good-looking foreigner who was taking him for a ride, Hannah suspected. For ten minutes she and Elstone talked about Lily, and the cold case review, before he asked if there was any news about Shona Whiteley.

"Our colleagues are still looking into the possibility that Shona has gone somewhere of her own free will." Her vagueness was deliberate. She didn't want to say anything that risked complicating the task for Ryan Borthwick and his team.

"I pray that Nigel is luckier than me." Elstone's eyes were haunted. "For weeks, months, I hoped Lily had run away of her own accord, but I never really believed it. She'd never have made us suffer like that. What's that fashionable word? *Closure.* It's all I can hope for now, that sooner or later the truth will come to light. Only yesterday, I was saying to Joanna, my old PA, that…"

"Joanna Footit?" Hannah interrupted.

"That's right. She went out for a while with Nigel."

"You're still in touch with her?"

"Not *still* in touch, but in touch *again*," he said fussily. "I hadn't clapped eyes on her for twenty years."

"Really?" Hannah couldn't hide her astonishment. "You met her yesterday, after all that time?"

"Absolutely. Jolly good to see her. Nice girl, Joanna." He turned pink with embarrassment, and lowered his voice. "She had…mental health issues, you know. Desperately sad. Good to see she seems to be making a fresh start."

It didn't take long to draw the story out of him, and learn that Joanna's sudden reappearance was no coincidence. News of Shona's disappearance had brought her hurrying back to the Lakes. By the sound of it, she was busily renewing old acquaintances. Especially those who had been around at the time of the Dungeon House killings.

"You don't think…she hoped to rekindle her romance with Nigel Whiteley?"

Gray spread his arms. "Who knows? I'll be honest with you, Chief Inspector. I've never really understood what goes on inside women's heads."

"You're not alone, Mr Elstone, trust me. Now, about Joanna's health. She lost her hair, didn't she?"

"Yes, poor girl. It was caused by stress, after she was involved in a fatal car accident. I didn't know her in those days, but apparently, she'd had lovely red hair, very thick and down to her shoulders. She'd started wearing a wig before she joined me, but it wasn't terribly satisfactory. Her constant complaint was that it was too heavy. I suppose because she'd tried to replicate her old hair style. Once, when she was running down the office stairs, she tripped, and it came adrift. Dreadfully embarrassing for her. I suppose they are much better made these days."

Another link in the chain. Hannah supposed the wig had fallen off as she was running away from the Dungeon House. Though why hadn't it been found?

"She's staying in the area at the moment, you say. Any idea where, and for how long?"

"In Ravenglass, at a guest house called Saltcoats View. She said she'd be staying for at least a fortnight."

Brilliant. Joanna Footit could answer some of the questions about exactly what had happened on the night of the killings at the Dungeon House. Who better than the Cold Case Review Team to tidy up the loose ends? Not that this would solve the mystery of Lily's fate. Hannah made cautiously reassuring noises, but as she said goodbye to Gray Elstone, she was all too aware that the closure he yearned for seemed as far away as ever.

Hannah was tempted to head straight to Ravenglass after leaving Seascale. Even if it did end up as a late night, she could try and track down Joanna Footit, before an evening of indulgence at the Eskdale Arms, listening to Daniel talk about murder. The snag was that she'd committed to showing her face at a leaving do for a retiring member of the back office staff at Divisional HQ in Kendal, and for Hannah it was a matter of honour to keep such promises. Too often, senior officers skived out of such events, making flimsy last minute excuses. The troops deserved better. In any case, it might take time to find Joanna, and then set up an appointment. Best leave it until tomorrow.

The long journey home gave her a chance to mull over the day's events, and work out questions to put to Joanna Footit. The woman should have come forward at the time, and explained what she was doing at the Dungeon House that night. Why hadn't she uttered a peep? Perhaps the trauma of what she'd witnessed had tipped her over the edge. Had she seen Malcolm Whiteley kill his daughter and then himself, or tried to intervene? Perhaps she'd arrived in the quarry garden only to find two corpses.

What if Malcolm Whiteley had tried to kill Joanna as well? That might explain a good deal. If the terrified young woman had run off in a panic to escape a man who was armed and very dangerous, it was easy to understand how she'd lost her wig. It might have fallen off, or caught on a branch, or met a dozen other fates. She wouldn't have dared to stop and retrieve it if Whiteley was chasing her. Hearing a car might have stopped the gunman in his tracks. Conceivably, Joanna owed her life to the lucky chance of Anton Friend passing by at precisely the right moment.

At last she reached Kendal. As she reversed into the last vacant bay in the pub car park off Stramongate, another idea struck her with such startling force that she had to slam on her brakes to avoid ramming a brick wall.

It was ridiculous, surely. But a detective had to look at all the options. Had Joanna Footit not simply witnessed the killings at the Dungeon House, but taken part in them?

〉〉〉

"Lovely day, Joanna!" Alvaro Quiggin beamed as she walked through the door of the Saltcoats View. A pair of sunglasses lay on the counter in front of him. "I actually managed to fit in half an hour soaking up the sun on the patio. You've brought good weather with you, a real bonus."

She nodded absently. "You said the other day that you keep information about local events."

"Always keen to be of service to our guests. What would you like to know, timetable for La'al Ratty, opening hours at Muncaster Castle?"

"No, but I see there's a talk on next door this evening. A historian who used to be on television. Do you know any more about it?"

"Oh yes, I was thinking of popping round myself. He was a bit of a celebrity at one time, wasn't he? Daniel something or other. Not seen him on the box for ages, though. It's all about fashion, isn't it, the telly?"

Joanna—in common, she was sure, with You-Can-Call-Me-Al—hadn't the faintest idea of what went on in the mysterious world of television, but she murmured agreement out of politeness. He said he'd kept some details about the talk in his office, and he lifted the flap of the counter so that she could follow him inside.

"I cut something out of the newspaper," he said, rummaging though a sheaf of documents from a file marked *Local Events*. "Here you go. Yes, the bloke's called Daniel Kind, and he's talking about a book he's written. The history of murder. Sounds quite interesting. I'm rather partial to a good murder myself. How about you, Joanna?"

"What?" She was distracted. "Oh, yes, yes."

He peered at her. "Everything all right."

"It's just…that photograph." She pointed to a sun-faded colour photo pinned to a board at the back of the tiny office, next to a window overlooking the patio above the foreshore. A picture of a pretty girl with long blonde hair. "Her face looks…I mean, she sort of resembles someone I once knew."

He seemed taken aback, and hesitated before replying. "Is that right?"

"Yes. I could be mistaken, of course. It was a long time ago."

He nodded. "It's an old photo."

For once in his life, Quiggin didn't seem to be inclined to say too much, and, perverse as ever. Intrigued by this new-found reticence, Joanna decided to press him.

"It was very sad about this friend of mine. She was killed in a car crash, an absolute tragedy. Her name was Carina. Carina North"

After a long pause, he said quietly, "So you knew my daughter?"

Joanna opened her eyes wide. "Carrie was your daughter?"

"Don't look so surprised," he said softly. "I'm nothing much to look at, but her mother was beautiful. Too beautiful, that was the trouble. She dumped me when Carrie was only eighteen months old."

"Oh God, I'm so sorry."

He shrugged. "What really hurt was that I only saw my girl half a dozen times after that."

"Her mum re-married?"

"Yes, to this bloke she ran off with. Name of North, a used car dealer. That marriage didn't last, either. She was immature, let's face it. She was only seventeen when I got her pregnant. But I was too staid for her, and North soon ran out of money. She had a drug habit, you see, and it cost her a fortune to keep herself stoned."

Joanna nodded. "I remember Carrie saying about her mum, and drugs."

"You'd think the court would insist that a hard-working father would be allowed to see his child, wouldn't you?" He made no attempt to hide his bitterness. "What good are rights, if you can't enforce them, eh? Suzy played ducks and drakes with me for years. I never got any sort of justice. In the end, I gave up."

Joanna couldn't think of anything suitable to say, so she touched him lightly on the hand.

"Of course, I always thought that one day, Carrie and I would see more of each other. I wasn't to know I'd be denied the chance. Her mother was more interested in sex and drugs than bringing up our daughter. She had no control over Carrie, and let her run wild. Before long, she'd got mixed up with the wrong crowd…I…oh, sorry." Confusion spread over his face like a crimson birthmark. "You said the two of you were friends."

"To be honest, she was the friend of a friend. I can't say I knew her well. We met two or three times, that's all."

"But you liked her?" His eagerness was pathetic.

As a matter of fact, Joanna hadn't really cared for Carrie North. In the circumstances, however, a white lie was forgivable. "Oh yes, she was sweet. Bubbly, you know. Fun-loving."

"Really?"

"Definitely. And so very pretty." She indicated the photo. "I was jealous of her, to tell you the truth."

He smiled. "No need. You're a nice-looking lady yourself, Joanna. You've got character, anyone can see that."

The office was small and over-heated. Until a few minutes ago, You-Can-Call-Me-Al had seemed rather ridiculous to her. She'd never wondered what might be going on inside his head. As they'd come in to the office, he'd closed the door behind them. Quickly, she pulled it open again.

"I'm so sorry about Carrie," she said hurriedly, groping for words that might mean something to a bereaved father. "She was so young, with so much to live for. The way she lost her life was absolutely criminal."

As Joanna edged into the hallway, he turned to look at her. "You know what I think?"

"What's that....Al?"

He gestured to the cutting about Daniel Kind's talk. "What happened to Carrie that night was nothing short of murder."

〉〉〉

As the party grew rowdier, Hannah and Billie Frederick took their Diet Cokes into the small garden at the back of the pub, and Billie asked if there was any chance of a vacancy in the Cold Case Review Team.

"Would you be interested?" Hannah asked. "If we get the green light to make up for some of the cut-backs?"

"I'd jump at the chance," Billie said. "It would be brilliant to work with you, Hannah. No disrespect to Ryan, he's a nice guy, but I'd love to be part of a team run by another woman."

"Let's not worry about the gender politics, huh? It's a very young team since Greg moved on, and we can't expect Les to keep going forever. Maggie and Linz have fantastic potential, but I'd like someone else with..."

"A few grey hairs?" Billie shook her black curls. "Look somewhere else for those, Hannah. I'm staying with this colour till I'm seventy. Maybe eighty."

Hannah laughed. "But you've been climbing the ladder in the Federation."

"I'm ready to jump off before I'm pushed." She sighed. "The Federation is still important for me, Ordinary men and women on the Job need the best representation they can get. They get beaten and hospitalised, and then they see their numbers slashed, not to mention their pay and pensions. Someone needs to give a damn."

"Someone like you."

"Thanks, but my idealism's taken a battering. Too many dodgy things have gone on, up and down the country. The Fed became part of the problem, more interested in fighting cabinet ministers than criminals. Sure, the world is full of people in power who look out for themselves, and not the people they're supposed to serve, but maybe we've become as bad. The stable needs a bloody good cleansing. You could say I'm Fed up."

"People are trying to change things. You can be part of the solution."

"Talking to you about the Dungeon House and Lily Elstone has cleared my mind. I want to get back to what I joined the force to do. I was proud to be a Fed rep, but now I just want to focus on being a half-decent detective. I've heard all the jokes about cold case work being a dead end for dead heads, but I think it's exciting and worthwhile."

"Keep an eye on the intranet. I might be on an interview panel, so I can't make any promises, but you'd be a strong candidate." They clinked glasses. "That was a barnstorming speech—you'd make a good Home Secretary."

Billie hooted. "You should hear me when I've drunk something stronger."

"Okay, let's keep in close touch about Shona Whiteley."

"Sure. Before I forget, we've talked to her teachers, looking for clues to her plans for the Easter holidays. A long shot, but there's a chink of light. One of them has proved impossible to contact. He said he was going to spend his break hitch-hiking around Scotland, which may explain it. For all we know, he's holed up in some remote glen, with only the deer and the midges for company, but we've made enquiries about him. Turns out, at his last school, he was warned for getting too friendly with a fifteen-year-old female pupil."

Hannah raised her eyebrows. "What happened?"

"He offered the kid one-to-one tuition after hours, supposedly to help her improve her guitar playing. The parents became worried she was developing a crush on him, and he wasn't keeping her at arm's length. When they spoke to the head teacher, the guy protested his innocence, and nothing came of it. He was highly regarded, and there was no evidence that he'd misbehaved. The school was actually disappointed when he handed in his notice. They gave him a glowing reference, and there was no mention of the issue with the pupil. It had all blown over, but still—makes you think."

"No smoke without fire?" Hannah asked. "Four of the most dangerous words in the English language, but yes, it's worth looking at him. So who is this teacher?"

"This is what's so intriguing, there's a link with the past. His name is Josh Durham. Wasn't it his father's affair that provoked the Dungeon House killings?"

Chapter Fifteen

Joanna's head was buzzing as she mounted the stairs up to the meeting room on the first floor of the Eskdale Arms, trying not to spill her Pinot Grigio. She felt shivery with elation, deserving of a little treat. So much had happened so quickly, no wonder her brain was whirling. Nigel needed her. Later tonight, she meant to be with him again.

The upstairs room was crammed with people. She'd bought the very last ticket, and took the last free plastic chair. The man next to her smelled of stale alcohol, and she realised it was Scott Durham. Their eyes met, and she thought—or was this silly over-sensitivity?—that he was dismayed to find her beside him. Anyone would think he'd been caught in a trap. When he said hello, his demeanour didn't invite further conversation. But it was surely right to be sociable.

"I came here on impulse," she said brightly. "Have you heard him speak before?"

Scott shook his head. "He used to be on television. I caught his programmes once or twice."

"The history of murder," she whispered. "I don't suppose he's intending to talk about Malcolm Whiteley, by any chance?"

"If he does," Scott said in a low growl, "I'm leaving."

He turned his head, to indicate that the conversation was over. Joanna considered his profile. Not a bad-looking man to this day, despite the added weight, but the grubby, moth-eaten fisherman's jersey did him no favours. Did a guilty conscience plague him; was that why he'd let himself go? It had never crossed her mind before; the Dungeon House murders had turned her brain to mush. If the rumours were true, and Scott had been playing around with Mrs Whiteley, he might never have forgiven himself. Was he obsessed with the Whiteleys and the Dungeon House; was that why he pored over newspaper stories about young Shona's disappearance?

An elderly man called Broderick who was something important in what he called "the West Cumbrian history community" rapped on a table to silence the chatter, and introduced Daniel Kind. The speaker looked pleasant enough, but Joanna was suspicious of academics, especially Oxbridge types who led such a cosseted existence. They'd surely condescend to a woman who hadn't made it to university, however good her reason. At least this chap came from Manchester, and didn't speak in the plummy tones of wealth and privilege.

Murder had scarred her life, but for all its horrors, she couldn't help but be fascinated by it. What made one person make up his or her mind to do something so…so *final* as to kill another? Over the past twenty years, whenever she'd asked herself the question, she'd always found the answers unbearable.

As Daniel Kind talked about Thomas de Quincey, and something called the Ratcliffe Highway murder case, her thoughts drifted like lazy clouds. He was a good speaker, and his occasional wry jokes brought ripples of approval from his audience. History was all very well, but what really mattered was tonight and tomorrow, not yesterday. Malcolm Whiteley's name wasn't mentioned, thank goodness, and she luxuriated in her reverie until the lecture came to an end, and it was time for questions.

"You said there are supposed to be six motives for murder," a man in the audience said. "What are they?"

"A famous criminologist called Tennyson Jesse suggested half a dozen," Daniel said. "Gain, revenge, elimination, jealousy, conviction, and lust for killing."

The man raised his hand again. "That doesn't cater for assassinations."

"You're right," Daniel said. "It's a rough and ready analysis, but I'm talking about individual murder cases, not political killings or acts of terror like 9/11. The typical murder fits into one or other of Tennyson Jesse's categories, wouldn't you agree?"

Without stopping to think, Joanna blurted out. "Sometimes there's more than one reason to commit murder, isn't there?"

People sitting in front turned round to look at her. Joanna spotted Gray Elstone among the sea of inquisitive faces. He looked astonished, as if she was the last person in the world he expected to chip in with observations about homicide. At her side, Scott Durham stiffened. She didn't need to see his face to know he was unhappy. He hadn't settled all evening. Several times, he'd surreptitiously checked his phone, and he'd kept shifting in his chair. Joanna felt herself blushing.

Daniel Kind gave her a friendly nod. "Perfectly true."

"Like murdering your husband, and cashing in on the insurance?" a grey-haired woman in the front row suggested.

People laughed, someone asked a question about Doctor Crippen, and the discussion moved on. Scott Durham grunted something unintelligible, and heaved himself out of the chair, pushing through people standing at the back of the room, in the direction of the staircase. Heaven only knew what had got into him.

Not that it mattered in the least, not tonight of all nights. The night when she was going to get what she wanted.

›/›/›

As she unlocked her car, Hannah called back to Billie. "One thing you might like to check out."

"Go on."

"Whether Josh Durham ever taught at Lily Elstone's school."

Billie's eyes widened. "I'll get on to it first thing tomorrow."

"Thanks, Billie. Goodnight."

Was this the breakthrough they'd been waiting for? It was a cool, clear night, and Hannah found herself shivering. If Josh Durham was, by some chance, a serial abductor of under-age girls he taught, who had kidnapped Lily long before turning his attention to Shona Whiteley, Lily was bound to be dead, and Shona's life was in grave danger. If he hadn't killed her already.

Joanna scurried back to her room as soon as Broderick had given the vote of thanks to Daniel Kind. She had no time to hang around. Thank goodness You-Can-Call-Me-Al wasn't stationed behind his counter as usual. Getting herself ready took five minutes. After a final check of her make-up and hair in the bathroom mirror, she picked up her bag, and hurried downstairs. In a wild flight of fancy, she'd wondered about using the fire escape. But how could she explain dodging around like a fugitive from justice? Her luck held, and neither You-Can-Call-Me-Al nor any of the other guests were lurking downstairs. Nobody saw her slip through the side door. Before stepping into the Eskdale Arms, she'd squeezed her Polo into a tiny gap behind a brick wall. It wasn't overlooked, like the car park, and with Main Street full of people who'd come for the talk, she had no desire to bump into anyone she knew.

Just as well she'd only drunk one small glass of wine. As she switched on the engine, she felt giddy with excitement, all because she was hugging a secret. Catching sight of herself in the rearview mirror, she saw wide, bright eyes, slightly parted red lips. Secrets enthralled her, always had done. Even if the secret made her feel ashamed, just like in her younger days, long before her hairweave, when she'd started wearing a wig.

She swung the car out on to the road, and headed out of the village. Her mood was so light and breezy, she put on the radio, and sang "I Say a Little Prayer" along with Aretha Franklin. An anthem that captured her hopes and dreams. As the song said, forever, and ever, that's how it would be.

In next to no time, she'd arrived at the car park by the dunes of Drigg. There were no other vehicles, no late night dog walkers setting off for a stroll along the moonlit beach. She consulted her phone. Ten o'clock, dead on. She'd done exactly as she'd been asked. Five minutes passed, and the moon dipped behind the clouds. A shiver of disappointment ran down her spine. Surely Nigel wasn't playing a game with her?

Might he be waiting for her in the look-out post? It would be so romantic, but he'd said nothing about it. Besides, where was his car? The big BMW she'd seen parked outside Ravenglass Knoll was nowhere in sight.

She left the car, and looked and listened, but the night air was cold and dark and silent. Scrambling back into her seat, she played the voicemail message again. Nigel must have rung shortly after she left the Dungeon House. She always switched her mobile off while driving.

"*Can you meet me at the car park by the dunes at Drigg this evening, please? Ten o'clock.*"

That was all. He spoke in a hoarse whisper, as if afraid someone might overhear. The first time she'd listened, she'd been so thrilled that she hadn't stopped to wonder why.

She trembled as she put the phone into her bag. It *was* Nigel's voice, surely. Who else could it possibly be? Why would anyone pretend to be him? How ridiculous to upset herself for no reason. Better play the message one more time, just to make sure.

But when she listened again, it made her less sure. That breathy tone, well, it might almost have belonged to anyone. Possibly even a husky-voiced woman. Yet it had to be Nigel; nothing else made sense. She'd given him her phone number, and his parting words had been a promise to give her a ring when he had a chance. He hadn't said when, but of course he was on edge, waiting for news that Shona was safe and well.

Nigel wasn't the only person around her who knew the number. She'd given it to Gray Elstone, hoping they'd keep in touch, and she'd asked Robbie Dean to pass it on to Nigel. Come to that, she'd put the number down on the form when checking in at the guest house. Could Alvaro Quiggin have passed it on—to Scott Durham, for instance?

Tears pricked her eyes at the thought one of them might have played a horrid trick. A puerile prank, making fun of her because she still carried a torch for an old boyfriend. Was someone watching out there in the darkness right now, gloating because she'd fallen for it, hook, line, and sinker?

Her heart pounded, and she'd started sweating despite the chill outside. Oh God, her mascara might run. If this was a hoax, it was very cruel.

And then, thank God, she heard the sound of a vehicle, coming down the lane. She craned her neck, but the engine cut out before it entered her line of vision. She prayed it wasn't some security guard from the nuclear waste site. Or some pervy bloke. Or a couple wanting to be alone in a deserted car park.

She wound down her window, and heard footsteps approaching. Then she saw a dark figure in a crash helmet. Terror paralysed her as the man—she was sure it was a man—wrenched open her car door. A gloved hand grasped her wrist roughly, and tried to pull her out, but she was still wearing her seat belt.

Shutting her eyes, too frightened to scream, she felt a sharp point prick her neck. Her flesh punctured, and she let out a little cry. It wasn't really painful, but the shock was too much to bear.

"Look at me." The same hoarse whisper she'd heard on the voicemail message.

She forced herself to open her eyes. It wasn't Nigel who was staring at her. And it wasn't Nigel whose knife blade grazed her throat.

Chapter Sixteen

A thick morning mist smothered Tarn Fell and the land beneath the slopes. Looking out from the warmth of the kitchen, Hannah could see no more than two or three twisted, spectral blurs formed by thick tree branches. The cipher garden was otherwise invisible. No bird sang, no creature stirred, the world outside was silent grey nothingness.

The fog meant the drive to work would take longer, as she'd be forced to crawl along the meandering lanes of Brackdale. After checking the forecast last night, she'd set the alarm half an hour early, and slipped out of bed while Daniel remained dead to the world. His ability to sleep through any disturbance never ceased to amaze her. He'd arrived home late last night, and she hadn't waited up. The big surprise came as she was pouring her coffee. He sauntered in to the warm kitchen, wearing boxer shorts and a wide grin. A nice sight to greet her on a dismal day.

"Perfect timing," she said. "Toast's almost ready, and the coffee's made."

He swung his arms around her, and they kissed. She felt his solid body pressing against her, and forced herself to pull away before she yielded to temptation, and finished up very late for work.

"I was in Santon Bridge yesterday," she said, as the toaster beeped, and four slices of wholegrain popped up. "I almost came along to watch you perform."

"Don't feel bad about missing out." That grin made him look like a cheeky teenager. "The bedroom mirror will be perfect for that tonight."

Picking up a piece of toast, she flung it at him, but he caught it one-handed with infuriating nonchalance. He had the same love of cricket as his father, and as a teenager, he'd kept wicket for the county schoolboys' team.

"Behave."

He yawned. "I was on my best behaviour last night, and…"

"Can't keep it up forever?"

"Now you behave yourself. This evening, I'm at Gosforth, one glitzy venue after another. Can you cope without me?"

She made a derisive noise, and waved him into a chair. "Eat that toast, build up your strength for tomorrow night."

"What happened yesterday? I thought you were off to St Bees to grill old Loney."

"One thing led to another. That's police work for you." She summarised the progress she'd made. "I'd love to speak to this Footit woman."

"But she wasn't around when Lily Elstone disappeared, and strictly speaking, the Dungeon House killings aren't your concern."

She put on a sad face. "Nosey cow, aren't I?"

"Pleasantly inquisitive," he said. "See, I'm on my best behaviour now."

"Whatever. Yes, Dungeon House doesn't count as a cold case, because it's officially solved. Even so, I'd love to prove your dad was right, and show there was more to the whole affair than Desmond's gut told him. Serve the old bastard right if he suffers a belated bout of indigestion. If Ben had taken part in the inquiry, I bet he'd have discovered that the person Anton Friend saw that night was Joanna Footit."

Daniel rubbed his eyes. "You're sure it was her?"

"Who else could it have been? Weird that she's turned up in the neighbourhood after all this time."

"A tall woman, thin as a rake, and with long, thick red hair, who's currently staying in Ravenglass," he said dreamily. "You know what? She might just have been a member of my audience last night."

"Why would she turn up for a talk about history? I mean, I know your TV programmes were popular, but…"

"Not that popular, huh? Ah, you'd be surprised about the power of the telly." He smeared marmalade over his toast. "Admittedly, there's not a huge amount to do in Ravenglass on a spring evening. It makes Kendal look like Las Vegas. She may have fancied whiling away an hour or two before going back to her room."

"Hey, perhaps it wasn't your dazzling personality that tempted her out, but your subject matter. Murder in the past."

"She did ask an interesting question. Or perhaps she was simply making a statement of fact."

Hannah put down her mug. "I need to hear this."

He told her what Joanna had said. "Of course, she might not have anything specific in mind. Can there be more than one reason to murder someone? The answer has to be yes."

"She didn't elaborate?"

"Didn't utter another peep. She didn't hang around to chat afterwards, either."

"Don't tell me she missed out on a signed copy of your book?"

"Incredible, isn't it? Tossing away a once-in-a-lifetime opportunity." Another cheeky grin. "Perhaps she'll think better of it, and show up again tonight. Or perhaps not. She left the moment the last question was asked, as if she'd had enough. I caught sight of her making for the exit. She stands out in a crowd, she's so much taller than most women. At least six foot. And her whole appearance is…striking."

"Did you think she was wearing a wig?"

"Never crossed my mind. Not that I took a close look at her."

"Her hair may have grown back after all these years. I need to find out more about alopecia, but apparently its effects vary from person to person. Maybe she's had a professional hairweave. I'm not sure if they were widely available twenty years ago."

"Tell you one thing." He built up the suspense by biting off a large piece of toast, and chewing it with infuriating deliberation.

"The woman ruffled feathers when she spoke up. The guy sitting next to her seemed extremely pissed off by what she said. His face reddened and he gave her a very hard stare."

"Description?"

"Rumpled, fifties. Fairish hair, baggy jersey that had seen better days."

"Can you be more specific?"

"I deduced he'd spent many years in the Far East, smoked Trichinopoly cigars, and wore pink underpants." He shook his head. "Give me a break, Hannah, I was concentrating on the questions, not on profiling the people asking them."

"Okay, okay, I wondered if it was someone who knew Joanna from the old days."

"Such as?"

"Scott Durham springs to mind. The local artist. Hey Sherlock, I don't suppose you noticed any paint splashes on his jumper?"

"Sorry. Looks like my childhood dream of becoming a great detective is turning to dust. "

She gave him a goodbye kiss and murmured, "Not to worry. There are a few other things you're very good at."

The mist was clearing as Hannah joined the long queue tailing back from a red light on the outskirts of Kendal, but her brain was fogged with confusion. The Dungeon House killings, the presumed abduction and murder of Lily Elstone, and the disappearance of Shona Whiteley were three distinct cases, separated by time, but connected by a small group of people. If she could figure out the missing links, she could grope toward the truth—or, as regards the Dungeon House killings, the *whole* truth. But what mattered most was to find out what happened to Lily. Gray Elstone and his ex-wife deserved answers. Not knowing their daughter's fate must be a living nightmare.

As the lights turned to green, she found herself wondering how she'd feel once she was installed in her new flat. It was only five minutes from here. Saving time on commuting would be a huge bonus, but she'd miss Tarn Cottage. For the hundredth time she asked herself if she was making a mistake by insisting on independence, cutting off her nose to spite her face. Absence didn't necessarily make the heart grow fonder. What if Daniel found someone else? *Que sera sera.* Her decision was made.

When at long last she arrived at her desk, her diary was crowded with meetings and reminders to comply with tedious bits of bureaucracy, and her inbox flooded with emails. Anyone would think she'd been out of the office for a month, rather than twenty-four hours. Rather than tackle the backlog, she sought out Maggie Eyre.

"I bumped into Billie five minutes ago," Maggie said. "She told me about your conversation last night. Sorry I couldn't make it, by the way, but it was my grandparents' golden wedding party."

Family always came first with Maggie. "Any more news?"

"Josh Durham never taught at any school that Lily attended."

"Lots of music teachers given private tuition. If Josh…"

"Billie thought of that. She's rung up both Gray Elstone and Anya Jovetic to check. They paid for Lily to have extra lessons in everything from playing the violin to Mandarin Chinese. Money no object. Each parent is putting together a list of teachers they hired for Lily over the years. Sounds like the list runs for pages. So far, there's no sign of Josh Durham's name on it."

Hannah exhaled. "It was always a long shot. Any more news about where he might be right now?"

"Nothing, but the plan is to re-interview Lily's friends, see if they can shed any light."

"I'll tell you about yesterday." Hannah gave her a potted summary, and said, "I want to see Joanna Footit, and find out what she was doing outside the Dungeon House on the night of the shootings."

"You're sure it *was* her?"

"Anton Friend has stuck to the same story all these years. He may have been pissed, but the sight of someone almost diving under his wheels in the dark made a big impression. It must be Joanna."

"She had no reason to be there."

"What if Amber called her over, in a state of panic?"

"If she did, by the time Joanna arrived, Malcolm Whiteley had probably done his worst."

"True. I'm wondering why she kept quiet."

"You don't think she was…involved with Whiteley in some way?"

Hannah frowned. "All I've been told is that she fancied his nephew."

"Might have been a blind."

"In that case, she was a good actress."

"Some women are." Maggie paused. "Or how about this? What if Lysette Whiteley's lover wasn't a bloke—but a young woman?"

"Joanna?" Hannah mulled this over. "Seems unlikely."

"You never know." Maggie's cheeks reddened. "She might just have wanted…to experiment."

"I'll put in a call to her, and see if we can meet. And I'd better run the gauntlet with Cheryl again, see if she can tell me more about Joanna and Lysette. Fancy coming along to Ravenglass with me?"

Maggie's face fell. "I'd love to, but Linz and I are booked in for training on Information Security all afternoon."

"It's probably against the rules even to tell me that. Enjoy."

"Absolutely ridiculous." Cheryl's voice quivered with homophobic outrage. "Lysette would never look at another woman, not in that way. I knew her almost from the day she could walk, and she was perfectly normal in every respect. I can't imagine why people have to go around blackening…"

"We have to consider every possibility," Hannah interrupted. "However outlandish."

"Sounds to me like you're getting desperate." Cheryl sniffed. "Desmond Loney proved as useless as ever, presumably?"

"Pretty much." Hannah was glad to change the subject. "I'm hoping to talk to Joanna Footit shortly."

"Joanna? My God, what's she up to nowadays?"

"She's back in the Lakes on holiday, I'm told."

"She never had much luck, what with her health problems and her appearance. To say nothing about the car crash."

"Tell me more about the car crash."

"It was Robbie Dean's fault, or so Lysette told me. I was living in Manchester at the time. Robbie and Nigel Whiteley were bosom buddies, and one night they'd taken their girlfriends out to a club in Whitehaven. Robbie was showing off, and as they were driving back past Sellafield, the car veered off the road and into a tree. Robbie was badly injured, and the girl in the passenger seat was killed. Joanna and Nigel had been smooching in the back, and they weren't hurt, but the shock was devastating. And no sooner had she recovered and found herself a decent job with Gray Elstone, than her best friend was murdered. No wonder she lost the plot."

As Hannah put down the phone, the new admin assistant looked in. She was an Estonian girl who had moved to Cumbria after meeting a lad from Cleator Moor whilst he was over in Tallinn for a stag party. She was bright, spoke good English, and had interviewed well, but Hannah was yet to be convinced about her diligence.

"Sorry, ma'am. Joanna Footit isn't at the guest house. I tried to leave a message, but the owner isn't sure when she'll be coming back. He wonders if she has moved elsewhere."

"You're not telling me she's done a bunk?" The girl looked mystified. "Left in a hurry to avoid paying her bills?"

"She paid in advance with her credit card, so she is not trying to dodge payment."

"Then why leave suddenly?"

"The owner says he does not have an idea."

"What makes him think she might have left permanently?"

"He was not clear. She has left some of her things in her room."

"Then she must be coming back."

"Her bed was not slept in last night. And her car is missing."

"She was in Ravenglass yesterday evening. Someone…saw her." The girl shrugged helplessly, and Hannah gave up. "Thanks, Edita, it's all right. I'll take over from here."

If you want a job doing, do it yourself. Delegation had never been Hannah's strong point. Inside two minutes, she was talking to the proprietor of the Saltcoats View Guest House. Alvaro Quiggin sounded wary, and no wonder. It isn't every day you receive a phone call from a detective chief inspector.

"I told the other young lady." He paused, as if anxious to phrase his reply with care. "Joanna left no message. I suppose she will come back, I simply don't know."

"How many of her belongings are left in the room?"

"How would I know? I haven't rifled through them, it wouldn't be…appropriate." Hannah visualised him puffing his chest out with self-righteous outrage. Why did people so often try to take the moral high ground when talking to the police? It was totally counter-productive. "She might walk back through the door at any moment."

"In the meantime, you've no idea where she may be?"

He hesitated, as if tempted to retort *I'm not her keeper.*

"None whatsoever."

Yet he'd referred to her as Joanna, not Ms Footit. Was Quiggin a naturally informal guy, on first name terms with any guest who booked in for a day or two? Or had he got to know this particular woman well, and if so, what was his interest in her?

"Has she done this before?"

"No, this is the first time her bed has been undisturbed, and she hasn't eaten breakfast. Come to that, I didn't see her car when I locked up last night."

"Were you surprised?"

"Not exactly. She used to live in Holmrook, she knows people round here. She may be staying with friends. If she had a few drinks, she probably decided it wasn't safe to drive home."

"Without letting you know?"

"She's perfectly entitled to come and go as she pleases."

"I believe she attended a lecture in the Eskdale Arms last night."

"You are very well informed, Detective Chief Inspector." He sounded disconcerted. "She mentioned the talk to me yesterday evening, it was given by a historian. I had some information about it, and we had a brief chat. I'd thought about dropping in myself."

"You didn't see her there?"

"In the end, I didn't bother with the talk. In this job, there's always plenty to be done. I mended a broken wardrobe instead." A nervous laugh. "Never a dull moment, eh?"

Hannah said, "This talk—the subject was murder, wasn't it?"

"The *history* of murder," he corrected. "The speaker used to present a series on television."

"Did Ms Footit say why she was interested?"

"I assumed she merely wanted to pass the time."

"She didn't mention doing anything else afterwards—like visiting friends?"

"No, and I didn't ask." He cleared his throat. "She's not… done anything, has she?"

"I simply want a quick word with her."

"You'll have the opportunity shortly, I presume. I still expect her back, even if she's found somewhere else to stay, if only to collect her things. I'm sure she isn't in hiding. She doesn't strike me as that sort of person."

"What sort of person is she?"

"Pleasant. And…enthusiastic, I suppose. Yes, pleased to be back in the area where she grew up, and keen to make the most of her time here. Now, if you'll excuse me, someone has been waiting patiently to ask about vacancies…."

Hannah asked him to confirm Joanna's phone number and car registration from her booking details, and left it there. She tried the mobile, but it went straight to voicemail.

Les Bryant poked his head around her door. "Going to this meeting about the new Communications Strategy?"

"Nobody told me about it."

He sniggered. "Nothing would surprise me in this place."

"I'm scheduled for a briefing on the Transparency Agenda, plus catch-ups with Finance and HR either side of lunch. Not to mention ten minutes ruled out for that photo shoot for the new ID cards to get us in and out of the building, and an hour's online course about…"

"A fun life you lead. Makes me sad that I'm a self-employed consultant, missing out on so many treats."

"Aren't I the lucky one? Whatever happened to what Desmond loves to call *good old-fashioned bobbying?*"

"Who cares, as long the crime stats are moving in the right direction? Not the powers-that-be, for sure." He stepped out into the corridor. "See you later."

Hannah asked herself, not for the first time, whether she simply was not cut out for management. In her twenties, she'd been regarded as a high flyer, and she'd risen fast. Perhaps too fast. Before long her career nose-dived, and before she could catch her breath, she found herself relegated to reviewing cold cases. A career cul-de-sac, yes, but she loved delving into the past. It wasn't just that it helped her to understand why historical research bewitched Daniel. She had so much more autonomy than colleagues investigating crimes in the here and now, and management responsibilities were a price worth paying. With a small, over-stretched team, she had the luxury of getting her hands dirty with proper detective work. How exhilarating to deliver justice to people who had waited years to learn the truth about a crime that once seemed insoluble. Was Joanna Footit one of those people, or did she know more than anyone alive about what had actually happened twenty years ago at the Dungeon House? Hannah needed to know.

So…what to do next?

Good Hannah was duty-bound to attend the various activities scheduled for her, even if the online course was one more wearisome example of "sheep-dip training." Bad Hannah would suffer a severe memory lapse—why not blame deficiencies in the IT system? They were a reliable scapegoat. She could race off to

Ravenglass before anyone trapped her in a corner, and started blathering away about key performance indicators.

Good Hannah never stood a chance. Her evil twin opened the door, and chased after Les.

> > >

"So what's our plan of action?" Les asked, as they caught a glimpse of the Irish Sea through the drizzle.

He'd spent the journey regaling her with anecdotes of his life as a young policeman in Yorkshire. Hannah let his reminiscences drift over her, like a kid luxuriating in a surfeit of bedtime stories.

"Here's my carefully considered strategy. Play it by ear, and see what happens."

He laughed. "You're a woman after my own heart. We need a slice of luck. Think of how they finally caught the Yorkshire Ripper, the Black Panther, and the rest. A good detective happens to be in the right place at the right time. Sat behind a desk is never the right place, not for the likes of you and me."

As they parked at Ravenglass station. Les said, "Five past twelve. Don't know about you, but my stomach's already rumbling."

"Quick bite before we talk to the chap at the guest house? Want to try the Eskdale Arms?"

"You read my mind."

"Let's make a dash for it." The rain was now teeming down. "Last one to the bar pays for lunch."

Given the state of Les' knees, it was an unfair contest, and she was ordering at the counter by the time he lumbered up, puffing and grunting as though he'd run a marathon.

"So this is where Lysette and Amber Whiteley ate their last meal," she whispered, as Les' eyes feasted on the voluptuous Polish barmaid.

Les sniffed. "Not really a selling point. Decent place, mind."

She wasn't quite sure if he was approving the location, the menu, or the barmaid. Ravenglass was gorgeous, even on a murky day. Hannah had the police officer's habit of checking out her surroundings, but she forced herself to concentrate on fellow customers, rather than the view. Two men at a table by the window caught her eye. They were sipping pints, and talking quietly. Both were in their fifties. One was no oil painting, but his companion was good-looking in a haggard, bleary-eyed way. A fair-haired, blue-eyed bloke who'd seen better days. So had his fisherman's jersey. She'd googled Scott Durham, and taken a look at his website. His photo suggested someone younger and sexier, but this was him, no question. He only lived round the corner, and his pasty complexion suggested more time spent at his local than catching up on his beauty sleep. Imagining him twenty years younger, however, Hannah saw why Lysette Whiteley had been smitten. Allegedly.

Durham's companion was speaking. Hannah tried to shut out every sound except his voice, and her concentration was rewarded when she caught her own name.

"….called herself DCI Scarlett. But why would she want….?"

His voice was so low that it wasn't easy to recognise, but it could only be the man she'd spoken to on the phone. Alvaro Quiggin—what a brilliant name. Les was still mesmerised by the barmaid's cleavage, so she elbowed him in the ribs, and nodded toward the two men. All of a sudden, she was no longer hungry. The pangs she felt were curiosity, pure and simple. Durham and Quiggin were worried, and she had an aching desire to understand why.

Only one way to find out.

Chapter Seventeen

"Mr Quiggin?"

The guest house owner looked up sharply. Hannah suspected that he wasn't often approached by strange women in bars. That comb-over…

"I'm DCI Hannah Scarlett. We spoke earlier."

His small eyes opened very wide, but what struck Hannah was his companion's reaction. The colour drained from Scott Durham's face as she introduced herself. She rarely had such an effect on even the most incompetent of criminals. The artist was panic-stricken. She couldn't resist a cheap flourish.

"And this is Mr Durham, I presume?"

He seemed incapable of speech. Quiggin rose, and extended his hand.

"Hello, Chief Inspector. Yes, I'm Alvaro Quiggin. This is a surprise, I must say." He cleared his throat. "When we talked on the phone, you never mentioned you'd be visiting Ravenglass in person."

"No," Hannah agreed. "I didn't."

Les had torn himself away from the barmaid, and as Hannah introduced him, Quiggin shifted in his chair.

"Didn't you say you were calling from Kendal? Surely the two of you haven't come all this way simply because one of my lady guests didn't sleep in her own bedroom last night?" He gave an uneasy laugh. "I mean, if that's enough to get the police out, Main Street would forever be choked with panda cars."

"Ms Footit still hasn't turned up?"

"No, but I can't tell you any more than I did when we spoke."

Scott Durham found his voice. "Why do you want to talk to Joanna?"

"Mind if we join you?" Les pulled up a couple of chairs without waiting for a reply.

"You'll appreciate," Hannah said, "that we can't divulge confidential information. As I said, I'm in charge of a team reviewing certain old files."

"Old files?" Durham seemed to relax fractionally. "I don't understand. Joanna's been living in Lancashire for the past twenty years."

"Have you seen her since she came back?"

"Well…." He seemed afraid of a booby-trap. "Well—yes, I suppose I have."

"You suppose?" She waited as the Polish girl served their baguettes. "Don't you know for certain?"

"Sorry…I mean, yes, we've bumped into each other once or twice. Passed the time of day, so to speak. That's all I can…"

Quiggin interrupted. "If you ask me, she's catching up with old friends at this very moment."

"Nostalgic about old times, is she?" Hannah asked. "That's odd. When she lived here, she was involved in a fatal car crash, and suffered a breakdown. No sooner had she recovered from that than her closest friend was murdered. I'm not surprised she left the area. It's harder to understand why she returned."

"She…she'd heard about her old boyfriend, Nigel Whiteley," Scott Durham muttered. "He's in the news lately, you must know. This fuss about his daughter. I'd guess she's dreamed of rekindling their romance. I wouldn't put it past her. Joanna's a sweet girl—woman—but she was always desperately naive. She's already got more than she bargained for."

"Meaning what?" Les demanded.

Durham shot Quiggin a quick glance. "Oh, nothing."

If he was trying to deflect attention away from himself, he was succeeding. Les moved closer to him, and repeated, "More than she bargained for?"

"Like I say, it was nothing. I suppose she had no idea Al was Carrie's father."

Quiggin swallowed some beer, and put his tankard down with exaggerated care. "I'm not with you."

Durham's eyebrows rose. "Al, don't tell me you didn't know?" he said. "She has an unusual surname, I presumed you realised who she was."

"Who she was?"

"Joanna was the other passenger."

"She was…Nigel Whiteley's girlfriend?"

"That's right. As the chief inspector says, it took her a long time to recover."

The conversation had raced away down a fresh track, and Hannah needed to keep up. "The *other* passenger?"

"Yes," Scott Durham said. "Four people were in the car on the night of the crash. Nigel and Joanna, and Robbie Dean and his girlfriend. She was known as Carrie North, but Al here was her dad."

"My wife left me long before Carrie died," Quiggin muttered. "She married again, though it didn't last. She made Carrie take the husband's surname."

"Were you living here at the time of the accident?"

"No, I only moved to Ravenglass three and a half years ago, when the guest house came on the market. Before then, I lived in the North East, where Carrie was born. She'd lived in Carlisle for years, that's where her mother moved with her fancy man." He breathed out. "My wife did everything in her power to destroy my relationship with Carrie. At the time she died, I was a stranger to her. My only child."

"Why move here? Plenty of guest houses in the north east."

"It sounds stupid and sentimental," he muttered. "She's buried not far away, in Gosforth. I liked Ravenglass, and I liked the idea of being close to her. Simple as that."

"You didn't realise Joanna was in the car when your daughter died?"

"No." He was gazing toward the bar, but Hannah was sure he wasn't ogling the Polish barmaid. "No, I'd forgotten the name, that's all. It's Carrie who needs remembering. If I don't remember her, who will?"

Hannah caught Les giving an almost imperceptible nod toward Scott Durham. Quite right; she mustn't allow herself to be side-tracked. "As you say, Carrie was your only child. And Mr Durham, you have one son, don't you?"

Durham coloured, but didn't reply directly. "You said you were reviewing old files, Chief Inspector. Surely not in connection with the car crash?"

"No, a couple of other things. A girl went missing three years ago, and…"

"Gray Elstone's daughter?" Quiggin interrupted. "Joanna Footit knew Gray. But I can't see how she can possibly…"

"What was the other thing?" Scott Durham asked. "Surely not the Dungeon House case?"

"Why do you say *surely not*?" Hannah lowered her voice, as if about to impart a secret. "To be frank, there are one or two loose ends…"

"Loose ends? After all this time? You can't be serious. Everyone knows what happened. Malcolm Whiteley went crazy with his rifle. End of."

"You were here that night, weren't you, Mr Durham?" Hannah indicated their surroundings. "Dining with Mrs Whiteley and her daughter. Along with Joanna Footit and Gray Elstone."

"Is that a crime?" Durham snapped. "You make it sound like I should feel guilty. As it happens, a police inspector and his lady friend were with us. Why not talk to him? Maybe he should have realised what Whiteley was about to do, and saved two innocent lives."

Without intending to, he'd struck a nerve. The killings had gnawed at Ben Kind. Hannah knew he'd beaten himself up, wondering if anything he might have done would have made a difference; he was that sort of man. Yet Whiteley's rampage had come out of the blue—hadn't it?

"Mrs Whiteley didn't have an inkling of what her husband was capable of?"

"Obviously not. Otherwise, she and her daughter would never have gone back home that night, would they?"

His reply verged on condescending. Time to regain the initiative.

"Surely she confided in you?"

The blue eyes were chilly with disdain. "We were friends, but she wasn't likely to discuss her marriage with me."

"You painted together, didn't you? She attended your art group, and you gave her personal tuition. I understood you were...close."

"Then you understood wrong." He folded his arms. "Don't think I wasn't aware of the rumours swirling around after that bastard shot Lysette. Let me tell you this, Chief Inspector. There wasn't an iota of truth in any of them. That's all I intend to say about her. In my opinion, she and Amber should be left to rest in peace."

Quiggin made a performance of consulting his wrist watch, and then stood up. "I have to go. A family of guests will be arriving any minute."

"Thanks for your time." Hannah handed him a card. "Perhaps Joanna Footit will turn up as well. If she does, could you let me know, and ask her to give me a ring?"

He gave her a curt nod, and said, "I'll see you later, Scott. And don't worry, eh?"

Hannah expected that Scott Durham would seize the opportunity to follow him out of the door, but he stayed put. Studying his fingernails, as if trying to come to a decision.

Les said, "Something worrying you, Mr Durham?"

He shot them a furtive glance. "I wonder...perhaps we could go to my cottage? It's only a few doors down the road. I'd prefer to continue this conversation in private, if you don't mind."

They told him they'd be round in ten minutes. The rain had eased off, and they walked along the Green so that Hannah could call

Divisional HQ to learn the latest about Josh Durham without being overheard.

"What do you reckon?" she asked as she dialled.

"He's hiding something," Les diagnosed. "About the son, rather than the Dungeon House."

"And Quiggin?" Hannah asked as she dialled.

"Would he hate Joanna because she survived that car crash, while his darling daughter died?" He shrugged. "Funny bugger, that one."

Hannah asked to be put through to Billie Frederick, who sounded cock-a-hoop.

"We've struck oil! The Jovetic woman has remembered that Lily took part in a pantomime the Christmas before she disappeared. Two of her school teachers were in the cast, along with several pupils, but the show was organised by a charity, and guess who was on the committee?"

"Not Josh Durham?" Hannah squeezed the required amount of wonder into her question, and was rewarded by a hoot of glee.

"Bull's eye! So they did know each other, after all."

"Les and I have just met Josh's dad, and he wants to talk to us in private."

"Fantastic!"

"Let's see how much he knows about his son's interest in young girls. As soon as we're done, I'll ring you back."

She stuffed her phone into her bag, and they strolled down Main Street to Scott Durham's cottage. Pretty at a distance, but on closer inspection, like its owner, it was showing its age. Grubby windows, peeling paint. Making money as an artist in the Lakes wasn't easy, with so much competition. It didn't help if you drank away a large chunk of your earnings.

"This way."

Durham motioned them into the studio. Jazz music was playing in the background. *Mood Indigo*. She and Les sat on a sofa facing the estuary. On an easel was a not-quite-finished view of Buttermere at sunset. Paintbrushes were everywhere, and half a dozen folders of pictures lay on a vast rectangular table in the middle of the room. All around was the paraphernalia of the modern commercial artist's trade, a computer, scanner and printer, and a sophisticated-looking camera on a tripod.

"I photograph the views I want to paint." Scott Durham's haggard expression lightened; he was talking about his passion in life. "It's vital to capture what I've seen, before subtle changes creep in. The quality of light alters so quickly, it can change in a few minutes, especially during that magical hour before sunset."

"Yes," she agreed. "Time passes, and it makes a difference. Which is why we like to review investigations. Take a look with fresh eyes."

He grimaced. "I suppose you're wondering why I asked you here."

"We're all ears, Mr Durham."

"It's about my son, Josh." Her calm nod made clear this was no surprise.

"You're…aware of him, then?"

"Yes, we are."

"What—what do you know?"

"We'll make quicker progress," she said, "if the two of us ask the questions, and you answer them. Why don't you tell us about Josh? Start at the beginning."

Durham sighed. An intelligent man, Hannah surmised, brought low by melancholy and resentment. As if he'd failed to play a good hand of cards to best advantage. Life's mishaps had defeated him, and he didn't think it was fair.

"Josh was always a solitary lad. I suppose his upbringing didn't help. His mother was diagnosed with cancer when he was young, and she struggled with the disease for an eternity until it finally beat her. Once she was gone, Josh was all I had left. Along with my art, of course. That helped, but I was miserable as sin, and I wasn't the best father. His refuge was the guitar, mine was painting."

"You never re-married?"

"I'm coming to that," he said. "I was sure that it would do Josh good if the two of us had female company. I wasn't looking for someone to replace his mother, that would be crass. Just someone to help create a normal family environment for him. And I won't lie, I also wanted a lover, someone to keep my mind off what I lost when Trish died, a woman as different from her as possible. Preferably, to be blunt, someone who was gagging for it in bed."

Hannah tried to look non-judgmental, and failed. He said, "I know what you're thinking."

"I doubt it, Mr Durham."

"You're thinking Lysette Whiteley fitted the bill, but you're way off beam. I don't mind admitting, I slept with a dozen or more women who were members of my art group, or came to me for lessons in watercolour technique. Lysette wasn't one of them. I fancied her, and we got on like a house on fire, but she always stayed out of reach. With hindsight, I suspect the idea of illicit romance turned her on, but she baulked at the prospect of turning fantasy into reality. I don't think morality had much to do with it. More likely, she was frightened of Malcolm, and guessed what he was capable of, if he discovered she'd been unfaithful. I was wary of him myself. Not that I expected him to go on a shooting spree, I hasten to add. But he had a lot of money, and a vicious streak, and he could have made life difficult for me if he'd wanted."

"You and Lysette Whiteley were Just Good Friends?" Les asked.

"Please, there's no need for cynicism. It was a long time ago, why would I lie?"

"Okay, keep talking."

"The shootings came as a bolt from the blue. Utterly shocking. It was such an extraordinary experience. To know that people were pointing the finger at me…the atmosphere in the local community was dreadful, the whole business was quite surreal."

He turned his back on them, and stared out at the little boats on the water, while *I Ain't Got Nothing But the Blues* filled the silence. Hannah leaned forward, about to fire another question, but Les laid a restraining hand on her arm.

"Nobody said it to my face," Scott Durham said, "but I knew what everyone was saying behind my back. Because I'd been screwing Lysette, I was indirectly responsible for three deaths. That's life in a small community for you. People I'd known all my life crossed the street to avoid me. Worst of all, Josh suffered. Kids at school made fun of him, they can be so cruel at that age. It was so fucking unfair."

Hannah couldn't keep the scepticism out of her voice. "You gave Malcolm Whiteley no reason to be jealous?"

"None." He pushed a weary hand through his hair. A gesture, Hannah guessed, that had made plenty of hearts flutter in his younger days. "Well, no *real* reason. Lysette was a passionate woman, and there was always a *frisson* between us. I suppose she enjoyed keeping me interested."

"And you were interested?"

"Perhaps I made my enthusiasm for her too obvious, and it was my fault that tongues wagged. No smoke without fire, that old lie. But there was no fire. I swear it."

Hannah shrugged. "Tell us more about Josh."

"Sorry, yes." He exhaled. "I simply must get this off my chest, or I'll go crazy. Eighteen months after the Dungeon House, I met someone. Her name was Wendy, and she worked as a classroom assistant. A divorcee, with two daughters. One girl was twelve, the other fourteen. I saw the chance of building a proper family life for Josh. Wendy and I took it slowly at first, but eventually she and her kids moved into the cottage. It seemed like a dream come true."

Dreams-come-true and real life didn't mix, in Hannah's opinion. "And then?"

"The younger girl was difficult. She'd been very close to her father, even though he was a loser, a redundant computer programmer who proved his manliness by blacking Wendy's eye every time he was turned down for a job. Though he took care never to hit her in front of the children. I did my best with the kid, but she never took to me. Or Josh. Whereas the older girl, Millie, was lovely. Angelic to look at, with a sweet personality, like her mother. I was so glad that she and Josh got on well. Then her sister spilled the beans. She'd caught the two of them in bed together one afternoon while Wendy and I went out for a walk."

"I see."

"They insisted nothing really happened, and they were just mucking about. Teenage experimentation, it's common enough. We managed to sweep it under the carpet, but a few weeks later, we found the younger kid in tears. She said Josh had put his hand up her skirt. He denied it, but Millie turned against him. Was there some jealousy between the two girls, were they competing for his attention? If I say it myself, he was a very handsome boy. I was never sure where the truth lay, but it all became too much for Wendy. She and her kids moved out, and Josh and I found ourselves back at square one. I assumed he was just going through a phase, and that I was to blame for any problems he had in relationships with girls."

"Were there other…incidents?"

"With young girls, you mean? One or two, yes. Same pattern, they were daughters of women I was seeing. Thankfully, no harm was done."

How can you be so sure? Hannah wondered. She was conscious of Les simmering with anger by her side. But this wasn't the moment for a debate about the trauma caused by abuse, or the damage done by turning a blind eye.

"At university, Josh never lacked girlfriends, but none lasted. The only career he ever wanted was teaching, and he showed a gift for bringing the best out of his pupils."

"It didn't cross your mind that he had an ulterior motive?"

"To get closer to young girls? No, that's horribly unfair. The best teachers are born, not trained. Josh is brilliant with kids of both sexes, and believe me, he's never had any sexual interest in boys. He's not like that. He just…seems to feel more comfortable around young people."

Hannah and Les exchanged glances. Better tread carefully. Say the wrong thing, and doting Dad would clam up in an instant. If he suspected Josh of kidnapping and killing Lily, he must be going through hell. As for Shona, was she alive or dead? The first priority was to focus on the living. If there was the faintest chance of saving the girl, Hannah couldn't risk blowing it.

"There was," she groped for an anodyne term, "…an incident at his last school."

"You've heard about that? Inevitable, I suppose, it was only a question of time before it came out. That's the trouble, stories are so easily exaggerated in the telling. That business was nothing like as bad as it seemed. Six of one and half a dozen of the other. Yes, a teacher is in a position of trust, but these things are never as simple as they seem, or as the tabloids would have you believe."

"No?" Les asked.

"The girl was bonkers about him. He did his best, but she wouldn't leave him alone." He added defiantly, "It's not as if Josh is on the sex offenders' register."

Only a question of time. Hannah said, "He resigned from his job."

"It was the right thing to do. For the girl, for the school, for him. Not an admission of guilt, but a chance to make a fresh start."

"So he moved schools, and met Shona Whiteley."

"He's only been teaching her since the autumn term. Their paths didn't cross before that."

"You don't socialise with Nigel Whiteley?"

"God, no. He's given me a wide berth ever since…Lysette and Amber died. I lost no sleep over that, we never knew each other well. The truth is, we've nothing in common. Nigel is a cold fish, and I doubt if he's got an artistic bone in his body. He just has pots of money." He coughed. "Sorry, I sound envious, and I suppose I am. Nigel is probably as ruthless a businessman as Malcolm, just more effective. Saying that, we do share one or two things. Each of us lost a wife we cared for deeply, and we're both devoted to our children."

"I hear he's distraught about Shona," Hannah said. "Naturally."

Scott Durham shut his eyes for a moment. "I can imagine. What father wouldn't be heartbroken if his daughter went missing?"

"When did you become aware that your son was…interested in Shona?"

Anguish was scrawled in the lines on his face. "You make it sound as though I figured it all out ages ago. Far from it. Even now, I'm not certain. There's no proof…"

"Tell us about Josh and Shona."

"I need a drink." He stood up. "Would either of you like one?"

"No thanks."

Opening a cupboard crammed with watercolour paper, pens and paints, he pulled out a half bottle of brandy and tumbler hidden behind them, and poured himself a generous measure.

"Josh mentioned her to me casually. He didn't know Nigel before they met at a parents' evening. Josh played guitar at the barbecue that terrible day, but I doubt Nigel recognised him. Josh told me Shona was very talented, and I didn't think any more about it until her name started cropping up in conversation. I was worried that…he might be taking too close an interest in her. He reassured me, and I believed him."

Yes, Hannah thought, people believe what they want to believe. Especially when it comes to their children. She wondered, as she'd wondered a hundred times before, what it was like to be a parent, and whether she'd ever find out. She'd fallen pregnant once, while she was living with Marc Amos, but a miscarriage had put paid to the prospect of motherhood, although not, she hoped, forever. Some might say her split from Marc meant that losing the child was a blessing in disguise. Not for Hannah. Every now and then, her dreams were haunted by the child-who-never-was.

"When did you suspect something was wrong?"

"Not until news broke that Shona was missing. The instant I heard, I rang Josh on his mobile. He'd told me he'd be away over Easter, and would be out of contact. Later, it dawned on me that he'd been unusually vague about his itinerary. I began to worry myself sick, and left two or three increasingly frantic messages, asking him to ring me, the minute he had a chance."

"No response?"

"Eventually, he did phone back, though the mobile number that came up was different." Hannah's stomach knotted. A new pay-as-you-go was the phone of choice for people with something to hide. "He sounded breathless, but happy. Told me not to worry, and that everything would work out fine. I asked him if he was with Shona, and he pretended he hadn't heard. Just repeated that he was having the time of his life, and he'd get in touch again as soon as he could. He rang off before I could utter another word, and I haven't heard from him since. Of course, it's entirely possible he and Shona may not be together."

"You don't really believe that, do you, Mr Durham?"

He groaned. "I don't know what to believe."

Les said, "You're seriously suggesting that you don't know his present whereabouts?"

"I don't have a clue. If I did, I'd tell you. Honestly, I can see it's for the best. If he has…gone somewhere with this girl, he's just living out some fantasy. It's a bad mistake, and he'll get into trouble, but there will be a way through. He's misguided, not wicked." He paused, as if scratching round in search of reassurance. "Nobody's been hurt. Nobody has died."

"Let's hope not," Hannah said.

He crouched in front of them, his expression that of a man begging for mercy. "You don't know Josh. He's a gentle soul. He'd never harm anyone, far less a kid like Shona. I suppose she flattered his ego, that's the way teenage girls…"

"And Lily Elstone?" Les demanded. "Are you saying he didn't hurt her?"

"My son had nothing to do with Lily's disappearance."

"He knew her, didn't he?"

Scott Durham finished the brandy, and re-filled his tumbler. "Josh never taught at her school."

"Lily's father is your accountant, isn't he?" Les asked.

"Totally irrelevant. Gray and I don't mix socially. Ours is a purely business relationship, always has been. We have nothing in common. I'm not sure Josh has even been in his company since…well, possibly not since the afternoon of the barbecue."

Hannah played her ace. "You knew Josh and Lily were both involved with a charity pantomime?"

Durham deflated like a punctured balloon. So he did know, and was probably just praying they hadn't done their research thoroughly.

"All right, Chief Inspector. You win. Josh did have a fleeting acquaintance with Lily, but categorically, that's as far as it went."

"How can you be certain?"

"He told me about the panto at the time, just as a matter of interest, because I knew Gray. He had nothing to hide."

You're wriggling. "What did he say about Lily?"

"Oh, that she was a sweet kid. He felt sorry for her, because her mother was a nightmare. Totally controlling, couldn't stop interfering. She made herself deeply unpopular with everyone playing in the concert. He told me Lily loathed her mum, and dreamed that one day she'd be able to live with Gray."

"So Lily confided in your son?"

"Please don't try to trap me into making admissions I don't intend, Chief Inspector." He wanted to sound dignified, but the brandy—plus whatever he'd drunk earlier—meant that *admissions* was hopelessly slurred. "She said the same to anyone she spoke to, as I understand it."

This chimed with evidence from Lily's friends. More than one girl had reported that she hated Anya, and this level of undisguised hostility—along with experience of meeting the appalling woman—had encouraged detectives on the original enquiry to suspect Lily of running away. But why escape from Gray, not Anya, and why leave without her passport or money? No, the voluntary disappearance theory didn't stack up. Especially after three years without a confirmed sighting. She'd been abducted; no other explanation made sense.

"Did you discuss Lily's disappearance?"

"Yes, the day the news broke. I was with him that evening."

For the first time, a glimmer of satisfaction lit the blue eyes. He looked like a man about to score a point.

"You remember it clearly?"

"I certainly do. As it happens, I was visiting Josh in hospital."
He sounded almost triumphant. "He'd broken his leg, falling
off a concert platform a couple of days earlier. His leg was in
plaster, and he'd also chipped his vertebrae. At one time, the
medics were seriously worried. It took a lot of hard work and
physio to get him back on his feet again, but thank goodness,
he made a full recovery."

"I see."

"I hope so, Chief Inspector. My boy may have made mistakes,
but he'd never physically harm a young girl, or do anything
against her will. I'd stake my life on it. If you think he kidnapped
poor Lily Elstone, you couldn't be more wrong."

Chapter Eighteen

"Win a few, lose a few, huh?" Les said.

They'd turned right out of the artist's cottage, heading through the flood gates and on to the beach. Now they were walking into a stiff breeze as they made their way back toward the guest house. The rain had eased off for the moment, but sepia clouds promised an imminent downpour.

"I'd have laid good money on Josh Durham being responsible for Lily's disappearance as well as Shona's,"

"Just as well you're not a gambler, eh?"

"Did you believe him?"

"Why lie about his son's accident, when we can check? He's not that stupid. Refusing to admit he had an affair with Lysette Whiteley is different. He's banking on the fact that nothing can be proved after all this time."

"Everyone assumed he and Lysette were lovers, so what does he have to gain by claiming otherwise?"

"He's in denial. He can't bear to face the fact that, indirectly, the affair provoked Malcolm Whiteley's killing spree." Les kicked at a pebble. "Weak as dishwater, that's Durham."

They clambered over the rocks, and toward the Green. "I'll call the office and ask for a check on hospital records," Hannah said. "Let's see if Josh does have an alibi for Lily's abduction. And we may have an update on his current whereabouts."

Billie greeted Hannah with the glee of a hunter who has scented her prey. "Things are really coming together. A neighbour saw Josh leaving home in his car half an hour before Shona said goodbye to her old man. The timings fit, he'd have taken twenty minutes plus to reach the Dungeon House. And his car's been found abandoned in a back street near Liverpool Lime Street station. Chances are, he and Shona caught a train to London."

"The location may be a blind," Hannah said. "Lime Street is walking distance from the ferry terminal. They might have headed for Ireland or the Isle of Man. Keep me posted?"

"You bet."

Hannah turned to Les. "Shall we see if there's any sign of Joanna yet? I can't imagine what she's playing at."

"Perhaps she nipped off for a quick leg-over with Nigel Whiteley."

"His daughter's missing. Surely he's got enough on his plate."

"Maybe, maybe not. An old flame turns up on his doorstep, and she's still got the hots for him. It's one way to take his mind off things."

"That's how men's minds work, is it?"

"Thought you'd been around long enough to realise."

"Thank God I'm a woman."

"I guess Ben Kind's boy is glad, too."

She rang the bell at the guest house. Alvaro Quiggin greeted them with gloomy resignation, and waved them into the cluttered cubby-hole that served as his office.

"This is just a quick call," Hannah said. "We wondered if…"

"Joanna isn't back, and she hasn't been in touch." Quiggin glanced at the wall clock. "It's still early afternoon. No need to send out a search party just yet."

"Would you mind if we had a quick look in her room?"

"I suppose I could object, but what's the point?" He sighed heavily, and turned to Les. "Something wrong?"

Les was staring at a photograph stuffed behind a box labelled *Invoices*. "Who's that?"

A flush came to Quiggin's sallow cheeks. "My daughter, Carina."

"Carrie North?" Les sounded incredulous.

"To me, she'll always be Carina Quiggin."

The moment Hannah took a proper look at the photo, light dawned. Les had been struck by a startling resemblance between Carrie North and Lily Elstone. Or at least between Carrie and Lily as she appeared in her last known picture. The shoulder-length blonde hair, the big grey eyes, and the rosebud mouth were almost identical. At first glance, the two teenage girls might have been sisters. Even twins.

"Well spotted," Hannah said, as they returned to the station car park. A cursory search of Joanna's room had proved fruitless; her suitcase and plenty of clothes were there, but nothing to indicate where she might be. The discovery that Quiggin's daughter was a dead ringer for Gray Elstone's girl, however, gave them plenty to chew over.

"Like I said, it's about being in the right place at the right time." Les fastened his seat belt. "What do you make of it?"

"When you look closely, the girls' appearances are only super-ficially similar," Hannah said. "Carrie North had a bigger nose, and her jaw wasn't so pointed. It's not a family resemblance."

Les said drily, "So we can rule out the possibility of Quiggin being Lily's real father?"

Hannah couldn't help laughing. "I reckon so. Anya Jovetic married Gray Elstone because he was rich and desperate. Quiggin might be desperate, but that wouldn't be enough for her. The girls' hair is done in the same style, and that counts for a lot."

Her phone trilled. Billie Frederick could scarcely manage to contain her excitement. "Got the bastard!"

"Jesus, that was quick."

"Good work, eh? You were right. Well, close enough. He and Shona are in Northern Ireland, not the Republic. Holed up in a B&B not far from the Giant's Causeway. The owner has been in touch. Sounds as if she loves playing the detective. Certainly, she's mastered the art of covert surveillance. She's even managed to photograph the pair of them with her mobile, and email the pictures to the PSNI. No question, it's Shona. Gazing into Durham's eyes as though the sun shines out of his arse."

"She looks okay?"

"Blooming. They are posing as a married couple, very lovey-dovey. They booked in with false ID, and Shona's claiming to be twenty-one. She has the figure to get away with it. Seems they planned their getaway carefully, not that it had a prayer of working out for them in the long run. Since they arrived, they've not bothered much with the scenery. They spend most of their time shagging, according to the owner. A woman in the room next door complained about the noise. Even at this time of day, they're tucked up in bed together."

Hannah breathed out. Scott Durham hadn't been so wide of the mark; Josh hadn't killed the girl, thank God. But he'd finish up in prison, beyond a doubt.

"So they can't sneak off?"

"The landlady's on guard downstairs, and the PSNI are due to arrive mob-handed any minute now. Lucky for us that the runaways are still in the UK, there's much less red tape to fret about. Shona and Durham will be separated straight away, and DI Borthwick and another colleague will get over there on the next available flight. If only every miss-per inquiry had such a positive outcome, eh?"

"If only, yes." Hannah pictured Lily Elstone in her mind. "Does Nigel Whiteley know?"

"Not yet, it's next job on the list. Unfortunately, Grizzly is stuck in the magistrates' in Barrow, and I'm not sure when…"

"If it helps," Hannah broke in, "Les and I can see him. Ravenglass Knoll is only down the road, and we wanted to speak to Nigel anyway."

"Terrific," Billie said. "Always good to kill two birds with one stone."

>>>

Tears glistened in Nigel Whiteley's eyes as he absorbed the news that his daughter was safe. He'd invited Hannah and Les into the living room, and they sat together while the rain poured down outside, and Hannah explained what would happen next. Standard practice was for Shona to be detained for her own protection, while the medics made sure she was okay. Life would become more complicated if the girl declined to answer questions for fear of incriminating her boyfriend, or proved reluctant to return home, but Nigel didn't fall into the trap of ranting about bureaucracy or making wild threats against the man who had stolen his daughter.

"I blame myself." He'd poured himself a generous measure of whisky, and tried in vain to persuade his visitors to join him. "Let's be honest, I'm her dad. I should have paid more attention to what was going on. How did I not realise, how come I didn't pick up the signs?"

"There weren't many signs," Les said. "The two of them were much more discreet and careful than the vast majority of couples in cases like this."

"It never crossed my mind that she'd do anything so…so crazy, and not say a word. As if she didn't care about me." He sounded dazed, still coming to terms with the news. "I'll have to think about whether she should move to a new school. Perhaps it won't be necessary, with Josh Durham out of the way. She has to understand the game is over."

"Teenage girls sometimes live in a fantasy world."

"Shona isn't a fantasist." He was speaking almost to himself. "She just knows what she wants, and sets about getting it. Ironic, huh? It's in her genes, it's the one lesson in life I've taught her, and now it's come back to haunt me."

"Don't blame yourself," Hannah said. "Josh Durham is the criminal, not you. A schoolgirl ought to be safe with a teacher."

"I suppose you're right." He let out a sigh. "Oh well, we'll survive, and I'm not sure Josh Durham will. Presumably he's finished? No job, years in the nick?"

"Racing certainty," Les said.

"Tough on his father," Nigel said. "I never cared for Scott, to be truthful, but it's no joke, losing your only child. There's a special bond between a parent and an only one, believe me. I've coped with plenty of shit in my life—my dad's illness, my uncle committing murder, my wife being slowly destroyed by a cancer in her brain. But this past week has been as tough as any. Not knowing if I'd ever clap eyes on Shona again. Not having any control."

Hannah had met plenty of rich businessmen—and quite a few senior police officers, come to that—who thrived on exerting control. To her, it seemed like the last word in futility. Sooner or later they all discovered that some things in life simply couldn't be controlled.

"Griselda will be here as soon as she can. Of course she'll keep you updated on developments. In case you were wondering, there's really no point in your dashing off to Northern Ireland. All being well, Shona will be back in England soon."

"Don't worry," he murmured. "There are bound to be procedures you need to follow. I'll curb my impatience. I just can't wait to see her home again."

Hannah made a non-committal noise. In all likelihood, Shona would return to Ravenglass Knoll soon, but it was too early to give assurances.

Nigel Whiteley stood up, and offered his hand. "All's well that ends well, eh? I'm very grateful to you for coming here to tell me in person, Chief Inspector. I'm sure your time's very valuable."

As Hannah and Les followed him out into the hall, she said, "There was something else."

Nigel Whiteley stopped in his tracks. "What was that?"

"It's about Joanna Footit. A name from your past, I gather."

He stared at her. "Joanna? What about her?"

"Have you seen her?"

"As a matter of fact, she came to see me." He rubbed his chin. "Only yesterday. The first time we'd met in twenty years."

"Since the shootings?"

"Yes. Joanna is staying nearby, and she wanted to catch up." He hesitated. "She'd seen the news about Shona, and….well, I wish I'd been more hospitable, but the worry about Shona left me distracted. I must let Jo know the good news."

"You know where she is?"

"Staying in Ravenglass, at a local guest house. Why do you ask?"

"It's only that she didn't spend last night there, and her whereabouts aren't clear."

He screwed up his face. "I don't understand. What has Joanna got to do with anything?"

"We're anxious to ask her one or two questions, that's all."

"Questions?"

"Routine," Les said, contriving to make it sound anything but routine.

"I'm completely baffled." He scratched his head, to emphasise the point. "I can't imagine what you would want to ask Jo, or where she might be, if she isn't at the guest house. Unless…"

"Unless?" Hannah asked.

"Unless it's something to do with…what my uncle did."

"Go on."

Nigel groaned. "Christ, sometimes I wonder if I'll ever be allowed to forget that this lovely house was a murder scene."

Hannah gave him a moment to collect his thoughts before prompting him. "You were saying?"

"I was startled to hear from Joanna after all this time, but it was good to see her again. I've often wondered how she was coping. We went out together briefly at one time."

"You were both in that fatal crash. In the car driven by Robbie Dean."

He gave her a penetrating look. "You have done your homework, Chief Inspector. Why in God's name are you dredging up such a painful episode from the past?"

"It's my job, Mr Whiteley. I'm in charge of the Cold Case Review Unit."

"Ah, I see." He mulled this over, like a barrister in court, processing new evidence. She suspected he could think on his feet as fast as any legal eagle. Years of working as a claims farmer must have given him plenty of practice. "But the car crash isn't a 'cold case', is it? Nor is what my uncle did. Everyone knows what happened here all those years ago."

"Do they?" Time to detonate a grenade? Hannah made a snap decision. "Not everyone knows that Joanna Footit was here that night."

Nigel Whiteley's eyes widened, but he said nothing.

"Did you know that, Mr Whiteley?"

"Tell you what." he said, giving a humourless smile. "Let's go back into the living room. I could do with another drink, if you don't mind."

Without waiting for a reply, he led them back, and gulped down some more whisky. Hannah couldn't blame him for wanting to fortify his nerves, but she could recognise a strong character when she saw one. Nigel Whiteley wouldn't shoot his mouth off without taking time to think. He'd never blurt out a stupid, blatant lie, as Alvaro Quiggin had, when asked if he'd realised Joanna was one of the survivors of the car crash. Easy to see why Whiteley was so much richer.

Better give him a shove. "When did you find out?"

"Not until yesterday," he said. "It came as a bolt from the blue."

Yes! She'd been right. Joanna Footit was the person Anton Friend had seen on the night of the shootings.

"I can imagine," she said. "What did she tell you?"

"Very little." He seemed unsure what to say. "Are you sure you won't have a drink? Tea, coffee?"

"No, thank you. About Joanna…"

"Yes, yes. She became flustered, a bit hyper. I think…she was trying to explain why she'd run away from the Lake District. Not that she owed me an explanation."

"She thought you deserved to know?"

He gave a helpless smile. "Jo was a sweet girl, Chief Inspector, but her moods swung rapidly. I felt sorry for her, just like I did in the old days, but pity isn't conducive to romance. The truth is, Joanna never had much luck. The car crash put paid to our brief romance. She had a breakdown, and turned into a stranger. Edgy, frightened of her own shadow. I was only a lad, and to be honest, I couldn't handle it."

"Her health improved, eventually."

"Yes." He hesitated. "She became more like the old Jo. The day of the barbecue, we spent time together."

"You had a meal that evening, along with Lysette Whiteley and her daughter."

"Along with several others, yes. Afterwards, Jo and I went for a walk in the moonlight. Quite romantic, but we did nothing more than hold hands."

"Is that so?"

"Yes." He coughed. For a man who did not, Hannah suspected, embarrass easily, he seemed rather uncomfortable. "Jo suggested we go off to Drigg. I don't know if you're familiar with the place, but there's a long beach, and extensive sand dunes. We'd....well, that was the first place where we ever made love. She made it fairly plain she'd like me to—um—rekindle things between us."

"And?"

"I told her I had to get back home. My dad was very poorly at the time, and I needed to be there."

"That was an excuse?"

"Listen," he said earnestly, "the last thing I wanted was to be unkind. I was fond of Joanna, and she knew I wasn't seeing anyone else. Amber pestered me, God rest her soul, but she was too young for me. The snag was, I simply wasn't ready to resume my relationship with Jo. To be totally honest, I doubt I'd ever have been ready. She was too...intense."

"So you weren't tempted?"

"I'm not saying that." His teeth flashed. "I was a young man, with a young man's libido. Joanna had found herself a good job, and was ready to settle down, but that wasn't for me. I was young, ambitious, and hopelessly immature. I'd left Malcolm's company, and started working in claims. I needed to focus my energies on my career. A wife and a tribe of snotty-nosed kids didn't form part of the plan. So I gave Jo a peck on the cheek, and cycled back home."

"What did Joanna do after you separated?"

"At the time, I assumed she'd simply headed back to Holmrook, and gone to bed."

"Why come here instead? It was too late for a social call, did she offer any explanation?"

"I'm still not clear, she was rather muddled." He spread his arms vaguely. "Typical of Joanna, I'm afraid, and I certainly didn't subject her to a Spanish inquisition. I've spent the last twenty years trying to forget what Malcolm did."

"Did Amber phone Joanna? Was she asking for help when your uncle ran amok?"

He clenched his fist. "That must be it. Yes, I bet you're spot on. They were very close, those two. Joanna was like Amber's big sister."

Les didn't look convinced. "Why wouldn't Amber ring 999?"

"Your guess is as good as mine." Nigel said. "Malcolm was Amber's dad, don't forget. If she called before he started shooting, perhaps she thought Jo could talk some sense into him. Who knows?"

"What did Joanna tell you about the events of that night?"

"She said she…had a bad feeling about what had happened at the barbecue. Malcolm's drunkenness. His nasty temper. I suspect Amber confided in Jo, told her that Lysette was seeing Scott Durham."

"What do you know about their affair?" Les said. "Their *alleged* affair?"

"No more than anyone else. It wasn't common knowledge until after the shootings. I certainly had no idea. Like I said, I scarcely knew Scott Durham, and Lysette was my aunt. She wasn't going to tell me her secrets."

Les grunted. "Sorry, I interrupted. You were telling us about what Joanna did, the night of the shootings."

"What she *told* me she did," Nigel corrected. "When she arrived at the house, she said, the front door was ajar, and she heard a commotion from the direction of the quarry garden. Amber was screaming her head off. Jo wasn't sure if there'd been a burglary, she was frantic. When she pushed the door open, she saw Lysette's body, sprawled across the floor. Blood was spattered everywhere. She said it was like staring into an abattoir." He swallowed some whisky. "In a blind panic, she ran out toward the quarry garden, and saw two figures on the path at the top of the quarry. Malcolm and Amber. He was waving his rifle around like a maniac."

He wiped his mouth. "Sorry, it's dreadful, reliving that night, even after so many years. This is why I didn't want Joanna to go on about it. What was done was done. I just hope Malcolm is still rotting in hell."

"Take your time, Mr Whiteley," Hannah said. "It's been an emotional few days for you. Can I get you anything, a glass of water?"

"No, no, I'll be fine." Gritting his teeth, he looked up at her. "This is a wonderful day. You've brought me the best news I've ever received. Shona is safe and well. The very least I can do is to answer your questions."

"Thanks." She was battling to suppress her impatience. *Gently does it.*

"Joanna said she was rooted to the spot. In front of her eyes, Malcolm and Amber struggled, and Amber fell over the edge."

"Her father pushed her?"

"God knows. Jo didn't seem sure whether it was accidental or deliberate. I doubt it changes anything. We'll never know."

"How did Joanna Footit see what happened?" Les asked. "At that time of night, surely it was pitch black."

"The quarry garden was still a work-in-progress, but Malcolm had already installed lights along the length of the path. They had motion sensors, a security feature. She had no trouble seeing him and Amber, but they couldn't see her. Obviously, she was frightened out of her wits, and started to run for her life. She hadn't got very far when she heard a shot. Only later did she realise that was Malcolm, killing himself."

"What did she do then?" This was Hannah.

"Legged it all the way home."

"Had she cycled there?"

Nigel looked confused. "I'm not sure. She didn't say."

"Why didn't she call the police, raise the alarm?"

"I asked her that." Nigel shook his head. "She didn't give me a straight answer."

"If you ask me, the whole experience was so shocking, it caused her to have a total breakdown."

"She was interviewed by the police," Les said. "I've read her statement."

"Yes?" Nigel's face was blank. "All of us who had anything to do with Malcolm were interviewed. She must have been in a poor way when she spoke to your colleagues. I'm sure she said nothing about her visit to the Dungeon House, or I'd have heard about it."

"The statement fills less than two sides of paper, but there's no hint that she wasn't fit to be questioned."

"On the surface, she may have seemed okay, but inside…"

"She was asked about the barbecue and the meal in the pub. She also confirmed that you and she went your separate ways after your walk on the shore."

Nigel nodded. "Of course."

"You and she didn't meet after the shootings?" Hannah asked.

"We never had a chance. I heard she wasn't well, and I thought if I got in touch, I'd do more harm than good. I heard a rumour she'd taken some of her mum's sleeping pills, and had to be rushed into hospital. The next I knew, she'd left the area."

"You never tried to get in touch with her?"

"No, Chief Inspector. Does that sound heartless?" He drained his glass. "You need to understand, it was a crazy time. The media were all over us as a family. Press, television. My uncle, aunt, and cousin were dead, and my father was dying. He and Malcolm didn't get on, but the whole business traumatised him. I'm sure it shortened his life. Not long afterwards, we buried him too. I always thought of him as Malcolm's final victim."

He stood up. "And now, Chief Inspector, if you don't mind, I've got a raging headache, and I'd better take something for it before I keel over. Will you excuse me? I'm thrilled about Shona, but right now, so much has happened so quickly that I feel like I've been through a threshing machine."

Chapter Nineteen

"Why aren't you looking smug?" Les demanded, as they walked back to the car. "You were dead right about the Footit woman."

"Time enough to pat myself on the back when we've cleared everything up," Hannah said. "Hello—see that?"

She was pointing to the name painted on a white van parked outside the garage block. *Deano Garden Services.* Two men came into view from behind the van. One was shaven-headed, and in his early twenties; his companion was squat and hairy, a low-browed older man. Both wore blue overalls; they were carrying a driftwood bench along a path between the trees.

"Let's have a word," Les said.

Hannah sprinted toward them, calling, "Mr Dean?"

The men halted, and lowered the bench to the ground. The lad with the shaved head treated her to a toothy leer. "Boss ain't here. Friend of his, darling? You can come in the woods with us for a picnic as long as you get rid of your grandad."

She shrivelled him with a look. "We'd like a quick word with Mr Dean."

The older man glowered. "Who wants him?"

"Cumbria Constabulary. DCI Scarlett, this is Mr Bryant."

"Oh yeah?" the lad jeered. "What's the boss been doing, then?"

"Where is he today?"

The older man spat on the ground. "Back at his place."

"Not working today?"

"Sorting out some tax stuff, he told us," the lad said. "Has he been on the fiddle?"

"Thanks very much for your help." Turning on her heel, she returned to the car.

"Want to pay Deano a visit?" Les asked.

"Lower Drigg isn't far from here. Joanna has spent the last few days meeting up with people from her past, and she was in Dean's car when Quiggin's daughter was killed. He might point us in the right direction, and the sooner we find her, the happier I'll be."

"Reckon she's done a runner?"

"God knows."

"She went to Daniel's lecture, and asked a cryptic question about motive. The shootings were playing on her mind. Chances are, she decided she couldn't handle it anymore, and decided to get out of the Lakes."

"Leaving all her stuff in her room? Why not tell Quiggin?"

"She's flaky."

Hannah frowned. "Yes, but…"

"You always want a rational answer for everything, don't you?" Les sighed. "People aren't rational."

"If you're about to say *especially women*, forget it, unless you fancy walking back to Kendal. What do you make of the story she told Nigel about the night of the shootings?"

"Weird." Les buckled his seat belt. "Why keep quiet all these years?"

"Nigel might be right. She was having a breakdown. After what she witnessed, hardly surprising."

"If that is what she witnessed," Les said.

"You think she lied to Nigel?"

"We'll only find out if we get to talk to her."

"Agreed. But let's have a word with Gray Elstone before we call on Dean. You never know, perhaps she's run off with her old boss."

Two fathers with missing daughters, but only one with cause to celebrate. When Hannah phoned the accountant's office, Yindee said that Elstone was in a meeting with a client. When pressed, she conceded that he might become free in the next half an hour. Her manner was off-hand, and when they arrived at the office, she was in the middle of a furious row with Gray's PA. The older woman, cheeks flaming with temper, stomped back into her room as the detectives introduced themselves, and slammed the door behind her. Yindee picked up her mobile, and started texting, as if Hannah and Les were invisible.

Moments later, Gray Elstone's door opened, and a thickset man wearing an anorak and a surly expression marched out. Perhaps he'd just been advised that the Revenue was planning to double his tax bill, He didn't spare the two detectives a glance before clumping down the stairs in heavy boots.

"Chief Inspector." Gray gave Hannah a sorrowful smile as she introduced Les. "To what do I owe this unexpected pleasure?"

"We won't take up much of your time, Mr Elstone. I'm sure you're busy." Out of the corner of her eye, she saw Yindee was still texting. "This is my colleague, Les Bryant."

"Yindee's offered you a drink?"

"I think she was just about to," Les lied cheerfully. "Mine's coffee with two sugars, and the Chief Inspector usually likes a cup of Earl Grey at this time of the afternoon. Milk, not lemon, if that's all right."

"Okay." Yindee put her phone away in her bag, a sulky child deprived of a favourite toy.

Elstone led them into his office. "My apologies if you've been kept waiting. That client you saw is a hill farmer. Having a rough time of it financially, I'm afraid. The old agricultural way of life is becoming untenable, though it pains me to say it. Now, how can I help you?"

"A couple of things," Hannah said. "First, you might like to know that Shona Whiteley has been located. Early indications are that she's safe and well."

Elstone gaped at them. "Are you saying that she wasn't kidnapped, after all?"

"I'm afraid we can't divulge anything more at this stage."

"Good grief." He gnawed at a fingernail. "That is a turn-up. Of course, I…I'm pleased for her father. It's a desperate business, to have your only child go missing. I don't suppose there's any connection?"

"It's very early days yet, but as far as we can tell at this stage, there is no link between what has happened to Shona, and Lily's disappearance."

"Ah. I see." For a horrible moment, Hannah thought he was going to burst into tears, but he fought to compose himself. Well, as I say, I'm glad it has turned out for the best. At least, for Nigel."

"There's something else. We spoke yesterday about Joanna Footit. Do you happen to know where she is right now?"

He rubbed his chin, as if to aid his memory. "She's staying in Ravenglass."

"Not anymore," Les said. "The last time she was seen was yesterday evening. She didn't check out of the guest house, and her things are still in her room, or so it would seem, but her bed wasn't slept in. Her car has also vanished."

Gray's tufted eyebrows lifted. "That doesn't sound like Joanna."

"Really? She's had problems over the years."

"Yes, yes, that's true. Poor girl—poor woman, rather. I hope… nothing has happened to her."

"Did Joanna talk to you about what happened at the Dungeon House all those years ago?"

"No, no, she didn't." His fingernails strayed toward to his mouth again. "Why do you ask? This has nothing to do with the kidnapping of Lily."

"This is another unexplained disappearance of a female in West Cumbria, Mr Elstone. We can't afford to ignore any angle, no matter how…"

"Tangential?"

Excellent word, much better than *far-fetched.* "That's right," she said gratefully.

"Malcolm….did what he did on the Saturday night, and the bodies were found by Robbie Dean the next day. It caused a sensation. Something like that would make headlines in a large city, but in this part of the world…well, the news flew around in a matter of hours. It was quite appalling. I mean, he was my major client. As for Joanna, she didn't come into work on the Monday."

"She took the day off sick?"

"Not just that one day. Amber Whiteley was a close friend of hers, so I understood perfectly. We'd all been together at the barbecue. I could hardly expect her to come in, and behave as if nothing had happened."

"Did she get in touch, let you know how she was feeling?"

A shake of the head. "No, her mother kept me in the picture by phone. I offered to pop round, pay a welfare visit, but she said Joanna wasn't up to it. I felt sorry for her. Decent people, the Footits."

"And?"

"Joanna sent in a sick note. Stress, anxiety, something along those lines. Then her mum rang up, and said Joanna had taken an overdose. They found her semi-conscious, and rushed her to hospital. Her stomach was pumped, or whatever they do in these cases." His expression was a blend of distress and distaste. "Quite dreadful. The next I heard was that she'd decided to leave the district. She wanted to make a fresh start somewhere else. Her parents were desperately worried, but what could they do? She was a grown woman, and there was no question of sectioning her. But there was just no reasoning with her."

"Did she say goodbye to you?"

"Not a word."

"So you never discussed what happened at the Dungeon House?"

"Nor anything else." He folded his arms. "It was a shame. I'd gone the extra miles as an employer, making it clear that I'd hold the job open for as long as she needed to get herself back on her feet."

"Upsetting."

A quick, opportunistic nibble of the thumbnail. "Yes, it… did disappoint me. But it was nothing personal. After everything that had happened here, she simply needed to get away."

"Very understanding," Les said. "Not every employer would be so fair-minded. Some would bear a grudge."

Elstone blanched, and Hannah found herself itching to give him the benefit of the doubt. She couldn't help feeling sorry for the man. This was a weakness in a detective, she knew, one of the reasons why her career was never likely to reach the giddy heights.

"It was lovely to see her again." Elstone sounded a note of defiance. "A lot of water has flowed under the bridge. But her main aim was to meet Nigel again. She'd already bumped into Scott Durham. Have you spoken to Scott or Nigel?"

"We've come here straight from Ravenglass Knoll," Hannah said.

"Nigel must be ecstatic that Shona is safe. Lucky devil." The mask slipped, and Hannah glimpsed his bitterness, raw and ugly as a gaping wound. Seconds later, the bland professional expression was back in place. "I do apologise, Chief Inspector. Your people are doing their utmost, I'm sure. It just seems… hopeless. The ultimate lost cause."

"When we first spoke," Hannah said gently, "I explained that case reviews usually take time. We need to take a fresh look at all the evidence…"

"And consider any fresh evidence," Les interrupted. "Speaking of which, Mr Quiggin from Ravenglass is a client of yours. How did he come to appoint you as his accountant?"

Elstone looked baffled. "In the usual way, as I recall. Word of mouth recommendation is still the best way to pick up work in a rural community. I keep advertising to the bare minimum, and never bother with all this social media gubbins. Leave it to the big city firms, that's my motto."

"Who recommended him?"

"I really can't remember." Elstone pondered. "Wait. On second thoughts, he simply rang up out of the blue, and asked if I'd act for him. This was shortly after he bought the guest house."

"Did he ever meet Lily?"

"I'm not…yes, yes, I think he did. We bumped into him one Saturday morning, as I recall. Anya had graciously allowed Lily to visit me, and I took her over to Muncaster Castle, and then down to Ravenglass for fish and chips, and a stroll along the front. Why on earth do you ask?"

"Just curious. You know that Lily bears a conspicuous resemblance to his daughter?"

Elstone swallowed. "I don't understand your point. Alvaro's daughter died years ago. He has a horror of talking about it. What can this have to do with Lily?"

"Almost certainly nothing," Hannah said quickly. "I expect it's just a strange coincidence."

Elstone's voice shook. "Do police officers really believe in coincidences, Chief Inspector?"

⟩⟩⟩

"Not sure I do," Les said, as they walked back to the car park. "Believe in coincidences, that is. How about you, Hannah? Friend Quiggin's quite strange, don't you think? Even stranger than Elstone."

"Two lonely men, I'd say."

"Know your problem, Hannah? You're too quick to sympathise. No offence, but for a moment back there, I thought you were going to offer Elstone a shoulder to cry on."

Hannah bridled. "You're forgetting he's lost his daughter."

"I'm not forgetting his ex is pointing a well-manicured finger at the bloke," he retorted. "Sure, she's vindictive, but even vindictive people aren't always wrong. I'm not saying Elstone did anything to Lily, but we can't rule it out."

Before she could answer, her mobile sang. The call was from Maggie Eyre, sounding as breathless as if she'd just run a half-marathon.

"Bad news about Joanna Footit, ma'am."

"What's happened?"

"Her car has been found close to Drigg beach."

"Drigg? We're just round the corner, at Seascale. Any sign of her?"

"She left some clothes on the driver's seat. Along with a note saying *Sorry*."

Chapter Twenty

"People harp on about the Yorkshire coast being bleak," Les said. "Load of bollocks. Whitby in winter is like the Costa del Sol, compared to this God-forsaken spot."

They were walking back to the car through a fierce shower. Gulls wailed up above, and the wind moaned as it whipped sand over the dunes of Drigg. Behind them, a police tape cordoned off Joanna's vehicle. The force's policy on missing persons included a lengthy procedure for dealing with situations like this, and two constables were conducting a risk assessment before deciding on next steps.

"Don't be such a misery. On a sunny day, Drigg is glorious. Years ago, I spent an afternoon walking along the beach, then back over the dunes. It was so peaceful, I hardly saw another soul. I started wondering where everyone was."

"Steering clear of nuclear fall-out," Les grumbled. "What's your guess? Has Joanna Footit drowned herself or done a Reggie Perrin?"

"Or been kidnapped?"

"You reckon?"

She opened the car door. "Why leave a note hinting at suicide, along with her jacket, jeans, and sandals, and then do a flit?"

"We've agreed she's flaky."

"Your adjective, not mine."

"Okay," Les said, as he squeezed into his seat. "Assume I've done her an injustice, and her head's screwed on right. A woman with something to hide has an incentive to fake her own death, and start a fresh life elsewhere. You can interpret the note in two ways. *Sorry* might be shorthand for *I mean to kill myself and there's nothing you can do to stop me.* Or she could be apologising for something else."

"Keeping quiet after the Dungeon House shootings, for example." Hannah said. "As for suicide, she may have chosen this spot to disappear for a very personal reason."

"Because this was where she had her first shag with Nigel Whiteley?"

"Ah, Les, you have such a delicate way with words. She'd just met her former boyfriend for the first time in twenty years, and he was too distracted by his daughter's disappearance to make a fuss of her. If she felt mortified by his indifference, she might choose somewhere with romantic associations to end her life."

"Seems a bit drastic."

"Suicide *is* drastic. There's another angle we need to consider. Robbie Dean lives close by. Coincidence, probably, but it's worth checking out. When I was last here, Lower Drigg amounted to two or three buildings and half a dozen sheep, so his place can't be hard to find."

"Yeah, I'm guessing they've not built an executive estate overlooking the dumps of nuclear sludge. Shall we have a chat with him?"

She nodded. Time to meet the man responsible for the death of Alvaro Quiggin's daughter.

〉〉〉

Robbie Dean's cottage didn't boast a name, a number or a doorbell. Neither the unkempt patch of lawn nor the cracked pane in the front window made a compelling case for his skills as gardener and handyman, but Hannah supposed he didn't rely on passing trade. Few people who ventured along that lonely, winding lane would be tempted to make a return visit. The best that could be said of it was that the dunes lining the horizon obscured the view of Sellafield's brooding bulk. In the chill and wet of this miserable afternoon, the exposed and featureless landscape between the dunes and the lane was very green, but hardly pleasant.

They splashed up the path, and moments after Les knocked, Dean opened the door, a strongly-built man wearing a Black Sabbath hoodie, corduroy jeans, and Doc Martens. Had he been expecting them? If so, he didn't look in the mood to offer coffee and cake.

"Mr Dean?" Hannah flourished her card and made the introductions. "Hope you don't mind if we trouble you for a couple of minutes?"

"Would it make any difference if I did mind?" he demanded.

"You don't seem surprised to see us," Les said.

"One of my lads rang. Said you'd been asking for me, up at Ravenglass Knoll."

Hannah had taught herself to resist jumping to instant conclusions about people. Ben Kind's mantra was that first impressions counted, but not for everything. A good detective always looked beneath the surface. So she told herself to give Robbie Dean the benefit of the doubt, despite the unpleasant glare darkening his face.

She shook her wet hair. "May we step inside for a moment?"

A weary shrug. "Follow me."

As he motioned them into the front room, Hannah caught sight of the kitchen through an open door at the end of the hall. A pile of dirty dishes rose up from the sink. Not a house-proud man, then, but a moment's glance around the sitting room gave a clue to what he cared about. There was a small sofa and two armchairs, but the room was dominated by a huge glass-topped cabinet, long, and deep, on sturdy wooden legs. Inside the cabinet was an array of memorabilia: gold medals in brown boxes, small silver trophies and brass plaques recording team and personal triumphs, gaudy football match programmes, and as a centrepiece, a peaked cap.

Les scrutinised the cap as if it were a religious relic. "You were a schoolboy international?"

"Uh-huh." He was still tight-lipped, defensive.

"Worth a few bob, this stuff. Hope you've got good security."

"Not many people get out this way," Dean said. "I've got CCTV, and the barbed wire keeps out the dog walkers and their animals. Anyone who tried to burgle me would be very sorry."

Hannah didn't doubt it, but now wasn't the time to deliver a lecture on crime prevention or the legal definition of reasonable force. Dean was obviously ready and willing to take the law in his hands if the need arose. One man's have-a-go hero is another man's sociopath, she thought. Framed photographs and press cuttings hung on three walls. One photo showed a young Robbie Dean looking lean and mean in a blue football strip; others featured teams of teenagers. She picked him out in the front row of two of them, staring at the camera with a ball at his feet. How old was he in those shots—fifteen, sixteen? The cuttings seemed to be a mix of match reports recording his triumphs on the pitch, and gossip paragraphs linking him with leading clubs. Snippets of journalistic hyperbole caught her eye: *nerveless… ice-coal finisher…never missed a penalty kick.* The front window didn't let in too much light, but the clippings were yellow with age. They dated back almost a quarter of a century.

"You were a star," she said

For a fleeting moment, she saw something other than hostility in his eyes. "Yeah, the Press reckoned I could go all the way. So did my coaches, more to the point. Never happened."

"You were injured in a car crash, I believe."

The scowl returned. "Been doing your homework?"

"It's quite simple, Mr Dean. Your name cropped up in connection with Joanna Footit. She was travelling with you on the night of the collision, I believe."

"What about it?" His tone was derisive. "Don't tell me old Jo is in trouble with the law."

"Not at all. We're concerned for her safety. Her car has been found abandoned nearby. In the public car park."

"So she's gone for a walk on the beach. Or a swim." He glanced through the window. "Could've chosen a nicer day for it."

"She was last seen yesterday evening. The signs are that she didn't spend the night at the guest house where she is staying. If she went for a walk last night, what's happened to her?"

"Don't ask me."

"We are asking you, Mr Dean. You knew her years ago, and since she came back to Cumbria, she's been catching up with old friends and acquaintances."

"All right, she did come here," he said grudgingly. "Wanted to see Nigel Whiteley, and she'd found out I worked for him. Why don't you ask Nige?"

"We saw him earlier this afternoon, but he couldn't help."

"Me neither." He grimaced. "Try the bloke she used to work for. Elstone."

"We've already spoken to Mr Elstone."

"Been busy, haven't you? Perhaps she's done a runner."

"It doesn't seem likely."

"Why not?" he demanded. "Jo was always a bit mental. She was only here five minutes, but I could see she hadn't changed."

"Is that what you reckon?" Les asked. "Did you know her well enough to judge?"

"She was Nige's girlfriend. I saw enough of her to tell."

"Sure she didn't come here again last night?" Les made a performance of surveying the room. "You're on your own here, right? Quite nice to have a cosy catch-up with an old flame."

Dean laughed. "She wasn't my old flame, I told you. Not my type, even when she was a spring chicken. No, she didn't come to see me last night, or today. Take a look round the place if you think I've got her tucked up in bed or summat."

Hannah was about to say that wouldn't be necessary, but Les was too quick for her. "Thanks, don't mind if we do. This'll only take a couple of minutes."

"Hope so. I need to finish my VAT returns, or those bastards will be on my back. You two interrupted me."

〉〉〉

The cottage wasn't large. Apart from the squalid kitchen and a large pantry filled with rubbish, rickety old chairs and half-used tins of paint, there was a back room on the ground floor that Dean used as his office. A couple of spreadsheets and a laptop on his desk and a battered old filing cabinet crammed with invoices and correspondence were the only signs that he ran a business. Upstairs were two bedrooms, one with a bed still unmade, and a bathroom. Les poked around in a wardrobe and cupboard, but found nothing of interest. From the first floor window at the back, Hannah looked down on outbuildings large enough to hold three or four vehicles. Dean followed her gaze.

"My equipment's kept there, plus my vans and a trailer. Half empty right now. A lot of the stuff is out with the lads at Nige's place."

"May we have a quick look?"

"It's only a garage."

"All the same."

She knew even before he said yes that their chances of finding any hint of Joanna Footit's whereabouts were negligible, and so it proved. There was a workbench and plenty of tools in the garage, and although he kept them much cleaner and tidier than the pots and pans he cooked with, she felt consumed by frustration as she followed Dean back through the kitchen door.

"Quiet place, this," Les said. "You don't even have a telly."

"Got rid of it. There was nothing on but a load of crap."

"You don't follow the footie? Plenty to watch nowadays. Not just homegrown teams. La Liga, Serie A, and I don't know what. Don't you miss it all?"

"Been there, done that, got the football shirt." He considered Les. "As for the rest, the telly's full of shitty cop dramas."

"Even shitty cops need to relax. What do you do for company, how's your social life?"

A withering glance. "There are pubs not too far away,"

Les refused to give up. "Funny about Nigel Whiteley, isn't it?"

"What d'you mean?"

"A bloke who can afford to pick and choose, wanting to live in the house where his uncle committed murder?"

"Takes all sorts."

As Dean unlocked the front door to let them out, Hannah said thanks, and couldn't resist adding, "You've been extremely helpful. I'm sure you're concerned about your old friend. We'll let you know the outcome of our search for her."

At least she managed to provoked a response, however baleful. "Joanna will be fine, you can stake your life on that. She's lucky, that one."

"Lucky?"

For the first time since he'd admitted them, he seemed uncertain. Finally, he tapped his damaged leg. "She walked away from that car crash without a scratch. Same as Nige, he's always led a charmed life. Not like Carrie. Or me."

He slammed the door behind them, and Hannah winked at Les. "Salt of the earth, would you say, just a shade taciturn?"

"Miserable bastard. No wonder he lives alone, who in their right mind could put up with that?"

"Not likely that Joanna parked where she did simply because she wanted to be in his neighbourhood, is it?"

"Nah. We passed a station when we drove through Drigg, didn't we? Maybe she got away by train."

"On the Cumbrian Coast Line? You might be right, Drigg's a request stop." Hannah considered. "If she found shelter overnight, she could have caught a train this morning. For all we know, she could be in the north of Scotland or on the Eurostar by now."

"Did she ask her old chum Dean to put her up? Stranger things have happened, but he won't admit it any time soon." Les peered up at the sky. "Looks like it's going to pee down even harder. What next?"

"There's nothing more we can do about Joanna. We need to let them get on with the search. Time to get back to basics."

"Lily Elstone?"

"Exactly. It's her disappearance we're supposed to be reviewing, after all."

He opened the car door on the driver's side. "Yeah, but my instinct is the same as yours. Joanna Footit worked for Lily's dad, she was at the Dungeon House when Malcolm Whiteley went berserk. Hard to believe there's no connection whatsoever."

The back of Hannah's neck prickled as they belted up. Was Robbie Dean watching, waiting for them to move off? She refused to turn, and look in the direction of the cottage. The trill of her mobile distracted her, and she smiled with relief when she saw the caller's number.

"Daniel," she murmured to Les.

"Hope your day is going better than mine," she said into the phone. "We've found one and lost another. The good news is that Shona Whiteley has turned up safe and well in Northern Ireland with Scott Durham's son. The bad news is that Joanna Footit's vanished."

"Never a dull moment, huh?"

"You can say that again. Les and I are at Drigg, where her car was found, with some of her clothes and a note saying *Sorry*. Not clear yet whether she's killed herself or wandered off on a mysterious frolic of her own."

"I'd hate to think I drive my audience to suicide," he said. "That puts my mishaps into perspective. There's been a flood at the pub where I'm speaking tonight. Collapsed drain. They've had to cancel the talk. Edwin Broderick has offered to take me out for a meal, but if you're in the mood for something to eat before trekking back home, we could meet up."

"A quick bite?" She glanced at Les, who patted his stomach, and gave her a thumbs-up sign. "If it's okay with Mr Bryant, it's fine by me. The Eskdale Arms?"

"Perfect. When shall I see you?"

"Give us three quarters of an hour. I want another word with Joanna's landlord. It's only fair to warn him that his guest isn't coming back to collect the rest of her things any time soon."

"Very caring of you, but…"

"Talk to you later," she said.

She ended the call, and rang Maggie to give her a quick update. "Do me a favour, and run a quick PNC check on Quiggin. Let's see if he's got any history."

>>>

"Quiggin was freaked out by Lily's resemblance to his daughter, you think?" Les asked, as they sped away from Lower Drigg.

"Stranger things have happened."

"Why take her? What would he do once he had her?"

"That's always the question, when a man abducts a pretty teenager. There is no plan, just a route map to disaster. The girl is frightened. She screams. The man panics...."

He digested this. "Anyone ever said that you have too much imagination for a detective?"

"Frequently."

"They were wrong. Just make sure your ideas don't run too far ahead of the evidence."

Moments after they reached Ravenglass, Maggie called back. "I've just spoken to Billie. Shona and Durham have been picked up. No aggravation from him, bucketfuls of tears from her. Perfect outcome, eh?"

Not for Josh Durham and his father, Hannah thought. "Any joy with Quiggin?"

"Depends what you wanted to hear. He doesn't have a record."

Hannah wasn't too surprised. If Quiggin had abducted Lily, she didn't suppose it was because he was a sexual predator. Unless, that is, the reason for the breakdown of his marriage was that he'd taken an unhealthy interest in Carrie. It might be worth tracking down the ex-wife, and seeing what she had to say.

When he opened the door to them, Quiggin swayed slightly, as if the sight of them knocked him off balance. Judging by the smell of his breath, he'd had a drink or two since their last conversation. Alcohol might loosen his tongue.

"Chief Inspector! I wasn't expecting to see you again."

"Just called for a quick update." This was so vague as to be meaningless, but Quiggin nodded, as if reassured. "May we...?"

"All right." He sounded exhausted, and his shoulders slumped as he accompanied them down the passageway. Squeezing into his tiny office, Hannah found it hard to tear her eyes away from the photograph of the dead daughter. She'd have been over forty now. The same age as Joanna Footit.

"If you're wondering," he said, "I've not heard from Joanna. I presume there's still no sign of her?"

"We simply wanted to let you know," Hannah said disingenuously, "there has been a development."

"Oh yes?" He seemed agitated. The bottle of Johnnie Walker and empty tumbler on his desk might explain his twitchiness. Or perhaps there was another reason.

"Her car has been found by the dunes at Drigg. Seems like she left it there overnight."

"You don't think…she's done anything silly, do you?"

"Like what?"

"Well…harming herself." He coughed, as if embarrassed. "Committing suicide."

"It's too early to rule anything in or out. Did she seem depressed to you?"

"On the contrary." His brow furrowed. "She did say something about putting things right."

"Putting things right? How, exactly?"

Quiggin scrunched his unlovely features into a parody of a man racking his brains. "Oh, I can't remember. Something about being glad to be back in the Lake District, a chance to put things right. She said it in passing, and I didn't cross-examine her."

"Is she an attractive woman, would you say?"

"I'm not sure what you mean."

Hannah said quietly, "It's a straightforward question, Mr Quiggin."

"Are you suggesting that I harassed the poor woman? Propositioned her, or something?"

"I'm not suggesting anything. But you found her attractive?"

"Just because I'm single, I'm fair game, am I?" His face was bright red. "I don't mess about with my guests. It wouldn't be…. seemly. Or sensible, given that people can rant and rave about the slightest thing on the Internet. I suppose you've read that review of this place when that Scottish woman made a fuss, and said I was creepy?"

The drink was talking. They might be getting somewhere.

"I'm not aware of that."

"I've had enough of women, let me tell you." His voice was shaking. "Most of those I've met have been bad news. I'm happier on my own."

"All I asked was whether she was attractive."

"The answer is no, not really." His voice was shaking. "If you want the truth, she looked rather odd. Very tall and thin, with lots of vivid red hair. Perhaps she dyes it, I don't know about these things. All I can tell you is this. She seemed like a nice woman, and I tried to make her welcome. Satisfied?"

"Have you any idea what she did after she left here for that talk in the pub about the history of murder?"

"None whatsoever." His jaw jutted forward. "That's…that's my last word on the subject. Now, if that's all…"

Les picked up the photograph of Carrie North. "Does this remind you of anyone, Mr Quiggin?"

"Put that down!" Quiggin reached out, and snatched the picture from Les' hand, tearing it slightly. Tears formed in the man's eyes. "Now see what you've done! I think you'd better leave."

"Sorry, Mr Quiggin, we don't want to upset you," Hannah said. "It's just that there is a strong resemblance between your daughter in this photo and…"

"She has my wife's features, not mine. You're not suggesting some other man was her father?" He was crying now. "It's an absolute lie!"

"No, no. We're not suggesting anything like that." Hannah kept her voice calm, although her thoughts were racing. "Please don't upset yourself, Mr Quiggin. I wasn't referring to your wife, but to Lily Elstone."

He wiped his face with his shirt sleeve. "Gray's girl? She was much younger."

"Lily's looks were mature for her years."

He looked at her as if she were insane. "I'm not with you. Lily was short. Carrie was blond, Lily wasn't."

"Lily dyed her hair blond shortly before she went missing," Les said.

"Give me a second." The scrunched-up expression of concentration reappeared. "Lily was much younger. Carrie was a woman, not a schoolgirl. You surely can't believe it's important."

Hannah felt an urge to bang her head against the wall. Surely Quiggin wasn't a good enough actor to lie so plausibly? It seemed they were no further forward as regards either Lily Elstone's fate or Joanna's.

She said quietly, "When we deal with old, difficult cases, we need to look at every possible angle. That's all we are doing. I'm sorry about your photograph."

Quiggin shut his eyes. "It's all right, Chief Inspector. I'm overwrought, that's all. I've had a few drinks today, but still I can't forget. You see, today is the anniversary."

"Anniversary?"

"Of the day Carrie died."

> > >

"Coincidences?" Hannah asked once they were outside. "Or something else?"

It was drizzling again, and Les hitched up his coat collar. "Hate to say it, but I reckon he's telling the truth about Lily."

"We'll soon find out. Let's see if Gray Elstone is still in the office."

Her call went straight through to the accountant. Yindee had probably gone home in a huff by now. Hannah told him about the discovery of Joanna's abandoned car.

"Good God, that's dreadful! The poor thing. I never imagined she would…it must all have become too much."

"One possibility is that she's left the area voluntarily."

"Why would she do that? It doesn't make sense."

"We don't have any answers at the moment, I'm afraid, but our colleagues are doing all they can to find out where she is."

He made a gulping noise. "I told you, she has a history of attempting suicide. For all I know, there have been other incidents during the past twenty years. I wonder..."

"Yes?"

"I wonder if she came back here to say goodbye."

"We're keeping an open mind, Mr Elstone." He mumbled something inarticulate in reply. "By the way, there was something else. This resemblance between your daughter and Carrie, the girl who died in the crash."

"Yes, yes, I've been thinking about that. I did wonder if you were implying that Alvaro Quiggin was in some way responsible for snatching Lily. I have to say I find it impossible to believe. He's not like that."

He's not like that. Hannah had often heard it said about people who proved eventually to be very much like that. "When Lily met him, was her hair blond, the same colour as when she disappeared?"

"Why do you ask?" When Hannah didn't answer, he fell silent for a few moments. "No, I'm certain that it wasn't. She wanted to change things in her life. She was fed up of Anya, and her dearest wish was to get away from her, and come and live with me."

"And she dyed her hair shortly before her disappearance?"

"Oh yes. Only a day or two before. Then she insisted on having her picture taken. She loved posing for the camera. *The new me*, that's how she described the look."

"I see. Thanks, you've been helpful."

"I'm reluctant to say this, Chief Inspector, but all this talk about photographs doesn't seem likely to get you anywhere."

"I understand the point you're making, Mr Elstone." She went through the usual rigmarole about needing to consider the case from every angle. It was the truth, so why did it sound so false when she tried to explain? As she ended the call, she felt her stomach churn. They were no closer to finding Lily Elstone, and now someone else was missing.

◇◇◇

"Cheer up," Les said, as they walked into the pub. "Your feller will be here in a minute. What are you having?"

His eyes wandered toward the bar, where an elderly customer was ogling the Polish barmaid and her equally well-endowed colleague, but Hannah's main concern was to make sure Scott Durham wasn't here, drowning his sorrows. After talking to one man whose daughter was dead, and another whose daughter had disappeared never to return, she could do without a close encounter with a man whose son would soon be locked up for years. There was only so much gloom and doom you could take in one afternoon. Let someone else break the bad news.

A table next to the window was free. Leave the men to drink in the view of the barmaids; she'd rather contemplate the estuary. Even on this grey, grim day, there was something magical about the shimmer of light on the waves. She was only vaguely aware of the village's past, but the Romans had known what they were doing when they'd chosen to build a port here.

"Here he is," Les said, as Daniel strolled into the bar. "The history man. What do you fancy? I'm buying."

Hannah laughed. "I see there's a two-for-one offer on the light bites."

Daniel grinned. "Orange juice for me, please. I can't face water, I've seen enough in the past hour to last a lifetime. Thank God the drains didn't collapse during my talk. Half the audience might have drowned."

He dropped a kiss on Hannah's cold cheek. "You look tired. Rough day?"

"I'm just hoping Joanna Footit hasn't actually drowned."

He squeezed her hand. "Want to tell me about it?"

While Les bought drinks and food, she recounted the events of her day. Daniel was a good listener, and his intensity when he concentrated was flattering. Would he be equally interested in her once she moved out of Tarn Cottage?

"This photograph of Carina North," he said. "There's a close likeness to Lily Elstone despite the age gap?"

"At first glance, definitely. Lily inherited her mother's good looks. She'd have passed for nineteen or twenty, no problem."

"Did Robbie Dean know Lily?"

"Doubtful. Elstone doesn't do his accounts, and I'm sure they don't mix in the same circles. Dean doesn't come over as a social animal. Why?"

"Carrie was Dean's girlfriend. What if he saw Lily, and was spooked by the resemblance?"

Les banged his fist on the table. "Good call. We focused on Quiggin because he was Carrie's father. But Dean..."

"Was responsible for Carrie's death," Hannah interrupted. "Nobody's mentioned any other relationships with women. That car crash changed his life. It ruined his career in football, but he also lost his girlfriend. It's easy to assume a man like that doesn't care about anyone but himself, those are the vibes he gives out. But what if he was obsessed with Carrie?"

"And what if years later," Les muttered, "he knocked a pretty girl off his bike, only to find she was Carrie's lookalike?"

"There's more," Daniel said. "I asked about Dean because I've been talking to Edwin Broderick about Dean's granddad."

Hannah sipped her drink. "His granddad?"

"Yes, the lad's parents died young, and he went to live with his grandparents. Old Joe Dean's cottage at Lower Drigg was his pride and joy. He bought it before the Second World War broke out, and his attitude was that an Englishman's home was his castle." Daniel leaned back in his chair. He hadn't touched his drink or meal. "Edwin is an expert on war-time Cumbria. He's told me all about the Barrow Blitz, when the Luftwaffe tried to destroy the shipyards at Barrow-in-Furness in the early years of the war. Not far down the coast from here."

"Fascinating," Les said, "but can we get back to Robbie Dean?"

"The gun range at Eskmeals was a target for the German bombers." A dreamy look drifted across Daniel's face, a look Hannah had seen before when he was transported in his mind to a different place and time. "So was an explosives factory at Calder Hall, the site that became the nuclear plant. Munitions works were dotted around West Cumbria. Drigg had one, for instance. The Luftwaffe would have loved to destroy it. How do you think Grandad Dean reacted?"

"Get on with it," Hannah said. "The suspense is killing us"

"The old man was scared stiff that enemy bombers would reduce his home to rubble. An Anderson shelter in the garden wasn't good enough for him. He decided, to quote Edwin, *to convert his cellars into the biggest bloody private air raid shelter for miles around. Folk said it was more like an underground palace than a place of refuge.*"

Daniel paused, his dark eyes glittering with barely suppressed excitement. "I'm guessing Robbie Dean didn't show you round downstairs?"

Chapter Twenty-one

On waking, Joanna fooled herself for a moment that this was merely one more nightmare. She was lying on an uncomfortable old mattress in a small, square room that smelled of urine. Dim light from a naked bulb shone on whitewashed walls and a rough stone floor. There were no windows, but one wall had a steel door. An old-fashioned cylinder radiator stood against the opposite wall, but no warmth came from it. It was like being trapped inside a freezer. The room was bare, apart from a dirty white duvet draped across her body, and a vile plastic toilet. She must be below ground, but the ceiling seemed high for a cellar. An extractor unit was set in it, adjacent to a small oblong panel of sheet metal. A trapdoor? No, it wasn't big enough for a child to squeeze through, let alone a grown man or woman.

The duvet was scant use or comfort in a room so dank. Numb with cold and misery, she shifted her position. There was a pressure on her right wrist from a tight leather bracelet with a lock and buckle. She felt woozy, and her face hurt, where he'd ripped off the tape gagging her. A sour taste lingered in her mouth, and her throat was sore where the knife had nicked it. Something scratched her left ankle, and when she shrugged aside the duvet to take a look, her gorge rose. This was nothing like the bad dreams she'd endured a thousand times before. He had tethered her to a rusty chain, and stripped off most of her clothes, leaving only her cotton under-shirt, bra, and knickers.

The chain was locked to an iron ring fixed into the wall behind her, and when she moved, the link bit into her flesh. She retched, but there was nothing inside her to vomit up. Her stomach felt burnt and empty. She'd been sick after the stranger seized her, she remembered now.

After dragging her out of her car, he'd tied her wrists with cord, and forced her to drink from a flask. She was shaking so much that some of the liquid spilled down her jaw instead of going into her mouth, angering him so that he pulled her hair hard, and brought tears to her eyes. The stuff smelled foul, and tasted bitter.

"Please," she'd gasped. "Why are you doing this to me?"

The man in the crash helmet gave no answer. He just took a roll of masking tape from the pocket of his anorak, and tore off a strip. Knowing that if she screamed, nobody would hear, and he'd make her suffer even more, she'd remained limp and unresisting as he taped her mouth shut.

As he tugged her trousers down, she'd felt his hands on her bare thighs. At last, she realised she'd been right. This wasn't Nigel. But it wasn't a stranger, either.

> > >

Joanna heard the metal panel in the ceiling slide open. Scared and exhausted, she'd dozed fitfully, but the sudden clatter reminded her that this nightmare was only just beginning. For a few seconds, she dared not open her eyes, terrified of what she might see. When she forced herself to look up, she saw a face framed in the opening. No, the metal panel wasn't a trapdoor. More like something from a sick peep-show.

Robbie Dean was watching her.

"Why?" She sounded like an old, hoarse woman.

"You should never have come back."

"I…I didn't…"

"You've ruined everything." His voice trembled with temper; he sounded like a child on the brink of a tantrum.

Despite her weakness, she summoned up the strength to protest. "I haven't…I never meant to bother you."

Why did he hate her? She'd never done him any harm. There was a strange wariness in his expression. She tried to persuade herself his rage wasn't caused by hate, but by uncertainty, as if he didn't know what to do.

His face disappeared, and the panel slid back into place. He was furious, yes, but that wasn't all. He sounded—nonsensical as it seemed to Joanna, chained to the wall of a mouldy cellar—on the verge of tears.

Hungry and feeble and afraid, she closed her eyes. Jumbled images swam through her mind. Robbie laughing in the car, seconds before it swerved off the road. Robbie, spotting her at the Dungeon House, the morning after the night before. Robbie, groping her in the darkness on the beach at Seascale. The rough touch of his calloused hands when he pulled down her trousers had triggered a long-buried memory. Had he raped her? He'd left her knickers on, and she didn't feel sore between her legs, but…

What was that? The rattle of a key in a lock. The door was opening. Robbie limped into the little room. He was breathing hard. She craned her neck, trying to see what lay on the other side of the door, but he shut it behind him with exaggerated care.

"So," he said.

One question she must ask, however much she feared the answer.

"What…what are you going to do with me?"

"Wait and see."

"If you let me go, I won't tell people about this," she whispered. "Not a word, not to anyone. I can keep a secret, nobody knows that better than you. This can be…just between us."

He glared as if she were out of her mind. "You don't understand. It's the story of your fucking life."

"I know, I'm stupid." Desperation was making her talk. If she kept the conversation going, he might relent. "Tell me, help me to understand."

"You're in the punishment cell."

"The punishment cell?" She looked around. "Are we underneath your cottage? Why would you want to punish me, Robbie?"

He groaned, as if the question was obtuse. "I don't want to hurt you."

Despite knowing she mustn't provoke his temper, her own anger welled up. "Hurt me? How do you think I feel right now?"

"Don't make it any worse for yourself. You can't escape. I can do anything I want down here. I could have fucked you all night, and you couldn't have done a fucking thing to stop me."

"But you didn't," she breathed.

"No." He spat out the word, and for all her helplessness, she felt a surge of relief. "I'll only hurt you if I need to. But you have to obey the rules."

"The rules?"

"If you don't…that's what this punishment cell is for."

"But I haven't broken any rules." She squinted at him through aching eyes. He seemed distracted, as if keeping a woman against her will in an underground prison wasn't the most urgent problem on his mind. "What's this all about? Nobody's going to pay a ransom for me."

"Same old Joanna." There were dark rings under his eyes, and his haggard features had aged ten years in twenty-four hours, but an odd touch of triumph sounded in his voice. "Got it all wrong as usual."

"Why am I wrong?"

"It's not money that I care about." He sucked the foetid air into his lungs. "Remember Carrie? She came back to be with me."

⟩⟩⟩

Joanna was locked up and alone again. Robbie had left her without another word, and when she heard the key turn in the padlock on the door, she wondered if he meant her to starve to death. He was mad, must be. Carrie North had been dead and gone for twenty-odd years. He was living in an insane world of his own, and for some unfathomable reason, he'd taken her prisoner.

As she drifted off to sleep, in her head she heard again the raucous chatter from that smoke-filled car, as it hurtled through the darkened countryside. Robbie, reeling out one dirty joke after another, while he kept one hand on the wheel and another up Carrie's skirt. Joanna hardly listened. They'd all had a lot to drink, and she was content to snuggle up to Nigel, while his hands explored inside her satin top.

Was it the car crashing or the rattle of the padlock that woke her? She'd no idea how many hours had passed. Time didn't exist in this stinking hell. Opening her eyes, she saw Robbie Dean framed in the doorway.

"You need to drink some water. And to eat. Not too much, mind, otherwise you'll spew it out."

"Thank you." Her voice was faint and scratchy. He was a monster, but she mustn't enrage him, not while he had her at his mercy.

"Come into the living room if you want. But you have to promise to behave."

"The…living room?"

"Yeah, it's where we spend most of the time. This place…" indicating their surroundings, "is the punishment cell. For Carrie, if she breaks the rules."

"I don't understand."

He made an exasperated noise. "You never understand, do you, Joanna? Listen, are you going to behave yourself? Do as I say, or you'll regret it."

"Yes, yes." She was whimpering. "Please. I'll behave."

"Five minutes."

He shut the door with a bang, and once again she heard him lock her in. Shivering, she pulled the duvet back over her skinny frame. Absurd as it was, she counted the seconds, to see if he was lying, but before she'd got to six minutes, he started unlocking the door. As he stepped inside the room, she saw that one of his hands held a short length of knotted cord, the other clutched a Stanley knife. Unable to help herself, she gave a yelp of alarm.

"Shut it."

"I'm sorry."

"There's something for you next door. Will you be good?"

She nodded, too scared to speak.

"You'd better be. All right, keep still. I won't cut you unless you force me to."

When he took a step toward her, she flinched, but managed to keep her mouth shut. Holding the knotted end of the cord, he fitted it into a loop in the leather wrist bracelet. She felt him pull it tight before unfastening the ankle chain, and when he jerked her forward, she didn't resist. He gave a grunt of satisfaction, and ridiculously, she felt something close to joy. Perhaps he was telling the truth, and he didn't mean to hurt her, provided she did as she was told.

He shepherded her through the steel door, and she blinked at the unexpected brightness. They were at one end of a long, broad passageway. Recessed ceiling lights shone on smartly painted cream walls, and a brown carpet. This was so different from the punishment cell; they might have strayed into the corridor of a three star hotel. Except that two doors on the left hand side of the passageway had large, imposing bolts as well as padlocks, and were made of steel.

Robbie's limp seemed worse than it had when she'd called at the cottage—was it only yesterday? He shuffled along like a weary, haggard pensioner. Joanna's eyes adjusted, and she saw that further down the corridor was a bank of four small CCTV screens. The pictures were in black and white, and before she could make out what they showed, Robbie slid the bolt on the second steel door. Opening it, he yanked the cord tethering her.

"Inside."

Joanna's eyes widened as she stumbled forward. She was in a large, well-heated room, furnished in a surreal pastiche of opulence. Colossal black leather sofa, plasma screen television, even a cocktail bar padded in matching black leather and two bar stools. The carpet was thick and cream-coloured, but not very clean. On top of the bar counter stood a jug of water and a tumbler, and there were four slices of buttered toast on a plain dinner plate. The two internal doors were made of steel and padlocked. Iron rings were screwed into each of the four walls, and linked to each of them was a long chain connected to something that looked like half of a pair of handcuffs.

He chained her leg to one of the rings, and then unfastened the cord from her wrist with the efficiency of long practice. She could walk, but not as far as the door. He motioned her to sit on one of the bar stools.

"Comfier, huh?" He forced a grin. "My very own Dungeon House."

She felt dazed, as if he'd clubbed her on the head. For a moment she thought she was going to fall off the stool, but she managed to keep her balance. His boast did give her a glimmer of insight. Robbie had created a subterranean parody of the pampered lifestyle led by the Whiteleys.

He pointed to the food and drink on the counter. "Get summat inside you."

"Thank you." She ventured a timid smile, and nibbled a piece of toast. She'd read that captives who establish a bond with their kidnappers stand a better chance of survival. And one thing she did know, with sudden, blinding clarity, was that she very much wanted to survive. "Would you like to tell me…?"

Putting a calloused forefinger to his lips, he said, "Don't talk. Just eat."

He hobbled over to the door. At eye level, he'd put an observation panel. It reminded her of those prison doors you saw in films and on television. A few seconds later, she was alone again. Nervous of being sick, she took little bites of toast, washing them down with gulps of water. Her stomach still hurt, but she kept the food down. That was better. It was so warm that she felt drowsy, but she splashed a few drops of the precious water on to her face to help her keep awake. She needed to think, try to work out a way to escape. For all her weakness and confusion, her brain hadn't quite stopped functioning. Frightened as she was, she told herself she must subdue her panic at being locked up in a confined space. Her life depended on it.

A loud noise broke through her thoughts. One of the internal doors behind her was opening. She craned her neck to see what was happening.

In the doorway, hands on slender hips, stood a young woman with shoulder-length blond hair and vivid crimson lipstick. She wore a very short white dress with a low top revealing plenty of pale flesh. Carrie North had returned to life.

> > >

"You do realise, don't you?" Les said. "This is the longest of long shots?"

"We can leave it for today, if you want," Hannah said. They were back inside the car, watching the rain as it bludgeoned the windscreen. A poor day was turning into a vile evening, but she didn't care. They'd asked Dean if the cottage had a cellar, and he'd said no. Why not mention the air raid shelter, if he had nothing to hide? Perhaps it no longer existed, perhaps he was just a miserable, uncommunicative sod, but instinct told her he was keeping a secret. She couldn't help feeling excited; they might at last be getting somewhere. They'd left Daniel in the pub, finishing his chicken salad, and Les had offered to take a turn behind the wheel. "Or we can call Divisional HQ, and run it past the Brief for a quick decision," she said.

Les snorted with derision. Hannah's new boss, appointed in a temporary capacity after the unmourned departure of his predecessor, was notoriously cautious. One of the Fed reps had nicknamed him the Brief, because he was as cautious as any lawyer. The Brief would wet himself if there was any prospect of a complaint about police harassment from a self-righteous Robbie Dean.

"'This man committed his one and only crime almost a quarter of a century ago, and he paid a high price'." Les, an unexpectedly good mimic, captured the Brief's gift for sounding more like defence counsel than a detective. "'He's already allowed you to look round his home, without any hint of compulsion. Turn up again ninety minutes later, and you run the risk that he'll slam the door in your face, and get on to m'learned friends first thing tomorrow. And the last thing we want is litigation, isn't it?"

Hannah laughed. "Perish the thought."

"All right, let's rattle Dean's cage. Doesn't matter if we spook him. Our last visit probably did the damage. This rain's lashing down, and if we don't get a move on, we'll find ourselves marooned. Don't know about you, but an overnight in Little Drigg isn't on my bucket list."

"For all we know, Dean's cellar flooded years ago. Or was bricked up."

"Fine. The minute he shows us the evidence, we're out of there."

"Who are you?" the young woman demanded.

"My name's Joanna Footit," she stammered. "And you…?"

"He calls me Carrie." Her voice shook with contempt. Her gaunt features reminded Joanna of Carrie North's skinny *chic*, but despite her appearance, she sounded nothing like Carrie. She was better educated, for a start. "Really, I'm Lily. Lily Elstone."

"Oh my God! He's tried to turn you into…"

"Carrie North, yeah. A fucking dead bitch." Lily paused. "You knew her?"

"Yes, yes. I was with her in Robbie's car…when she died."

"Is that why he brought you here?"

"I was tricked. I was sent a message pretending to be from… someone else. Then Robbie made me drink some horrible stuff…"

"Chloral hydrate," Lily said. "Tastes like shit, huh? Trust me, I know."

"Three whole years you've been here?" Joanna struggled to grasp the enormity of it. Robbie Dean, a kidnapper. A successful kidnapper, too. Everyone else believed Lily was dead. Down here, you might as well be. His elaborate precautions made escape impossible.

"Yeah. Stinks like a pig sty, this place, doesn't it? Don't worry, you get used to anything in time. The first year is the worst, you'll find."

Her laugh was harsh, but Joanna told herself the girl didn't mean to be unkind. "What happened?"

"He knocked me off my bike, and next thing I know, I'm trussed up like a fucking chicken in some underground Alcatraz."

Joanna breathed out. "What has he done to you?"

"All sorts." Lily rolled up the left sleeve of her dress. A livid scar ran down her arm from elbow to wrist. "That's for when I bit him." She lifted up her skirt, and pointed to a faded red mark below her thigh. "That was when I tried to get out of this shit-hole. There's more, but I'd need to know you better."

Her laughter was raw. Joanna didn't know what to say. Gray's daughter: it was too much to take in. At least he missed her, and thought about her all the time. Would anybody even notice her own disappearance? Might Nigel raise the alarm? Was it too much to hope that he'd suspect Robbie had taken her, and ride to the rescue?

"Don't worry," Lily said. "He won't rape you. Probably won't even try. He gave up with me ages ago. And, no offence, but I'm the one who looks like his long lost love."

"Gave up?"

"Can't manage it, can he?" The crimson lips curved in a brutal smile. "But don't make fun of him. I called him an old softy once. Big mistake."

"He tortured you." Horror after horror. How had this poor girl survived? She must be so strong.

"Sort of." The smile vanished. "It's not all one-way traffic, though. He's smart, but not that smart. Now and then, I get the better of him. Small victories, tiny really, but they keep me sane. More or less."

"Robbie's the one who is mad."

Lily gave the cocktail bar a withering look. "Yeah, I guess you might just have a point. Anyway, there are two of us now, and only one of him. Besides, he's on the edge."

"The edge?"

"Yeah, he's changed this past day or two. Don't ask me why. He seems knackered. And he's getting careless."

"Really?"

"Not so long ago, he wouldn't have dreamed of letting me walk around without my chain. It's like he's losing heart. Any idea why he's brought you here?"

"No, no, I can't imagine."

Lily was trying to be strong, Joanna thought, but her thin arms were shaking. "I only hope, like, he's not thinking of... doing something really rash."

"What do you mean?" Joanna's voice was scarcely audible. "Oh God, what can we do?"

"We don't have a choice," Lily said. "It's kill or be killed."

"That's Nigel Whiteley!" Hannah said, as a black BMW shot out onto the main road ahead of them. "See the personalised number plate?"

"Hard to see anything in this rain."

"Trust me, it's him. That lane he came from is the back road to Ravenglass Knoll."

"You'd expect him to be staying at home. Waiting to hear more about Shona. And he's had a fair bit to drink."

"Must be something special to bring him out in this weather."

"He's driving like a man with a plane to catch. Hey, he's turning left."

"To Drigg? Better put my foot down."

"Not in these conditions, please. We don't want to end up skidding into a hedge."

Les turned into the Drigg road with exaggerated care. No sign of the BMW. "He might be on his way to Seascale. Paying a call on Gray Elstone?"

"No, it's quicker to stay on the main road."

"You think he's off to see Robbie Dean?"

"His old pal, yes. They go back a long way. " A phrase of Cheryl's floated into her head. *The two of them used to watch porn together.* "He knows Dean better than anyone."

Les groaned. "What d'you reckon? We've little or nothing to go on. If we march in, and find Nigel and Robbie are having a cosy get-together to celebrate the good news about young Shona, we'll both...shit!"

A white van heading from the direction of Drigg overtook a parked car on a bend just ahead of them. Speeding straight toward them. Les wrenched the steering wheel, and their car skidded across the road, but the van was too fast. At the moment of impact, Hannah glimpsed the name on the side.

Deano Garden Services.

〉〉〉

Time passed. To Joanna, it seemed an eternity before the observation panel in the door slid open. Looking up, she saw Robbie Dean peering at her from the passageway. He said nothing, and neither did she. She heard a sound—shuffling feet?—and the panel slid back into place.

Slowly, slowly, slowly, the steel door swung open. Joanna held her breath as the man stepped inside. The instant he crossed the threshold, Lily, standing on the far side of the door, brought down on his head the chain she held in both hands. The noise made as his skull broke was sickening. He screamed in agony, and fell on to his knees. Without hesitating, Lily smashed him again with the chain, right across the face, and then on the back of his head. His squeal made Joanna think of a dying pig. Blood spilled from his wounds, spattering on the wall, and disfiguring the cream carpet on which he sprawled.

Joanna gasped in horror, and Lily froze before she could land another lethal blow with the chain. Their plan had been simple. They'd agreed it was foolproof. Attack Robbie, steal his keys, and find a way out.

Only one problem. The body wasn't Robbie Dean's.

"Omigod!" Lily shrieked. "Who is he?"

Robbie stepped in from the passageway, and ripped the chain out of her hands. Tottering, Lily caught her foot on the man's arm, and tumbled to the floor, landing an inch or two away from the body. Rocking on his heels, Robbie watched her, and the dark, spreading pool on the carpet.

"Saved me a job, huh?" Mockery glinted in the deep-set eyes. "You killed lover boy."

"Nigel," Joanna whispered.

Nigel Whiteley's face was mangled, his skull crushed. Half-blinded with tears, she turned her head away. She was too exhausted to weep.

Chapter Twenty-two

"What are you going to do with us?" Lily's voice faltered as she dragged herself back on to her feet.

When Robbie said nothing, she collapsed on to the sofa, and started to sob. The bravado had vanished; all the fight had drained out of her. After waiting so long for her chance to escape, Robbie had outfoxed her. Outfoxed us, Joanna corrected herself. He'd guessed they'd try something, and taken a step back to allow Nigel to enter the room first. Good manners weren't in his make-up; he must have been using his friend as a decoy. The ruse had saved his life, and destroyed Nigel's.

Robbie sat on one of the bar stools, swinging his legs. He didn't speak until Lily forced herself to look him in the eye again.

"What'd you like me to do with you?"

He'd won, and they were at his mercy. Yet in his moment of triumph, it seemed to Joanna that he was distracted, almost bored. A strange thought popped into her head. *He's lost hope, just like us.*

"Nigel was your friend," she said.

The legs stopped swinging. "You reckon?"

"Why did you let him die? Anyone would think you…hated him."

"You were always fucking dense, Joanna. Never mind that you looked down on Carrie 'cause she never got into college. Why ask me about Nige? You know what he was like."

His contempt stung like a whiplash. *You know what he was like.* Was that right? Yes, she supposed so. It just hurt too much to face the truth.

"So you meant us to kill him?"

"Go to the top of the class." He gave a slow handclap. In the quiet of the underground room, the sound was unnaturally loud. "Nige deserved it, after ruining everything. Same as he always did."

"What do you mean?"

Dragging his attention away from Lily, he considered Joanna, as if she were an insect, waiting to be swatted. "He wanted a turn at the wheel, remember? Desperate to find out what it was like, driving a BMW. Grabbed me by the shoulder, so I spun off the road. Carrie was killed, and I was crippled. You and him walked away without a scratch."

"He was only messing about." Her breath was coming in jerky gasps. Her recollection of that night was fuzzy. She'd had too much to drink. "You were driving too fast. Anyway, you had concussion. Your memory's not reliable."

"I remember," he said. "You're the one who lost her marbles, not me."

"Robbie, we all suffered. I was ill for years."

"Nige was fine." He sniffed noisily, wiping his nose with the back of a hairy hand. "You know he was just practising with you? Told me himself. You were too young."

"You're wrong. It was Amber who was too young."

"Nah, Nige liked them older. Much older. That wife of his was ancient, that's why they only had the one kid." He sniggered, as if making her writhe was the last pleasure left for him to take. "You were up against the lovely Lysette. You had no chance."

"No." Her voice was shrill. "No!"

"Followed him that night, didn't you? When he gave you the brush off?"

"He never...."

"Hey, I was there. Watching the two of you, after you left the pub and went for a walk on the beach. All very lovey-dovey, but he was stringing you along. You were his alibi, just like the way Lysette started flirting with his dad. The minute Nige got shut of you, he went to her."

"It's not true!"

"Bollocks. You followed him." There wasn't a shred of pity in his voice, she thought. He despised weakness, and she was weak. Always had been, most of all where Nigel was concerned. "I saw you. You waited half a minute, then jumped on your bike, and pedalled after him. Bet you started wetting yourself when he wound up at the Dungeon House. Suppose you thought he fancied shagging Amber."

Her eyes widened. She wanted to scream in protest, but could not make a sound.

"Went tits-up, didn't it? For once in his life. Nige was always such a lucky bugger." He jerked a thumb toward the battered corpse. "Till tonight, anyway."

Lily said feebly, "What is this? What are you talking about?"

"History lesson. Once upon a time at the Dungeon House."

"I don't get it."

He shrugged and turned away from her. The spell was broken, Joanna thought. For three years, he'd obsessed over this girl, but then she'd tried to kill him. Now she was no better than Joanna.

"Nige was waiting in the summer house for Lysette, but Malcolm shot her. Amber ran off to the quarry garden, and Nige went up there to find out what all the commotion was about. Nige and Amber finished up together on the top path. She'd realised what was happening was his fault, as much as Malcolm's. He'd been shagging her mum in secret, and using her and you as a blind. She went all hysterical, and started punching him with her little fists. Until he pushed her over the edge."

"You can't be sure of that!" Joanna cried.

"You saw him yourself, you said so the next morning."

"I…I was confused. How could I be certain what I saw? It was dark, and so frightening.…Nigel would never have meant to…"

"He meant it, all right."

"You don't know that!"

"Nige told me," Robbie Dean said. "Yeah, I wormed the truth out of him. He fessed up when I went round to see him on the Sunday. Not twenty-four hours after he murdered Amber."

›〉〉

"Will he be okay?" Hannah asked the ginger-haired paramedic, as her male colleague helped the driver of Dean's van to his feet. He was the troglodyte Hannah and Les had met up at Ravenglass Knoll. His shaven-headed sidekick was sitting on his haunches at the side of the road, swearing at the rain.

The traffic crew had closed the road, and the blue flashing lights of ambulance and traffic patrol car had tempted a handful of onlookers to brave the downpour, but there was precious little for them to see. Their car had mounted the pavement, front wing badly dented but otherwise unscathed, and safe to drive away. The van was a write-off. Having caught the car a glancing blow as Les tried desperately to avoid a head-on collision, it had swerved straight into a low garden wall.

"Broken ribs, shoulder, and nose," the paramedic murmured, "but it looks worse than it really is."

"Yeah, he wasn't exactly Jude Law before he got covered in blood."

"You know him?"

"Les and I had a brief encounter with this pair earlier today."

The paramedic considered the wrecked van. "Lucky devil, he got off lightly. All four of you did. Even so, take what I said seriously. Whiplash symptoms often don't present for six to twelve hours. If you experience any discomfort…"

"Right, thanks, got the message." Hannah clapped the woman on the back. Her neck was fine, but she felt spaced out. The collision had shocked her, but she couldn't risk being carted off to hospital for a better-safe-than-sorry check up. "Go and tend to your patient. I'll have a quick word with his pal."

When the drenched lad saw Hannah approaching, he rubbed his left arm with a theatrical grimace, and the swearing became an incoherent moan. She diagnosed a young man feeling sorry for himself rather than someone in serious pain. No doubt he was hoping to blag his way to a bit of compensation. Folk like him had helped to make Nigel Whiteley rich.

"There, there. Now, why were you in such a tearing hurry?"

"The boss gave us a bonus, like, and we were off to have a few bevvies."

"A bonus? What for?"

"Don't ask me. Never happened before. We turned up as usual, to put the equipment in the store for the night, but he said he'd sort it out. Told us to piss off, and treat ourselves. He gave us a hundred quid each."

"Generous."

"Obvious, innit?" He gave a salacious wink, and she guessed he wanted to embarrass her, petty revenge for the loss of his night in the pub with the troglodyte. "Bet he had a woman there. Dirty bugger wanted us out of the way so he could hurry up, and get his leg over."

> > >

Joanna's temples were throbbing, and the smell in the room was making her nauseous. They were sharing a tomb with a dead man. Soon Robbie would murder her, and Lily too. What use did he have for either of them? She must keep him talking, whatever the cost. At times in the past, she'd scarcely cared whether she lived or died. Now, when she was in danger through no fault of her own, she cared with a wild desperation.

Robbie said, "Nige would've killed you, that night, if he'd caught you. Lucky you ran for your life, and he was too busy keeping out of Malcolm's way to chase you."

"I was terrified," she said. "In shock. I wept all night long, but I knew I had to go back, and collect my bike. I'd left it on the drive. I needed my wig, too. It caught on a branch when I was running, and I didn't have time to rescue it. I heard the rifle shot, but I didn't know Malcolm had shot himself. Or what I'd find there the next morning."

"You found me."

True. She'd arrived at the Dungeon House as Robbie turned up to tidy after the barbecue. To her, everything had seemed unreal, out of focus. But Robbie was never one to panic. Not even after stumbling across three corpses, and a young woman half out of her mind. He'd interrogated her like a QC at the Old Bailey.

"You weren't making sense, blathering about Malcolm, and Nigel, and Amber. It's a miracle I figured out what you'd seen."

"I was petrified."

"Did you a favour, didn't I? Let you go, and never told the police you'd been there." He grinned. "You've a lot to thank me for, Joanna. I kept you out of so much shit."

"I never…"

"Said thank you? Well, now's your chance." He waved his hand. "Nah, doesn't matter. Nothing matters now. Soon as the police finished asking me questions, I drove straight round to see Nige. He was expecting the cops to turn up with the handcuffs, but they never showed. It was an open goal. I told him it'd work out fine. We did a deal. I'd look after him, and he'd look after me."

"Look after you?"

"Money, Joanna, loads of it. I was stony broke. No money, no girlfriend, nothing to look forward to. Nige was coming in to a fortune. The Dungeon House was sure to go to his dad, there was no-one else. But he was dying, and Nige thought he'd inherit the lot. Course, he wanted to spite Malcolm, kill his daughter in revenge after Malcolm blew Lysette's head off. And he was shutting Amber up, when if she stayed alive, she'd tell everyone it was his fault. Then there was the cash. Nigel, the millionaire. Yeah, he'd lots of reasons to kill the girl."

Deep down, yes, the truth had lain buried in her subconscious. When you care for someone the way she'd cared for Nigel, you understand what they care about, even if you refuse to accept it. And he loved money, more than anything. More even than Lysette.

"I never believed," she began, "I never believed he'd do… something so awful on the spur of the moment. You've no idea what it was like at the Dungeon House that night. Malcolm bellowing like a wounded tiger, Amber screaming fit to burst. Two intruders in the grounds, Nigel and me. It was chaos. Madness."

Robbie looked at the corpse on the carpet. "Liked taking chances, did Nige. He was set up for life with the wife of a rich man, but Malcolm stole that from him. He didn't think twice about killing Amber when he had the chance. Nobody had any idea what he'd done, except you, and you were too crazy to matter. He was sure you'd top yourself, but you had a breakdown, and then fucked off to Manchester, and that was just as good."

"What about me?" Lily said in a small voice. "Where do I come in?"

"Missed Carrie, didn't I?" He gave her a hard stare. "Haven't you listened to a word I've said? Nigel was too busy to spend any more time watching mucky films with his old mate. Never mind. Once I turned the old air raid shelter into a home from home, all I needed was Carrie to share it with. You were perfect. When I saw your face, your hair….well, I had to go for it. That's one thing Nigel taught me. The moment you're given a chance in life, grab it. Even as a kid, he loved to think of himself as a psycho. But even psychos run out of luck in the end. You brought him bad luck, Joanna. You should never have come back."

"You sent me that message, pretending to be Nigel."

"He asked me to. When you went to see him, he panicked, big style. Not like him, but he lost the plot after Shona went missing."

"I didn't mean to threaten him!" Surely Nigel couldn't have been afraid of her? The mask of friendliness hadn't slipped once, even when she'd dared to make a cryptic reference to what had happened that night at the Dungeon House. "All I said was…"

"Who gives a shit?" Robbie interrupted. "He knew he'd never be safe with you around. So he begged me to take care of you."

A long silence.

"Did he know about Lily?"

Joanna's voice was barely audible. She'd been so loyal to Nigel for so long. Never said that he was to blame for the accident. Never told anyone—except Robbie, of course, when her head was still spinning—about what she'd witnessed at the Dungeon House. She'd paid such a price, suffered such torments. Her health had been ruined, her whole life blown to pieces. How could Nigel, of all people, betray her? It was beyond her worst imagining.

Robbie shrugged. "We never spoke about her. Some things men don't talk about. You're a woman, you wouldn't understand. He guessed, even if he didn't know I'd kept her alive."

"But he…wanted you to keep me here?"

"Nah, you're kidding yourself. He wanted me to finish you off, said it was the only way he'd be safe." He paused for effect. "Wanted me to drown you, off Drigg Point. Make it look like suicide."

She swallowed hard. "You didn't do it, though. You brought me here."

"Nige has ordered me around for years." His voice was hard. "Killing you was never going to work. If he'd thought straight, he'd never have suggested it. I only agreed 'cause he said he'd let the police know I took Lily. Of all the days to threaten me. He'd forgotten tonight is the anniversary."

"Anniversary?"

"Don't' tell me you've forgotten too? Of the accident, stupid."

"Oh." She exhaled. "Sorry. It…slipped my mind."

"He might as well have told the police. They've come sniffing round already."

"The police?" Her heartbeat quickened.

He laughed; a cruel, discordant noise. "You look as though you've wet yourself. No need to get excited. I showed them over the house, and they buggered off again."

She bent her head. Was that the last hope gone?

"Nige should have trusted me, but the cops went to see him." Robbie was almost shouting. "His daughter's been found, but did he thank his lucky stars? Not Nige, he came here to throw his weight around. That's when I knew everything had changed. He'd messed up, and I was paying the price."

He walked across the room, and kicked the corpse's torso. "Well, he paid too. Least he didn't die in vain. Now I know there's nobody I can trust."

The tear-streaked girl cringed under his gaze. Joanna could read her mind. *He still hasn't answered the question. What is he going to do with us?*

Robbie was a mind-reader too. "It's over. Nige's fault, as usual."

Jangling the keys in his pocket, he strode out of the room. Joanna was paralysed, and so was Lily. They didn't even twitch when the steel door crashed shut behind him.

"It's not every day they have this much excitement in Drigg, ma'am," Azeem, a traffic sergeant with a Yorkshire accent broader than Les Bryant's, was with Hannah in her car. The road was open again, and the giant young constable and Les were standing outside in the teeming rain, talking to the recovery vehicle's driver. He'd loaded the wrecked van, which was ready to make its final journey.

"First, a woman goes missing, and leaves her things and a mysterious note in her car. Now a POLAC with a DCI in the passenger seat. Glad you weren't driving, ma'am, We'd have had to call out the Superintendent, and on a night like this..."

"Too right," Hannah said. A police accident had to be investigated by an officer of a higher rank than the driver involved. She'd have made herself unpopular, even though nobody could doubt who was to blame. "Talking about that misper, would you mind lending us a hand? We were making for Lower Drigg. An old acquaintance of the woman has a cottage there."

Azeem pondered. Hannah had met him a couple of times at force-wide conferences, and they'd agreed there was more to traffic work than catching people who thought speed limits didn't apply to them. Some senior detectives condescended to traffic officers, but she'd often found their input helped to solve serious crimes. Not many burglars walked to their work, for one thing, and ANPR provided clues to all manner of offences. Checking driver details with the help of automatic number plate recognition threw up countless cases of people driving without insurance, or a valid MOT certificate, or whatever, and experience showed that those who broke one law often broke others. Azeem had all the instincts of a good detective.

"Deano, you mean?" He pointed to the recovery lorry. "The gardener those scrotes work for?"

"Spot on. Robbie Dean is our man. We called there this afternoon, and didn't find anything untoward. What he didn't tell us is that there's a large air raid shelter under the premises. There's probably nothing in it, but, Les and I want to check it out. He won't be overjoyed to see us, and it'd be useful to have a uniformed presence. Just in case."

"Glad to help, ma'am." Azeem lowered his window and called to his colleague. "Ready, Beefy? We've got work to do."

"What's in the other room?" Joanna asked.

The five minutes since Robbie's departure felt like five hours. She'd spent the time trying to calm Lily down. For years, the girl had dreamed of the day when she killed her captor, and made her escape. The chance had come and gone, and now they were incarcerated with only a corpse for company.

"It's the bedroom. There's no way out." Lily managed a wan smile. "Trust me, I've checked."

"What is this place?"

"An old air raid shelter. His grandad built it, and he tarted it up, so he could be here with this Carrie, the girl who died."

"He'll come back."

"No way, you heard what he said." She pointed at Nigel's body. "This bastard ruined it all for him."

"What do you think he will do, then?"

Lily shivered. "I've lost count of the number of times he's said that he couldn't bear to lose me. Lose Carrie, I mean. Life wouldn't be worth living, those were his words."

This time, Robbie Dean wasn't answering the door. Nigel Whiteley's BMW was parked on the verge in front of the cottage, but there were no lights in the windows, no sign that anyone was inside. With Azeem and Beefy stationed in the lane, Hannah and Les walked round the house, but found nothing. The outbuildings were locked, and when they peered through the single cobwebbed window, there was no obvious means of access to the air raid shelter.

Les indicated a rusty garden roller. "I'd like to move that, see if it's covering something. Or maybe there's a way down underneath the van."

"Yeah, there was a lot of clutter in that pantry, if you remember. He lives like a slob, but the rubbish might also hide any trapdoor leading to a staircase."

"Time to invoke the Ways and Means Act?"

Code for finding an excuse—any excuse—to make an entry. They might even rely on the law that allowed the emergency service to force their way into a private house if there was a reasonable belief it was necessary to save life or avert serious harm. Whatever. All Hannah cared about was getting inside the cottage. She'd convinced herself that Joanna was there. What she couldn't guess was whether the woman was dead or alive.

"His other van is parked here, so he can't have gone far."

"He and Whiteley are hiding inside," Les said. "Pound to a penny."

"He should answer the door, then." Hannah kicked at it. "Tell you what, I'm not sure even Beefy could shift something this heavy."

"The kitchen window at the back," Les suggested. "Not double glazed, but not too big, either."

"I can squeeze through it, no problem."

"Not sure that's conduct befitting a DCI," he said.

"Story of my life."

"Chances are, it's alarmed."

"Who cares?" Hannah said. "Not me. Let's do it."

Inside two minutes, the window was open, and she'd managed to wriggle through without straining her ligaments or putting her back out. All the time she kept listening. Was Dean lurking in a dark corner, ready to attack an intruder?

If he really had kidnapped Joanna Footit, he was dangerous, and probably deranged. As she got her bearings, it crossed her mind that this wasn't the cleverest move she'd ever made. Even with Azeem and Beefy in support, so much could go so wrong. And yet.

To wait would be disastrous. For reasons she didn't yet understand, today had seen events racing toward a crisis. Joanna hadn't drowned herself. The note was a crude attempt to throw the police off the track. Something dark and terrible had taken place, and Robbie and Nigel Whiteley were at the centre of it.

"Mr Dean!" she called. "DCI Scarlett. We need to talk to you. Is that all right?"

No answer. She inched forward.

"Ma'am, wait!"

Azeeem was trying to squeeze through the window. Taller and bulkier than Hannah, he had no chance. She waved him back.

"Let me open the front door for you."

"Our man might be lying in wait outside the kitchen."

"Mr Dean!" she called again. "Are you there?"

Nothing. The quiet in the cottage made her flesh creep. She listened intently, but couldn't hear breathing. He wasn't hiding from them, she's stake her life on it. Nobody could be so still, so silent.

She advanced toward the kitchen door. Was some horror film ogre lurking behind it? She pulled the handle with a flourish. The hallway beyond was unlit. With infinite caution, she peered around the door.

Hanging in the hallway, at the bottom of the stairs, was the body of a man, cold and dead. Robbie Dean had put his neck inside a noose suspended from the high ceiling. On the floor was the rickety chair he'd stood on, before kicking it away to allow his neck to snap. On his head was his beloved football cap.

Chapter Twenty-three

"You can still change your mind," Daniel said.

Hannah leaned over, and dropped a kiss on his cheek. They were out in the cipher garden, making the most of a bottle of Chablis and a shimmering sunset. All through a long day at Divisional HQ, she'd been dreading this conversation. So many lines she'd rehearsed in her head. Now, when the moment came to deliver them, every single one seemed clunky and false.

"Thanks, but I've almost finished packing. All the arrangements are made. I pick up the keys from the solicitor tomorrow morning, and hey presto! I'm a householder again."

"Arrangements can be undone." He put his hand on her leg. "Stay here with me. Let the flat out, there will be plenty of takers. "

She moved his hand away. "Sorry."

"I'll let you into a secret," he said. "I've hoped you'd think again about the flat, right from day one."

A heron landed on a branch above the pool. Serene and elegant, it contemplated the view with the air of a feudal lord surveying his fiefdom.

"As soon as I've settled in, you can come over. I'll cook a meal. And I hope you'll invite me back here soon. This place is utterly magical."

"Isn't it?" The heron had seen enough, and flapped its wings. Daniel's eyes followed its flight as it rose above the trees, before disappearing toward the fell. "So your mind's made up?"

Oh God, now was the time to make her little speech. "After all those years with Marc, I need to spend some time living in my own space. It wasn't until he moved out that I began to realise life with him had been suffocating me. Not his fault, at least not entirely. Living together simply didn't suit us as much as I used to pretend to myself." She ran a finger around the rim of her glass. "I like my own company, I discovered. Don't get me wrong. I like yours, too, but right now, I need time by myself."

"I'll take that as a 'yes,' then."

"Nothing's changed between us, Daniel. My staying here was always meant to be temporary. We agreed that on day one."

"I suppose you're right,"

She stretched her arms luxuriantly. "*As usual*, didn't you mean to add?"

"Don't push it." A reluctant smile. "Seriously, I understand what you're saying."

"Yes, I think you do."

"I've enjoyed these last few weeks."

"Me too." She sipped her wine, and counted the lilies on the pool.

"Blissful, isn't it? Such a pity real life keeps getting in the way."

"It doesn't have to."

"It does, you know. We can't spend all our lives in an idyll, that never works. We'd get itchy feet, even in somewhere as close to Paradise as Tarn Fold. It's battling through all the crap the outside world flings at us that makes this such a perfect place for escape. Even if only for hours at a time."

"Talking about the crappy outside world, how much sleep did you get last night?"

Ever since that extraordinary day at Lower Drigg, she'd been plagued by insomnia. In the space of a few hours, she'd survived a car crash, discovered a suicide, and—eventually—helped the rescue team to set Joanna Footit and Lily Elstone free from that vile subterranean tomb, and to recover the body of Nigel Whiteley. She'd seen things beneath the cottage that she'd never forget, but she knew they must be put to the back of her mind. Dean had been as dangerous as he was inadequate, and he mustn't be allowed to mess up her life from beyond the grave. Or mess up the lives of his two captives.

She'd refused to look at any of the dozens of films he'd made of poor, defenceless Lily Elstone, and her top priority was to make sure they were destroyed. They weren't a fit subject for study by academics or psychiatrists in Hannah's opinion, and for as long as they existed, there was a risk they'd be copied, circulated and salivated over. Lily deserved better, after all she had endured. She must be left in peace while she rebuilt her life, back in the open air after three years underground.

The story had caused a sensation, and the last few days had become a dizzying whirl. Colleagues and journalists alike lavished praise on her leadership of the Cold Case team, and there was much glib talk about happy endings. But when night came, and she lay in bed next to Daniel, her mind crowded with hateful images. A man in a noose, his tongue poking out. A wild-eyed girl who'd not seen daylight for years. A corpse with a crushed face.

"Enough. Four or five hours, maybe." This was a lie, but the truth would only make him plead with her to stay here. New flat, fresh start—that was the way to conquer the demons of darkness.

"Will you see that counsellor?" he asked. "Give it a go, you've nothing to lose."

"I'd rather sort things out for myself. Then I'll feel I've achieved something. I know I'm stubborn...."

"Bloody intransigent, more like. I blame my dad. He was pig-headed, too. He was a bad influence on you."

"Think you don't take after him?" she teased. "If not for Ben, things would have turned out very differently for Joanna Footit and Lily Elstone. He didn't go along with the consensus about the Dungeon House, and he was proved right."

"Thanks to you, trusting his instinct."

"Don't be modest. If you hadn't come up with that tit-bit from Edwin about the air raid shelter, Les and I would never have dashed back to the cottage." She lifted her glass. "To the Kinds, father and son. Good detectives."

"What's the latest on Lily?"

"Early days, but the signs are hopeful. I'm not sure you ever get over an ordeal like that, but she's strong-willed. Had to be, to keep her sanity in that hell-hole, held captive by a nutcase who saw her as the reincarnation of the only person he ever loved."

"She must be strong, if she's refused to go back to live with her mother, Has she moved in with Gray Elstone yet?"

"Uh-huh. It's all too much for the woman he was planning to marry. Yindee didn't fancy playing second fiddle to Lily, and she's found herself another sucker. Turns out she'd got very friendly with a financier Elstone acts for. He was supposed to be helping her to set up in business, modeling with clay. Her idea of client relations involved sleeping with him, and now she's moved in with him. Narrow escape for Elstone, if you ask me. As for Anya Jovetic, she and Lily had a tense and unhappy reunion. The upshot is that Anya's washed her hands of the kid, and is heading off to France with her new bloke. Oh, and guess what I heard today?"

"Surprise me," he said lazily.

"Gray asked Joanna to help look after Lily. She and the girl formed a strong bond in the short time they were together."

"Strong enough to conspire to kill a man."

"They were desperate. It was an act of courage, not a crime. With Yindee out of the picture, Joanna and her old boss seem to be hitting it off. She spent all those years fantasising about a cold, selfish murderer. Elstone may not be handsome, or even be the best of accountants, but he's got to be a massive improvement on Nigel Whiteley."

"Has Joanna told you any more about that night at the Dungeon House?"

Hannah sighed. "I'm not sure she even knows for certain what she did see. It was pandemonium that night. It didn't help that she'd been drinking at the barbecue, and then during dinner. If she'd sworn in court that she'd seen Nigel push Amber to her death, counsel for the defence would have had a field day with her. You'd never establish intention to kill on such flimsy eyewitness evidence. Yes, she should have come forward, just as she should have told someone that Nigel was largely to blame for the car crash that killed Carrie, but it's not fair to judge her for keeping quiet. She was severely damaged by everything she went through. Thank God there's no need for a trial."

"You're convinced Nigel was a psychopathic murderer?"

"Absolutely. He killed Amber on impulse, but I'm sure he meant to do it. That's why he lost his nerve so badly when Joanna came back to haunt him. He was a risk-taker, bold and decisive, but he didn't always think through the implications of what he was doing. Joanna was too good for him. I don't believe for a minute that he cared for her, he was too cold and callous."

"He cared for Lysette Whiteley."

"Really? I'd say the real attraction was that she was married to his uncle, and Malcolm treated his dying brother despicably. Sure, he had a thing for older women, but screwing Lysette was about revenge as much as lust."

"How is Shona?"

"Still adamant that Josh Durham is the love of her life, and she'll stick by him, however long they bang him up for."

"Who knows? She might just mean it."

"She's a child, Daniel. Savvy and spoiled, but above all, a child. Josh Durham took full advantage of her vulnerability. His father's telling any reporter who cares to listen that it was true love, but it makes no difference. Josh will go to jail. At present she's holed up on the other side of the Pennines, in Robin Hood's Bay. A distant cousin of Nigel's has offered to take care of her. She'll need almost as much professional support as Lily. At least Lily has a home to go to. As if it wasn't enough to be abducted by a school teacher, Shona has to come to terms with her father's death."

"Do you think the Press will get hold of Joanna's story about Nigel killing Amber? So far the coverage about Shona's rescue has been as positive as the stories about Lily and Joanna. No suggestion that Shona's dad was a murderer."

"I'm praying it stays that way. Nigel was loathsome, but he's dead now, and looking after the living matters far more than denouncing the dead. Apparently, the media are offering Lily big bucks for her story, but Gray told them where to go. Good for him. The Elstones don't need more money, just time to get to know each other again."

"And Joanna?"

"Now she has a chance of happiness with Gray. Let's hope she grabs it. People call her an oddball, but that's unfair. She just sees the good in others. Sometimes when there isn't any, unfortunately. Gray will make sure she doesn't complicate matters by feeding the vultures with her story."

"All's well that ends well, then?"

She sighed. "Those were Les' very words this afternoon. Not sure I see it that way, even if Dean and Whiteley are no loss. Josh's reputation is in tatters, but I feel for his father. Shona's an orphan, a poor little rich girl, and although Lily's free at last, it'll take a hell of a lot of love and hard work to ease her back to anything remotely close to normality. Things may work out for Gray and Joanna, but it's early days. Two lives lost, others changed forever. Not your textbook happy-ever-after."

"Any news about Quiggin?"

"He's put his guest house on the market. The reason he moved to the western Lakes was to feel closer to Carrie, but Dean's ruined it for him. He's struggling to cope with the idea that Lily was kidnapped and held captive because she looked rather like Carrie. He never even knew there was a resemblance."

The sun had vanished, leaving a faint orange glow to remember it by. Daniel closed his eyes, but she didn't try to fathom what he was thinking. However well you knew someone, there remained so much you'd never understand. A lesson Joanna Footit had learned the hard way.

"I'm going inside."

He opened his eyes. "Chilly?"

"It's not the breeze. I'm ready for an early night."

"Sure, you've had a long day, and there's a lot to do tomorrow. You must be wiped out. At least you might get a decent night's sleep."

"No chance. I'm fizzing with energy. You'd better be, too, or else."

She ran into the cottage and, after a moment's wondering, he followed her.

Author's Note

As with the other books in this series, I've made a few changes to the detailed topography of the setting in order to avoid confusion between my fictional world and real life. Ravenglass Knoll does not exist (in fact, its quarry garden was inspired by a visit to a beautiful garden in Cheshire); nor does Lower Drigg. The characters who appear are imaginary, and not intended to resemble any living (or dead) person; the same applies to the events of the story. The organisations and businesses mentioned are fictitious, with a few obvious exceptions, such as the Sellafield nuclear plant, and Muncaster Castle. My description of Cumbria Constabulary, and the people who work for it, is intended as a portrayal of an imagined equivalent of the real force, and Hannah and her colleagues do not represent real life counterparts. Similarly, the murders and kidnappings in the story are not based on abductions, family annihilations, or other events in real life. The Eskdale Arms, Saltcoats View, and Scott Durham's cottage were all invented for the purpose of the story.

I have, once again, been fortunate to receive a great deal of help in writing this book, and trying to strike a sensible and entertaining balance between invention and authenticity. My researches in Ravenglass and the surrounding area were assisted by several people, but I'd like to make special mention of my gratitude toward Neil Anderson of Rosegarth Guest House, and Mark A. Pearce, a gifted local artist, who gave me a great deal of invaluable information about life and work in the locality. Details about Rosegarth, and Mark's work are available online; I can recommend both. Liz Gilbey supplied me with photos and insight relating to western Cumbria with her customary generosity. Gary and Linda Stratmann gave me welcome help in relation to Malcolm Whiteley's weaponry, whilst Roger Forsdyke's guidance on police procedure proved as invaluable as ever.

I'd also like to thank my agent, James Wills, and my publishers here and overseas, for all their support. Most of all, my thanks go to my readers, not least those who take the trouble to get in touch with kind words about the books. Your continuing enthusiasm for the Lake District Mysteries is as rewarding as it is motivational.

Martin Edwards
www.martinedwardsbooks.com

To receive a free catalog of Poisoned Pen Press titles, please provide your name and address in one of the following ways:

Phone: 1-800-421-3976
Facsimile: 1-480-949-1707
Email: info@poisonedpenpress.com
Website: www.poisonedpenpress.com

Poisoned Pen Press
6962 E. First Ave. Ste 103
Scottsdale, AZ 85251